Slippers
wed album

NEVER LET GO

Laura Phillips

A KISMET™ Romance

METEOR PUBLISHING CORPORATION
Bensalem, Pennsylvania

KISMET™ is a trademark of Meteor Publishing Corporation

Copyright © 1990 Laura M. Phillips
Cover Art copyright © 1990 Alex Zwarenstein

First Printing December 1990.

ISBN: 1-878702-21-1

For Kevin, who helped me spread my wings

LAURA PHILLIPS

Laura Phillips is a former reporter and news editor who began writing fiction after her first child was born. She lives in Kansas City, Missouri, with her husband, three children and assorted pets. When she isn't writing or doing Mommy jobs, she can be found in the backyard garden.

ONE

"Touch that and I'll break your arm."

Kelly Smith jerked her finger back from the doorbell. She looked around and saw no one. Even so, she knew that Ryan Matthews was the man who had shouted. There was no mistaking that voice.

Who did he think he was, yelling at her like that? He had invited her here. Or maybe he wasn't yelling at her, she thought, as the one-sided argument continued.

"You swine," the bimbo said. *"You wouldn't."*

What?

Kelly cocked her head to the side as she looked up and down the street, then stepped off the porch and peered around the corner of the big stone house. Located on a dead-end street in south Kansas City, the old house was part of what was once a large estate. Now it was conspicuous among the wood-frame ranch houses that surrounded it. The converted carriage house at the end of the drive was the only other structure in the neighborhood from that era.

The curtain fluttered in the open window to her right. Childish giggles floated out when the deep, vibrant voice changed to a falsetto. Kelly leaned closer to the window. She could see Ryan seated on the edge of the couch, reading with exaggerated expression from a sheet of paper. His voice squeaked and he wriggled his wide shoulders, fluffed his wavy brown hair, and batted his eyelashes. At his feet, a chubby toddler pulled at his shoelaces. Two pairs of feet clad in Mickey Mouse sandals were the only visible parts of the other Webster children.

Well, at least he was reading to them. Too many parents didn't bother, she thought. Her opinion of him went up two notches. As Ryan's voice grew quieter, she strained to catch the words.

"No," Bambi retorted, her blue eyes flashing with stubborn independence. "I'll carry it."

Kelly suppressed a slight shiver at the sound of his voice. She had felt that same tingle when his sister introduced them last winter. Kelly had arrived that day for her monthly appointment. Mr. Matthews answered the door and called to his sister. They exchanged pleasantries. Then he disappeared into the family room with the children.

Several days later she bumped into him at a movie rental store. She ended up spending the evening with the entire family, eating chips and watching a couple of hit comedies. Several times she noticed Ryan watching her, just as she studied him when he was not looking. He asked her to dinner the next night, but cancelled just hours before their date. By dinner time, he was on a plane to Europe to replace a correspondent who had been injured in a car wreck.

That was it, the full scope of their relationship, if it could even be called that. The ridiculous part was that Ryan Matthews had popped into her dreams after that with alarming regularity.

Then one evening, he was there on the television screen. Microphone in hand, he stood amidst the rubble that had been a classroom hours before. His voice broke when he described the human toll.

Kelly saw him on the news again from time to time, reporting from various parts of the world. A famine. An important conference in Africa. An interview with an American in a Belfast jail.

He had been a pleasant fantasy, a safe one for someone who had no intention of ever getting seriously involved with a man again. She had never expected to meet him again, let alone have him as a client.

Although it wasn't unusual for her clients to call her at home, the message Ryan Matthews left on her answering machine two days ago had surprised her. She had thought the man capable of coping with anything, even the sudden inheritance of three preschoolers. "Call me," he had said, his vibrant voice caressing her senses even while she recognized its note of strain. "No matter how late it is. I desperately need some advice. By the way, how do you heat a bottle when the microwave is broken?"

That had been enough to set her fingers dialing before the machine could go on to the next message.

Mr. Matthews had sounded frazzled. After Kelly warned him to *never* heat a baby bottle in the microwave because it didn't heat evenly, she suggested they set up an appointment *soon*.

Although his new family was on her list of clients for the year, she had not yet begun making regular appointments. It usually took a couple of weeks for the Early Childhood Center at the local school district to organize itself, and school had just begun three days before.

She had heard through the grapevine about the accident that killed Mr. Matthews's sister. She had assumed that an aunt or grandmother had been appointed guardian of the Webster children. But her supervisor told her later that Ryan Matthews was taking care of the children, that he'd resigned his overseas job with the network. Kelly's co-workers had ranted about his devilish good looks. He was nice to look at, Kelly agreed as his voice invaded her thoughts again.

"—be stupid." Dirk's voice vibrated with barely controlled anger. "You're tired, but we can't afford to rest any longer. The general probably has his dogs out after us by now."

"I can take care of myself," the stupid blonde said.

"Like you did this morning? If it weren't for me, you'd be the entertainment in the general's barracks tonight."

What was he reading to those children? It didn't sound like anything from the children's section of the public library. Kelly could hear a child's giggle bubbling out. She stifled one herself as she watched him do an impression of the nefarious "general."

"Or maybe the general would keep you for himself."

Bambi jerked her head away and reached for the

*camera bag, her hands stopping midway, then
clutching at the bag jerkily.*

"Oh my God," she shrilled.

Dirk turned the bag and saw the bullet hole.

*Bambi gasped as she pulled the camera from the
bag and saw the shattered lens. Slowly, she turned
it over and touched the hole where the bullet had
exited.*

"Uh-oh. It broke." The child sounded worried.
Kelly smiled, thinking how quickly children become
wrapped up in stories. She knew she shouldn't be
eavesdropping, but for once, she let her curiosity
overcome her good sense.

*"It's ruined," said Bimbo, I mean Bambi. "The
camera, the film. There's no evidence now, no photos of the outlaw general and the U.S. senator. I
can't prove a da—a darn thing."*

"Forget the story, Bambi. It's not worth it."

"It's my life, Dirk."

*"And mine," he said through clenched teeth. "Or
does that matter to you."*

"I'm sorry," she whispered, turning toward him.

*Dirk cupped her face in his hands and lowered
his lips to hers, touching, caressing, deepening until
neither could remember the fear of the flight through
the forest or the rain or anything but their over-
whelming need.*

"Yuck," Kelly whispered, making a mental note
to suggest he choose more appropriate stories to read
to the children. Whatever he liked to read himself,
the *Conquest of Bambi* wasn't suitable for preschoolers. But how was she to bring up the subject without
revealing that she had been snooping on the porch?

"Uncle Ryan," a small voice called.

"What?"

"I heard something outside. I think she's here."

Kelly could hear footsteps moving closer to the window and she shrank back toward the door, her heart pounding.

Eavesdropping. That's what she was doing. Shamelessly eavesdropping, and peeping through the curtains to boot. After a brief second of panic, she reached for the doorbell, jabbing it quickly. Maybe they would think that she had just arrived.

Four-year-old Eric peeked out the window. Kelly smiled and waved.

"It's her," he shouted before disappearing.

The lock clicked and rasped, then the door swung wide open. Kelly found herself staring through the screen door into a pair of shadowed brown eyes that bored into her own with an unnerving intensity. A spark of recognition warmed his expression into a smile. She flushed guiltily, while a thousand tiny moths fluttered in her chest.

Her instincts told her to turn around and run, that those eyes were even more warm and dangerous in reality. Instead, she stood her ground and forced a smile. She told herself she was being ridiculous. He was just a man, like any other, a client accompanied by three gurgling and chattering chaperones.

"I'm glad you're here. We've all been excited about your visit, haven't we, kids?" Mr. Matthews smiled and reached for the screen door handle. Eric beat him to it and fumbled for a minute before he managed to open it. He held it while Kelly stepped dropping a crushed insect. "Hold him, Uncle Ryan. I'm gonna get a big Nody fly."

Eric hopped down from the couch and scurried out of the room. Ryan rolled his eyes and was surprised to find Kelly laughing, not watching him with the disdainful expression he expected. It was an infectious sound, and Ryan found himself chuckling, too.

"He names all the big flies 'Nody.' " Ryan explained.

"What does he call the little ones?"

Ryan's grin widened.

"Plain Old Little Fly."

Kelly slipped the beads and strings back into a box and put them in the huge tote bag on the floor. Then she pulled out a pegboard.

"Last time I was here Eric and Rachel were collecting worms," she said as she led Rachel into the next room.

"They still do." He lifted Rachel into a chair at the big wooden table and kissed her forehead.

"Rachel, would you put the red pegs in the red holes?" Kelly asked.

Rachel reached into the bag of pegs and toyed with the pieces. Then she held out the bag and deliberately dropped it onto the floor. Puzzled, Kelly picked up the bag. She picked out a red peg and placed it on the pegboard. Then she handed a peg to Rachel, but the child just set it on the table.

Kelly met Ryan's eyes across the table, hers questioning, his dimmed with resignation.

"You know your colors, Rachel," he said. "Put the red peg in the red hole."

"That's okay," Kelly said, setting the bag of pegs

on the table. "You can play with them if you want to. Your uncle and I will go into the other room and talk."

They returned to the family room, she to the couch and he to the recliner.

"Mr. Matthews," she began.

"Call me Ryan," he said. "Anyone who sees our dirty laundry should be on a first-name basis."

"Call me Kelly, the kids do. Do you know much about the Early Childhood Program?" she asked.

"Not much."

"Okay, we'll start with the basics." She pulled a sheaf of papers out of her oversize bag. During the next few minutes, she explained the program and handed over pamphlets and information sheets.

"So, you're a social worker in a sense," Ryan said.

"Not really," she explained. "I guess I'm a cross between a teacher and a guidance counselor. I help parents to be the best parents they can. I used to teach first grade in my hometown, but when this program began, I applied for a job in Kansas City."

"Why is that? Did a room full of six-year-olds make you crazy?"

"No, I loved teaching," she said quietly. "I just felt I could do more good this way."

That was her standard answer. Only her parents knew the real reason why she had changed jobs. It was too personal, too painful. Besides, she didn't need anyone's sympathy. She had accepted the lot that fate had dealt her, and she was making the best of it.

"How is that?" Ryan was leaning forward, his

eyes alert with interest. Kelly knew then why he had been such an arresting presence on the television screen. She also understood how he had dredged such painful admissions from the people he had interviewed.

"We do developmental screening. If there's a problem, like a speech delay, then we help the parents find therapists or doctors. It gives the child a chance to catch up before kindergarten. If we get them off to a good start, they'll do better all through school."

As she finished speaking, she crossed to the doorway to check on Rachel. Kelly smiled as she watched Rachel slip a yellow peg into the last empty hole, then methodically empty the pegboard. Eric was busy with crayons and a coloring book at the other end of the table.

Kelly nodded in answer to Ryan's questioning look and returned to her seat.

She toyed with the strap of her tote bag, wondering how to broach the question of how well the children were dealing with the deaths of their parents. She was saved by Ryan's next words.

"Rachel still thinks her mommy and daddy will come home," he said as he rested his elbows on his knees and dropped his forehead into his hands. Abruptly, he stood and walked to the window, brushing his hand through his hair.

Kelly nodded. Tears of compassion welled up in her eyes, but she willed herself not to cry. "And the others?"

"Sarah seems to be all right. I guess she's too little to really know what's going on. At first she cried a lot and I couldn't seem to comfort her no matter how much I held her and rocked her. My housekeeper, Mrs. Yates, says I'm not shaped right. And Eric is still wetting the bed at night. The doctor says the kids are still adjusting to all the changes. I know I am. Thank God Mrs. Yates lives at the carriage house, and I can call her when I get in trouble.''

Kelly tilted her head to the side, watching Ryan's restless pacing. ''Most parents have nine months to adjust to each new addition. You got three children on short notice.''

''They didn't come with a training manual, either.''

Ryan flopped back into his seat, leaning forward, resting his forearms on his knees again. As he moved, Kelly's eyes were drawn to the lean muscles exposed below the rolled-up shirt sleeves.

''Sometimes I think I'm going to go crazy if I don't get some peace and quiet. But when they're not here, I miss the noise.''

''I know what you mean,'' she said.

''How many children do you have?''

Ryan thought he imagined the brief shadow that flickered across her face.

''None of my own. But I have seven nieces and six nephews. And as the oldest girl in my family, I helped raise my younger sisters. There were six of us,'' she added before he could ask.

''Six?'' Ryan's eyes were wide with horror.

''Six girls and one big brother. I wouldn't dream of having more than five myself,'' she teased.

Ryan looked out the window. ''I hadn't planned to have any,'' he said. ''Now I know what I would have missed.''

"It's none of my business, but why did you leave your job and move here to live with the kids? Don't they have any other relatives to take care of them?"

For a moment, Kelly thought he wasn't going to answer her, and she was sorry she had spoken. "Never mind, I shouldn't have asked."

"No. It's all right. I'm getting used to the questions." Ryan leaned back in his chair, his fingers restlessly tapping on the upholstered arm. "I didn't even have to think about it. It's what my sister wanted. We were twins, you know. We never had anyone but each other. I had to come back. I owed it to Sharon and I owe it to her kids. They deserve a full-time parent who will love them and hug them and listen to them. There wasn't anyone else who would do that for them."

Kelly nodded slowly.

"That's what I would have done," she said. "I would do the same in an instant for my nieces and nephews."

They stared at one another for a moment in quiet understanding until a shout and a crash from the other room distracted them.

Ryan leaped from his chair and ran into the other room, with Kelly close on his heels. He dragged Eric and Rachel apart and quieted their screams with a piercing whistle.

"What was all that about?" he asked.

"She hit me."

"He hit me."

"She won't share."

"It's mine."

Before the explanations could descend into a full-scale war, Ryan sent the children to their separate rooms to cool off. Running his hands through his hair, he gave Kelly a rueful smile.

"It's been a good day. They've usually had three or four fights by this time. Why do they fight this much? Is that normal?"

"I hope it is," Kelly replied as she set a chair upright. "We always fought a lot in my family. My father would yell at us and my mother would tell him to be quiet and let the kids settle it. As long as we didn't break the furniture or seriously hurt one another, she didn't interfere."

While Kelly picked up the rest of the spilled pegs, she could feel him watching her. She turned her back to him, mustering her inner defenses. He was just a man, like any other, a client. No, a little voice in her head insisted, he's Ryan Matthews. And he's very different from any man you've ever known.

As she stood up, she backed into Ryan, who had moved closer, probably to help her retrieve the scattered toys. His steadying hands were warm, lingering on her arms a moment longer than necessary. Kelly's startled glance over her shoulder caught the quick, answering flare in Ryan's eyes. Then he released her and turned away, leaving Kelly wondering if she had imagined it.

"Here's another one," he said, his voice impersonal and unaffected. He bent and plucked a blue peg from the edge of the heating duct, then dropped it into Kelly's bag.

While Kelly gathered her things, she pulled herself together enough mentally to finish her assignment and make her escape. No matter what her personal feelings for the man, she had a responsibility to the school district and the family. Next time, though, she resolved to keep all the children in the room with her, even if they were pulling one another's hair out.

"By the way," she said. "There's a group meeting next week at the center. Babysitting is free. We're having a speaker this time. He's a child psychologist."

Ryan wondered if she was trying to find a nice way to tell him that he needed to find a therapist to help the kids deal with the death of their parents.

"What will he be talking about?"

Kelly grinned. "Sibling rivalry."

Ryan smiled back his relief. "Now, that's a problem. I'll try to come. I'm supposed to meet with my agent next week, but I think I can rearrange my schedule."

"Your agent?"

Ryan hesitated, then shrugged. "I'm writing a book. I always wanted to, but I never had time before."

"How do you find the time now?"

"That's the trouble," he said. "I don't. I'm way behind and my agent is unhappy, to say the least."

Kelly could feel the beginnings of a laugh stirring and she struggled to control it.

"What are you writing?" she asked innocently.

"It's kind of an adventure novel, a cross between *Raiders of the Lost Ark* and *The Spy Who Came In From the Cold*. Hal says he thinks he's found a publisher who wants it if the rest of the book is as good as the first three chapters."

That must be it, Kelly thought. Bambi the Bimbo Takes Moscow. "How wonderful for you," she said aloud, hoping she didn't sound as insincere as she thought she did. "I have to go. Maybe I'll see you at the group meeting."

She stowed the pegboard in the bag and walked to the front door.

"About the next appointment," Ryan said as he followed her, "I'm not sure what my schedule is going to be."

"I could call you in a couple of weeks," she said as she stepped onto the porch. He followed her down the steps.

"Sure," Ryan said. "Watch out for the truck."

Kelly waved, then headed for her car, stepping carefully around the toy dump truck at the end of the sidewalk. As she inserted the key in the lock, she saw Ryan scoop up the dump truck. He flashed a camera-perfect grin when he noticed she was watching him.

"And by the way," she called back. "I think you're doing a great job with the kids."

"Yeah?" He sounded unsure, as if he thought she was just saying that to bolster his confidence.

"Really, you are," she said. "There's just one thing—"

Kelly unlocked her car door, biting her lip. She almost changed her mind. Then she blurted it out, the question that had been hovering in the back of her mind for the last hour. Only it didn't come out quite right.

"There's just one thing I'm curious about. How cozy do Dirk and Bambi get before the general catches them?"

TWO

The dump truck crashed to the sidewalk. Kelly winced as it bounced onto its side and a toy wheel rolled into the marigolds. She met Ryan's startled stare across the hood of the car. As his eyes narrowed with comprehension, Kelly regretted the impulsive question and groaned softly.

"Ryan? Mr. Matthews?" Kelly slowly placed her bag on the hood of the car, then started back toward the sidewalk. One look at Ryan stopped her. "Mr. Matthews, that's not exactly what I mean. It just didn't sound like the kind of thing you should read to children."

There was not a trace of warmth left in his eyes, only wariness, as if Kelly had suddenly become an adversary. Damn it! Why did she feel so defensive? She wasn't the one who had been reading trash to those kids. She was just trying to help.

She sounded like the spokesperson for the Moral Decency League, a little voice inside her head told her. Besides, eavesdropping was not exactly a virtue.

With catlike grace, Ryan stalked halfway across the driveway, then stopped inches away from Kelly. Although he stood still, his muscles were tensed as if ready to spring at her if she said an untoward word. Thrusting his hands deeply into his pockets, he faced her, jaw clenched.

Then his voice, low and demanding, broke the spell.

"How long were you on the front porch."

Kelly felt the warm flush of color flood her face and she looked away, focusing on a squirrel across the yard. It swished its bushy tail, then scampered up the trunk of a maple tree. Kelly wished she could follow it and hide among the leaves.

"Not long." She resisted the childish urge to cross her fingers to secretly negate the lie.

"Long enough."

"I couldn't help hearing," she said, trying to explain. "The window was open and you were practically shouting."

"Yeah?"

Kelly's gaze darted to his face at his rueful tone. The corners of his mouth curved upwards slightly. Kelly wondered then if Ryan realized how devastating that contrite half-smile was.

"I guess I didn't realize it was time for you to be here," he said. "Otherwise, I would have been reading about Winnie the Pooh and Tigger and the rest of the gang."

"Really?" Kelly's tone was skeptical.

"Probably not," Ryan admitted. "I'm starting to have nightmares about being stuck in the honey tree with the three little kittens."

"Not good." Kelly shook her head, trying to frown but utterly failing.

"Well, are you going to turn me in?"

Ryan's tone was an attempt at lightness, but Kelly sensed the underlying tension that tightened his brows.

"Turn you in? To whom?"

"To Child Welfare Services." Noting Kelly's puzzlement, he explained, a note of bitterness creeping into his voice. "For contributing to the delinquency of minors, for being an immoral influence on impressionable minds."

Kelly's brows lifted.

"You're joking," she said. "Aren't you?"

"No."

"Have you had some kind of trouble with Children's Services?"

"Not yet. Should I be worried?"

Kelly smiled reassuringly. "No. I doubt that Bambi the Bimbo will turn them into little ax murderers. I really think you're doing great with the kids, considering you've only been a father for a couple of months."

"Not a father, just—" Ryan halted mid-sentence and looked back toward the house. "Wait here, just a minute."

Kelly watched him run onto the porch and leap inside. She couldn't help but smile when she imagined what he might find inside. She remembered the kind of havoc she and her brother and sisters had created when left to their own devices for a few minutes. No wonder her mother had developed premature gray hair.

But Ryan Matthews was another story. He was a puzzle. He obviously cared deeply for his nephew and nieces. Otherwise, he wouldn't have left his job and moved here. The house was charming, but no match for the glamour capitals of the world. And life in the suburbs was pretty boring, compared with what Ryan was accustomed to.

Why had he given all that up? He could have hired a nanny to take care of the kids while he was working. He could have done a lot of things. With his experience and good looks, he surely could have gotten a job as a news anchor someplace. Or maybe that's what he was waiting for. The right offer. Why else would he be hanging around here?

She leaned back against the car and watched the front door. Within seconds, Ryan was there. Kelly felt her breath catch when his eyes captured hers and she responded to his grin with a shaky smile.

"So, how cozy do they get?" she persisted.

"Pretty cozy." Ryan's grin was downright wicked as he winked. Kelly laughed in relief at his lighter mood while she wondered why he had been so worried. Not just worried. Stricken.

"I wouldn't read that part to the children," she said.

"No, you wouldn't," he said, taking a step toward her. Kelly held her breath for an instant, feeling as if he was reaching out and caressing her with his eyes. "And neither would I."

"I didn't think so," she said. "Just the same, I'd stick to Pooh and Peter Rabbit and the like."

"Spoken like a true teacher."

Kelly shrugged. "That's what I am. I guess maybe I just don't know when to shut up."

"Or maybe you just care a lot."

"Maybe too much," she said. "A lot of people would have told me to mind my own business and don't come back."

"Not me." The statement was a caress, or so it seemed to Kelly in her overly aware state. Then again, she thought, she was probably imagining things, conjuring up fantasies from a year's worth of restless nights.

"I have to go," she said. "I'm late for my next appointment." She headed for the driver's seat, grabbing her bag from the hood. As she slid behind the wheel and buckled her seat belt, she saw his battered running shoes by the open car door.

Her gaze followed the faded denim up, pausing on the lean hips, then darting uneasily to his face.

"How about dinner?" he asked.

"I can't."

"Tomorrow?"

"No."

"Working?"

"No, it's not that. I don't date clients."

"I guess most of their wives would object," he said. "Sorry, bad joke. We're barbecuing tomorrow night. Come over then. You could give me some extra lessons in parenting."

"You could always read a book."

"I've read fifteen, no sixteen. And now I'm really confused."

"They're like that. Everyone has a different theory. Ryan, you just have to follow your instincts and use a little common sense. You're really doing fine, considering you've only been at this for a couple of months.''

"Apparently not good enough," he muttered.

Kelly leaned out the window to get a clearer look at his face. "What makes you say that?"

He splayed his hands on his hips and stared at her, searching, testing her sincerity.

"There's another relative who wants custody. I don't think she would be good for them. She's great at buying them things and putting them on display for her friends. But I've never once seen her hug them.''

"Yet, you're afraid she can take them away?"

"Yes.''

"Do you really want to keep the kids?''

"More than anything I've ever wanted in my life. My sister was the only person who I could ever really depend on. I owe it to her to see that her kids get the best possible care.'' Bracing his hands on his knees, he bent down to challenge her with those dark, gypsy eyes. "With a few lessons from you, I could win an uncle of the year contest.''

Kelly could feel herself weakening.

"Okay. What time is the barbecue?''

"Six o'clock. And bring your bag of tricks.''

Kelly laid the infant across her knees, crooning softly and patting gently. But nothing would quiet her. The tiny legs shot out straight, then doubled up tight. Kelly's heart contracted as she watched the tiny fists flail.

Resigned, she handed the screaming child back to the nursery attendant. "I'll go get her mother."

"I think that's best," the older woman said. "It's colic. My oldest boy had it."

Kelly let herself out of the nursery and headed down the hallway toward the library. It was always like this on group meeting nights. One or two of the children either came down with a stomach ache or couldn't bear being separated from their mothers.

The group meetings were supposed to allow the parents of young children free time to talk with one another and with trained professionals. The Early Childhood Center provided free babysitting. Kelly almost always volunteered to help out in the nursery.

She slipped quietly into the library, not wanting to interrupt the program. Peering carefully around the room, she located the infant's mother then walked over and gently tapped her arm.

"It's the baby," the woman whispered before Kelly could speak. At Kelly's nod, she sighed deeply, then gathered up her things.

As Kelly turned to leave, she caught a glimpse of Ryan Matthews. He was staring at her. She could feel a slow flush suffuse her body. She tried to wipe the silly grin off her face, but she couldn't. Irritated, she wondered how he could affect her that way from across a crowded room.

It had been bad enough that night at the barbecue. Every time he had looked at her, she had felt like a piece of meat on a stick. No, not like that. Like she was sitting in the sunshine on a warm day in March. She was glad she had left early, before the real sun dimmed. As it was, it had been a fun evening.

Hurrying into the hallway, she told herself she was being ridiculous again. He wasn't the only one that had stared at her when she slipped into the room. Twenty people had watched her nervously, hoping that it was not their child that was causing all the ruckus this time.

So, why was she so concerned about a particular pair of plain old brown eyes? No, not plain. Mischievous, warm, gypsy eyes. Afraid of the answer, she darted back into the nursery and threw herself into a raucous game of ring-around-a-rosy.

Distracting her thoughts was not so easy an hour later. She had just sent the last child home with his parents. As she began to tidy up, she heard a noise at the door. Turning, she saw Ryan leaning against the jamb. A surge of excitement ran through her midsection, leaving quivering sensations behind.

"Hello, Ryan," she said, hoping she at least sounded normal. "Did you like the program?"

He smiled, and walked toward her. Kelly quickly moved to the left and started sorting a clutter of blocks, toy cars, and puzzle pieces into their proper containers.

"Dr. Bartholomew had a few good tips." Ryan's voice came from directly above her. His battered running shoe was only a few inches away from the spot where she was kneeling. Slowly, Kelly's eyes followed the white stripe up the side of his blue sweatpants. When she reached Ryan's muscled thigh, she looked away again and dropped a car into the block box.

"Wrong one," Ryan said as he crouched and

retrieved the car. He put it in its proper place and went to work on the rest of the mess.

Kelly could not help but smile to herself as she watched him gather up the brightly colored rings and stack them on the yellow post.

"We try to get Dr. Bartholomew to speak here at least once a year. He's pretty good with kids," she said.

"He ought to be. He has half a dozen of his own. The youngest is in the sixth grade."

"You know him?" Really, the man was amazing. Was there anyone who was anyone that he hadn't interviewed?

"Not really. I talked to him for a bit when everyone was leaving. I know of a couple of stations that might run an interview with someone like him."

"Oh?" Right on the mark again, Kelly, she thought. "I thought you were writing now."

"I am," Ryan said. "And I did some freelance TV work when I was in college. I could do some now, at least until something more permanent comes along. Where do the crayons go?"

Until something more permanent comes along.

So, he's not planning on staying here. That didn't surprise her, but the depth of disappointment did.

"The crayons?" Ryan held out the shoebox full of broken crayons. His eyes held a question, one Kelly chose to ignore.

"On the top shelf," she said, then turned away.

When the toys were all in place, Ryan stood restlessly fidgeting in the middle of the room.

"I need to talk to you for a minute," he said, frowning.

"Is there a problem with the kids?" Kelly asked.

"Not exactly. I was wondering if I could ask a favor? It's for Rachel."

"Sure, if I can help." Kelly leaned back against the wall, crossing her arms. "What is it?"

"I was wondering if you could tell me what to get Rachel for her birthday. I'm not sure what is appropriate. Do I get her toy dishes or is that a sexist notion? Should I get her a football or a toy tool set and show her that gender has nothing to do with a person's job? Or do I get her something educational like one of those talking computers? Or something simple like a paint set to encourage her to be creative? I don't know. I've never done this before, not like this. I've always been Uncle Ryan who sends them a package in the mail. I never saw their faces when they opened them."

While he weighed the comparative merits of a chalkboard and an erector set, she watched the play of emotions across his face.

Finally, he ran out of steam. "I'm making too much of this, aren't I?"

She nodded. "What does Rachel want?"

"Everything," he said, throwing his arms wide.

Kelly smiled. "Does she have a doll?"

He thought for a moment, then a shadow crossed his face.

"What is it?" Kelly asked.

"I brought her one last winter when I came to visit. The accident, it was in the car then. Sharon—"

Kelly looked down at her hands, swallowing the lump in her throat.

"My sister left it in the car, I guess, when she

and her husband dropped the kids off at their grand-mother's house. The doll was torn up pretty badly in the accident. I didn't think it was a good idea to give it back to her like that.''

"So, get her another one.''

"Do you think that's a good idea? Won't it remind her of the accident? Well, not that. But her doll dis-appeared at the same time as her parents.''

Kelly closed the gap between them and laid a hand on his arm. For one shocked instant, her eyes met his. Then she jerked her hand back, still tingling from the charged touch.

"I don't mean get her the same doll,'' Kelly con-tinued, her voice husky with emotion. "Get her one that's soft and huggable, though. There are some nice ones in the toy stores. I think Rachel needs something to hug and take care of.''

"She's only three. She needs somebody to take care of her, not the other way around. That's what I'm here for.''

Kelly shrugged. "Kids learn by pretending. Play-ing with dolls is one way kids learn to deal with other people. But there are lots of other things you could get her.''

"What about a toy tool set?''

"Why not? A woman needs to know how to use a hammer and a drill.''

"Do you?'' Ryan challenged.

"Of course. My dad's a woodshop teacher.''

"An equal opportunity woodshop teacher?''

"Of course. One with a broken drill.''

Ryan laughed. It was a deep chuckling that reminded Kelly of her father when he was amused and trying hard not to show how much. "You didn't," Ryan said.

Kelly nodded. "I accidentally sawed the cord when I was helping him make a birdhouse. Dad was furious, more with himself than me, though, because he hadn't seen the cord either and he was supposed to be teaching me how to use the tools properly."

"So, did you buy your dad a new drill?"

"No, he taught me how to put a new cord on." Kelly noticed that Ryan had edged closer while they were talking. He now stood just inches from her, looking down at her with that half-smile that stole her breath.

"You have all sorts of hidden talents," he said softly, barely above a whisper.

"All sorts."

Ryan ran his finger lightly along her jaw line. "Lady, are you flirting with me?"

Kelly swallowed, but the lump was still there. She tried to ignore the soft tingling where he touched her.

"I don't flirt," she whispered.

"Why not?" His eyes were dark pools that mesmerized her with their gentleness.

"I have my reasons," she said, pulling back against the wall, then slipping away to the left. "And one of them is, I don't need the complications in my life."

"And the others?" He half-turned to face her again.

"That's my business." Kelly pulled her purse and a sweater out of the cabinet and walked to the door.

"I think I'd like flirting with you." Halting in her tracks, Kelly pivoted, a slow anger starting to burn.

Why was he doing this, stirring up emotions she thought she would never feel again? Emotions she could not allow herself to feel again. Why was she letting him?

"I think you'd like flirting with the old woman in a shoe, if it got you what you wanted," she said, striving for a light tone.

"And that is?" Ryan was wearing that half smile again.

Kelly shrugged. "A little information. An interview. A prime-time spot in the news."

Ryan pushed a tiny chair up to the table, then opened the door, standing aside for Kelly to pass. After a moment's hesitation, she stepped into the hall.

"You couldn't do that for me, even if I wanted you to," he whispered near her ear as she brushed past him.

The feathering brush of his breath in her hair nearly distracted her, and she stepped away, struggling for control over the fluttering weakness in her limbs.

"No, I'm just the one who's giving you advice about a birthday present."

"And that's all?"

"That and a few parenting tips you could get from a good book. What else is there?"

"This," he said, capturing her chin and lifting it with his fingers as he drew closer and closer. Kelly's eyes widened in surprise. She stiffened as Ryan's lips touched her gently once, twice, then drew away. While her brain screamed a warning, her senses threatened betrayal. Ryan's tenderness was her undoing as his mouth descended a third time in a lingering kiss that turned her bones to gelatin.

When Ryan's head lifted, Kelly realized she was clinging to his shoulders. Self-consciously, she withdrew her hands, resisting the urge to smooth the rumpled spots in the fabric of his sweatshirt. When she started to look away, Ryan turned her head back with a gentle, burning touch to her cheek.

"What else is there?" he repeated. "I think you already know."

"No," she whispered as she pulled away. "You're wrong."

"That kiss told me I'm right," he insisted.

Hours later, the words echoed in Kelly's brain as she lay awake in her twin bed, staring at the shadows on the ceiling.

For the life of her, she couldn't figure out what to do. She only knew that she was becoming too involved with Ryan Matthews. The worst part was that she was no longer sure she minded.

It was a problem she still struggled with two weeks later as she rang the bell at Ryan's house. She had almost decided to cancel, but she knew she could not disappoint Rachel by not coming to her birthday party. Kelly was just beginning to make friends with the shy, withdrawn child.

Kelly stared at the tall, stately woman who opened the door. A pair of sharp, blue eyes surveyed her, and registered mild approval. "Come in. I'm Amanda Webster. John, the children's father, was my son."

As Kelly entered the living room, she could see the bitter lines that creased the corners of Mrs. Webster's mouth, lines that the screen door had blurred moments before.

"I was sorry to hear about the accident," Kelly said. "Your son and Sharon were wonderful people." Mrs. Webster accepted the condolences with a regal nod and excused herself for a moment.

Kelly slipped into the dining room and laid her brightly wrapped present on the table with the others. She could hear Eric's excited shrieks, coupled with Rachel's laughter, and she turned to the open window. Ryan jumped out from behind the old maple tree and roared, sending the two older children running.

"It's such a shame," Mrs. Webster said as she took a place beside Kelly. "Those children have turned into wild animals since he's been here."

The older woman fussed with the curtains, which were flapping wildly in the breeze. Finally, she pushed the window closed, then straightened the silverware on the table that was laid out in readiness for the birthday celebration. Kelly looked around for something to do, but before she could move, Mrs. Webster spoke again.

"I hope you'll be able to do something about Ryan."

Kelly met the calculating blue eyes across the table.

"Do something?" she asked, careful to maintain a bland tone of voice. It was beginning to make sense—Ryan's paranoia about Child Welfare Services, his plea for her help, all the books he had read. There was more to this than an inexperienced bachelor's concern about managing an instant family.

"It's not right. What does he know about children? He's a *journalist*. He's completely unqualified."

"He's not an experienced parent, no," Kelly said.

"He has no experience with children and no idea of how to rear a child properly. Do you know what he was reading to those children when I got here?"

Alarmed, Kelly immediately thought of the day she had eavesdropped on Ryan's storytelling.

"What was Ryan—Mr. Matthews reading?" Kelly noticed Mrs. Webster's raised brows at her use of Ryan's first name.

"Mr. Matthews," she said, punctuating each syllable. "Was reading them a story he wrote himself."

No, she thought. Not that. He wouldn't do that. He said he wouldn't, not anymore. At least not *those* parts.

"Yes," Kelly struggled to hide her growing disquiet, and she reached out to turn the vase of flowers that stood on the table between them. "He said he had been doing some writing lately. What was the story about?"

"It was a ridiculous article about some crackpot psychologist and his theories. Really, now. Is that the sort of thing to read to children?" Mrs. Webster turned the flowers back around.

"Perhaps he just needs a little more time to adjust and a little training in parenting. That's my job."

Mrs. Webster's hands stopped in the midst of moving a daisy to another spot in the vase. "That is what Mr. Matthews said. I don't think there's much hope."

She tucked the daisy into place and stepped into

the kitchen. Kelly went to the back door and waved to Ryan. Seeing her, he called to the children and scooped up Sarah, who was toddling along at his heels.

"I'm sorry I'm late," Kelly said when Ryan entered the house. "I had to stop by my apartment to change clothes. The baby had an accident in my lap during my last appointment today."

"That's okay. Mrs. Yates just went after the cake. She figured it would be safer at her house than here." Kelly watched the plump, white-haired woman step across the yard, holding the cake in front of her and talking to the two children dancing around her.

That's what grandmothers are supposed to look like, Kelly thought, mentally comparing the kindly housekeeper to the impeccably dressed woman in the next room.

"Coming through," Mrs. Yates warned. "You kids get back. How's a body to make it through with you two gallivanting all over the place?"

"Come on, let's wash up," Kelly said, marshalling the children into the bathroom. While she wiped away the worst of the grime that coated their faces, she listened to their chatter. By the time they were finished, the three adults were seated silently around the table. Ryan lighted the candles and held Rachel over the cake, her untied shoelace dangling into a glass of milk.

"Put that child down," Mrs. Webster ordered.

Ryan cast her a long-suffering look. "How else is she going to blow out the candles. She's too short to reach the cake on her own."

"We have to sing first," Eric insisted.

"That's right," Ryan said as he plopped Rachel into a chair at the head of the table and led an off-key rendition of "Happy Birthday." Then, ignoring Mrs. Webster's scowl, he held Rachel over the dessert bowls and helped her blow out the candles.

Kelly smiled as Rachel squealed over a set of toy dishes from Mrs. Yates, a toy fire truck from Eric and little Sarah, and a battery-powered toy drill from Ryan. Kelly clipped the frilly barrette that was her present to Rachel into the child's hair. Her heart did a little flip-flop when Rachel hugged her.

Then Rachel modeled the lace-edged velvet dress that Grandmother Webster gave her. "It's just perfect for church services," the older woman intoned. "I'm taking her with me next Sunday. The ladies from the S.P.A.M. have been asking about the children."

"Spam?" Mrs. Yates wore a puzzled frown. "Spam? Now, isn't that the canned meat?"

Grandmother Webster breathed an audible sigh. "S.P.A.M.," she spelled. "The Society for Preservation of Morality in America. We meet each Sunday for luncheon."

"Oh, yes, now I remember." Mrs. Yates nodded as she shuffled the child on her lap, then captured a little hand just before it dipped into the cake icing. "Isn't that the group that picketed at the high school? Some kind of trouble over a book in the library."

"*Huckleberry Finn*, wasn't it?" Kelly interjected.

"Completely unsuitable," Mrs. Webster said. "If you had read—"

"More cake, anyone," Mrs. Yates interrupted.

Kelly noticed Ryan's clenched jaw and she attempted to change the subject.

"Ryan? Isn't there another present?"

"More presents?" Eric's eyes were sparkling with excitement. "One for me?"

"No," Ryan said. "One for Rachel. It's her birthday."

He deposited Rachel in a chair and retrieved a brightly wrapped box from the bottom of the sideboard. Kelly held her breath as Rachel slowly tore away the wrappings and lifted the lid of the box.

Rachel's face slowly creased into a broad smile.

"A dolly," she whispered.

"Rachel needed a new dolly," Eric said. "Her old one got lost."

For one horrible moment of silence the adults looked uncomfortably at one another and then at Rachel.

The three-year-old nodded.

"My dolly went with Mommy and Daddy."

"And now you have a new dolly," Mrs. Yates said. She picked up the doll and held it at arms' length, looking it over, pointing out all the wonderful characteristics. She snuggled it close, grinning. "Oh, what a pretty baby."

Then, she carefully handed it over to Rachel, who clutched it tightly to her chest before scrambling up into Ryan's lap.

Ryan mouthed a soundless "thank you" across the table. Kelly smiled back, forgetting for an instant about the disapproving woman who sat with them.

THREE

As Kelly scooped chocolate ice cream from the carton and dropped it into the bowl, she remembered about the day she had stood alone on the porch, an outsider listening in on a private family scene. With each passing day, she felt less like an outsider and more like a favorite aunt. No, she thought determinedly, make that a favorite cousin. The connotations of the former were too much for her overactive imagination to handle these days.

Not that Ryan had given her any cause for her imaginings, at least not since that night at the school. He had probably taken her word that the kiss was a mistake.

She had seen him exactly six times since then, and he had not touched her once. In fact, he seemed to be avoiding all physical contact with her. But at least they were becoming friends, and that was much safer, she thought. Besides the birthday party, they had taken the kids to the park, had shopped for winter clothes, and had picked out a swing set. They had spent hours teaching Eric to play badminton, with limited success. And she had rocked little Sarah to sleep, holding her long after her eyelids had drooped closed.

She kept telling herself that the novelty of it all would wear off. She would soon go back to what she usually did in her spare time before she took on the project of training Ryan to be a father.

What did she do in her spare time that was so important? Suddenly, a quiet evening of reading professional journals didn't have much appeal.

"Kelly?" A pleasurable warmth filled her at the sound of Ryan's voice.

"In the kitchen," she called. The problem was that she enjoyed being a part of a family too much. Maybe she should never have left Harrington. At least she had all those nieces and nephews to fuss over in her hometown. Her real reason for leaving Harrington came to mind, but she firmly thrust it away again.

"There you are." Ryan picked up the ice cream carton and turned it around. "Chocolate, huh? I thought strawberry was your favorite."

"This is for Mrs. Yates. She was bathing Sarah when the rest of us had ours."

"She's tucking Sarah in now." Ryan's hand bumped hers as they both reached for a spoon. Kelly heard Ryan's sharp intake of breath at the contact. She would have jerked her hand back, but he held it trapped in his own for an instant. Then, he gently squeezed it and released her.

Kelly could feel his eyes on her as she took a spoon from the drawer and stuck it into the ice cream. "Do you think they'll like the swing set as much as they like the sandbox?" he asked.

"I'm sure they will if you ever get it assembled," Kelly answered as she put the ice cream back into the freezer. "Maybe Mrs. Yates knows someone you could hire to put it together."

"You don't think I can do it?" Ryan was blocking her path now. His large frame seemed to fill the little kitchen. He might have intimidated Kelly as he stood there with his hands on his hips, challenging her. But she saw the laughter twinkling in his eyes and she responded in kind.

"Not if your performance today is any indication."

"I made some progress," he said.

"Only after you barked at me and then begged me to help."

"Begged? I never beg," he said, backing Kelly against the counter. "I don't need to."

Ryan's wolfish grin told Kelly that the next move was hers, but so was the risk that went with it.

"You can't tickle me into submission like you do the kids," she said as she edged away warily. "You wouldn't dare."

Ryan's expression was quickly shuttered. "You're right. I wouldn't." He turned his back on her and reached into the refrigerator.

"I'll be back in a minute," she told him, then picked up the ice cream and sought out Mrs. Yates. By the time the older woman was settled in the living room with a magazine and her snack, Kelly had summoned up the courage to return to the kitchen and face Ryan.

When she walked in, he was staring out the window, the opened beer sitting forgotten on the counter. Her first impulse was to hug away the tension in those strong shoulders. But she suppressed it. He wouldn't want that, not from her.

"Is there any soda left in the refrigerator?" she asked.

"Sure. Help yourself," he said, turning around. "And then I think we need to talk about something."

Kelly reached for a soda, refusing to look at Ryan. "About what?"

She pulled on the can, but nothing happened. She glanced up at Ryan, who was then watching her over the top of the opened door. "It's stuck," she said in explanation, then lifted the shelf above the can to free it. When she released the shelf it collapsed, spilling plastic bowls, fruit, and picante sauce all over her and the floor.

Ryan swore, then joined her in retrieving the food. Fortunately, most of it had remained in the containers. "I forgot about the shelf. It broke last week. Mrs. Yates must have used that can to prop it up."

"Just my luck," Kelly said with a giggle. She took Ryan's proffered hand and struggled to her feet, slipping on a dollop of cottage cheese.

Grasping her firmly about the waist, Ryan lifted her out of the mess and deposited her across the room in the corner. Kelly nervously tried to back out of his arms, but stopped when she felt the wall behind her.

"You can let me go now," she said. "I don't think I'll fall again."

"Not yet. Not until you answer one question."

"I'll answer your question. Just let me go."

But he didn't release her. He took a deep breath and held it for an instant. Then he asked, "Are you afraid of me or just men in general?"

Startled at his perceptiveness, Kelly mouthed a quick denial. But she could see that he didn't believe her. Moreover, his thumb found the pulse point in her wrist and slowly stroked it, sending tremors up her arm.

"I've watched you with the kids. With them, you're affectionate and warm and loving. You hug them and kiss them all the time. But with me you're reserved. You don't touch me and you shy away every time I come near you. And now, you're shaking like a leaf."

My God, he knew. She didn't know how, but he did. Kelly was frightened at that moment, not of him, but of the emotion that swelled in her chest, closing off her breath. She saw her reflection in his eyes, then noticed how dark those eyes were now, darker than she remembered. He was watching her with an intensity that thrilled her, yet fed her fear. It was like sitting in the front seat of a roller coaster, waiting for the ride to begin.

"Why should I be afraid?" she asked, dismayed at the tremor in her voice.

"You tell me." His voice was gentle, kind. Kelly wanted to tell him, but she couldn't. Not yet. Not until she was sure he would understand why her dreams had died not once, but twice. She couldn't say anything until she was in firm control of her emotions. So, she strived for a jesting tone.

"Well," she began slowly, "it could be that I'm

afraid you'll think I'm just another one of your fans.''

Ryan laughed softly. ''I'm a newsman, not a rock star. Newsmen don't have fan clubs. Of course, now that I'm going to be an author I'll need one. You could start a fan club, and everyone would pay ten dollars in dues. We could run away to Tahiti with the money.''

Now he was stroking the other wrist. Kelly struggled to follow the twisted conversation, but her mind was settling into a warm lethargy. ''Do you think there would be enough money to get to Tahiti?'' She pulled her hands away, but he only captured them again.

''Cincinnati, maybe.'' His head lowered, and Kelly fought the urge to meet him halfway. She stood perfectly still, holding the stiff pose in the hope that he would back away.

His lips never touched hers. Instead, she felt a caressing touch on her fingers. Opening her eyes, she watched him kiss her knuckles, then slip the top of her forefinger into his mouth, sucking away a smear of chocolate ice cream.

An electric charge jolted through Kelly at the intimate gesture. She started to pull her hand back.

''No,'' Ryan whispered. He licked the tip of the next finger, then turned her hand palm side up. His eyes never leaving hers, he kissed her palm, then laid it against his cheek.

''Trust me, Kelly. I don't bite.''

Kelly responded with a tremulous smile. ''Said the spider to the fly,'' she whispered. ''And we both know what happened to the fly.''

Ryan released her hand, his smile broadening when Kelly let it linger for an instant longer.

"Who is the spider, and who is the fly?" he asked. He backed away and reached for the paper towels. Together, they cleaned up the rest of the mess. When they finished, Kelly had regained most of her composure.

While Ryan headed upstairs to check on the children, Kelly joined Mrs. Yates in the living room. They were laughing over a ridiculously short mini-skirt in a newspaper advertisement when Ryan joined them.

"My stars! That skirt leaves a bit exposed to the wind," Mrs. Yates exclaimed. "Who in their right mind would wear something like that anyway?"

"Wear what?" Ryan asked as he leaned against the door jamb.

"Never mind," Kelly answered. "You don't have the legs for it, anyway."

"How do you know? You've never seen my legs." The spark of amusement lit his eyes, belying his pretended indignation.

Mrs. Yates snorted as she turned the page. "Real people don't have legs like that, just those skinny models who don't eat enough to keep a mouse alive."

"Come on," he said. "There's something I want to show you."

"What?" Kelly asked.

"Just come," he said, holding out his hand. Then, almost as an afterthought, he added, "You, too, Mrs. Yates."

The older woman shook her head. "If you can

manage without me, then I'll stay here. I'd like to finish this article."

Kelly cast her a suspicious look, knowing full well that Mrs. Yates was making up an excuse. She rose from the couch and reluctantly took Ryan's hand. But as she skirted the coffee table and headed for the doorway, Kelly realized she was being unfair. The woman was probably tired. A second look confirmed the fact. Mrs. Yates yawned surreptitiously behind the newspaper.

"Give me a woman with meat on her bones," Ryan whispered as he pantomimed the ungainly gait of a circus fat lady. Giggling, Kelly followed him through the dining room, then upstairs to the children's bedrooms. When Kelly's steps faltered, he urged her on. "Just to the door. But be quiet. I don't want her to hear us."

Her curiosity piqued, Kelly followed him. They stopped just outside Rachel's open door.

"Good, she's still doing it," Ryan said, his voice brimming with satisfaction. "I was afraid she would stop before you saw her."

"Doing what?"

As soon as her curious eyes located Rachel, Kelly had her answer. In the far corner of the room, Rachel was standing at the edge of her bed with the new doll, hugging it and singing a garbled tune. Then she tucked it into bed. Pulling the covers up to the doll's chin, she kissed it.

Ryan and Kelly watched her repeat the sequence three times before they tiptoed away and found Mrs. Yates supervising Eric as he brushed his teeth, her tiredness evidently forgotten as she chastised the child for not brushing in the back. Finding everything under control, Kelly and Ryan plopped down in the living room; he on the couch and she in the opposite chair.

"You have good instincts, Kelly."

"Thank you," she murmured as they smiled at one another, basking in the small victory they found in Rachel's delight with the doll.

"You should have children of your own," he said.

For an instant she stiffened, then relaxed again, remembering that he had no way of knowing how much remarks like that could hurt her.

"I have scores of children," she said, making light of the issue.

"You would make a good mother. You always say the right things, do the right things."

"I have five younger sisters," she said more sharply than she intended. "I got plenty of practice."

Ryan started to speak, then clamped his mouth shut as Mrs. Yates entered the room.

"Already asleep," she said. "And this body's heading home to do the same."

"If you'd like to take the day off tomorrow and visit your daughter, that'd be fine," Ryan told the older woman, as she sagged onto the other end of the couch. "I don't have any appointments outside the house. Kelly's coming over to run some screening tests on the kids."

Kelly gave Ryan an approving smile. She was glad he had noticed the older woman's fatigue. "I guess you could use a rest after the last couple of days."

"I suppose so," Mrs. Yates said. "But tests? Aren't they a bit little to be taking tests?"

Kelly smiled. "They're fun tests. I check to see if they know the difference between in and out, and over and under, and things like that. We use the tests to catch kids that are behind in speech or motor skills. If they are, we teach the parents how to help their children catch up or help them find a professional therapist."

"I see," Mrs. Yates said, while giving the impression that she didn't understand at all. "Well, I'm off."

"I'll walk out with you," Kelly said as she retrieved both their jackets from the hall closet. "I've got to get an early start tomorrow."

During the short drive to her apartment, her uneasiness resurfaced. She wondered again whether she was wise to become so involved with Ryan and his family. For several years now, she had kept the boundaries clear between her personal and professional lives. Lately, she had been ignoring all of her own rules. A daily stop at Ryan's house had become part of her routine. More often than not, she stayed until the children were tucked in. And she loved it all, especially feeding Sarah, even if the child did spit spinach in Kelly's face.

Was it the children or Ryan himself that drew her?

She suspected it was both, but was afraid to delve more deeply into her own motives. For now, she would just go upstairs, take a nice hot bath, and work on her thesis for an hour or two, maybe longer. She knew if she didn't start spending more time on it, she would never finish it and thus would not get her master's degree. And maybe if she focused her thoughts in that direction, she would be able to put the whole situation with Ryan into perspective.

The telephone was ringing when Kelly reached her apartment door, and she fumbled with the lock hurriedly. As the door swung open, she heard her voice on the answering machine, followed by Ryan's vibrant tone. "Call me as soon as you get in. It's important."

She dropped her purse and carry-all on the floor and grabbed the receiver.

"Don't hang up," she said just as she heard the click on the line. While the machine whirred and clicked as it reset itself for the next call, Kelly quickly dialed his number.

"So much for perspective," she muttered tensely.

Ryan answered halfway through the first ring.

"Is something wrong? Are the kids okay?" she asked before he had a chance to speak.

"They're fine," he said. "I guess I hung up too soon."

"I was just coming in the door. You said it was important. I thought maybe someone got hurt and you needed me."

"You're half right. That's why I called."

Kelly knit her brow in confusion. "Ryan, you're not making any sense."

"I just didn't want you to be upset."

"Why should I be upset?" A sudden thought struck her even as she spoke. "You're not going to drop out of the program are you?"

"No, it's nothing like that. I just wanted to apologize for that stupid remark about you having children. It's none of my business, and it obviously upset you."

Kelly sagged against the wall, closing her eyes. "It's no big deal," she said. "It was a compliment, really."

"That's the way I meant it. But you just clammed up, and then you left before I could figure out what was wrong. I thought I'd better straighten things out right away."

"It's all right," she insisted.

"Good, then you'll be here in the morning?"

"Yes, but don't expect me until about ten. I have an appointment at the school, and I have some paperwork to do." She paused to gather courage for the suggestion she was about to make. "Maybe you should consider getting another parent educator."

"You said you weren't upset."

"I'm not. But I'm losing my objectivity."

"We need you. The kids trust you."

"But we're not supposed to have relatives and close friends on our client lists," she said. "I'd still visit the children, if it's all right with you. Besides, you know that the school district is lending me to the Harrington district for the second half of the year. They only have one parent educator, and she's going on maternity leave right after New Year's."

"You mentioned it," he said in a tight voice. "But that's not for several months."

"Two months," she corrected.

"The children know you," he repeated. "They trust you. I asked for you specifically because they already knew you. They've already had enough disruptions in their lives lately. If you won't do it, I'll drop out of the program. It's as simple as that.''

Kelly's mouth dropped open. ''That's blackmail,'' she accused. ''Emotional blackmail.''

''Well?''

''All right. All right. Have it your way.''

''This time, it's the best way for the kids.''

''Maybe you're right,'' she said with a surprising sense of relief. What if he had agreed with her? She knew she'd miss her evenings with the children. Face it, she'd miss him, too. She wasn't sure she'd have the courage to drop by if there was no professional reason for her to be there.

''Good. So, are we still friends?'' There was an uncertain note in Ryan's voice that sent a rush of warmth surging through Kelly's veins.

''Of course, we're friends,'' she said softly.

''Good, then I'll see you in the morning.''

''Ryan,'' she started quickly, before he could hang up.

''Yes?''

''Ryan, the time I spend with the kids is special. Maybe it's because they need so much. Maybe it's because I really feel like I can give them something no one else can.''

''You do.''

When Kelly hung up the receiver, she touched the button on her answering machine to play back her messages from that day. There were two calls from salesmen and a reminder from her thesis advisor, urging her to call him with a progress report. Kelly groaned and cast her eye over the pile of files and envelopes on the corner desk. Then Ryan's voice filled her ears as the machine replayed his message.

She settled down to work at her desk, but couldn't keep her mind on the task. Finally, she gave up and headed for the shower, certain that the hot water would dispel her restlessness.

As she towelled her hair dry, she mentally reviewed her schedule for the next few weeks and sorted her activities into those she could skip and those she couldn't. The result was a decision to spend less time at the stone house and more time on her thesis. As she readied herself for bed, she thought that was probably a good thing anyway for all concerned. Ryan, she suspected, was beginning to rely too heavily on her. He needed more time on his own with the kids. He had to learn to trust his own judgment.

And her? She met her eyes in the reflection in the mirror, searching them for answers. Then she touched her cheek wonderingly, remembering the feel of Ryan's kiss. Just the memory made her tremble. That alone frightened her. It made her feel so vulnerable.

That night she dreamed that she was in Harrington, standing on her parents' front porch with Brian. She was trying to explain why she didn't want to stay married, although there really wasn't much to explain. It was painfully obvious that they really didn't have a marriage anymore. They even lived in different houses, she in her parents' home and he in the cozy farmhouse they once shared. They had tried, but they weren't the same people anymore, not after losing their baby. Not when they knew there could be no more babies. They had turned away from each other, blaming themselves and one another, unable to admit that no one was truly responsible for a quirk of nature.

Yet deep inside, Kelly knew that Brian needed a wife who was a whole woman, one who could give him the healthy children he deserved. But when he turned around, moving with dream-distorted slowness, the face was Bradley's. He wore the shocked, disappointed look that had warned her that he, too, had found her wanting, that he couldn't marry her, that an adopted baby wouldn't be good enough. Then she blinked, and the face was Ryan's.

Kelly awoke with a start. Trembling with the after-effects of the nightmare, she brushed her hands over her eyes, then stared into the darkness. Did all men ache to see little miniatures of themselves running about their feet? Did Ryan? Was it just another facet of the male ego? Or was it, as Brian had explained, a natural biological urge?

Kelly remembered her mother's words years ago when the pain had been at its worst. *Some man will love you for yourself—not these small-town tyrants, but a man that's sure enough of himself that he doesn't need to prove himself that way.* Maybe it was time she stopped hiding, she thought, remembering the marvelous but frightening feelings Ryan's touch could arouse. Maybe he was the one, maybe he wasn't. She'd never find out if she kept shying away every time he came near her. In time, she would have the answers to her questions. Only time was not something she had in abundance.

Wide awake now, she stared at the clock. Five A.M. Rolling out of bed, she flicked off the alarm and headed for the shower. If she hurried, she could get in a couple of hours of work on her thesis before her first appointment that morning. Somehow she had to finish it before she left for the temporary assignment in Harrington in January. Maybe by then she would know, too, whether Ryan Matthews was meant to be a friend or something more.

However, balancing the two objectives proved to be harder than Kelly had expected. True to her word, Kelly spent the next two weeks in a flurry of activity. When she wasn't making her rounds of the households assigned to her, she was reviewing notes for her thesis and writing the rough draft. It was coming along better than she had expected. The question of her relationship with Ryan was as unsettled as ever.

The most difficult point came when it was time to write the section of her thesis concerning the Webster children. She had written the rest of the rough draft and rewritten it with few major problems. But she had put this section aside time and time again. The others were just names in the files, pages in a report. Eric, Rachel, and Sarah were different. She had seen them cry and had wiped away their tears. She had held them and told them bedtime stories. She only hoped that the insight she gained from her close relationship with the family compensated for her obvious lack of objectivity.

As she added their case history, salty tears dropped onto the paper. Kelly was glad that her co-workers had already left the converted classroom that served as an office for the parent educators.

Staring out the window as she wiped her tears, Kelly wished she were leaving then, too. At that moment, she couldn't summon up the barest amount of enthusiasm for the work ahead of her. The idea of spending the evening bawling over a stack of papers had little appeal, particularly when the alternative was to play auntie to three very adorable children.

Nevertheless, she had to work tonight and probably a dozen more nights before she was finished. With a deep sigh, she returned to her desk, kicked off her shoes, and propped her feet up on an opened drawer. Setting aside the Webster case history again, she reached for the top file on the stack on her desk, deciding to work on another weak point in the thesis. She rejected that file and three others before she found the one she wanted. She read the notes in the margins and compared the child's scores on tests taken before and after his parents were divorced. Her interest piqued, she compared them with the charts she had already drawn up, then began taking notes.

When the late afternoon glow faded, she flipped on the overhead lights and returned to her desk. Some time later, she heard the janitor locking up the outside doors. She smiled absently at him when he came into the room to pull the shades. The man fumbled with the one on the end for a minute, then left it as it was, a foot or so higher than the others.

A tapping at the window jarred Kelly's attention abruptly away from the files about an hour later. As she started and turned, she saw a hand on the glass below the recalcitrant shade. Before she could reach the telephone to call the security guard, a face joined the hand framed in the aluminum-edged glass.

She sagged back in relief as she recognized Ryan.

She tried to fix a stern glare on her face, but found she couldn't. So instead, she sauntered to the window, attempting to hide her delight at his appearance. She tugged at the handle, but nothing happened.

"It figures," she muttered, then shook her head at Ryan's questioning gaze. After a moment, the window pulled open part way.

"What are you doing here?" she asked, her pleasure adding a lilt in her voice. The light streaming through the window revealed Ryan's answering smile.

"Looking for you."

"Why?"

"I thought you might like to have dinner with me."

"I wish I could," she said. "But I have to finish rewriting this section tonight. I only have a couple of days left before I have to show the rough draft to my advisor."

"You aren't going to eat?"

"I had an apple a little while ago. I'll eat something else when I get home."

"You won't have to. I came prepared." Grinning widely, Ryan held up a pair of brown paper sacks.

"Take-out?"

"Chinese." He handed her one of the sacks, edging it carefully through the window opening. "I wasn't sure what you like, so I got chicken cashew, Szechuan pork, mushroom beef, and shrimp pea pod. You don't get the tea unless you let me in."

"You're tempting me."

"I hope so," he said. For an instant, Ryan's cinnamon eyes blazed with a fiery heat that had nothing to do with the food. Kelly stared, startled by the intensity of her reaction. Then Ryan shuttered his eyes, leaving Kelly wondering if she had conjured that look from her imagination.

Yet, there was a hoarse note in his voice when he asked her which door to use. Kelly directed him around the side of the building to the east entrance. She headed down the hallway at a half-run. When she reached the door he was already there, scraping the mud from his shoes on the edge of the sidewalk and brushing broken bits of shrubbery off his thighs.

"You could have called, you know. Then you wouldn't have had to traipse through the bushes."

Ryan gave his jeans one last brush, then joined her at the open door. "I didn't want to give you a chance to say no."

In the semidarkness of the doorway, Kelly couldn't read his expression, but her body responded, nevertheless, with a trembling warmth. Not trusting her voice, she stepped inside to let him pass, then secured the door.

"How's the thesis coming along?" Ryan asked as they made their way up the empty hallway to the converted classroom that served as the office for the Early Childhood Center.

"Most of the rough draft is finished. I'm just rewriting a weak section now." Kelly led the way into the room and stopped at the formica-topped work table where she had left the bag of food.

As she unpacked the white cardboard cartons, releasing the aromatic scents of savory dishes, she realized how hungry she was.

"Are there any plates in that bag?" she asked as Ryan removed napkins, chopsticks, and plastic pouches of hot mustard, soy sauce, and duck sauce. Then, he pulled out a large Styrofoam cup with green Chinese figures and a pagoda printed on the side.

Ryan turned the bag upside down, dropping a handful of extra tea bags onto the table, but nothing else. "No forks either," he answered. "The chopsticks will have to do."

Kelly looked askance at the cellophane wrapped utensils and wished she had paid more attention when her brother had tried to teach her to use them. But it didn't make sense to fumble with sticks, when a perfectly good fork was available.

"I'll check the cafeteria," was all she said.

She was out the door before he could argue, only to return a couple of minutes later with nothing but two Styrofoam coffee cups. He was standing by her desk, his back to her, thumbing through the stack of typed and scribbled sheets that made up the rough draft of her thesis. When he heard her footsteps in the room, he returned to the table, a neutral expression fixed on his face.

"Find anything?" he asked.

"The cafeteria was locked," she explained. "There wasn't anything in the teacher's lounge either, just these and instant coffee. I just hope you're better with chopsticks than I am."

"I could always feed you," he suggested blandly as he opened the Styrofoam take-out package that contained fried wontons and egg rolls. The mischievous gleam in his eyes belied his innocent tone.

"I'll manage," Kelly replied, her voice a trifle breathless. She reached for an egg roll, careful to avoid touching Ryan. His amused expression indicated he had noticed her studied caution, which only made her feel more uncertain and a bit foolish. In silence, she poured the still steaming tea into the small cups and handed one to Ryan.

"So, what did you think?"

"About what?"

"My thesis. You were reading it when I was gone." It wasn't an accusation, but a statement of fact, and Ryan took it as such.

"I couldn't say without reading the whole thing," he prevaricated.

"But?"

Kelly licked a bit of spicy sauce from the corner of her mouth. As her eyes met Ryan's, the naked longing reflected in their cinnamon depths ignited a matching quiver in her mid-section.

"But what?" His answer was slow, almost distracted, but his eyes continued to watch her intently.

"That's one of those tactful answers that says you're trying to be polite, but you think it's terrible." She reached for the cooling tea, not out of thirst, but to drench her increasingly fevered senses. If Ryan kept casting her those unguarded looks, she was likely to melt onto her chair like a pat of butter in the sunshine.

"Actually, it's pretty good, at least as much as I read," he reassured her. "It just sounds pretty clinical. I'm not used to thinking of the kids in those terms."

"Neither am I." She took a deep breath and let it out slowly. "That's why I'm having so much trouble with that section."

They finished off the appetizers in silence. As

Kelly munched on the last of her egg roll, she watched Ryan tear off the top of the Styrofoam container and use it for a bowl for the rice and cashew chicken. Kelly followed suit with the Szechuan pork and tore the paper packaging off a pair of wooden chopsticks. She watched Ryan deftly scoop a bite into his mouth, then she gamely attacked her own food. Finally, she stabbed the piece of meat that had persistently eluded the grasp of her chopsticks.

"Where did you get the idea to do a thesis on the grieving process of children? Surely not from us. After all, you must have been working on this for months."

A sad smile touched Kelly's lips, and she saw the answering quirk in Ryan's eyebrows.

"Don't tell me you're really an orphan and those teachers are the imaginary parents you dreamed up when you were growing up in a convent."

Kelly's smile widened. "No. I guess Joey Nichols gave me the idea. He was in my first grade class when I began my master's work. He was very bright and excelled in his schoolwork until halfway through the year. After his father died, his schoolwork suffered. He became loud and disruptive. He was angry with the world."

"Did he get over it?"

Kelly stabbed another piece of pork. "Eventually, I suppose. I never really knew. The family moved away over the summer."

"Do you think Eric and Rachel will ever get over their parents' deaths?"

The bite stopped halfway to her mouth. "Have you?"

Ryan nibbled thoughtfully on the end of the chopstick before answering.

"No. Sometimes I still feel like I'm there for a visit and I'm waiting for Sharon and John to come home, only they can't. I wish they could. And the kids miss their mommy and daddy."

Kelly found herself staring at her own food as she struggled for the right words. "I think they're better already. They know you love them, and they're learning to trust you."

"I just hope I can always be there for them."

Kelly looked up, startled by the sharp edge to Ryan's voice. She noticed the sudden lines of strain around his mouth that hadn't been there a moment ago.

"Why wouldn't you be?"

"Oh, I plan to be," he said. "But I got a call from a Child Welfare officer today."

Kelly knit her brows in puzzlement. "Why would they be calling you? They don't have any jurisdiction over guardianship appointments, particularly in cases like yours when it's set up in the will."

"Maybe someone filed a complaint?"

"Who would do that?" Kelly knew the answer as soon as the words left her mouth. "Mrs. Webster?"

Ryan toyed absently with his food while his eyes glittered with controlled anger. "She's made no bones about the fact that she thinks I'm completely incapable of raising her grandchildren. She complains about everything, from what they eat, to the clothes they wear, to the games they play. If she had her way, they'd be locked up inside that mansion of hers with an army of nannies."

Kelly might have laughed at the mental picture he drew, if she hadn't noticed his pained expression.

"She can't be that bad. Her son turned out all right."

Ryan's answering smile was brief, never reaching his eyes.

"Yes, but Mr. Webster was alive then to control her. He died several years ago, and then it was up to John to try to keep her from meddling."

"Poor John."

"Yes, and now poor me."

"Do you think she'll cause any real trouble?" Kelly's concern spilled over into her voice, eliciting a faint smile of appreciation from Ryan.

"I'm sure that she'll try."

"What will you do?"

Ryan reached for the soy sauce and tore a corner of the package with his strong, white teeth. "I guess I'll just have to get respectable."

"How will you do that, write inspirational adventure novels?"

Ryan pretended to ignore her jest, but she could tell by the slant of his shoulders that her quip had eased some of his tension.

"I could do that," he said solemnly. "But it wouldn't be enough to satisfy her. No, the only thing that might work would be to get married. You know, provide the children with a mother figure. Are you doing anything Friday afternoon?"

FOUR

Kelly almost choked on the bit of rice she'd managed to maneuver into her mouth.

"What?" she gasped, then realized instantly that he was following her cue and making light of the problem.

"It does sound kind of extreme, doesn't it?" His voice was calm, well schooled from his years as an interviewer, but he pushed the rice in his dish around in circles, drawing and tapping repeatedly.

"Yes. Besides, do you think that would stop her?"

"Probably not."

"Oh, well," Kelly teased. "I guess I'll have to find some other way to get Mom and Aunt Elsie off my back. They're still trying to marry me off to some nice, dependable, but boring man."

"I knew there was a good reason why you left Harrington. It wasn't just to go back to college, was it?"

"Nope, it was to escape from the pressure. You

can't imagine what it's like when they start match-making.''

"I take it they had someone in mind for you?"

Kelly rolled her eyes outrageously. "They set me up with several before I finally escaped."

"Anything serious?"

Kelly shrugged. "Nothing I couldn't recover from." She hoped he hadn't noticed the catch in her voice, but he had.

"There was one that was serious, wasn't there?"

A wary edge crept into Kelly's banter as she struggled to maintain a light tone.

"What makes you say that?" She could tell by his expression that she hadn't fooled him.

"Your eyes. They're too wise, too compassionate for an innocent."

"It was a long time ago."

"What happened?"

Kelly pushed the makeshift plate away and started closing the containers. "It didn't work out." Subject closed.

"Why not?" Ryan persisted.

She shrugged and flashed an irritated glance in his direction. "It doesn't matter now. It was all over and done with years ago. He's happily married now and expecting a baby."

"He doesn't know what he let slip away."

Kelly couldn't resist the smile. "Evidently."

Leaning across the table, he captured her fidgeting fingers in a strong clasp. "Well, I know. And I think you're very special." Slowly and with infinite care, he kissed her fingers, then enclosed them again in his own.

This time Kelly didn't stiffen. Instead, she reveled in the seeping warmth that pushed the past a little bit farther away, a past that was receding a tiny step with every moment spent in Ryan's company. *Maybe it was her turn to let go and to get on with her life.*

"I just hope," Ryan said, "that we can get beyond whatever or whoever hurt you."

Kelly sighed, still entranced by the sincerity in his voice, but afraid of stepping further into what she knew was dangerous territory. She wasn't sure he would understand. Some losses were permanent. They could never be repaired or replaced. She tried to pull her hand away. But he held it firmly, forcing her to meet his eyes—not by any show of strength, but by his sheer presence.

"I don't want to push you. Maybe sometime you'll trust me enough to tell me about it." And his eyes reflected compassion and a sense of purpose Kelly could not define.

"Maybe," she answered, trying to marshal her senses and return to normalcy. "Maybe soon, but now I have to get back to work. Do you want to save the extras for lunch tomorrow?"

He met her abrupt change of subject with nothing more than a raised pair of eyebrows. "No. You take it. At least I know you'll have something besides an apple."

"Ryan Matthews, you're worse than my mother," she said as she stuffed the containers of leftovers into a paper bag. After a quick trip to the teachers' lounge to deposit the bag in the small refrigerator, she returned to the room. In her absence, Ryan had cleaned up the rest of their mess.

• "Do you mind if I stick around for a while? I won't bother you." He pulled a paperback from his jacket pocket and held it up. "I'm checking out my competition."

Kelly dubiously eyed the flashy cover with its embossed sword and barely clothed bodies. "It looks—interesting. But with your experience, you should be writing something serious, investigating congressmen or something like that."

Ryan shook his head. "I tried that. There's no money in it."

"So, you're selling out?"

Flashing a wicked grin, Ryan nodded. "That's one way to put it. Now, get to work or we'll be here all night. And that, I think, would be difficult to explain to the principal."

For the next half hour Kelly worked her way steadily through the stack of files, making notes and scribbling changes in the margins of the typed pages. Then, she moved to the next desk so she could retype them.

Within a few minutes she was wincing every other stroke and wishing she hadn't defied her mother and taken art class instead of typing. She still couldn't draw a straight line, but there were times when typing skills would come in handy. Now was one of them.

While she waited for the correction fluid to dry over yet another error, she turned to find Ryan watching her, his feet propped comfortably on one of the desks.

"Why don't you come over to the house and use my word processor? You'll only have to type the whole thing once. Then you can just change the parts you want and the machine takes care of the rest.''

Kelly declined politely, but firmly. ''I'd probably screw up your word processor and erase every other chapter of your book.''

Ryan shook his head. ''That wouldn't happen. I guarantee it.''

''I'll think about it.''

He eased his feet to the floor and joined her at the typewriter. Reaching around her, he rolled the paper out of the machine. ''In the meantime, why don't you pack all this up and get some rest.'' He lightly brushed the darkened smudges under her eyes.

''I have been burning the candle at both ends,'' she admitted as Ryan gathered up the stack of notes and manuscript pages.

''Tonight, you'll get to bed early, probably before ten-thirty. I'm taking all this hostage. You can't have it back until you get a good night's sleep. And then, you can use my word processor and printer,'' he said, holding up his hand to forestall the protest forming in her brain. ''You've helped me a lot. Now it's my turn to help you.''

Again, that curious warmth suffused every cell of her body, leaving Kelly with an unfamiliar sense of well-being and security. And she wasn't sure that was good. She didn't like losing control over any aspect of her life, and Ryan had certainly taken control in this matter. On the other hand, everyone needed to lean on someone once in a while. Just so it didn't get out of hand.

''I said I'd think about it,'' she replied softly. But she already knew what her decision would be.

"I'm not upset, Mother," Kelly insisted the next day as she cradled the telephone receiver on her shoulder. While she spoke, her hands ripped the lettuce into shreds and dropped the pieces into a bowl. "I'm happy for them. I know Brian always wanted a son."

"He made that painfully obvious, didn't he?" Her mother's concern carried over the line despite the crackle of static. Kelly didn't miss the bite of sarcasm, either.

Marta Simms divided the fault for her daughter's divorce, the one blight on the family's name, equally between Kelly and her ex-husband. Mrs. Simms still saw the world in black and white, with very few shades of gray in between. Having reared a houseful of children despite several miscarriages, she couldn't understand how the death of one small infant could tear a marriage apart, magnifying the problems instead of overshadowing them.

"It wasn't like that, Mom."

"So why haven't you come home for a visit?"

"Certainly not because I'm afraid of seeing Brian. I've been busy. I'll come for Christmas. And then, you know, I'll be replacing Debbie at the Early Childhood Center for a couple of months."

"What about Thanksgiving?"

"I—um—have plans. You remember the family I told you about, the three kids whose parents were killed this summer."

"Yes, the ones living with that nice-looking television reporter."

Kelly smiled into the receiver.

"Yes, well, I promised to spend Thanksgiving with them. It's their first real holiday without their parents. You won't even miss me with all of the others there."

"Of course, I'll miss you. But I understand."

Kelly could just see the wheels turning in her mother's matchmaking mind. "Do you?" she queried skeptically.

"Of course. I'm just worried about you."

"Why? Because of Brian's new baby? Or because you think this reporter might be husband material?" Kelly could tell from the long pause that she had hit the mark.

"Your father and I, well, we're wondering whether you're becoming too involved with this family. You know, you were so terribly hurt when you lost the baby. Then, between the divorce and that awful Bradley Jenkins, you were feeling pretty low." The thought of Bradley made Kelly groan aloud. Another old friend from high school, he had been anxious to step in after the divorce and take Brian's place. That is, until he learned that she couldn't have children and give him the requisite heir to the family chain of hardware stores.

"And you know I wanted a houseful of children, right? You're thinking it would all work out nicely if I married that reporter, former reporter, really. Nice try, Mom. I know what I'm doing and husband-hunting isn't part of the plan."

But as she hung up the phone, she wondered if she really did know what she was doing. Despite all her assurances to her mother, she was depressed by the news of Brian's new child. It reminded her of how little time they had with their child, Brian's first, and the marriage that hadn't survived the loss.

Thrusting the memories aside, she reached for the phone again and dialed Ryan's number. He sounded preoccupied when he answered.

"Is this a bad time?" she asked. "This really isn't that important."

Ryan's denial was firm and reassuring, automatically lifting her spirits. "Had a rough day?" The obvious note of concern in his voice almost made her ashamed of herself.

"Not the best," she agreed. "How are the kids?"

"Asleep. I was just starting chapter seven."

"Then I won't keep you."

"Are you all right? You sound kind of strange. You're not getting sick are you?"

"I'm fine, just tired, I guess."

Ryan was not convinced, but Kelly sidestepped his questions. She didn't want to explain why her mother's phone call had unsettled her. It was too complicated.

"Will I see you tomorrow?" Ryan asked.

"I'll be there first thing in the morning. Did you forget about the appointment?"

"No. I just didn't want you to."

"I wouldn't. Besides, you kidnapped most of my thesis."

"I could start typing it in," Ryan offered.

"No. I haven't even said I'd use your word processor."

"You will," he said. His confidence would have been irritating if Kelly hadn't been distracted by the earlier phone call.

"All right. I will."

As Ryan replaced the receiver a few minutes later, he wondered what had upset Kelly. She hadn't been her usual cheerful self. He drummed his fingers thoughtfully on the desk for a few seconds, then returned his attention to the word processor. But for the next couple of hours, his nagging concern about Kelly disrupted his thoughts.

Finally he gave up, stored the information, and flipped the computer switch to "off." He picked up a stack of printouts and started reading. Ryan's brow furrowed as he skimmed the pages a third time. Then he pulled a red pencil out of the drawer and began writing. Thirty seconds later, he dropped the entire stack into the trash can. He turned the word processor back on, then went into the kitchen to pour another cup of coffee while the machine warmed up.

This was driving him crazy. Even a cold shower had not helped much. He couldn't write. He couldn't think of anything but Kelly. Kelly rocking the baby. Kelly laughing as she flopped onto the ground in a game of ring-around-a-rosy. Kelly with her back pinned against the refrigerator, her hands trembling in his. Kelly playing with the children, her eyes filled with that strange yearning he sometimes glimpsed before she thought to hide it from him. The odd note of sadness in her voice on the telephone was the most disturbing of all.

On the way back to the study, he thought he heard a soft whimper. Pausing outside the girls' room, he noticed that Sarah had kicked her covers off. He retrieved the stuffed bear from the floor and tucked it in at Sarah's side. As he pulled the covers up to her chin, the child rolled over on her side and snuggled up against the bear.

As Ryan turned to leave, Sarah whimpered again, then broke into a plaintive wail. He set the coffee down on the dresser and picked her up. He stroked her back soothingly and swayed gently as he sang a nonsensical tune. When she had quieted, Ryan tucked her back into bed and handed her the ever-present bottle, still half-filled with water. Before leaving the room, he checked on Rachel, but she was sleeping soundly, undisturbed by the crying.

A few moments later, Ryan was back at his desk, his fingers flying over the keyboard, the steaming cup of coffee forgotten.

When Dirk awoke, he was alone in the bed. The only signs that Bambi had been there were an indentation in the pillow and the musky scent of their lovemaking.

The moonlight streamed through the open balcony door. Dirk knew he had closed the door earlier. She must be out there, staring at the mountains, wondering if the others had gotten out in time.

He swung his legs over the edge of the bed and pulled on his pants. He reached for his shirt, but it was no longer slung over the chair.

Then a shadow fell across the bed, and he turned to see Bambi, her delectable body framed by the moonlight streaming through the doorway. His shirt hung loosely about her body, its tails ending at the curve of her thighs.

"We should leave tomorrow," he said.

"And do what?" she asked in a strained voice.

"Keep on wondering? No, I have to know if they escaped."

"If they did, they'll know where to find us. If they didn't, there's nothing we can do to help them. Nothing anyone can do."

Bambi nodded slowly, then glided towards him, letting the front of the shirt fall open. When Dirk reached out to her, she pushed him backwards into the chair, then climbed into his lap.

"You feel good, love," Dirk whispered as his arms closed around her. He gasped as she—

A wail from across the hallway rose in a crescendo, followed shortly by a second cry in a different voice. Closing his eyes in frustration, Ryan took a deep breath, then pushed himself back from the desk and headed across the hall.

"I'd love to stop and talk, dear, but my daughter is expecting me," Mrs. Yates called from the next yard. "Just ring the bell again and wait. He probably has the baby in the tub. It's easier to get her breakfast off her that way."

"I'm sure it's something like that," Kelly called back. She watched the older woman climb into her car and back out of the drive. Then she turned back to the door and started to knock, halting when she heard the noises coming from the other side.

Kelly could hear the children whispering and scuttling about on the other side of the heavy oak door.

What was going on? She had been waiting for several minutes, but Ryan had not come to the door even though she had rung twice. He must be home.

The car was in the driveway, and the children were obviously there. She could hear them talking.

So where was Ryan?

Then she heard the rasping of the lock and she sighed with relief. After a couple more clatters and bangs, the door opened and Eric's pajama-clad figure popped into view. A purple smear, probably jelly, stained his front.

"Hi, Kelly," he said.

"Hello, Eric. Where's your Uncle Ryan?"

"He's sleeping. You brought toys," his eyes rested on the bulging bag on Kelly's shoulder. "Come inside," he said. "We can play until Uncle Ryan wakes up."

Kelly wondered if now was the time for a lecture on opening the door to strangers. No, she decided, as she looked around, then stepped over a pile of newspapers and through a maze of building blocks, dump trucks, and toy dishes. There was a lump of something brown on the table, and the smell of peanut butter permeated the air. Now was the time to rescue the carpet and anything else that was in danger of being ruined. The lecture could wait.

She set her bag down beside the kitchen table and searched for a dishcloth to wipe away the milk that was dripping from the counter onto a chair that was shoved up against the kitchen cabinet.

"Wouldn't this set Grandmother Webster's teeth on edge," Kelly muttered.

Ryan must sleep like a log. Either that or he was ill.

Frowning, she went in search of Eric, who had

disappeared already. She found him in the girls' room, showing Rachel a puzzle from Kelly's bag.

"Is Uncle Ryan still in bed?"

"No." Eric said. "He's sleeping in the rocking chair."

"Go wake him up and tell him that I'm here," Kelly suggested.

Eric shook his head slowly. "Uncle Ryan is grouchy."

Kelly smiled her understanding. She wasn't exactly a morning person herself. "Is he always grouchy in the morning?"

A wide grin split the little boy's face. "Always. Mrs. Yates says he's a growly bear. Tell Rachel to wake him up."

Kelly smiled at the little girl that had quietly sidled up to her.

"Will you show me where Uncle Ryan is?" Kelly asked.

Rachel hesitated. "Okay." She held out her small hand and haltingly led Rachel down the hallway and into a room Kelly had not been into before.

As Kelly stepped through the doorway, she hoped that Ryan was not one of those men who slept in the buff. Blushing at the picture that popped into her mind, she stopped. What am I doing standing here in Ryan Matthews's bedroom wondering what he sleeps in? Acting like an idiot, a little voice in her head answered.

Rachel's gentle tug on her hand halted Kelly's mental wanderings. "This is your uncle's room?"

"No. It's Mommy and Daddy's room. Uncle Ryan just sleeps here."

The bed was empty, Kelly thought, until a lump at the edge moved. Then a furry head peeked out from under the covers. The cat slowly climbed out, stretched and yawned.

Then Kelly saw Ryan in the far corner, stretched out in an overstuffed rocker. Little Sarah was sprawled out, her wispy blond hair curling up against the dark hair on Ryan's chest. Her body gently lifted and fell with his breathing. She whimpered, then wriggled and stuffed a tiny thumb into her mouth and sucked, making faint smacking sounds.

A teething ring and a tube of infant gum gel lay on the floor next to the chair, evidence of what must have been a rough night for both of them. The rest of the room was a strange mixture of tasteful design and masculine clutter. Like the rest of the house, disorder reigned in Ryan's bedroom. It wasn't the chaotic disorder the children left behind. The over-stuffed clutter indicated to Kelly that Ryan had not yet moved his things into the drawers, but was living out of the suitcases and boxes that were stacked about.

The room was scented with a cruious mixture of cedar and cologne, along with another strange odor that Kelly soon identified as soured milk.

"Time to eat, Uncle Ryan," Rachel called. Kelly picked up the little girl before she could dart over to wake him.

"Just let them sleep a little longer," she said as she watched them. Ryan looked vulnerable, his body relaxed and his lids closed over the probing eyes that always seemed to see too much. She smiled wryly. Even in sleep, Ryan's features were deceptive. If there was one thing Kelly knew, it was that Ryan Matthews was anything but vulnerable, except maybe where the children were concerned.

For a moment, she imagined what it would be like to be a part of all this, to have children to care for, a man to love and who loved her. She sighed, thinking that this was as close as she was likely to come to that state. She had accepted long ago that she was different. For her, the dream could not come true.

Still, she lingered for an instant longer, then turned away regretfully.

"I'm hungry," Rachel said, tugging on her sleeve.

"Okay, sweetheart. Let's go find some cereal." Kelly carried Rachel into the kitchen and set her down in a chair before she called out to Eric. When the two children were eating, she slipped back into Ryan's bedroom to check on Sarah.

Whimpering louder now, Sarah shifted her head restlessly from side to side. As Kelly approached, Sarah blinked, then watched her with a wary stare.

"Hello, little one." Kelly reached down, and Sarah smiled in recognition and held up her arms. The now familiar rush of emotion brought tears to Kelly's eyes, but she blinked them back as she lifted the child.

Her fingers burned where they brushed against Ryan's chest. She tried to ignore the little moan of pleasure he emitted when she touched him. What she could not ignore was the gaping front of the robe that left nothing to the imagination. Ryan's nakedness was unsettling, and she quelled the sudden trembling in her limbs.

She sat Sarah on her feet in the middle of the floor

and grabbed a sheet from the bed. As she draped it across Ryan, she was thankful that the toddler was the only witness to the heated blush that suffused Kelly's face. Holding Sarah away from her, she went in search of a clean diaper. She gave the child a lightning quick bath, dressed her, and then deposited her in the playpen with a bottle. Checking the clock, she decided to wake up Ryan. She still had a half hour before she needed to leave, but he might need some time to get himself together before he was awake enough to manage the children.

As she approached the chair, she saw that the sheet had slipped, and she quickly pulled it into place again, then stood back.

"Ryan? Ryan wake up."

He didn't move.

"Ryan?" Kelly touched his shoulder, pulled her hand back, then rested it on his shoulder again. His skin was enticingly warm there, smoothly laid over the firm muscles. She leaned over and gave him a little shake.

"Wake up. You have to take care of the kids."

A pair of strong hands grabbed her forearms and she sprawled across his chest in an undignified heap, her feet dangling over the edge of the chair. She knew her skirt was hiked dangerously high because she could feel the cool air up on her thighs. She struggled to right herself, but Ryan only held her tighter.

"No," he murmured into her hair. "You feel good here. You belong here."

Kelly's heart lurched, then dropped into the pit of her stomach. She could hear his heartbeat echoing the pounding in his own veins. He was dreaming. He had to be. He wouldn't be talking like that to her if he were awake, would he? He had never said anything like that before. Cautiously, she started to move away again, but his arms held her tightly in place.

She couldn't think there with her body pressed so intimately against his bare flesh. She could only feel. For the moment, she gave in to her traitorous instincts and relaxed against Ryan's warmth. She would think later, rationalize it all away. For now, she could not move away any more than she could willfully stop breathing.

"Kelly?" he whispered, his breath fanning her ear while his hand found the sensitive nerve at the base of her neck and stroked it. Shivers of excitement skimmed along her nerves.

Kelly turned her face toward him, and in a single movement, he turned her over, cradling her on his lap. When his lips finally met hers, all thoughts of the past and the future were gone. There was only now.

Her one arm was trapped between them, but Kelly slid the other hand sensuously up his chest to clasp his shoulder. Gradually the kiss deepened. With a soft sigh, Kelly parted her lips and melted with the sweetness of it.

When Ryan finally lifted his head, Kelly moaned her protest.

"The kids?" His breath fanned her neck, sending shivers down her spine.

"Hmmm?" She nuzzled against his chest. "Oh, yes. They're eating cereal. Eric let me in."

Ryan groaned. "I'm sorry."

Sorry? Kelly's eyes flew open and she started to sit up, but he pulled her back.

"Sorry I didn't wake up," he said as he ran a long finger up her leg. "No. I take that back. I like waking up this way better."

"I need to check on the kids."

"They'll be all right for another minute. I can hear them. They're not too loud and they're not too quiet."

Kelly couldn't help but smile. "You're learning."

"That's two I owe you," he said.

"What do you mean?"

He captured her finger before it could finish tracing the pattern across his chest.

"The doll. And this morning. You could have yelled at me, told me to get off my lazy duff."

"You obviously had a rough night. I found the teething ring on the floor. I washed it and put it back in the freezer. You might need it again later."

"Thanks," he said, kissing her nose.

"Is this how you thank all the household help?"

His eyes darkened. "No, this is what I want to do every time I see you. Only it isn't enough."

This kiss was different, more intense, and their breathing was ragged when they drew apart.

"Kelly, I—" Whatever he had been about to say was lost as his attention focused behind Kelly.

She turned in his lap to see Grandmother Webster standing just inside the doorway. The triumphant gleam in Grandmother Webster's eyes was something Kelly would remember for a long time afterwards.

FIVE

Ryan's arms tightened around Kelly's waist when he heard her startled gasp, and her eyes followed his to the doorway. The sight of the silver-haired martinet abruptly chilled his overheated senses.

While he instinctively schooled his expression into a poker face, his mind whirred from the question of how she had gotten in to how long had she been there, and then on to the matter of how she could turn the situation to her advantage.

And all the while, his glance swung back and forth between the two women—one an enemy or the next thing to it, the other a friend and something more, although he wasn't quite sure what. Kelly tried to pull away, but he held her possessively, unashamedly, despite the censure in the older woman's knowing stare.

He wasn't about to start acting like a teenager caught in the backseat of his father's car, even if he felt like one. No, damn it. He wasn't an oversexed adolescent. He was a responsible man who had just been awakened by a taste of heaven itself. He wasn't about to let an old woman's bitterness take that away from him.

Across the room, his wary eyes met the steel-blue gleam of his adversary's. For a moment, neither wavered. Then Ryan noticed the deepening lines around the older woman's mouth, her shadowed eyes.

Mrs. Webster hesitated for an instant, seeming to struggle with second thoughts as her eyes rested on Kelly's chagrined expression. Her outrage won out over any softer feelings she might have.

"How dare you leave those children alone downstairs where you can't even hear them!" She advanced into the room, her finger pointing accusingly at the two of them, still ensconced in the chair. "One of them could choke to death, and you wouldn't even know it."

Kelly flushed and pursed her lips, biting off whatever retort was hovering on the edge of her tongue. She awkwardly maneuvered herself out of Ryan's lap, brushing aside his efforts at helping her. She headed for the door, but Ryan's hand on her wrist stopped her before she could take a second step. "No," he said. "You stay. She's leaving."

"Not this time," Mrs. Webster interjected.

Kelly tried again to escape. "I should check on the kids," she said, but neither Ryan nor Mrs. Webster paid any attention. He didn't release her wrist either.

"Didn't your mother teach you that it's impolite to walk into someone's house uninvited?" Ryan asked, his voice deceptively calm, his eyes narrowing as he struggled to hide his anger. "How did you get in? I didn't hear the doorbell."

The older woman's mouth quirked slightly at his clipped tone. "I'm not surprised. You seemed too busy to notice much of anything." Her smirk was infuriating, but her fingers rubbed in agitation at the heavy gold bracelets that jangled at her wrists. Noting the nervous movement, Ryan's spirits climbed a step or two. Maybe he could salvage the situation.

"Do you still have a key to the house?" he persisted.

"How I got into the house is not the issue. Your behavior is," her voice quavered, but whether it was from anger, nervousness, or unease, Ryan couldn't tell. The woman had been hiding her emotions behind a social mask for too many years. She was too hard to read.

"I've known all along that you are quite incapable of providing a proper home for my grandchildren," she continued. "It was only a matter of time before you proved it. I'm just grateful that I arrived before something terrible happened to one of them. It's just as I've thought all along."

Ryan heaved himself to his feet, tugging at the sheet and winding it more closely around him to cover what the gaping robe did not. "Which is?" he questioned as he mentally acknowledged the irony of defending his morality while he was wrapped in a sheet.

"Despite your good intentions and your tutoring—" Her brows lifted in Kelly's direction before she continued. "I don't doubt that you care for these children as much as you can care for anyone. But obviously neither of you has the remotest idea of what raising children entails. It's not just keeping them clean and fed. It's teaching them to be moral, productive citizens. What kind of an example are you setting? My word, it's not even nine o'clock in the morning. Or were you just saying goodbye to Miss Smith?''

"What I was or wasn't doing with Kelly is none of your damn business—'' Ryan ground out between clenched teeth while he clutched at the slipping sheet and cursed it beneath his breath. Kelly's warm hand on his arm stilled his mutterings for an instant. He listened with growing irritation to her effort to diffuse the crackling tension in the room.

"I realize what you think, and I know what you saw a few minutes ago. But you've obviously misunderstood. I didn't sleep here. You can verify that with Mrs. Yates.'' Kelly's color was paler than usual. Her voice was pitched a bit high, but other than that she appeared in perfect control. She retrieved a tube of teething gel from under the chair and handed it to Mrs. Webster, remaining opposite the woman. With her back to Ryan, he could no longer read her expressions. Ryan took advantage of the moment and pulled his robe closed, knotted the belt, and let the sheet slide to the floor.

"That doesn't explain what you're doing here.''

"Sarah is teething and Ryan was evidently up with her a lot last night. When I got here, he was still asleep, so the kids let me in. I fed them and then came upstairs to—''

"You don't need to explain to her,'' Ryan interrupted as he tossed the sheet into the corner. "She wouldn't believe you anyway."

The gold bracelets jangled as Mrs. Webster held up her hands. "No, please continue."

"I came up here to wake up Ryan before I left. I guess he was dreaming because he was muttering something—I couldn't tell what—and when I reached over to shake him, he grabbed me. It wasn't passion you witnessed. It was just a dream."

From where he stood, Ryan couldn't see either of their faces, so he moved closer and to the side, hovering protectively near Kelly. But she seemed to neither need nor want his help.

Mrs. Webster, however, was thoughtful in a calculated sort of way.

"So, it isn't likely that such a scene would be repeated?"

"No," Kelly said, her chin thrust high.

"I see. Well, you at least are dressed. That's something in your favor." Mrs. Webster stalked around Kelly and over to the dresser. She picked up a garish paperback and frowned first at the book and then at Kelly. "It doesn't change the fact that the children could have walked in on you, or that they were unattended downstairs while the two of you necked, dream or not."

"You're determined to think the worst, aren't you?" Kelly's voice quivered with anger now, and with what Ryan hoped was reaction to the other unsettled emotions that he had so recently stirred. "You're wrong about Ryan, and you're wrong about me. And you've obviously made a few other incorrect assumptions. That's between the two of you to settle. I have another appointment.''

With heartrending regret, Ryan watched Kelly stalk out of the room with carefully controlled dignity and disappear into the hallway. Her footsteps quickened to a run when she neared the stairs. He listened for the safe click of her low heels on the tiles below before he breathed again.

The older woman's eyes followed Kelly for a moment before returning to Ryan, who bent to dig through a clothes basket.

''I'll see you downstairs when you're dressed,'' she said.

Ryan's voice followed her out into the hallway, stopping her in her tracks for an instant. ''Leave her out of this. You can say what you like to me, but leave her alone.''

''Your Miss Smith is no wilting flower, Ryan. She didn't faint on the stairs. I doubt if she'll do so in the hallway or on the front porch.''

''No, but she can be hurt all the same. And that's something I won't allow.''

Mrs. Webster hesitated, glancing down the hallway. Then she slowly stepped back into Ryan's room. ''I'm afraid there's no way you can prevent that at this point, unless you decide to act sensibly.'' Her strong features screwed into a distasteful grimace. ''Don't ask me to apologize for spoiling your little seduction. Despite what you may think, I believe she deserves much better than you. Perhaps this will bring her to her senses.''

Ryan regarded her with suspicion and mild surprise. Then he simply shook his head in reply. It would serve no purpose to try to explain. She wouldn't believe him anyway, and he'd probably make matters worse. On the other hand, he could not let that self-righteous witch brand Kelly with the same brush that she tarred him with, wrong as it was. Yet, how could he explain to someone with a closed mind what he didn't understand yet himself?

All he knew was that Kelly provided the spark that had brought laughter back to this house and to his life. For a man of words, he was remarkably unable to define the scope of his feelings for this woman, not even in his own mind. He only knew they went beyond anything he had experienced before.

When he finally spoke, it was only to tell Mrs. Webster to meet him in the study downstairs. He should have known better than to expect her compliance.

"No. I'm late for the society board meeting already. We'll settle this now."

Ryan nodded slowly. "If that's the way you want it. I'm changing the locks today. You are free to visit your grandchildren anytime, but you'll have to ring the doorbell and wait for someone to let you in."

"That won't be necessary. I'm taking the children home with me. You'll have time to pack their things before I return from my meeting."

"No." His refusal was adamant, his tone brooking no argument. Even the formidable Grandmother Webster was startled for an instant, but then her eyes narrowed.

"Surely, you know that I can prove you unfit."

"It's your word against mine."

The smug smile widened.

"I didn't come alone. Emily Vanderhoff, of the banking branch of the Vanderhoffs, is waiting downstairs. I'm sure she can add two and two and come up with four."

At that moment, the impact of her words struck at his heart. Like a fool, he had inadvertently handed her the pretext for a custody suit on a silver platter. It didn't matter that Emily What's-her-name hadn't been part of the scene in the bedroom. Unless he was very lucky, the old bat could hear and see well enough to back up Mrs. Webster's story.

He had practically given the children away. It would be difficult, perhaps impossible, to win against the combined odds of Mrs. Webster's accusations and her money. What could he give them except love? He knew they needed love and reassurance more than anything else, but could he convince the judge that they wouldn't get it from their grandmother. If she really cared as much as she claimed, she wouldn't go to that committee meeting at all. She'd be packing their bags herself, if she was any kind of grandmother at all.

Resolution followed hard on the heels of panic, and he thanked God that she evidently wasn't. He had to win. He couldn't abandon his sister's children to the dispassionate care of this martinet.

"You're not taking the children," he repeated. "Now, if you'll excuse me, I'd like to get dressed."

"I'm not finished," she said.

Ryan reached for a pair of jeans lying crumpled on the floor and started to untie the robe. He smiled weakly as the door slammed behind him.

*   *   *

Kelly started when she heard the door slam upstairs. She glanced at the bird-like woman that was engaged in a game of Itsy-bitsy-spider with Sarah and Rachel. Emily Vanderhoff was a surprising mixture of pixie and age-earned wisdom, all wrapped into an elegantly tailored pink wool suit. Kelly had found her doling out second helpings of cereal in the kitchen, acting quite at home as she dug through the box in search of the cereal prize.

Instantly drawn to the woman's candid charm, Kelly wished they had met under different circumstances. But Emily, as she had insisted being called, was a longtime friend of Mrs. Webster's. What's more, the woman couldn't help but agree with her friend, particularly when she heard her side of the story. And Kelly was quite sure Emily would be treated to a detailed description of the scene in the bedroom. On the face of things, Kelly had to admit that Grandmother Webster did have a point about leaving the children unattended. It didn't matter that Kelly had only intended to be gone a minute. She was gone longer than that. Much longer.

So, it was a worried smile that she gave Emily in response to the children's cheering at the end of the game. Her spine stiffened when she heard the footsteps on the tile at the bottom of the stairs—not the soft, muffled tread of Ryan's sneakers—but the sharp, clacking sounds of Mrs. Webster's expensive pumps.

"Find me the telephone book," she ordered as she passed through the doorway. "Where is that Yates woman, anyway?"

"I don't think there is one in here," Kelly said. "Try the study."

"Nonsense. My son always kept one near each of the phones. It's in one of these cabinets here," she said as she started opening drawers and rifling through the contents. Not finding it, she started on the lower cabinets.

"Margie, whatever do you need a telephone directory for?" Emily asked.

"I need to call my attorney and have him start custody proceedings immediately. I should be able to work in an appointment this afternoon after the Red Cross meeting."

Kelly's heart contracted as she turned away, struggling for control over the tears welling up in her eyes. She felt so responsible for this mess. If only she hadn't touched Ryan, hadn't fallen into his lap like an eager puppy. If she'd gone to the door and shouted at him, there wouldn't have been anything for Mrs. Webster to see. Instead, she had chosen the gentle touch, the peaceful wakening, and had let her body's urges overrule her good sense.

"You can call him from a pay phone," Ryan said from across the room.

Mrs. Webster straightened and closed the cabinet door. "Very well. Emily, let's go. We're running late as it is, but we'll just have to be late. I hope you don't mind."

"We needn't go at all," her friend argued as she surveyed the uneasy expressions of her companions. "Perhaps if you sat down and talked—"

"There's nothing to talk about," Mrs. Webster insisted. "I'll just get my purse from the living room and meet you at the door. Oh, and you might want to brush the cereal off your lapel.''

Emily's eyes followed her friend's back through the doorway, then met Kelly's apologetically. Without a word, Ryan left the room, presumably for the front door as well.

Emily cleared her throat daintily as she brushed lightly at her jacket with her finger. Instead of leaving, too, she came closer to Kelly, joining her at the sink.

"I know it's difficult to understand her," Emily began, speaking in a low tone so the children would not hear. "But things have not always been easy for Margie. In fact, she's really had a difficult life. And now with both her husband and son gone, she's lost her sense of balance. She means well, but she will do anything to get her way in this and for all the wrong reasons."

"Why are you telling me this?" She searched Emily's face for a clue, but found only gentle compassion in her wrinkled expression.

"She has spoken of you and of Ryan. She has suspected for several weeks that you were attracted to one another. I don't doubt that, particularly when you blush like that." Kelly looked away, embarrassed that she wore her emotions so close to the surface. After a moment, Emily continued. "She'll use that if she can, along with anything else that comes to mind. She would even try to damage your career, if she thought it would get her what she wants."

Kelly's startled eyes flew back to Emily. "I hadn't thought of that."

Emily nodded slowly, then turned away. "Well, you should."

"Emily?" The older woman pivoted, her hands halted halfway between picking up her purse and slinging its strap over her shoulder.

"Yes?"

"How long have you known Mrs. Webster?"

Emily smiled. "Since we were girls."

Kelly's spirits sagged. Despite the other woman's kindly appearance, she would be loyal to her friend. Perhaps she was even doing Mrs. Webster's bidding now, trying to convince Kelly that she should stay away from the children and not get involved in this fight. She was warning her off.

Emily evidently read her thoughts. "I hope Margie is right about you and Ryan. I've watched him off and on these past few years when he was visiting John and Sharon. He seemed envious of them."

Kelly couldn't contain her surprise, and it was a moment before she could speak. "They had a lot to envy," Kelly said, gesturing toward the children. "And they had each other."

For a moment, Kelly let herself remember what it was like to be so close to another person, to share the same dreams and plan for the future. But she closed the door to that image as quickly as she had opened it. There was no happy ending to that memory.

"Things will work themselves out," Emily said. "Margie will come around, given time. Now, I must be going."

Kelly stood motionless for a moment, wondering if she had heard the other woman right. Mrs. Web-

ster would come around? She was the immovable
object incarnate. Or did Emily, who knew Mrs.
Webster so well, understand the situation better than
the rest of them? Being an outsider, she could perhaps see more clearly the paths they should choose.
And if her words were anything to go by, she thought
the children should be with Ryan, not her friend.

Several minutes later, Kelly was hanging up the
kitchen telephone extension when Ryan walked into
the room. She quickly slid her notebook into her big
blue bag and slung the strap over her shoulder.

"I cancelled my next appointment," she explained,
neglecting to add that she'd cancelled everything else
for the morning as well. "I couldn't have made it
there in time anyway. The kids have eaten and
they're coloring now. Sarah's tried to draw on the
wall twice, but there's only one mark that I couldn't
get off, and—" her voice trailed off as she realized
she was rattling.

"Please," Ryan said as he gently grasped her
upper arms, staying her movement towards the door.
"Don't leave."

"I think I'd better." She couldn't look at him.

"Not yet. We need to talk." She could feel the
heat of his fingers through the thin fabric of her
blouse, and she fought the rising warmth that flooded
her. The knot in her throat grew tighter.

"Do you think she'll really do it?" Kelly asked.

"Take the kids away? She'll try," Ryan whispered, then pulled her along to the living room, closing the doors behind them. "Did the kids hear?" he
asked when he was sure they were out of earshot.

Kelly shook her head. "I don't think so. Emily

NEVER LET GO / 97

gave them more cereal and then played singing games with them. I didn't hear anything until the door slammed upstairs. I didn't hear anything when you left the kitchen, either.''

"That's good. I don't want that witch to upset them. I don't know what I'm going to do when she comes back for them this afternoon.''

"You're not going to let her take them!''

"Of course not. She doesn't have custody yet, and she never will if I have anything to say about it. I wouldn't trust her to take them to the park.'' He strode across the room while jerking his fingers through his hair, leaving it even more mussed than ever. "Damn. They'll both swear I was upstairs having my wicked way with you and that I'm too irresponsible to raise them.''

"Well, when you put it that way, it sounds pretty bad,'' Kelly replied. "But you may not need to worry about Emily.''

Ryan's eyebrows lifted at her use of the prominent Mrs. Vanderhoff's first name.

"She seemed too friendly to be against you.''

Ryan's doubting expression spurred her on. "She didn't say she was on your side, at least not in so many words. But she said Mrs. Webster would eventually come around. I guess she meant that she would accept that you're the kids' guardian and make the best of it.''

Ryan was not convinced, even after Kelly recounted her conversation in the kitchen with the older lady.

"They're up to something. Mrs. Vanderhoff and Margaret Webster are old friends. They grew up in the same neighborhood. They're old money and as loyal as old dogs."

Kelly shook her head. "You could be right, but Emily was very convincing. She seemed worried about Mrs. Webster."

"Did she say so?"

"Nothing in so many words. It was just a general impression I got. She likes you, though."

"I don't trust her," Ryan insisted.

"I wonder if you've forgotten how to trust. You've been a journalist for too long."

"What's that supposed to mean?"

"I just mean that you've spent so much time with politicians and crooks and terrorists that you think everyone is hiding something. You've forgotten what it's like to be around normal people."

"I trust my instincts," Ryan said. "And my instincts tell me that I can't trust Margaret Webster's best friend to keep her mouth shut about what happened here today. I can't depend on anyone but myself."

Stung, she turned away, biting back the angry retort that sprang to her lips. And what about her, Kelly wondered. Didn't he know she'd walk through fire for those kids? For him? Perhaps he didn't care.

In an instant, he had crushed her to his chest, squeezing her so tightly she could feel the buttons on his shirt pressing against her cheek.

"I'm sorry to put you through this," he muttered in her hair. "I had no idea that she would show up. Even if I did, I would have kissed you anyway. I don't think I could have stopped myself."

Kelly pushed against his chest, struggling to

escape from his embrace before she thoroughly disgraced herself by bursting into tears or, worse yet, by giving in to her body's insistent urges and kissing the ticking vein at his throat.

"You don't have to say that," she said. "What's done, is done. I only hope it works out right in the end."

Ryan closed his eyes and pulled her back against his chest, resting his chin on the top of her head as he released a deep sigh. "It will," he said. "It has to."

They stood wrapped together there for a few moments before the muffled giggles penetrated the comforting silence. Then they drew apart, both self-conscious and not yet comfortable with the subtly changing nature of their relationship. They were conspirators, stealing hidden moments of rapture in a world of jealous grandmothers and teddy bears. And for now, their moment was up.

"Come in here," Ryan ordered, his grin belying the stern tone of his voice.

Kelly smiled openly at the children as she reached for her bag, wondering when it had slipped from her shoulder.

"Sarah marked on the wall again," Rachel said.

Ryan was trying to look stern, but failing miserably. Giving up, he gathered the children in his arms and hugged them as if it would be his last. "Uncle Ryan will clean it up."

Feeling like an intruder all of the sudden, Kelly headed for the door. "I'll call you in a day or two," she said.

"Don't wait that long," Ryan answered.

When she paused in the doorway, her body silhouetted against the panel of sunlight, Ryan's throat tightened with emotion.

"Ryan? I could explain to her again what happened."

"No," he said. "It wouldn't make any difference. She's been waiting for something like this for months."

"I think I should stop coming over," she said. "I'll arrange to have another parent educator assigned to you."

"No," he shouted, then reached down to pick up Sarah, who had started visibly at the sound and burst into tears. Then he continued, more quietly, his exasperation apparent. "I don't want another parent educator. I want you." As the words left his mouth, he realized how true they were. He wanted her, needed her desperately. And the idea scared the hell out of him.

Kelly shook her head. "I think this is best. She'll probably hire someone to watch us. I'd rather not give her any more ammunition to take to court."

Ryan couldn't help but admit that she was right. It didn't matter that theirs was supposed to be a professional relationship. Sexual sparks flew every time they were together. Today's incident was proof that they could no longer pretend the sparks didn't exist.

His answer was slow in coming. "You're probably right."

"I already got my notes out of the study. If you could print out the pages that are on the computer, I'll pick them up on Friday."

"I won't be here on Friday."

"I know. Mrs. Yates can give them to me."

Ryan closed his eyes and nodded. When he opened them again, she was gone. He heard her car start and the crunch of gravel as it left the driveway, then the distant hum of the engine as it traveled away from him.

He was surprised at the empty ache he felt already, knowing she wouldn't be back. He couldn't accept it. He wouldn't. He'd settle this custody problem, then he'd call her up and ask her for a date. A real date with flowers and candlelight, not a stolen moment with the kids around the corner or a janitor outside the classroom doorway.

Then he pulled himself together and tried to make some sense of the wild clamoring around him. After he listened to each of them in turn, including Sarah's nonsensical garbling, he led the children back to the table and cleared the considerable mess they had made. When they were safely occupied in their rooms with their toys, he reached for the phone to call his attorney.

Kelly read the paragraph a third time, but it still didn't make sense. She decided she must have left out a line or two when she typed it. Either that or her brain was more scrambled than she thought. Whatever the case, she'd done enough proofreading for now. She still had a day or two before she had to meet with her thesis advisor.

Sighing, she shoved the typed page back into the folder and tucked it into her bag amidst the lacing beads, colored blocks, and various other children's paraphernalia. It was a good thing that she hadn't thrown out her handwritten rough draft. She could go over it tonight and pencil in the part she had left out. And then she'd retype it. Again.

She started to work on the stack of reports on her desk, but didn't get far before her stomach's nagging hunger turned to a loud rumble, reminding her that she had skipped both breakfast and lunch. When her supervisor started laughing, she decided it was time to quit for the day and get a sandwich. Within five minutes, she had said goodbye to her supervisor and two other stragglers and was evading the janitor's mop on her way down the hallway.

She searched the parking lot for the ancient blue Mustang that had been parked outside her house or wherever she happened to be working every day for the last two weeks—she first noticed it the evening after Mrs. Webster's big blowup at Ryan's house. At first, she ignored it and its short driver, who constantly hid behind newspapers. Then she got angry and tried to lose him, succeeding once, but causing a minor traffic jam in the process. After that, she amused herself by waving at him, and once she walked back to his car to tell him not to bother to get the newspaper out because she'd only be a minute or two.

She barely noticed the battered brown sedan that pulled up to the curb, until its driver shouted her name loudly enough to shake the leaves off the faded shrubbery.

Startled, she spun back around, dropping two books in the process. By the time she had bent to pick them up, the man was thrusting an envelope in her face.

"Miss Smith," he bellowed, only a shade more quietly than the last time.

"Yes?"

"You've been served," he said as he stuffed the envelope into her open bag and hurried back to his car.

"Served?" Kelly asked the empty air in front of her. Was this a court summons? Was it legally binding if the man put it in her bag instead of her hand? On television, they employed an endless variety of ruses to get someone to take those papers. Or was that just television?

Kelly was still gaping after the slight man with the loud voice when his engine roared to life and he sped away, ignoring the speed limit signs in the empty school parking lot as he squealed around light poles and onto the street. She wondered if he always drove like a demon or whether he thought she would shoot him for delivering the envelope, whatever it contained.

But then, she knew what it was. She had been expecting something like this for the last week. Its appearance was almost an anticlimax to the worry of the last few days, during which she had tossed about ideas in her mind that ranged from running back home to the relative safety of Harrington, to invading Mrs. Webster's home and forcing her to listen to a thing or two. In the end, she had decided that her best course was to do exactly what she had been doing about the situation—nothing.

But her shoulders drooped when she turned back toward her car and trudged the remaining ten steps to the door. She set the books on the hood and dug about in her bag until she located the keys. She studiously avoided looking at the envelope until after she was in the car. And then she held it poised in her fingertips for several moments before gathering the courage to slit open the envelope and read the contents.

After she did, she wished she hadn't. She'd never seen a court summons before, but this one was surely different than what she had imagined. As she turned page after page, her heart sank into the pit of her stomach. It was worse than she had expected. Margaret Webster had distorted everything. Worse yet, she had dug into Kelly's past and discovered facts Kelly wanted to forget. Those were distorted, too, and mixed in with several downright lies.

Kelly barely remembered driving home. All she could think of was getting to the telephone and calling Ryan. Her fingers trembled as she dialed the number. When she heard his mellow timbred voice, she was suddenly at a loss for words. She had to take a deep breath before she could respond to his insistent string of "hellos."

"Ryan, it's Kelly."

"I've wanted to call you," he said. "But I didn't think I'd better. Someone's been following me and I was afraid the line was bugged."

"That's not legal, is it?" Kelly was astonished at the lengths Margaret Webster would go to get her own way. Ryan apparently wasn't surprised at all.

"What difference does that make?"

"Ryan, someone's been following me, too."

"Damn her! I was afraid of that."

"And I was served with court papers this afternoon."

There was a long silence on the line. Kelly could hear childish murmurs in the background, but the only sound from Ryan was a muffled expletive followed by a long sigh.

"Meet me in the park in an hour," he said.

When Kelly arrived at the park, there was no sign of Ryan. The playground was deserted except for a couple of teenage girls deep in conversation at one of the picnic tables. She zipped her coat against the wind and locked the car before heading over to the swing set.

Halfway there, she spotted a familiar set of shoulders propped up against the trunk of an ancient maple. Looking back, Kelly located the blue Mustang as it pulled into the spot next to hers and for once stifled the urge to wave. Then she strolled over to Ryan's tree, stopping a few feet in front of him.

He looked good, as good as the flat image that had haunted her days and nights. Except the 3-D, real-life version was warm and alive, not just a dancing figment of memory. Even in the wrinkled, gray sweatsuit, even with shadows beneath his eyes, he looked better to her than any man she had ever seen before.

He flicked the ash from his half-smoked cigarette

onto the ground between them. He checked the brown grass for live sparks, then lifted his eyes slowly, lingering on her exposed calves, then the open neck of the wool coat. When his eyes finally held hers, she tried to read his expression. She was afraid to believe what she saw, afraid that if she closed her eyes and opened them, the fiery light of desire that flickered between them would be gone. She swayed imperceptibly toward him, but caught herself before her feet could put her wishes into motion.

Guiltily, she glanced back at the blue Mustang, then realized that the balding shadow was too far away to see what she instinctively knew was for her eyes alone. It was all she could do to keep from touching Ryan. But she couldn't. Not with the half bald man watching, waiting for just that.

"I've never seen you smoke before," she said, her voice husky.

A wry smile crossed his lips as he eyed the cigarette like some sort of nasty insect, then dropped it on the ground and crushed it with the toe of his running shoe. "I quit two years ago. I gave in yesterday and bought a pack." Then he bent and picked up the tattered remnants and tore them to bits, scattering them in the breeze.

"Why did you do that?"

"An old habit. I've been in a few spots where I didn't want to leave any traces behind."

Kelly nodded slowly, wondering about the places he had been, the dangers he had faced to bring the news to America's living rooms. She thought briefly that he must miss the excitement sometimes. But before she could voice her thoughts, he changed the subject.

"Did you bring the papers?"

Without a word, Kelly pulled the envelope from her bag and handed it to Ryan. "Let's sit at one of those tables," he said, indicating the nearby picnic shelter. When they had settled themselves opposite one another, he spread the papers on the table, weighting them down with his fingertips. Kelly sat immobile, barely breathing as she watched him read, or rather watched the wind play with the strands of hair that danced out of place and fluttered in a quick gust before lying down slightly askew.

"These are copies of the papers Mrs. Webster's attorney filed with the court," he said. "My guess is dear old Grandmother had them delivered to you, hoping to upset you and maybe put pressure on me." He folded them and thrust them back into the envelope, then tucked it into his pocket. "Do you know who delivered the papers?"

She shook her head and recounted the incident, describing the loud man who served the papers, along with the balding man in the Mustang who had been following her. "He's over there," she said, "behind the newspaper."

"That's an original disguise," Ryan said. "Mine's better. I didn't catch her until two days ago, although she's probably been watching me for longer than that."

"Her?"

A wry grin touched his lips. "I caught a whiff of Chanel No. 5, not that that's conclusive evidence." He pointed across the street to a brown sedan with dented front bumper and a long scratch extending from the front door to the rear wheel well. "She's over there."

"The brown car? That's it. The man who delivered the papers drove that car."

"Are you sure?"

"Positive. I recognize the battle scars."

Ryan swore softly and slammed his fist on the table. "It was *her*. God, I've got to find a way to stop this."

Kelly wrapped her two hands around the fist, squeezing lightly, offering what comfort she could. "She can't win."

"That's just it," he said. "She might." Kelly's heart turned over at the raw pain in his voice, the harsh, angry lines that creased his face. "When I first found out that John and Sharon wanted me to take the kids, I was floored. I thought they were cute, but I couldn't have three kids, all practically babies, trailing around after me, not in my line of work. But that first night, Rachel woke up crying. And when I held her and rocked her with her little body all curled up in my arms, I knew that I had to stay. All my life I've been chasing shadows, looking for someplace to belong. And here were these three kids, and they needed me. I realized I needed them even more."

"What are you going to do?"

"I'm not sure. My attorney said that I'd have a better chance of winning if I were married. The fact that I haven't lived in the same place for more than six months is another strike against me. On the face of it, their grandmother appears to offer the best home.''

"We know that's not true, but how do we prove it?''

For an answer, Ryan pulled his hand away and jumped back from the table. For a moment, he stood with his back to her. Then he combed his fingers through his hair and turned around, his face composed in an unreadable mask.

"There is one thing that might work,'' he offered. "We could get married.''

"*What?*'' For an instant, Kelly's world spun about crazily. Her breath stopped, then her heart took over, racing madly. Her brain kept telling her it was insanity, desperation speaking. Yet, he was watching her as if her answer mattered very much to him. But then, it did. He wouldn't have asked if he thought anything else would work.

"We wouldn't interfere with your life, at least not much. You'd still have your job and your master's work. And I know you like the kids. It would only be for a while, just until the court confirms the guardianship. Then we could both go our separate ways.''

"And what about the children then?'' she said. "They need stability, not a temporary mother who's going to walk out on them. They need a family, but it has to be permanent.''

"It might work out,'' Ryan said. "We've gotten along well so far. And try as you might, you can't deny that we're attracted to one another.''

"We're friends, Ryan. You can't build a marriage on friendship.''

"Friends don't tremble when they touch one

another. People who are just friends don't lie awake at night thinking about one another," he said, his voice almost a whisper.

"I don't," she lied. She could tell by the challenging lift of his brows that he knew it.

"I do," he admitted.

Kelly was silent for a long moment. "I do, too," she said finally.

"Then give it a chance. Give us all a chance."

Kelly smiled softly and shook her head. "No. It's not right. Besides, she'd see right through it, and so would the judge." When he didn't answer, she continued in a firm tone. "There has to be another way."

"You were married before."

Kelly nodded. Of course, he knew. That was one of the few accuracies in the court filings. He had her copy, which he said was indentical to the copy he had received. He would have read every word. "The rest wasn't true, at least not strictly true."

"I know that. The Kelly I know couldn't have done those things."

Kelly couldn't meet his eyes. The accusations in the court papers were partly true, but they were distorted beyond belief. Still, what would he think if he knew that she had abandoned her husband. Technically, that was what she had done. She'd abandoned him emotionally, locking herself away in her own pain, unable to see or understand his. And Brian had been right about one thing. She wasn't capable of being a wife, not really. It wasn't fair to pretend that she was, even for the sake of Ryan and his three charges. There always was a day of reckoning, a payment to be made for secrets and lies. And she was afraid that the cost would be too great this time for everyone involved.

"I know there's another way. We'll find it."

Ryan's expression was even more closed if possible. "You're right," he agreed, sounding almost relieved. "I guess I was just desperate."

Kelly frowned. He didn't have to be so agreeable.

"I'll try to keep you out of this," Ryan said. "But it may not be possible."

"I know. It's all right. It's as much my fault as it is yours. I got involved of my own free will. I could have said no."

The spark in his eyes flamed briefly before he shuttered them again, but his voice was cool. "I guess that was your first mistake."

"And what was the second?" she demanded, her spine stiff with indignation.

"No way," he said as he untangled himself from the picnic table bench. "I wouldn't touch that one with a telephone pole."

Coming around to her side, he drew her to her feet and dropped a companionable arm around her shoulders. His brown eyes danced with a devilish glint. "Shall we give our friends with the newspapers something to report?"

"Ryan, no. You have enough trouble already without—"

His lips brushed lightly over hers. "Might as well be hung for a sinner as a saint. Besides, I have an idea."

She found it hard to think clearly when he held

her so snugly against him, but a nagging suspicion niggled at her. "What idea?"

"Just play along," he whispered in her ear as he pulled her down the sidewalk that led toward her parked car and the nearby sleuth in the Mustang.

"Ryan Matthews," she muttered between gritted teeth. "What are you up to?"

"I'll tell you later, after I talk to my lawyer." He dropped another light kiss, on her nose this time. "Just pretend you adore me until we get to your car. While Mr. Mustang is busy taking pictures, I'll snitch his car keys and try to convince him to leave you alone."

Kelly stopped in her tracks. "That's the dumbest idea I've heard yet. Just what do you hope to accomplish? What are you going to do, bribe the man?" Her outburst ended on a high squeak as Ryan swung her up in his arms and flung her over his shoulder caveman style.

"Good lord, woman, you're heavy," he growled, tightening one arm around her legs and swatting her derriere with his free hand. "Don't wriggle so much or you'll make us both fall."

Kelly exercised what she considered to be monumental self-restraint and refrained from calling him the worst of the names that came to mind. "Put me down or I swear I'll do permanent damage to the most tender part of your anatomy."

"What's that?" Ryan answered calmly as he continued down the sidewalk. A furious tug at his ear warned him that she wasn't just playing along. She meant it. He stopped at the curb and slid her body slowly down the front of his, stopping just before her toes touched the ground. "Get ready to move," he said, then halted her sputtering outburst with a searing kiss.

Her bones really did melt, just like in the books her sisters read, or that's how it seemed. Kelly lost all track of time and place and even forgot about the chill wind whipping at her exposed legs. It wasn't until Ryan's head lifted and she met his bemused eyes that she remembered they were in a very public place. The whir of a camera's motor drive brought that fact home, as cold replaced the warmth in Ryan's gaze. "Go straight home," he ordered as he thrust her away. "I'll call you as soon as I work things out."

Then he was gone, striding angrily across the pavement. Kelly flushed hot, then cold, realizing he had done it for effect. The embrace, that soul-burning kiss, was just a distraction for . . . for what she didn't know. And God how she'd responded. Embarrassed and hurt, Kelly fumbled with the car keys and jammed at the lock. She repeated the maneuver with the ignition, while muttering a string of recriminations. As she pulled away from the curb, she saw Ryan jerk open the back of Mr. Mustang's camera and pull out the film, ruining the exposures in the bright sunlight.

Her brief feeling of relief vanished as she followed the one-way drive around the park and saw the other detective busily snapping shots with a telephoto lens. It had all been for nothing, and they'd only made matters worse, she thought, remembering Ryan's antics and the kiss, all probably captured on film in the second camera.

What had Ryan been thinking of? He knew the other detective was there. Or did he plan it this way? More confused than ever, she resolved to find out at the earliest opportunity just what this new idea of his was. The trouble was that she didn't know whether to wait for him to call or to risk calling him again.

On the way home, she stopped at the supermarket, strolling blankly through the aisles as she tried to calm her nerves and gather her scattered, frantic thoughts. Gradually, the absolute normalcy of her surroundings had the desired effect. By the time she made it to the produce department, she was capable of selecting the ingredients for a salad without dropping half of them on the floor. While she added items to the cart, she concentrated on the details of living through the next few days. With that in mind, she decided to stop at the office supply store for more typing paper. She had to meet with her thesis advisor the next day and wanted to be prepared to make any changes he suggested and get the final version typed and turned in. That, at least, was one problem in her life that was nearing resolution. Another week or two and she could place the thesis in the hands of the committee for approval, then sit back and wait for her grade and diploma. And with no nightly sessions at the books or typewriter, she'd have time to straighten out the rest of her life. With a sigh, she dropped a box of cereal into the cart and wished time really did heal all wounds, solve all problems, and that sort of thing. Somehow, she didn't think it would be that easy to sort things out.

When she finally made it home, she found a message from Ryan on her answering machine. When she called him back, he wasn't there. Mrs. Yates just said that he had gone to see his lawyer and would call her when he had some answers.

Hours later she had talked to two siding salesmen, a fund-raiser, and had hung up on an obscene phone caller. But she still hadn't heard from Ryan. So she turned on the machine and slouched on the lumpy couch with a racy paperback, one of her youngest sister's leftovers. When the phone rang again, she leaped to her feet without thinking, then flopped back, waiting edgily until her mother's voice came through the machine's speaker. Kelly's oldest sister was pregnant again, and the family was overjoyed. Kelly leaned back and closed her eyes in bittersweet frustration. Normally, she would have grabbed up the phone and asked for the details, when the baby was due, how her sister would handle pregnancy and another baby when the last one was only now starting to crawl. But not tonight. She was too emotional, too vulnerable after all the commotion late this afternoon. When the dial tone hummed and the machine kicked off, she sighed and picked up her book again.

She was getting ready for bed when the phone rang again. As Ryan's voice came over the speaker, she ran down the hallway and grabbed the receiver.

"Well?" she demanded. "What happened? What's going on?"

"Well," he repeated, dragging the word out as if he was reluctant to speak at all. "My idea wasn't such a good one. At least that's what my attorney said."

"You never did tell me what you were trying to

accomplish. But it had something to do with me and with the way you were acting in the park, didn't it?"

"I think it backfired."

"What backfired? Ryan, you're not making any sense."

The ensuing silence was heavy. "I guess I'm not," he finally said. "You see, I was trying to protect you."

"From what? Mrs. Webster?"

"I was afraid she'd make trouble for you. Your reputation is at stake here."

Kelly's eyes widened in amazement. Her reputation was at stake? That sounded like something out of a Victorian novel, or at best, an after-school special. "So is yours," she replied.

His dry laugh sounded harsh in her ear. "Personal or professional? I'm afraid my personal reputation was shot years ago, at least in Margaret Webster's mind."

"You don't need to protect me. This isn't the old West and I'm not going to be shunned because an old lady saw us kissing in the bedroom."

"Kelly," he grated out, his patience obviously wearing thin. "You work with young children. Margaret Webster could tell your supervisor, or maybe even a school board member or two, all about what she saw over here two weeks ago. And she'd probably exaggerate it and make up a thing or two, and there'd be no way to prove it wasn't all true. Do you know how that would make you look?"

Kelly leaned back against the wall and brushed the hair back from her face. "I know."

"At best, you'd get a formal reprimand, the letter

in the file, and all that business. They could fire you over this, and you'd never get another job as a parent educator, not with something like this hanging over your head.''

"Do you think I haven't thought of that?''

"Kelly, I can't let that happen to you,'' Ryan continued. "I know how much this job means to you. I know how much you love working with children.''

"Maybe I don't deserve the job,'' she fired back angrily. "If I could do something as irresponsible as necking in an armchair while three small children are alone in another room on another floor, I have no right to sit and tell other people how to raise their children. We're not supposed to say it, but when you get right down to it, that's what I do. I tell them the 'correct' way to feed their kids and the 'correct' way to play with them. What right do I have to do that? I'm not a mother. How should I know what it's really like?''

"Because you helped with your younger sisters and because you almost have a master's degree in early childhood development. And because you're damn good. I ought to know. Besides, you know it's not like you make it sound. You don't preach. You just help.''

Kelly couldn't help but smile into the receiver. He sounded so positive, so encouraging. She was ashamed of herself for complaining and wallowing in self-pity. He was trying to make her feel better, despite the fact he'd obviously had a bad day himself.

"Okay,'' she said. "You've convinced me. Now, will you tell me about this idea that backfired.''

"I don't think you want to know.''

"How bad could it be?"

"Well, I thought it was great, so great that I decided to lay the groundwork so everyone would believe it. That's why I kissed you and why I ripped the film out of that detective's camera."

"I still don't understand."

"I thought that if we pretended to be engaged, it would take some of the wind out of Mrs. Webster's sails," he explained. "I thought it would seem more stable than my present state and it would help you—"

Kelly interrupted. "You mean, I wouldn't look so much like a tramp if I were kissing my fiance instead of just some man I happened to know."

"That's not how I meant it."

"Yes, it is, but you have a good point there. I don't think it would help you any, though. Mrs. Webster would see right through a phony engagement. It wouldn't make any difference in the long run."

"That's what my lawyer said. He seems to think that I've made matters worse instead of better."

"He's probably right. The other detective, the one that was following you, was taking pictures, too."

"I know. I thought at the time that I could use it in our favor to convince the court that we weren't having an affair, but that we got carried away celebrating our engagement. It was another mistake, a major one."

"You'll find a way, or your lawyer will." Kelly reassured him. But as she lay awake later that night staring at the spider web of shadows the street light cast on her ceiling, she wondered if that was really possible now.

Kelly poured herself a cup of coffee and added a liberal dose of milk. She ambled over to the kitchen table and set the cup next to the stack of typed pages. She stared dejectedly at handwritten lines of red ink across the cover page of her thesis and thought back to the meeting in her advisor's office two days ago. What was it he said? Her ideas were good. Then he suggested a complete reorganization, rewrite, the whole bit. Which was, she supposed, a little better than chucking the whole thing and starting over.

With a sigh, she started thumbing through the thick stack, reading, making notes in the margins among the red scratches, and occasionally jotting a line in a spiral notebook. She was on page fourteen when the doorbell rang. She glanced up in mild surprise because she hadn't been expecting anyone. Nevertheless, she was grateful for the respite, even if it was only a vacuum cleaner salesman. Setting her pencil down, she headed for the door and peered through the tiny peephole. When she saw the distorted fish-eye version of Mrs. Yates, she exclaimed and flung the door open.

"Mrs. Yates, how nice to see you. Everything is all right, isn't it?" She held the door invitingly wide, stifling a smile as the heavy woman bustled in and pulled the scarf from hair that was more frazzled than normal.

"Well, it is and it isn't," she answered with her usual no nonsense tone. "The children aren't sick, if that's what you mean."

Kelly took her coat and laid it over the back of a chair. She followed her guest into the living room and grimaced when Mrs. Yates sank into the green armchair, the one that swallowed up its victims in its sagging depths.

"The couch is more comfortable," she offered when she met Mrs. Yates' wide-eyed glance.

"Never mind. I think I'm stuck here for the moment."

"Something is wrong, isn't it? Otherwise, you wouldn't be here." People came to Mrs. Yates, not the other way around, with the possible exception of her invalid sister.

"I'll get right to the point," the older woman began. "A social worker came to the house yesterday, some sniping do-gooder from the county. She was checking Ryan out for the judge that's going to hear the case."

"Already? I expected something like this, but not this quickly."

"Well, evidently Margaret's lawyer has convinced the judge that the kids are in some sort of danger, although what from I can't imagine. They're pushing the case through pretty quickly." Her worry was evident. "Anyway, she showed up without warning and things were already a zoo that day, what with Ryan trying to get an article done on time and the kids doing everything they could to get his attention and distract him. I'd been to my niece's house. She's pregnant, you know. I'd just gotten back and hadn't started on the house. Then five minutes after the woman got there, Sarah walks in naked as a jaybird and wets the carpet."

It would have been funny if the situation weren't so deadly serious, Kelly thought. But she could just imagine how the chaos appeared to the social worker. The report would be damning.

"I wondered," Mrs. Yates continued, "if there was something you could do. What with your position in the school district, you must have connections. Maybe you could persuade the social worker to come back again when we're better prepared for her. I wrote her phone number down." She dug around in her purse until she found the scrap of paper, then leaned forward, handing it to Kelly across the coffee table.

Kelly looked away, unable to face Mrs. Yates and tell her that her faith was misplaced. Evidently, the good lady was not in possession of all the facts. If she knew what had precipitated the custody suit in the first place, she wouldn't have considered asking. In fact, she probably wouldn't be speaking to her at all. In all honesty, she had to explain, at least a little bit. As little as possible, though.

"I'm afraid I'm part of the problem. Mrs. Webster thinks I'm a bad influence." That, she figured, was putting it mildly.

"Baloney! That woman has cottage cheese where her brains should be." Then her eyes narrowed accusingly. "That's why you haven't been over for three weeks. You're afraid you'll make things worse for Ryan. Well, let me tell you, you're making things worse by not being there. He misses you something terrible and he's been worse than a snarling dog. And the kids think you don't like them any more."

Kelly watched her hands, her feet, the wall, anything but Mrs. Yates. When the woman finally stopped speaking, she answered in a low, pained voice. "There's nothing I can do to help except stay away. I don't want Ryan to lose the kids and he could. She's having us both followed."

"I know that. I nearly tripped over the idiot on the stairs. Who in their right mind reads a newspaper in a stairwell?"

Kelly almost smiled. "He's not very good, is he?"

"Think about it," Mrs. Yates urged. "Maybe you'll come up with something. Now, if you'll help me up."

As Kelly ushered the older woman out the door, she felt even more guilty. The woman wouldn't be convinced. Her faith in Kelly's ability to right matters was a crushing weight. Kelly followed her down the hall a few minutes later in the hopes that a long, brisk walk would dispel some of the gloom.

Without thinking, her footsteps led her back to the neighborhood park where she and Ryan had met days before. She climbed the slope and stood in the spot where the second detective had snapped photos of Ryan ripping film from the other's camera. She could see the spot where they had stood clearly, too clearly for anyone who knew how to use a camera to mess up the shot.

Then she walked on. Twenty minutes later she reached the familiar street where Ryan lived. She sat down in the shelter of a mungo pine across the street and stared at the house, wondering what she could do to make things right for the people who lived inside it. Her heart tripped and she shrank back against the branches when Ryan stepped out into the front lawn to retrieve the newspaper. She didn't know why she sat there, hiding in the shrubbery like some sort of peeping Tom. She only knew that she was slowly working her way toward a decision. When feisty Eric ran out the door, scooped up the yellow car and hauled it awkwardly into the house, she had her answer.

She stood up and brushed the dirt and dead leaves from her crumpled jeans and started purposefully back up the street toward home to shower and change. She couldn't do what she had to dressed like this. She needed the composed lines of a well-cut dress, silk stockings, and high heels to give her much needed confidence for what she was about to do.

SEVEN

Kelly slowed her car to a crawl and squinted at the Mission Hills address she had hurriedly copied from the telephone book before leaving her apartment. Then she looked back at the brass numbers displayed discreetly on the post next to the wrought iron gates. Her throat suddenly dry, she turned the wheel and urged the ancient Chevrolet through the gates and up the drive towards the imposing front of Margaret Webster's brick mansion.

The sheer size of the place stunned her. Yet, she shouldn't have been surprised. Everything she had learned about the woman should have prepared her for this. Mrs. Webster's clothes, her jewelry—even the way she spoke reeked of old money. But this house was bigger than Kelly's old elementary school, and that building had housed six grades.

She tried not to gape as she drove slowly up the drive and around the fountain. She stopped directly behind an empty Mercedes and turned to look at the well-dressed passengers who were already heading up the sidewalk. Mrs. Webster, it seemed, already had guests.

While Kelly pondered whether to proceed with her plans or postpone them until there were no guests to overhear, a red-jacketed teenager drove the Mercedes around the fountain and onto the lawn. He parked it carefully next to a Rolls Royce.

Before she had time to shift her aging Chevy into gear and make her escape, another red-jacketed youth had opened her door and was offering to park her car.

"I'll put it around back next to the caterer's van," he suggested, eyeing the ripped upholstery with an interest that seemed almost morbid. "I don't think there's much room on the side lawn."

"There's really no need to park it at all," Kelly said. "I'll only be a few minutes."

"It's blocking the drive."

Kelly looked in the rearview mirror at the BMW that had pulled in behind her, followed by a sleek, black sportscar. More guests.

"All right." She handed him her keys as he helped her smoothly out of the car and up the steps, paying more attention to her legs than to where his own feet were landing.

Smiling his appreciation, the boy flashed a grin. "Just let me know when you're ready to leave and I'll get your car."

Kelly squared her shoulders, then headed for the front door. She had just stepped inside and handed her coat to a uniformed maid when a vaguely familiar voice called her name.

She pivoted slowly as she searched the crowded

room for the owner of the trilling voice. Who here besides Mrs. Webster would know her? The voice touched a chord of familiarity, but she couldn't place it until she spotted Emily Vanderhoff weaving purposefully through the clusters of people, her pink and gray silk dress shimmering lightly.

"This is such a lovely surprise," she said, reaching for Kelly's hand. Kelly stood stiff with unease while Emily chattered affectionately, then leaned close. "Smile and pretend you've been invited," Emily whispered, then drew back, and continued in a more normal tone. "Have you seen Margie yet?"

"No," Kelly answered, looking about her nervously. "I need to speak to her. It's important. I wouldn't crash her party otherwise."

"What, this?" Emily waved her hands deprecatingly at the elegant hordes and led Kelly through an archway toward the buffet table. "Margaret hasn't entertained since her son died. She owed so many invitations, and she decided to pay them all back at once. It's so much more efficient."

Kelly shook her head. "I should have called first. What I need to say requires privacy."

Emily frowned at the spiced shrimp she had just bitten, but Kelly wasn't sure if the woman was displeased with it or her.

"I'd better leave. I'll call her tomorrow and set up an appointment."

"No," Emily insisted. "This is probably the best way. Margie won't do anything foolish with all these people around."

"Like pay the parking attendants to throw me in the fountain?" Kelly suggested.

Emily's eyebrows lifted in wry amusement. "She's angry enough to do more than that," she warned. "I haven't seen her like this in years."

"Will she even talk to me?"

Emily frowned. "I'm not sure. Probably. We're about to find out."

Kelly glanced over her shoulder, then turned to watch Mrs. Webster's purposeful stride. She stopped twice to respond to remarks from her guests, then hurried on. Kelly had to hand it to her. She appeared calm, in perfect control. Only her eyes gave her away. The ice blue of her dress matched them perfectly, and they glittered with suppressed anger. She halted directly in front of them and eyed Kelly hostilely, then noticed the avidly curious glance from a blue-haired woman standing nearby. Mrs. Webster smiled brilliantly in reply, then turned back to Kelly, the smile still held stiffly in place.

"Miss Smith, I'm surprised you could make it. I thought you had other plans."

Emily pressed Kelly's arm firmly, halting the words that were on the tip of her tongue. Speaking quietly so the other guests could not hear, Emily drew Mrs. Webster even closer. "I was just telling Kelly that I hoped Ryan will meet you halfway. A compromise would be so much nicer than the scandal of a drawn-out custody battle, don't you think?"

Mrs. Webster cast a furious look at her friend, which Emily met with an imperious one of her own. "I don't think—" she began, but Emily interrupted.

"Perhaps you could talk about it in the library. I'm sure your guests can do without you for a few minutes. I think you should explain your concerns about Mr. Matthews to Kelly. She should be warned.''

Mrs. Webster glanced around her. ''Perhaps that would be best. Follow me.'' She turned and left the room without a backward glance. A light push from Emily propelled Kelly through the doorway after Mrs. Webster.

Kelly followed the older woman down a dark-panelled hallway and into a book-lined room dominated by a massive walnut desk, its surface cleared and gleaming from frequent polishing. A collection of antique weapons decorated the wall above the mantel.

''This was my husband's study,'' Mrs. Webster explained. ''I expected John to take it over whenever he and Sharon gave up on their silly notion of being independent. As if there weren't enough room in this house to have any privacy.'' Positioning herself in front of the fireplace, she motioned for Kelly to seat herself in the wing back chair to her left.

''Sit down and say what you came to say.''

Kelly took her place behind the chair, her fingertips pinching the upholstery. She only hoped her expression didn't reveal how nervous she was. ''I know you want to get back to your guests, so I'll be brief.''

''Please do.''

''It's wrong to try to take the children away from Ryan.''

''I would expect you to say that.''

Kelly met her gaze squarely, almost defiantly. As her fingers tightened into fists behind her back, she mentally counted to ten and then to ten again.

Shortly, she had her emotions under enough control to attempt to reason with Mrs. Webster.

"My job is working with young children," she began. "I do it because I love it and because I believe the program helps adults become better parents."

Kelly leaned slightly forward, her posture unconsciously emphasizing her complete sincerity. "I'll admit that at first I had my doubts about Ryan's ability to take care of those kids. But I've watched him with them. He may not be able to grill a cheese sandwich without burning it, but he knows how to make a child feel important and loved."

"Is that your professional opinion or your personal assessment?" The older woman's tone was cold and condescending. Rising indignation added more starch to Kelly's spine as she responded.

"My professional opinion is that Ryan Matthews is a wonderful guardian for your grandchildren."

"You're not exactly objective about the situation," Mrs. Webster said. "Remember, I'm the one who caught you in the bedroom."

"I'm not likely to forget it."

"Miss Smith," Mrs. Webster laid a knobby hand on Kelly's arm. "You're young. And you have a great passion for your work with children. I also suspect that you take in lost kittens and injured dogs. It's quite understandable how a young woman like you could be misled by a man like Ryan."

Kelly wasn't taken in by the other woman's sudden change of tactics or her patronizing tone. But curiosity made her play along.

"And what kind of man is Ryan?"

"Fascinating, exciting." Mrs. Webster spread her hands, gesturing while her eyes changed from cold to bitter. "In a shallow sort of way, of course. He's not the type to stick around for long, though. He'll be on to better prospects before you know it."

Kelly wasn't sure who was reaping the most insults, her or Ryan. She supposed that in Mrs. Webster's book, a self-supporting teacher didn't rank high on the scale of "prospects."

"You don't know him at all," Kelly replied, but Mrs. Webster didn't even seem to hear her. She seemed lost in her own thoughts, her own words.

"I'm not sleeping with him," Kelly continued. "I've done nothing to be ashamed of and nothing that would harm the children. I would never do that."

"Kelly," Mrs. Webster began, then stopped as she eased herself into the chair. The lines on her face were deeper. A drawn sadness haunted her expression. "Men like Ryan were not meant to settle down with a family. They're not capable of it. Oh, they may give it a try for a while, but soon the everyday sameness, the sheer normalness of it all begins to wear on them. They start to miss the excitement. In time, they miss it so much that they leave and go back to the life they love."

Mrs. Webster's words settled in the pit of Kelly's stomach. The same doubts had gnawed at Kelly's heart. Was that why she hadn't taken Ryan's desperate marriage proposal seriously? Because she had sensed a restlessness in Ryan? Because she was afraid to allow herself to become tied to another man who might later decide she couldn't give him the life he needed?

"No," Kelly thought. "He's different."

When her eyes focused again on Mrs. Webster's expression, she realized she must have spoken aloud. The older woman's next words confirmed it.

"I'm sure you think so now, dear. I thought that once myself."

Kelly was puzzled. "From what I've heard, you've always disliked Ryan."

"He's exactly like my first husband," Mrs. Webster said.

Speechless with shock, Kelly could only watch the fleeting expressions of remembered joy, vulnerable sadness, and hard anger flicker across the older woman's face. The anger won out, along with the bitterness of long-remembered pain and disillusionment.

"I married Lucas when I was nineteen." Her lip curled with bitter amusement. "I was as idealistic as you are now, but I soon learned better. The newspaper always came first. Finally, I gave him an ultimatum. He chose the newspaper, and I chose to divorce him."

"I see," Kelly said. "And you think Ryan is just like Lucas."

"He is."

"No," Kelly shook her head emphatically. "Ryan chose to come home. He chose to raise the children."

Mrs. Webster's lips curved into a humoring, pitying smile. "Only because he felt obligated to. It really wasn't a choice at all. It's only a matter of time before the restlessness becomes too great and he returns to the television screen. Next, he'll go to

Europe for just a short trip. Then, the trips will get longer and the places more remote and dangerous. And one day, he won't come back."

Kelly shook her head. "He's writing now. He's already sold a book and he's working on another. And even if he did decide to go back to television, he could work in the United States, in Kansas City, even."

"There are plenty of dangerous places in our own country for him to investigate. And what about the children?"

Kelly frowned. "What about them? Mrs. Yates is an excellent housekeeper, and she's wonderful with the children. And there are plenty of good day care centers."

Mrs. Webster stood up and crossed the room to the big desk. She halted behind it and tapped its gleaming surface. "Someday this will belong to Eric, or even Rachel or Sarah. They aren't like other children. They're Websters, heirs to the Webster Corp., real estate holdings, this house, and the tremendous obligations all of this entails. They must be prepared to handle it."

"They're just children," Kelly exclaimed, jumping to her feet.

"Children need guidance, not coddling."

Kelly nodded and settled her fists on her hips. "They do need guidance. But right now they need stability more than anything else. They're still grieving, but they're settling in with Ryan now. That's why I'm hoping that you and Ryan can come up with some sort of compromise."

"I'm not trying to cut him out of their lives,"

Mrs. Webster said. "He could visit them whenever it was convenient."

"For him or for you?"

"I'm sure I could come up with a workable plan."

Kelly shook her head, wondering why she had bothered to come. She understood better why Mrs. Webster disliked Ryan so much, but understanding didn't change much. Mrs. Webster was still firmly committed to taking the children away from Ryan. And her idea of a compromise was no compromise at all.

"I'm sorry you're involved in this," Mrs. Webster continued. "You must understand that I have no choice. I'm only acting in the best interests of the children. I hope you'll remember that when you're subpoenaed to testify."

"I'm sure I'll remember this conversation," Kelly said. "I would, however, appreciate it if you would get rid of the detective that's been following me."

Mrs. Webster looked startled. "You saw him?"

Kelly held back a grin. For the first time that evening, she felt in control of the situation. "I couldn't miss him. He's not very good."

"Well, no matter, I believe I have everything I need to win this case anyway. I'll call the agency in the morning," Mrs. Webster said, immediately throwing Kelly back into a state of unease. "My attorney suggested as much this afternoon."

Kelly nodded slowly, wondering what else Mrs. Webster's high-priced lawyer had said. But since the other woman wasn't likely to tell, Kelly didn't ask. "I should be going," she said. "I'm sure you want to get back to your guests."

"You're welcome to stay. They are several young people you might enjoy meeting. Just please refrain from mentioning my grandchildren. It's bad enough that Emily knows. I do not want the others to learn about this."

Kelly raised her brows, but offered no comment. She'd already said enough. Instead, she followed Mrs. Webster out of the room and made her way to the foyer. She had no intention of staying to socialize with Mrs. Webster's friends. She'd feel as out of place among them as her car was among the Mercedes and BMWs on the side lawn. She retrieved her coat and headed out the front door in search of her car. She shrugged aside the parking attendant's offer to re-upholster the seats at a bargain basement price, then slowly drove through the iron gates.

Unwilling to face the empty apartment, she headed for a shopping mall and bought a ticket for a Disney comedy. Then she splurged on popcorn, soda, and peanuts in an effort to thrust aside her worries for a couple of hours.

Instead, she sat among the laughing families and brooded. Even the magic of Disney couldn't lift her depression. Halfway through, she handed the un-opened package of peanuts to the harried mother sitting next to her, then walked out.

It took a moment for her eyes to adjust to the bright light of the theater foyer. Once she could see clearly again, she wandered aimlessly out into the mall and into a department store. While she was here, she figured she might as well look for a couple of blouses to replace the ones that were hopelessly stained. She'd learned quickly to carry a set of casual clothes in the car and change once she got to Ryan's house. Otherwise, her work clothes, no matter how baby-resistant, were eventually ruined.

She stared at the vast array of merchandise on the racks, but nothing leaped out and said "Buy me, I'm perfect." Maybe it was her mood. Or maybe it was the fact that she'd never gone clothes shopping alone before. Whatever the cause, shopping suddenly seemed more like work than the fun time she remembered.

She grabbed three blouses from a nearby rack and headed for the changing room. The fresh-faced salesgirl smiled and told Kelly she looked so slim, considering. Puzzled, Kelly just nodded and headed for the changing booth. Considering what? That Kelly was over twenty-five and not wide as a door?

Kelly hung the blouses on the wall hook inside the changing booth and sank onto the tiny stool. She stared glumly at her reflection in the full-length mirror, the ditsy salesgirl forgotten.

She wondered why she had ever thought that she could persuade Mrs. Webster to drop the custody suit. Going to her house had been a mistake, she thought. Then again, maybe not. At least she knew why the woman disliked Ryan so much.

But knowing only made Kelly feel worse. Mrs. Webster's dislike was the unreasonable kind that had nothing to do with Ryan and everything to do with old wounds. That made it even more difficult to deal with because Kelly couldn't reason away that kind of prejudice. Such emotions were beyond the scope of logic.

Yet what could she do? The custody battle threatened the family's future at a very delicate time. The children were beginning to recover from the loss of their parents. It would be cruel to jerk them out of their new-found security. But that's exactly what would happen if Kelly couldn't come up with another solution.

There was an answer, she knew. Marriage. Yet every time the thought crossed her mind, she thrust it away. She bounced to her feet and jerked the first blouse off the hanger. But the idea kept niggling at the edge of her conscience. Kelly and Ryan both had tried every reasonable solution they could think of, but nothing seemed to dent Mrs. Webster's resolve. The trip to Mrs. Webster's house had been a last-ditch effort that had obviously failed. It had probably made matters worse. It confirmed that Kelly had shed the professional distance that was necessary to her job.

Kelly groaned, but she didn't realize how loudly until the salesgirl spoke from the other side of the curtain.

"Are you all right?"

Kelly jumped, the voice startling her out of her thoughts. "Fine," she stammered.

"I'll stay close in case you need anything," the girl offered.

Kelly looked down at the jagged hem, then in the mirror at the mismatched row of buttons. She almost laughed, but then figured the girl would come right in to see what was so funny. It wasn't just the bad buttoning job. The blouse was ludicrously large, billowing about Kelly's slight frame like a sheet. She looked at the tag. A very expensive sheet.

Then the second tag caught her eye. Not only was

the blouse five sizes too large, but it was designed for someone very pregnant. She was worse than distracted. She was losing her mind. In less than a minute, Kelly was in her own clothes and handing the items to the concerned salesgirl. Then she headed resolutely for the other side of the store.

As she fingered a soft peach dress, an even more depressing thought struck her. No wonder Mrs. Webster had invited her to stay at the party. The more people who saw Kelly there, the more people Mrs. Webster could call on to testify that Kelly had become personally involved with the family.

No. It didn't mean a thing. Not even a crafty lawyer could make much out of her presence at the party. But, said the little devil on her shoulder, it was just another fact that added up to the whole picture of Kelly's involvement. Add that to the scene in the bedroom and a judge would draw the obvious conclusion.

She'd have to marry Ryan, no matter what the cost to herself. It was the only way to keep the kids from becoming permanent residents of the brick mansion with the fountain by the drive. Now, all she had to do was convince Ryan.

That shouldn't be too hard, she thought. After all, it was his idea in the first place. Ryan hadn't been all that serious about it at the time—he'd certainly taken her refusal well enough. But he would, in time, see there just weren't any alternatives.

A voice intruded, and Kelly turned. Another salesgirl asked if she wanted to try on the dress. Kelly shook her head and turned towards the exit.

Marriage. The idea alternately warmed and terrified her. Marry me, marry my family. That was fine for Kelly. But she feared Ryan would be stifled by the type of family life she had known throughout her growing up years. Her large, boisterous family would probably send him into hiding. Heck, they overwhelmed her sometimes, and she was used to them. Then again, maybe he needed a family of his own as much as she did. All she knew was that she might have a chance now to live the life she had dreamed of, the life she thought had been hers before her baby's death had ripped the ground from beneath her feet. And if it turned out that Ryan still couldn't resist the lure of adventure, well, then, she and the children would have each other until he decided to come home again.

She knew that was why she fought so hard against her own feelings, against the silken web that bound her more closely to Ryan every time they touched. Or maybe that was just an excuse. It was easier to hide behind reasons and excuses than to take a chance on feelings that might not last, or maybe weren't really there at all on his side. She had to admit, to herself at least, that she felt more alive with Ryan than she ever had in her life. It was almost as if she was falling in love.

In love.

Kelly ran full steam into a sturdy, graying man. But she barely noticed his efforts to steady her on her feet as she stumbled on by him.

It couldn't be. It shouldn't be. After Bradley's rejection, she had sworn she'd never care that way for a man again. Besides that, Ryan was a client. It was unethical to fall in love with a client. Not only that, it was stupid. Kelly sank onto a nearby bench. She frowned at the wildly churning emotions that chased one another through her mid-section. In time, her thoughts became more focused. She concentrated not on how she could have allowed herself to fall in love with Ryan, but on what she was going to do about it.

The safest thing was to do nothing. He need never know, and eventually she would get over it. She had gotten over Brian, so much so it didn't give her a twinge to think of him married and the father of a newborn baby. But she had simply replaced him in her heart with Bradley, whose defection had left her cold and empty, unwilling to try again. And she hadn't tried. Love had slipped in the back door this time.

She had just made up her mind to propose to the man, to suggest a businesslike arrangement for the sake of the children. Was she really thinking of marriage as a noble, selfless gesture that would bring stability to the lives of three precious children? Or was she selfishly using them to get Ryan? The questions danced round and round in her head, but no clear answers flew forth. It was too complicated. Everything was twisted into a maze of rights and wrongs and emotions and memories, both recent and more distant. Time alone could sort them into some sort of clear picture. Only time was the most precious and least available thing of all.

Shaking her head, she headed for her car. Minutes later, she was driving down the highway and wondering whether to go straight to Ryan's house or stop at her apartment first. Knowing her new-found resolve was liable to waver if she delayed, she headed straight for the stone house on the dead-end street. She rehearsed the words in her mind again as she rang the doorbell, determinedly thrusting back her nagging doubts of the sanity of what she was about to do. But when Ryan opened the door with a crying toddler in his arms, any remaining doubts flew away in the brisk breeze. Surprise and pleasure inter-mingled in Ryan's expression when he saw her stand-ing there under the porch light.

"It's about time," he said as he balanced Sarah on his hip and unlatched the screen. Kelly pulled open the screen and stepped inside, shutting the cold wind behind the heavy oak door.

"What do you mean?" she asked, puzzled by his manner. Taken alone, his words would have been a sign of irritation. But a faint twitch at the corners of his mouth indicated otherwise.

"I saw you this afternoon. You came out from behind the Henderson's bushes and stalked on up the street. What were you doing in my neighbor's shrubbery?"

Kelly forced herself to meet his half angry, half-confused glare. "I was thinking. And while I was in the bushes, I came up with an idea that I thought might help you. As it turns out, it was a stupid idea. I probably just made things worse."

Ryan shifted Sarah to his other side and tucked the flannel blanket around her more tightly, wincing when she let out an ear-piercing scream.

"I'll explain in a minute when it's quieter around here," Kelly said as she reached for her coat buttons, glancing around the room as she did so. The clutter of toys, scattered cushions, and torn papers was testimony to the difficult day Ryan had spent while she had whiled away the hours, trying to come to terms with her own feelings. She felt guilty, even though she knew there was nothing to feel guilty about. Still, she hadn't managed to do anything productive. Rather, she suspected her actions that evening might produce distinctly unpleasant results if she and Ryan didn't tread carefully over the next few weeks. Even her nocturnal trip here was suspect, but that couldn't be helped. There was just some things you couldn't do by telephone.

Leaning back against the wall, Ryan patted the howling child's back and crooned soothingly in her ear, but with little effect.

As soon as Kelly had shrugged out of her coat she held out her arms. "She's drooling," Ryan warned. "You'll end up with spots on your dress."

"It doesn't matter." Kelly pulled the child into her arms. "It's washable. In my line of work, my clothes have to be baby proof."

"She's still teething," Ryan explained. "She woke up crying a few minutes ago. I was just going to get the teething ring out of the freezer."

Kelly rocked the child gently in her arms. "Go ahead. We'll wait here." Her eyes lingered on his while he backed toward the doorway, then disappeared into the next room. Then, she laid Sarah down on the couch and coaxed her tiny fingers out of her mouth. Gingerly feeling along the gum line, she located the swollen nub where a tooth was trying to break through.

"Ouch," she muttered, jerking her hand back when Sarah bit down.

"What's the matter?" Ryan called from the doorway.

"Nothing much. I asked for it anyway. I should know by now to be more careful when looking for new teeth."

"Ah, she bit you." He nodded with wry understanding. "She got me this morning. Let's take her up to the nursery. I'll dig up some teething gel. Between that and the teething ring, she should be able to go back to sleep pretty soon, at least for a little while."

Kelly gathered up Sarah, whose loud wails had faded to quiet whimpers the minute she bit down on the ice-cold teething ring. "Can I carry her up, please?" Holding the unhappy child brought to mind all the things she'd never experienced with her own child, the sleepless nights as well as the unforgettable hurdles like her first step. Suddenly, it was doubly important that Ryan agree to the course of action she was about to suggest. It wasn't just for them. It was for Kelly, too, because she loved Ryan and because she loved and needed these children.

Ryan must have sensed her intensity. His eyes darkened with emotion as he reached out and touched Kelly's cheek, sending frissons of excitement shimmering through her body. "Of course, you can carry her," he said, his voice low and slightly husky. His hands burned where they touched when he helped her to her feet. Together, they climbed the stairs, Kelly with the child and Ryan with his hand resting gently at her waist.

Kelly couldn't help thinking how like a family they seemed as they tucked Sarah into her crib and wound the musical lamb. But with two doting adults to entertain her, Sarah took her own sweet time in getting to sleep. When she finally dozed off, Ryan and Kelly tiptoed out of the room and downstairs to the kitchen on the pretext of making coffee.

While Ryan measured the coffee into the filter, Kelly fidgeted nervously at the table, clicking the salt and pepper shakers together until Ryan's exasperated stare halted her movements. "Sorry," she murmured, unconsciously picking up the rhythmic tapping with her fingernails. She responded to his mundane comments with little more than absentminded grunts, until he set a carton of milk and a steaming mug of coffee in front of her.

"Talk," he ordered as he sat down opposite her. "Something is obviously bothering you. Spit it out."

Kelly stared down at the coffee, then poured a generous helping of milk into it and watched the colors swirl and blend.

"Could I have a spoon, please?" she asked in a small voice. She knew she was stalling, but now that the moment had arrived, she couldn't seem to summon the courage she needed. What if he didn't agree with her? Worse yet, what if he laughed?

Ryan placed a spoon in front of her, then returned to his seat and tapped the grained wooden tabletop with his forefinger. The tension in the room sizzled.

"The milk—"

"—won't spoil that fast," he finished for her. Then, muttering an indistinguishable imprecation, he raised his mug to his lips and took a tentative sip.

Watching him, Kelly took a deep breath, then blurted it out.

"I think we should get married."

Ryan sputtered on the coffee, spraying large drips on the table and on his shirt. Kelly stared in dismay while he tried to recover his wind and bring his coughing under control.

"Sorry," he gasped. "I wasn't expecting that."

Highly indignant with his reaction, Kelly exploded, all the pent-up tension and emotion from the last few days pouring forth.

"It was your idea in the first place. I'm not exactly thrilled about it, but I don't see that we have any other choice, unless you want to take your chances with the judge."

Ryan's eyes widened at her tirade, but Kelly left him no opening to speak.

"It's not as if I'm after your money. I'm not particularly crazy about your housekeeping habits, either. Nor am I one of those sex-starved bimbos from your books. I just think that the only way we're going to convince people that we're not having a cheap affair is to get married."

Ryan moved swiftly around the table and pushed her back into her chair. He leaned over her, gently tilting her chin and forcing her to look up at him.

"That's not what you said the other day. As I recall, you were adamantly opposed to marriage. This sudden change of heart is a surprise, that's all."

"Well, a lot's happened since then, and none of it good," she snapped.

Ryan's finger released her chin and he backed away. "She told you, didn't she?" He shook his head resignedly, already knowing the answer. "I told Mrs. Yates not to bother you with it," Ryan said. "I knew it would only worry you."

Kelly rolled her eyes. In the midst of her fears about proposing to Ryan, she had temporarily forgotten Mrs. Yates's detailed account of the social worker's visit. "I'm glad she told me, although I'm not sure whether what I did tonight made things better or worse. That's why I think marriage is the only answer." As a dark fear took hold, Kelly searched his face for a hint of rejection. "You do agree, don't you?"

Ryan released her arms, only to cup her face in his hands. "I think you'd better tell me what you did." Never quite releasing her, he pulled out the chair next to her and sat down, clasping her small hands in his own.

Briefly she described her day, beginning with Mrs. Yates's visit and finishing with Mrs. Webster's promise to call off the private detective.

"She thinks she has all the evidence she needs to win," Kelly explained. "She came right out and said so."

Ryan closed his eyes and sighed. "So, our best option is to present the judge with a couple of happily married parent figures. And maybe, just maybe, we can turn this so-called evidence of hers to our advantage."

"You mean, let Mrs. Webster prove things for us? The photos and her testimony about—" Kelly had to look away. "About that morning. If we were married, it would legitimize it all, wouldn't it?"

"We'd be just another young couple in love,"

Ryan answered dryly. "Who just happens to have an interfering relative. Not unusual at all."

"It just might work." With a sigh of relief, Kelly met Ryan's serious gaze.

"Do you think you can pull it off?" Ryan asked.

Kelly nodded. "What about when it's over, when the custody is settled permanently?"

"Then you're free to get on with your life, if that's what you really want. We could get a divorce." He kept his expression blank, but his eyes captured hers with an intensity that unnerved her.

While his eyes excited her, his words revived her anger. "It wouldn't be that simple. I can't just say, 'Well, kids, I've had a great time playing Mommy, but now it's time to move on to bigger and better things.' I'm not even sure I could walk away now if I had to."

"Good." Ryan squeezed her hands, then released them. "You could divorce me, but not them. You're committed to them. And in the meantime, who knows what can happen if we're forced to spend every day and every night together. We might like it." One eyebrow lifted speculatively, while his eyes danced with mischief.

Kelly started, suddenly realizing the full import of such a marriage. She thought she'd considered everything carefully. She had, really, logically and intellectually, weighing the pros and cons—or at least that's what she told herself. But the enormity of this commitment slammed into her stomach, leaving her slightly breathless. She had so much to gain—and so much to lose.

It wasn't just a matter of few weeks' pretense to

satisfy the legal system. It would change the course of five lives, not the least of which were three innocent children. There was a very real possibility that the marriage would last, that she and Ryan would remain together to provide the children with a lasting stability that would be impossible if they divorced. Ryan might even learn to love her someday. Also, the time might come when Ryan would want a child of his own.

She bolted out of the chair and paced the floor, oblivious to Ryan's troubled stare. She had to tell him. She couldn't make the choice for both of them. It wasn't right. Yet her heart cried out for silence, just for a little while until her newly discovered love could bask in his nearness without the risk of rejection. But no, she had to tell him now. Later might be too late.

"Ryan, do you want children?" she blurted out, still pacing.

EIGHT

Ryan cocked his head, his face a picture of puzzlement. "Isn't that what we've been talking about? Keeping the kids?"

"I mean," she said, standing with hand on hips. "We should talk about whether you want to have children of your own someday?"

He paled visibly. "You mean more kids? Aren't three enough?"

"Some men might not think so," she retorted, and her mind sprang to her ex-husband, then on to Bradley. He had thought more in terms of litters, whole packs of children, all with dimples that matched his own. He had been more than disappointed when he found that he'd have to settle for the vagaries of the adoption system or find another woman to marry. Looking back, it wasn't surprising that he had opted for the latter.

"Anyway," she continued. "I think we should talk about things like that. Babies, where we're going to live, who's paying the electric bill."

"I'll pay the electric bill and the gas and phone, too. You can buy groceries, if you want. We'll live here until we decide to move. And I can't even think about having more children. I don't know what I thought I'd do with the rest of my life, but raising kids wasn't part of the plan. I'm not sure I can survive the three I have now."

Kelly stared up at him, caught between relief and anger at his high-handed attitude.

"For someone who literally choked on the idea of marriage, you sure have things thought out."

Ryan threw his hands into the air, then fell backwards into a chair.

"I give up. What do you want?"

Kelly stared at the clean lines of his body, the warm brown eyes, now wide with exasperation. She knew darn well what she wanted. She just didn't have the guts to say it.

"I just want everyone to be happy," she half-whispered.

Ryan leaned forward, the exasperation fading to tenderness and something else, worry perhaps. "Do you want a baby?" he asked. "Or can you be happy mothering my three?"

Kelly frowned. "Very happy," she replied. "It's more than I ever expected, more than I dared dream of after what happened to Brian and I." And Bradley, she thought. But that humiliating episode didn't bear mentioning. She walked slowly to the counter and leaned heavily against it, unconsciously tapping her nails on the surface.

"Then why do you seem distinctly unhappy right now?" Ryan stepped behind her and pulled her against him. He trapped the tapping fingers within his own. His touch was almost her undoing. She tried to pull away, but he turned her almost effortlessly in his arms and tilted her chin upwards. "What is it? It's something to do with Brian, isn't it? Do you still want him?"

Still want Brian? How could Ryan even think that? Kelly didn't think she'd ever wanted Brian, even in the beginning, as much as she wanted Ryan right now. She shook her head mutely, but he didn't seem to notice. He probably didn't realize either that his tightening grip was starting to hurt. "He's married again, Kelly. He has a baby. You have to get on with your life."

"No, you're wrong," she blurted out, shoving against Ryan's chest. His grip slackened and she pulled away, shrinking from the fierce anger in his eyes.

"Then why did you come here tonight?"

"Ryan, there's a lot you don't know about my marriage to Brian."

"I don't think I want to know," Ryan replied.

"And I don't want to tell you," she said. "But that's the only way I can make you understand."

"Understand what? That you're willing to sacrifice yourself for a while to help me, but you can't forget your ex-husband?"

Kelly forced herself to meet his harsh stare. "Brian and I lost a child."

The words hung between them for an instant. Kelly was the first to look away and she closed her eyes and bit her lip to keep the sudden tears at bay. The tears were a surprise. She hadn't cried about that for such a long time. She'd come to terms with Melanie's death and gone on with her life. The same was true about the divorce. But somehow she had to convince Ryan of that.

"It was a difficult pregnancy. I spent the last six weeks in the hospital, but it wasn't enough. Melanie only lived two days."

Ryan pulled her close, but she pressed against his chest with her palms, rearing back so she could see his expression. She didn't want his sympathy now. She wanted him to understand the facts clearly.

"I nearly died myself," she said. "As it is, I can't have any more children. I've been to specialists. No operation, no marvel of modern medical technology is going to change that fact. I can't give you a child of your own."

Ryan cupped her face. "I'm not asking that."

"I know," Kelly swallowed. "But you might want one someday. Brian did." She tried to look away, but Ryan wouldn't let her.

"So he left and found someone else."

"No. I left." Ryan's disbelieving grunt urged her on. "All our plans were built around having a big family. We didn't have much else in common. We couldn't even help each other over losing the baby. Brian just wanted to try again and he couldn't see that no matter how much we tried, we couldn't make another baby together."

"What about adoption? I know the waiting lists are long, but surely that was an option."

Kelly's tone was distant and resigned as she remembered the arguments and Brian's blind obstinacy. "Not for Brian."

"So you sacrificed yourself for Brian's ego, the idiot. Doesn't he know what he's missing?"

"Brian has exactly what he wanted in the first place. The only difference is this time he picked someone who likes the same things he does. They have more in common than a fantasy."

Ryan sighed. His eyes were wary now. The anger was gone, but the well-remembered warmth hadn't returned yet. "Now I know why you chose to be an educator. Do you think you can stand to take on my three? Sharon's really. Do you think you can raise them like you would have raised your own daughter?"

Kelly nodded, the lump in her throat making speech impossible.

"Then we'll be a family," Ryan insisted, the corners of his mouth stealing into a smile. "Just the five of us. Well, six if you count Mrs. Yates."

"What about Grandmother Webster?"

Ryan glared down at her. "That's stretching things a bit."

Kelly let a moment's peaceful silence pass before she latched onto the second matter that had been troubling her. She wasn't sure she was ready to risk her heart so completely yet. She knew that once they made love she'd be lost. If he left, he'd hurt her a thousand times more than Brian or Bradley ever had.

"If we're going to be married," she began, "then I assume we'll be sharing the same bed because, if we don't, then Mrs. Webster will find out somehow. You know she will. You can't imagine what big mouths kids have. And there's this attraction between us. It's what got us into this trouble in the first place."

Kelly stared, fascinated by the fire igniting his eyes. She dodged the light kiss that he aimed for her lips, but which landed near her ear, sending weak shivers along her nerve endings.

"What are we talking about?" he asked. "Sex? Birth control? I thought you just finished telling me that's one little detail we don't have to worry about. Just think of the money we'll save."

Kelly thumped his chest in frustration. "Why do you have to make this so difficult? I just need to know what you expect. Not just now, but in the future. I don't know if you want—"

Ryan's forefinger on her lips stopped her bumbled attempt at confession. "I won't ask anything of you that you're not ready to give."

"It's not that," she tried again. "We're making a serious commitment. I want everything out in the open. No secrets, no surprises."

"No sudden attacks," he suggested with a glint of amusement. "Kelly, we don't have to share a bed, unless you want to, although to be quite honest, I hope we will. I want you to go on with your work, and I want you to finish your thesis. I don't want to interfere with that."

Kelly searched his expression for a clue to his real feelings, but she couldn't see beyond her own confusion.

"Ryan, I—"

"No buts," Ryan said. "Either we get married or we don't. Either we have a chance at keeping the kids or we don't. What will it be?"

When he put it that way, Kelly had very little choice but to agree. She only hoped that she wouldn't regret it later. She nodded her assent. She thought she saw a faint smile tease his lips, a leap of fire in his eyes, but it was hidden so quickly behind his carefully closed expression that Kelly decided it must be wishful thinking.

"I'm not Brian," he said. "Don't ever forget that."

At Kelly's nod, he pulled her closer. Sealing their bargain with a light, chaste kiss, Ryan propelled her into the living room and retrieved her coat. Surprised at his sudden change of mood, Kelly hung back and stole a quick glance at his expressionless face.

Shouldn't there be something more? Something like, *Thank you, Kelly, for pulling my chestnuts out of the fire,* or a simple *I love you for what you're doing.* No, that was asking too much. But Ryan had turned so distant, so businesslike. Kelly stared at him in confusion as she slipped on her coat and buttoned it.

"You'd better get home and get some sleep," Ryan ordered. "I'm sure our friend the detective is outside with one eye on the windows and the other on his watch. I'll take care of the arrangements and call you as soon as I have something firm. Is next Saturday too soon?"

Kelly swallowed hard.

"The hearing is the following week," he reminded her.

"Next Saturday will be fine."

But it wasn't. By Monday they realized that it would be impossible to arrange a proper wedding on such short notice. The church was booked solid for the next two weeks. And a church wedding in Kelly's hometown is what they decided upon. Ryan's lawyer insisted it would be appear more like a love match and less like a hurried, last ditch grab for respectability. Not much, Kelly supposed, but maybe all those sisters and cousins would make it more believable. Kelly hated the fact that Ryan had discussed the personal details of their relationship with the attorney, no matter how necessary it was. It only added to her sense of uneasiness, of unwanted exposure to the judgment of strangers who didn't really understand.

The day of the hearing arrived too soon, yet not soon enough. Seated in the judge's outer office, Kelly toyed nervously with her purse strap, while she tapped her heel into the sound-absorbing carpet and tried to ignore the self-possessed Mrs. Webster. She looked up sharply when a muffled giggle escaped from behind the thick, paneled door.

Ryan's hand tightened on hers. "They've been in there a long time."

Kelly consulted her watch. "Five minutes," she said. Yesterday a clerk had called and asked that they bring the children along so that the judge could meet them. Now the three of them and Mrs. Yates were closeted with the stout gray-haired man and, from the sound of it, having a good time. Good Lord, Kelly thought, I hope Eric doesn't mention Bambi and the stories. Ryan hadn't read one to the children in months. But four-year-olds had an infuriating tendency to forget what happened the day before and remember for months anything you'd rather they didn't.

Then the door opened and Kelly could see a grinning Eric shaking hands with the judge. "Bye, Jelly Belly," he said, while his sisters toddled shyly past. Kelly winced. Ryan groaned. Mrs. Webster beamed.

Before Ryan could launch into a lecture on name calling and tact, the judge raised a hand to forestall him. "They're delightful children," he said. "And that's what my grandchildren call me."

Kelly's spirits lifted at the sight of the warm, gray gentleman who ushered the children out the door and gave Mrs. Yates directions to the ice cream shop down the block. Then he excused himself and returned to his office, shutting the door. After a moment, a clerk emerged and led them to a conference room down the hall.

Frowning slightly, Mrs. Webster took a seat and whispered to the bland-faced attorney. Then she turned and glared at Ryan. "No child of mine would have said something like that to an adult. It's time someone took them in hand."

Before she could continue, the door opened and the stout judge entered, followed by a businesslike court reporter who quietly took a place in the corner. The judge himself had changed into his robes. By the looks of things, he'd changed more than that. Gone was the gentle grandfather, replaced by the stern judge. Even Mrs. Webster seemed suitably impressed. Seconds later, a harried man with thick glasses entered and took a seat on the other side of Ryan.

"I'm sorry, Judge Benson," the man said. "I was detained unexpectedly in juvenile court."

"Yes," the stout man cleared his throat then fixed

understanding eyes on Kelly and continued distract-
edly. "My clerk mentioned it. I'm sure Judge Mar-
low is quite grateful to you for disarming that young
man. Now, Miss Smith?"

Kelly tensed still more if that were possible.

"Miss Smith, I'd like to dispense with the formali-
ties. I've read all the reports and the filings. I'd like
to know why you're here today. For moral support,
I assume. Is that correct?"

Ryan's attorney cleared his throat. "Your honor,
if I may interject. Miss Smith has a vested interest
in the outcome of these proceedings. She and Mr.
Matthews are to be married in less than two weeks."

The judge nodded, then pointedly returned his
attention to Kelly. "And are you willing to assume
responsibility for these children, even though they
are not yours?"

Kelly nodded, choosing her words carefully. "Of
course. The children are my first interest. I love them
very much." Damn! Mrs. Webster's smirk warned
Kelly that her words didn't convey quite what she
had intended. "I'm from a large family myself. I
understand that I'm not just marrying Ryan, but I'm
taking on a ready-made family."

"Most brides would resent the lack of privacy.
Not to mention the added responsibilities. It's quite
a strain to put on a new marriage." The judge
cleared his throat again.

The bland faced man spoke before the judge could
continue. "My client has reason to believe that Miss
Smith and Mr. Matthews are marrying solely to
maintain custody of the three minor children and control over the trust fund in their names."

"That's bull." Ryan's eyes shot fire across the table.

Ryan's attorney pushed him back into his seat with a steely hand on the shoulder.

The judge eyed the tense combatants with mild irritation. "I had considered that. However, there is nothing in the case reports to indicate that Miss Smith is of a mercenary nature. However, I am concerned about the caseworker's report on the home situation. There seems to be a need for—shall we say organization, for lack of a better word."

"My feelings exactly," said Mrs. Webster, ignoring the judge's glare. "Half the time he lets those children run wild and do whatever they like. There's no structure, no lessons, no preparation for the life they'll be expected to lead."

"Your honor," Ryan's attorney interjected, "the caseworker arrived without notice at a particularly bad time. Mr. Matthews was struggling to meet a deadline with his publisher. He'd spent most of the night caring for a sick baby and had the flu himself. His housekeeper had been helping her pregnant niece and had just arrived. He could not call on Miss Smith for help because pressure from Mrs. Webster forced them to discontinue their relationship."

The judge fixed Kelly and Ryan with a piercing stare. "And yet the two of you plan to marry in two weeks?"

Ryan leaned forward. "Your honor. I would like to request another visit, either with that caseworker or another. She is welcome to arrive at any time, announced or unannounced."

The judge nodded. "I was about to suggest that.

However, Mr. Matthews, could you please explain how your household came to be in such a state as it was in during her first visit.''

Ryan frowned. ''A combination of things, really,'' he began. ''The flu. My deadline. And I had just suffered the biggest disappointment in my life. I'm afraid I didn't make a very good impression.'' He took Kelly's hand and squeezed it, a touching emphasis, she thought.

''Ms. Peterson's report indicates that. What kind of disappointment are you speaking of?''

''The night before I asked Kelly Smith to marry me. She turned me down. Evidently she thought I just wanted someone to mother the children. I was able to convince her otherwise.''

''Miss Smith?''

Kelly nodded. ''Mrs. Webster was having us both followed. I think she believed we were having an affair. But we weren't. I know she means well and that she is concerned about her grandchildren. But I don't think she understands that although Ryan's parenting style is very different from her own, it is not bad. In fact, he's very good with the children. That's what first attracted me to him.'' That at least was the truth, partly. Those warm, knowing brown eyes had helped, she thought.

Glancing over, she saw those eyes resting on her with a tense worry now.

''Miss Smith. Do you wish to have children of your own?''

She told herself it wasn't a trick question. There was no way the judge could know he'd touched a sore point. It was just another question to determine whether she had the children's best interests at heart.

"Do you mean," she asked, her voice trembling despite her attempt at control. "Do you mean would I favor my own child over Ryan's nephew and nieces?"

"To put it frankly, yes, that is the question."

"Any child in my home, in our home, would be loved. Every child deserves that most of all. And every child is special in some way. These children each have special talents, although they're not apparent yet. But what makes them special now is that they've lost their parents and they need to be reassured and to know that their world is still safe. They'll always need that. My mother claims that you can't stop being a parent."

The judge nodded. "It appears that you have thought this through, and I would assume that you and Mr. Matthews have discussed these matters."

"We have." Ryan's firm voice stiffened Kelly's weakening spine.

"Mr. Duncan," the judge turned to Mrs. Webster's attorney. "Do you have anything to add?"

"Nothing that was not listed in the complaint filed with the court."

"I do." All eyes swiveled to Mrs. Webster, who bristled with affront. "These two are rushing into marriage like a couple of young fools just to prevent me from gaining custody of my grandchildren. Miss Smith is sensible enough and knowledgeable enough about children. But she already has one failed marriage behind her, and I wouldn't give this marriage much chance of making it past the final custody decision. And Mr. Matthews is not a good influence.''

"Anything else.'' The judge's deadpan stare invited no elaboration.

"It's enough, isn't it. That and the reports from the private investigator and the fact that I caught them kissing upstairs in Ryan's bedroom.''

"Your honor, there is a reasonable explanation,'' Ryan's attorney began.

"I'm sure there is. However, it has no bearing on the outcome, so I suggest we don't concern ourselves with the whys and wherefores and get to the point. I'm ordering a second investigation of the home situation. I think we should wait in all fairness until after the wedding. We can, I'm sure, expect general chaos until then. Also, I'd like to know how Miss Smith settles into the household and how the children adjust to the changes. Mrs. Webster is to be allowed reasonable visitation rights. If need be, I can include a schedule in my order.''

"That won't be necessary,'' Kelly said. "I'm sure we can work it out among ourselves, can't we, Mrs. Webster? We all want what's best for the children. I believe that includes spending time with their grandmother.''

Deflated for the moment, Mrs. Webster nodded silently.

"Good,'' the judge said. "I had hoped the family could begin to work together on something.''

Kelly's second wedding day dawned all too soon, yet not soon enough. She'd been frantically busy during the last week, rearranging appointments and catching up on stacks of paperwork so she could stretch the weekend by a couple of days and take a short honeymoon. She'd scarcely had time to think about the enormous commitment she would make later that morning, let alone dwell on the pitfalls of such a marriage. And for that she was immensely grateful. But now there was nothing left to do but get dressed and get to the church on time. And if Kelly knew her family, she wouldn't even need to be responsible for that. In a couple of hours, her sisters would crowd into her room to help her dress and do her hair. And undoubtedly, they would have a lot to say about Kelly marrying a man she hadn't even had time to bring home to meet the folks until the day before the wedding.

She padded barefoot across the cold, wooden floor of her old room to stare out the window at the early morning mist that blanketed the sleepy streets of Harrington. Already, the muffled sounds of water running and pans clinking were wending their way up from the kitchen. She supposed she ought to go help her mother since there were so many extra mouths to feed that morning. But still she lingered, enjoying the last tidbit of peace and quiet she was likely to have for a long time.

A dozen warm, cozy memories sprang to mind, and she was glad her mother had talked Kelly and Ryan into having the wedding in Kelly's hometown. They were to be married in the brick church where she had been christened as a baby. Never mind that she had married Brian there in a wedding attended by half the town. This time was different. She was a mature woman going into this with her eyes open and no fantasies or delusions. It didn't matter that her husband-to-be wasn't madly in love with her. He liked her, trusted her. He obviously found her physically attractive. In time, he might even love her.

Then again, he might not. Her toes began to cramp in the chill of the room, so she dug around the edge of the bed until she located her slippers, then pulled on a robe. She carefully opened the door, then smiled when the hinges didn't creak like they used to. With half of his brood gone now, Dad must have more time for minor home repairs. But when the floorboards emitted a loud squawk halfway down the hall, Kelly decided that Dad hadn't gotten around to fixing everything. Or maybe there were some things that you didn't fix. You just put up with them.

Kelly stepped down the stairs as quietly as possible and joined her mother in the warm, cozy kitchen.

"Have a cup of coffee, dear," Marta Simms said as she dusted the flour from her hands. "I'll join you as soon as I put the rolls in the oven."

"Do you need any help?"

"Everything's under control," the older woman insisted. "Now, get your coffee and sit down."

Meekly following her mother's instructions, Kelly took two cups from the cabinet, added generous portions of milk, then poured the coffee. She carried both to the table and sat cross legged on one of the scarred oak chairs. She gingerly sipped at the hot brew while Marta Simms checked the oven temperature, then slid the tray of freshly made cinnamon rolls inside.

"Isn't there anything I can do to help, Mother?"

"Heavens, no, not on your wedding day. Just sit back and think about how happy you're going to be when all the fuss is over." Marta's eyes sparkled with excitement. There was nothing she liked better than organizing and accomplishing the impossible. Putting together a wedding in six days had been right up her alley.

"You think you know me pretty well, don't you?" Kelly teased.

Marta pursed her lips, but couldn't hold the frown for long. "You always enjoyed shop class more than those mother-daughter teas we went to. If you had your way, the two of you would have gotten married at the county courthouse, then taken the kids to the zoo for a honeymoon."

"That's a little extreme, isn't it?"

"Your wedding day should be something to remember, something to look back on."

Kelly eyed her mother suspiciously. "You didn't go wild with the decorations and a big reception, did you? I told you we wanted something quiet."

"Quiet and tasteful, you said."

"And?"

"And I've invited our friends and neighbors, some of your school friends. I've ordered a modest amount of flowers," she held up her palm before Kelly could interrupt. "Your father and I already paid for them, and we also paid Mr. Shillings from the newspaper to take some photographs."

Burying her face in her hands, Kelly sighed. "How many people did you invite?"

"I'm not sure. When you count husbands and wives, and of course, children, there won't be more than two hundred or so at the church. And I'm sure that they won't all come. With such short notice, a lot of people already had plans," she said accusingly.

All those people, Kelly thought as she allowed a muffled groan to escape. She had reluctantly agreed to allow her mother to make the arrangements, knowing that the warm, hometown wedding was bound to be more convincing than a courthouse quickie. But she had forgotten just how enthusiastically efficient the woman could be.

How can I get up there in front of all those people and pretend this wedding is the culmination of a passionate, whirlwind romance, she wondered. I'm not that good an actress. They'll ask questions, lots of questions, not at the wedding, but afterwards. Damn, why didn't I think of that?

"Excuse me, Mother," Kelly said as she pushed her chair back from the table and rose to her feet. "I need to talk to Ryan." I need to warn him, she added to herself. We need to get our stories straight.

"Now? You can't."

"Why not? And don't say anything about that stupid superstition about the groom seeing the bride before the wedding."

Amusement crinkled the laugh lines around Marta's eyes. "Ryan and your father went to Miller's Pond to fish."

Kelly sank back into her chair. "You're joking, aren't you? Please say you're joking."

"No, dear. They left about four-thirty. Don't worry, they'll be back in time to wash the fish smell off before the wedding."

"That's not what I'm worried about," Kelly retorted. Dad never took anyone fishing unless he wanted to have a serious conversation. Kelly's growing up years, like those of her siblings, had been punctuated by periodic jaunts to Miller's Pond. The last had been the day her divorce became final.

Marta's hazel eyes softened with understanding. "Ryan isn't a teenager, and your father isn't going to give him the third degree like he did with your prom date. He just wants to get to know the man you're going to marry. Under normal circumstances, there would have been plenty of time for a few weekends at the lake. As it is," she said with a wave of the hand.

"As it is," Kelly interrupted. "This is the best he could manage on short notice. I know, and I'm sorry about that, but it couldn't be helped."

Kelly squirmed under the force of the long, considering look her mother gave her. She forced herself to meet her mother's gaze, pretending a peace of mind that didn't exist. The slight lift of Marta's brow indicated she wasn't the least bit convinced.

"Pre-wedding jitters," Kelly finally suggested.

"Is that all it is?"

Kelly carried her cup to the counter to refill it. Standing with her back to her mother, she answered. "I wish it were that simple."

"Tell me."

Kelly opened her mouth to do so, but didn't know how to begin. She was saved for the moment by the oven timer.

"That'll be the coffee cake."

Kelly returned to her seat and winced when she

burned her tongue on the hot coffee. Quickly, she popped an ice cube out of the freezer and sucked on it, adding a second one to the steaming cup. While Marta bustled about the kitchen rearranging pans in the oven and resetting the timer, Kelly nursed her ice cube and prayed for the return of Ryan and her father. She even considered waking up the children and hiding behind the noisy confusion that followed them around. But she knew her mother would just create another opportunity to finish the conversation.

"Well?" The hazel eyes prodded insistently as Marta settled herself back into the chair.

Kelly crunched the rest of the ice cube beneath her teeth and swallowed it. "It's complicated."

"How complicated can it be? Either you love each other or you don't."

Kelly took a deep breath, then launched into a brief description of Ryan's custody problems. Heartened by her mother's nodding understanding, Kelly haltingly told how Mrs. Webster had caught her and Ryan necking.

"All this because of a simple kiss?" Kelly could see that her mother was still skeptical. "You're not telling me everything."

Kelly looked at the oven, willing the timer to buzz again, but it didn't cooperate. "The custody isn't final. And we both got the impression that the judge was swayed by the fact that I'm from a strong family background and that I'm trained in early childhood education."

"I don't think you realize what you're doing." Marta set her cup down with a sharp click. "You're all caught up in this fantasy about saving these children from their wicked grandmother, and you've clouded the real issue. Marriage is permanent, or at least it should be. What happened with Brian, well, it was a terrible tragedy that the two of you weren't mature enough to help each other and work out your problems. This time, though, I expect you to get it right. Either back out now, or make it work.''

''I can't back out. Ryan's depending on me.''

''So what? What is he to you, really? This is the rest of your life.''

''I love him, Mother. I can't walk away,'' Kelly admitted. ''I'm marrying him and, in a sense, I'm marrying the children. I don't have a choice, not really.''

The silence in the kitchen stretched, broken only by the ticking of the mantle clock in the next room. Kelly's confession hung between them, more revealing by what she didn't say than in what she did. Outside, a car door slammed, warning them that the men had returned. The two women stared at one another across the scarred tabletop, then stretched across to clasp hands.

''I wouldn't want to be in your shoes, child.''

When Ryan entered the room a few minutes later, he thought he had never seen two women drink coffee with such intensity before.

''You okay?'' he asked, dropping a hand onto Kelly's shoulder. Her eyes were red and watery as if she were trying to hold back tears.

''Fine,'' she replied with a falsely bright smile.

He saw the look that passed between the two women and furrowed his brow. Now he was really worried. The two of them had been talking about something serious, by the looks of things. He would have given anything to know what it was. He could make a few educated guesses, any one of which made him want to squirm—almost as much as he had felt like squirming under the force of his future father-in-law's skillful interrogation. Now Ryan knew how the people he had interviewed must have felt at times.

"Is Dad bringing the fish?" Kelly asked.

Ryan grimaced. "No. He's down the street arranging for a tow truck."

Marta's startled eyes met his. "Our car?"

"No. Mine."

Kelly groaned "What else could go wrong?"

"The timing belt slipped off."

Kelly brightened. "Oh. Well, that shouldn't take too long to fix."

Her mother wasn't so optimistic. "You probably can't get it into a shop before Monday."

Kelly set her cup down with a thud. "I guess that means the honeymoon will be right here."

Ryan exchanged a look with Marta. "I guess we should tell her," he said. "We're flying down to Hermann, that little German town with all the wineries. Marta arranged for a pilot."

"Kenny Mansard, remember him from high school? He has a plane out at Miller's Field. That's near Miller's Pond," she added for Ryan's benefit. "He's flying the two of you out as his wedding present."

"That sounds like fun," Kelly said into her cup. Then she met Ryan's eyes over the rim, with a mischievous quirk of her brow. "So how many fish did you catch?"

Ryan grinned. "Two."

Both women looked suitably surprised, impressed even. "We really did fish once I finished explaining that I was of sound mind and body and capable of providing financially for Kelly," he explained.

"I knew it," Kelly groaned. "I'm cursed."

"We all are," a voice called gaily from the doorway. And suddenly the room was flooded with so many people that for a moment Ryan couldn't even see Kelly. Ten minutes later, two more families poured in and everyone took turns hugging Kelly and shaking Ryan's hand. Then as the various nieces and nephews were sent to the basement where they would do the least damage, Kelly was able to make her way through the crowd to Ryan's side.

"Well," she whispered. "What do you think of my family?"

A bit overwhelmed at the moment, Ryan's only answer was a nervous smile and a vague expression of longing. He couldn't ever remember belonging anywhere or to anyone, unless you counted Sharon. All this hugging and chattering and confusion was a bit suffocating at first. But as Kelly's sisters dragged her from his side and led her upstairs, Ryan realized that he didn't mind much. In fact, he rationalized, it would probably be good for the kids to be part of a large, loving extended family.

He didn't see Kelly again until they were at the church, and then not alone. His chin dropped, then clamped shut when he peeked around the corner at the packed pews. Mrs. Simms, or Marta as she had insisted, had come through better than he had ever imagined. Kelly had tried to warn him. But this? At least half the town was here. Were these people all related to Kelly?

Then he spotted a squirming Eric in the second pew and the rising sense of panic faded away. Catching the child's eye, Ryan winked broadly then made a quick pig face. Mrs. Yates frowned at him, while Mrs. Webster glared from the pew behind them. For her, Ryan had a broad, triumphant smile. The crowd alone was impressive. He only hoped Kelly would make it through the vows without choking.

Damn! He hadn't even had a chance to talk to the minister. He was a minister, wasn't he? Or was he a pastor or, not a priest, surely. Of all the things to forget to ask. He hadn't even looked at the sign out front. He must be more nervous than he thought. Ryan darted into a room and picked up a hymnal off the shelf and checked the stamped imprint inside.

Presbyterian. Not that it mattered. They'd still be legally married if the man was a rabbi. But did Presbyterian weddings include the part that invited anyone with objections to speak up? That part made Ryan uneasy, considering Mrs. Webster's presence.

And then Kelly was there, standing with him in front of hundreds of people Ryan didn't know, and looking absolutely perfect. A little pale, but so beautiful he couldn't breathe for looking at her and thinking about how well the simple silk dress fit the curves of her body. And thinking about what was underneath that dress. He forgot all about Mrs. Webster and objections, even about all the strangers who were watching their intimate exchange.

Then Kelly was speaking, vowing with her eyes what Ryan knew couldn't be true. When it was his turn, he spoke with fervent confidence, meaning every word, knowing at that instant that he truly loved someone more than he ever could imagine was possible. Something shattered inside, and he found he was grinning like a fool while he slid the plain gold band onto her trembling finger, then held out his own hand to her. Properly ringed now, he pulled his wife into his arms and lowered his lips. Somewhere in the corner of his consciousness, he heard someone belatedly mutter, "You may kiss the bride."

One moment faded into the next. He was barely aware of walking the length of the church and next door to the reception hall. He felt only the soaring sensations that vibrated between him and Kelly, and he wished everyone would go away. Only they wouldn't. This was their celebration, too, and they wouldn't be deprived of a single tradition.

That part, Ryan thought, fitted nicely with his original plan to put on a convincing show. He wondered maliciously whether the guy taking all the pictures was another private detective, then someone introduced him as a local newspaperman. Kelly's smirk told Ryan that she knew exactly what he had been thinking. Which made him wonder if she knew what else he had been thinking over the last hour.

Then the muscles in her hand tensed, gripping his jacket sleeve. A tall, dark-haired man stopped in front of them.

"Congratulations," he said, holding out his hand. Kelly's fingers clenched even tighter as Ryan nodded his thanks and offered his own hand.

"Thanks, Brian," Kelly said, her voice a trifle

high. "Have you met Ryan yet? No? Ryan, this is Brian Smith. Brian, Ryan. Oh my that sounds silly."

Ryan looked from one to the other, his gaze halting on Kelly's fine features. Smith. Kelly Smith. Kelly's ex-husband's name was Brian. Reading his mind, she nodded.

A sharp stab of jealous anger pierced Ryan, though he kept his expression carefully controlled. He listened to Kelly's nervous questions about Brian's new family while his eyes sparred with Brian's. The other man seemed to be assessing Ryan. His expression wasn't open and friendly like that of the other guests. There was something remote, almost hostile in Brian's survey. It made Ryan wonder if there weren't some leftover feelings on Brian's side.

He was sure of it when Brian clasped Kelly's hands between his own. "I don't know how to say this," her ex-husband began. "I guess I'll start by apologizing."

"For what?" Kelly's voice quavered.

"You didn't deserve all that's happened the last few years. Lately, I've felt pretty guilty about things."

"Why?" Kelly asked, with an edge to her voice that seemed to confirm Ryan's suspicion that Kelly still cared for her ex-husband, maybe even loved him. "Because you have a beautiful baby now and you're happy?"

"Something like that," Brian muttered. "I acted like a jerk with you when I should have been helping you."

"Yes, you did," Kelly said with a glimmer of a smile. "I did some stupid things myself back then.

But I think that we both got what we needed in the long run.''

Brian cast an appraising glance in Ryan's direction. ''I hope so. In fact, this guy had better make damn sure of it.'' Giving Kelly a final nod, Brian turned on his heel and disappeared into the crowd.

''What was all that about?'' Ryan asked, sounding half confused, half angry.

Kelly, still staring at Brian's back, wiped the amusement from her face before turning to face Ryan.

''Who the hell does he think he is?'' Ryan continued. ''After everything he did to you, your ex-husband has the nerve to act like an overprotective big brother.''

Kelly shook her head. ''You don't have all the facts.'' Her voice was flat, conveying nothing as she turned her back and stalked away.

NINE

In a flash, Ryan was beside her, steering her away from an approaching sister and towards an empty space at the buffet table. "What are the facts? What else is there?"

Kelly reached for a cup of punch. "Later," she whispered, then turned to hug a bald-pated man. "Uncle Ralph, it's good to see you."

By mid-afternoon, Ryan was beginning to think that he'd never get a moment alone with his bride. The reception dragged on and on. Then it was too noisy in the small airplane for anything but a shouted conversation. By the time the plane touched down, he was almost rigid with frustration. While Ryan arranged for their pilot to pick them up two days later, Kelly climbed into the cab of the pickup truck that would carry them into the little German community of Hermann. Ryan climbed in next to her and pulled her close against his side, warding away his doubts with the temporary contact.

The short drive to the bed and breakfast inn was accomplished fairly quickly. All the while, their driver kept up a running commentary on the scenery and on the sights the town had to offer tourists— mostly antiques, history, and good food and local vintage wines. With Kelly snuggled close to him, Ryan could almost believe that everything would be all right, that the time alone together would give them a much needed opportunity to talk, to get everything out in the open.

But an hour later as he stared at the antique walnut bed in their room, he wasn't so sure. All he could think about was making love to Kelly. And that, he decided to his discomfort, was something that would have to wait until there were no ghosts between them. He loved her, but he wanted her whole and thinking of no one but him.

"What do you want to do now?" Ryan said as he set the two suitcases down, making a dull thud on the wooden floorboards. Bad choice of words, he thought.

"Go for a walk?" Kelly suggested quickly. She said something else, but he couldn't hear it for the roar of the freight train on the tracks across the street. While he waited for the noise to subside, he glanced around the romantic, Victorian bedroom.

"A walk sounds nice," Ryan answered and headed down the stairs, leaving Kelly with nothing to do but follow. After a brief conversation with their hostess, they slipped through the art gallery at the front of the house and out into a brick courtyard.

"Which way?" Ryan asked.

"Up the hill," was Kelly's immediate choice. "After all that sitting, I need the exercise."

Nodding his agreement, Ryan started across the intersection and up the steep hill. He didn't slow his steps until he realized that Kelly had lagged behind several yards, her shorter legs unable to keep pace with his long stride. His heart pounded hard in his chest. He felt a rising response someplace lower as he watched the healthy flush in her cheeks, then swung his glance lower to the rhythmic swing of her legs as she struggled to catch up with him.

He turned away and strode wordlessly at her side for the rest of the way up the hill to Market Street. They crossed and headed still farther up the hill until they reached the crest and gazed out between the houses to the river far below. They could see for miles in the cool, crisp air. But the chill of the breeze soon had them moving again, this time wandering through residential neighborhoods that were a charming mixture of old brick and newer frame houses.

They meandered up and down side streets, locating a cemetery that overlooked the rest of the hillside community. As they wandered among the markers in the older section, Ryan wondered about the lives of these people, whose names all sounded so German. That wasn't surprising, he reminded himself, considering the town's strong German heritage. Then they entered a section where the stones were smaller and closer spaced. The dates were closely spaced, too, at least they were on the stones that weren't so weathered they were illegible. The aging graves of children.

Turning abruptly, Kelly headed toward the road,

not looking back to see if Ryan had even noticed her flight. But he had, and he followed close on her heels. She stopped at the end of the cemetery drive and stared out into the distance. Ryan didn't spare a glance for the scenic view of the town. He couldn't see past Kelly's haunted expression.

"All those children," she whispered. "I wonder if their parents ever learned to stop grieving."

Ryan dropped a comforting arm around her shoulders and steered her downhill, farther away from the cemetery. He didn't know what to say, if anything he could say would make a difference.

"It's faded," she continued. "But it still hurts. I think it always will."

Ryan stopped, his restraining arm pulling Kelly to a halt as well. "Will you let me help?" he asked.

The corners of her lips curved upwards. "You already have," she answered. "I can't think of anyone I'd rather be with right now."

He had to ask. "Not even Brian?"

Frowning, Kelly tilted her head to one side. "I think you've gotten the wrong idea about Brian and me."

"Have I?"

"Ryan, I'm glad Brian is married again. I'm glad he has a child. I didn't love him the way I should have. Maybe someday we'll be friends again, but even that's going to take some time."

"So why does he act like your big brother."

Kelly rolled her eyes. "Because that's the way he's always acted. He's my older brother's best friend. I've known Brian since I was in diapers."

"And that's all? He doesn't still care for you?"

"Of course, he cares about me. I care about him. But not like you're thinking."

"You had a child together."

"And lost that child. If we had truly loved one another the way a husband and wife should, we would have been able to help one another over it. We would have found a solution to our problems. Instead, we turned away from each other and found our own answers."

"That's not necessarily true. Statistically, a couple stands a sixty percent chance of splitting up after their child dies."

Kelly eyed him warily, then shrugged. "I suppose you wrote an article about that, too."

"No. I've been doing some reading on the subject lately."

"Why? So you can analyze me?" Kelly threw her arms up in the air. "Here. I'll make it simple. First, I no longer am in love with my ex-husband. Second, I'm doing just fine without your amateur psychiatry," she half shouted. Flinging her hands up again, she turned and stalked on down the hill, leaving Ryan to follow or not.

He stared at her back, wanting her to turn around and wait for him. But she just kept going.

"Wait," he shouted. Kelly's steps slowed, then faltered before finally halting altogether. Ryan jogged after her, then planted his feet toe to toe with hers.

"Why were you so upset when you saw Brian at the wedding reception?"

Kelly hesitated, then drew a deep breath. "I wasn't sure what Brian would do. He's been very protective of me for most of my life. After the divorce, he used to check out anyone I dated. That's why I finally left Harrington, that and the match-making efforts of the rest of my family.''

"So you were afraid I wouldn't pass muster."

"I was afraid he'd start something. He punched one man I dated in the nose," she explained. "And I was afraid of what you'd think. You did get the wrong impression, too.''

Ryan captured a wisp of blowing hair and stroked it back into place. "I thought you still loved him, but you were settling on me because he was out of reach. And because of the kids.''

Kelly eyed him, her face set in a wary expression. "Isn't that why we got married? So the kids could stay with you.''

"There's more to it than that," Ryan insisted. "Admit it to yourself if you can't say it out loud. Neither of us could have made that kind of commitment if we didn't care for one another.''

Kelly closed her eyes. "Of course, we do. We wouldn't have gotten this far if we hated one another.''

Ryan sighed, then dropped an arm around her shoulders. "Come on," he said. "Let's get something to eat.''

Kelly's relief was almost depressing, Ryan thought. But he knew better than to keep pushing. He had to give her time to get used to him, time to learn to love him.

As they made their way back toward the business district, Ryan shortened his steps to accomodate Kelly. She pointed out an antique shop she wanted to visit the next day and charmed an elderly man who was sweeping the sidewalk. With Ryan she was edgy and preoccupied.

Even after they were seated in the nondescript restaurant, the air between them remained tense. It wasn't until after they had sampled several wines and made their choice that they began to relax. Ryan wasn't sure whether it was the effect of the alcohol or the reprieve from returning to their room.

Halfway through the meal, Ryan's hand brushed Kelly's as they both reached for a roll. He was shocked at the bolt of pure electricity that shot through his body. He could tell from her stunned expression that she was just as affected. Her face flushed with fiery heat, she dropped her eyes to her plate and concentrated on cutting a piece of meat.

Ryan tried to turn his attention to his meal as well, but found he no longer had an appetite for food. Kelly, too, was just pushing the food in circles on her plate.

Reaching deliberately across the table, he took the fork from her hand and dropped it into her plate. "Let's go," he said. He dropped some bills on the table, grabbed their coats and led her outside.

They walked back to the inn in silence. When they reached their room, Kelly flopped backwards onto the bed and kicked her shoes off. "We must have walked miles," she said.

Ryan eased himself into a chair and muttered his agreement while he eyed her slim form and fought the betraying desire that swept through him.

Then she turned her head, her eyes dancing with some private joke. Ryan couldn't hear what she said for the blood pounding loudly in his ears. Slowly, without ever meaning to, he left the chair, never taking his eyes from hers. And the mischief faded into desire as she watched his approach.

Three steps and he was almost there. Sparks crackled between them as Kelly's pose stiffened from casual exhaustion to tense anticipation. Then a loud squawk from the floor broke the intimate silence, and she released a quick nervous laugh.

"Just like home," she said, flushing from embarrassment or the wine or the sudden heat of the room—Ryan couldn't tell which. He stood over her, carefully avoiding the squeaky spot on the floor. When his fingertips touched her jaw line, she trembled visibly and tilted her face into his caress.

When Kelly jerked, her eyes popping open, he realized that the pounding in his ears was really a tapping on the door. Kelly slipped past him, leaving him staring foolishly at his tingling fingertips. He turned when the door clicked closed.

Kelly leaned back against the darkened wood and squeezed her eyes closed, clutching an ice bucket against the soft cotton blouse. "What are we going to do with this?"

"What? The ice?"

"No, this." Eyes open again, she held up a frosted bottle. "Champagne. Local vintage, of course."

"Champagne," he repeated dumbly, watching the gentle heaving of her breasts against the ice bucket.

"A gift from our hostess," Kelly explained in a subdued tone. "For our wedding night. I guess she meant well."

Ryan shrugged and turned away. He had to before she noticed that his jeans were becoming painfully tight. "I guess we could drink it. Wouldn't want to offend our hosts?"

He flung himself face down across the bed and groaned.

"Are you okay?" she asked.

"Tired," he lied.

"Why don't you take the bathroom first?" Kelly leaned over and picked up her overnight bag, offering him a brief, tantalizing glimpse of creamy, rounded flesh.

"You go ahead," he insisted. "I can't move just now." He didn't dare. He looked pointedly away and tried to think of something else, something completely unsexy, like an elephant show. Only it didn't work, not knowing that in a few minutes, an hour at the most, he and Kelly would be together under the sheets in this bed. It was that or one of them slept on the hardwood floor, and it damn well wasn't going to be him. He'd just have to grit his teeth and get himself under control. He was an adult, not a horny teenager.

Correction. He was a horny adult who was in danger of blowing everything. He knew Kelly was as attracted to him as he was to her. He knew he could caress her and coax her into making love to him. They'd come dangerously close before. But sex wasn't enough, not anymore and not with Kelly. She had to learn to love him. He didn't want to pressure her into anything. A moment's pleasure wasn't worth the resentment she'd feel. It would destroy everything he was trying to build.

The very idea of waiting was torture. But Kelly was worth the wait. He just had to put her at ease, show her how much he cared, give her time to realize how good things could be between them. In the meantime, he mused as he eyed the champagne bucket, he might have to put that ice to better use.

"Damn them." Kelly's furious mutterings penetrated the closed bathroom door.

Ryan half-raised himself. "What's wrong?" he called, while he tugged at the tight denim.

A moment's silence answered him. "Nothing," she finally answered. Then the sound of the shower muffled any further mutterings.

Twenty minutes later she tentatively peeked around the door. "Ryan?" Her face was flushed with embarrassment. "Could I borrow your robe? Or a shirt?"

"Forget your nightgown?" he teased.

Her dark scowl told him he'd better not push the issue. "I didn't. But somebody tampered with my luggage. My nightshirt's gone."

Ryan was off the bed in a flash. Her warning glare stopped him halfway across the room, and he realized how his behavior must appear to her. "I didn't hide your nightshirt," he said in what he hoped was his most sincere tone.

Kelly rolled her eyes. "I never thought you did. You're not that devious. It was probably Sandy."

"Sandy? Your sister?" Or was she a cousin. Ryan hadn't been able to keep track of who belonged with whom, although he supposed he'd sort them all out eventually. "Why would she do that?"

"Because that's what I did to her when she got married." A ghost of a smile teased the corner of her lips, only to be replaced by an exasperated stare.

"Now, will you please give me something to put on."

Ryan crossed out of sight to the closet and pulled a soft cotton shirt from the hanger. "I don't know if there's anything here that'll fit. Wrap a towel around you and come check."

"No way." The door slammed shut.

"Why not?" He slipped the collar of the shirt over the doorknob.

"It wouldn't cover enough." Her voice cracked just enough to let him know that she was as flustered as he was.

He smiled, then backed away, this time aiming for the noisy floorboard next to the bed. When the squawk sounded, the door whipped open and a slender, pale hand snatched the shirt, then slammed the door shut again.

A few moments later, Kelly sidled into the main room, dropped the overnight bag on the closet floor, then sat down demurely in the striped chair by the window. Ryan took one look at the moist, translucent trails her hair left on the shirt and headed for the shower. Turning the cold water on full blast, he gritted his teeth and counted backwards from one hundred. Then he recited the Gettysburg address and the preamble to the U.S. Constitution.

Finally, he shut the water off and slipped into a pair of baggy boxer shorts, struggling to not laugh out loud at his reflection in the mirror. He felt pretty ridiculous. He started to take them back off, then growled and grabbed his robe.

The bedroom was dark, except for the faint glow from a wall sconce near the door. He flipped the switch off, then treaded gingerly across the room, wincing when he hit the faulty board again. He thought he heard a muffled giggle, and he glared at the huddled mound on the far side of the bed.

The antique bed creaked loudly when he eased his frame under the covers, robe and all. It creaked again when he rolled to find a more comfortable position. Then it started shaking. At first, Ryan wondered whether the New Madrid Fault had decided to give way. Then he realized from the snuffling squeaks that Kelly was trying unsuccessfully to control a bad case of the giggles.

In answer, he rolled a couple of more times, then repeated the motion that brought the loudest noise from the complaining bed frame. A full-fledged peal of laughter was his reward.

"There that ought to convince them," he whispered. "Wouldn't want them to think the champagne was wasted."

Kelly sighed. "It seems a shame to waste it."

"You're right," he said, bounding out of bed, and flinging off the robe, which had only tangled around his legs. He reached for the lamp switch, then remembered his boxer shorts. Instead, he fumbled in the dark, then grabbed the bottle from the corner table. With surprising dexterity, he pried loose the cork, then grabbed for the discarded robe to catch the overflowing bubbles.

Suddenly, the room flooded with light.

"I'll get the glasses from the bathroom," Kelly offered. Her mouth twitched for an instant, but she didn't say anything else. Ryan stared down at the baggy boxer shorts and cringed.

Back in an instant, she joined him on the cabbage rose coverlet and allowed him to fill a glass for her, then another for him. Taking a sip, she wrinkled her nose. Then she downed the entire glass and held it out for more.

"Are you sure?"

"Very," she replied. "Otherwise, I'll never sleep."

Ryan watched her over the edge of his glass. The damp tendrils of hair were drying, curling tantalizingly about her face. As the overlarge shirt slipped to the side, he caught a glimpse of ribbon and lace.

"Does champagne make you sleepy?" he asked.

"Eventually." She downed half a glass, unaware the shirt had slipped further.

Bewitched, he watched the almost imperceptible sliding of the shirt, responding to her attempts at light conversation with more wit than he would have thought possible under the circumstances. When he could stand it no longer, he handed her his glass, then reached out and undid the next button.

"What are you doing?" Her voice trembled.

"What's this?" His finger lifted a flimsy strap.

Her blush deepened. But she didn't push his hands away. "I think it's a gift from Sandy."

He drew a deep, quivering breath, then carefully rebuttoned the shirt. He took both glasses from her and set them on the floor under the edge of the bed. "I think we'd better stop before something happens that you're not ready for." He snapped off the light and settled back onto the pillow and tried to remember the Gettysburg address.

Kelly sat motionless for several minutes, staring at his still form. He didn't want her, not the way she wanted him. And for a moment there, she hadn't cared. Angry at herself for her weakness, she laid down, hugging the edge of the bed. She didn't know how long they laid that way, both stiff as boards. She only knew that she felt terrible.

Reaching out, Ryan dragged her over to him, pulling her tight against his chest. She curled against him spoon fashion and sighed, relaxing by degrees. Without intending to, he began stroking her thigh with feather touches. When she turned in his arms, his lips found hers unerringly in the dark. His hands, his lips, touched and caressed, teased and worshipped until she moaned deep in her throat and pulled his mouth back to her with desperate strength.

Their bodies pressed close, not allowing a single speck of air to separate them. He was trembling. They both were trembling so much that the bed started shaking. Then a blaring noise split the night and jarred them both upright. Outside, across the street, a freight train raced past the house, rattling the windows.

This time, she couldn't stifle the laughter. She leaned against him, shaking, her tears wetting his chest. "God, what a night," she said shakily between giggles. Her laughter inflamed him still more, and he no longer cared whether she had let go of the past. He could only think of now, and she was here in his arms, warm and loving and touching him with trails of fire.

While the train roared by, he cupped her face and kissed the moisture away. "Not yet," he promised. "But it can be if you want."

"I want," she whispered into his ear.

Ryan drew a shuddering breath, then touched his lips to hers. "You're sure?"

Her answering kiss thrust away his doubts and made him forget any plans he had for wooing her slowly. She was here now, in his arms and in his bed, for better or for worse. And he couldn't stop now if he tried.

Then he tugged the coverlet from beneath her and laid it on the floor, well away from the betraying floorboard.

"No sound effects," he explained, then grabbed her arm and pulled her down to the floor, onto his lap. And then there was no need for words, only feelings, rising soaring feelings as fingers teased flesh and lips met and parted and met again. And then there was nothing between them, no clothes, no past, no present, no air.

Their first fight didn't occur until three weeks later. Kelly was involved in a rousing game of ring-around-a-rosy when Ryan leaned through the doorway.

"You have a phone call," he said. "It's your thesis advisor."

"Tell him I'll call back," she replied as she picked herself up off the floor, then reached for Sarah. "I have to change a diaper."

She should have known that it was only a momentary trade-off. Ryan was waiting for her when she finally made it downstairs half an hour later.

"You're supposed to call your advisor back this afternoon. The phone number's in the computer."

"Why there?" she asked.

Ryan's smug grin warned her she wouldn't like

the answer. "Because he wants you to outline the changes you've made so far. I put the phone number on the first page so you would have your latest draft on hand when you call him."

He disappeared around the corner. An instant later, Kelly heard the front door open. She dashed into the living room and shouted onto the porch. "Where are you going? You know I can't work that damned thing!"

"You could if you'd try," he shouted. He bent and retrieved the newspaper and flung it at the front door. The neighbor's cat yowled and jumped into the bushes when the paper bounced off the step below.

Kelly grabbed the paper and retreated inside the house before Ryan could reach the sidewalk. She was seated on the couch leafing through the front section when he stepped inside and pushed the door closed.

"Don't do that," he barked, ignoring the door when it swung back open.

"Do what?" Without looking up, she folded a page lengthwise.

"Don't you dare tear it."

Kelly's fingers stopped. "I just wanted to keep this article."

"Just wait until I've had a chance to read the paper."

Kelly shrugged. He had a point. He didn't like to read a paper with holes in it. "I'm sorry. I'll wait until later. It's just that if I don't take care of it when I think of it, I'll probably forget to clip it."

"Like you forgot to work on your thesis. Kelly, you're not going to make your deadline."

"So I'll get an extension. I have more important things to do right now." She rose from the couch and headed for the doorway. "Speaking of which, I promised the kids I'd make brownies."

Ryan grabbed her arm. "Forget the brownies."

"But I promised—"

"I'll make the damn brownies, all right?"

Kelly's eyes widened. "You? You can't boil an egg without burning it."

"That's not the point," Ryan shouted.

"Then what is the point? I'm trying to do my job and help around here. I'm doing the best I can."

"That's just it. You're doing too much. You can't replace their mother. You shouldn't be trying."

Kelly gasped. That stung. She spun on her heel and wrested her arms from him, but he caught at her wrists before she could make her escape.

"That's not what I meant."

Kelly stared at the wall, willing herself not to cry. "You said it. You must have meant it."

"You're trying too hard," he said. "You're neglecting your own work."

Kelly's anger flared. "No way. I haven't missed a single appointment or even one group meeting." Ryan tried to interrupt, but she ignored him. "I even got my paperwork caught up and most of my files transferred to the woman who's taking over my clients while I'm in Harrington. And I—"

"Kelly!" Ryan's shout silenced her. She was gathering her breath to shout back when a movement near the door caught her eye.

"Ryan, there's someone—"

"Kelly, will you just shut up and answer one question? Please?'' His hands rested squarely on her shoulders now. ''How much have you worked on your thesis in the last three weeks?''

''We can talk about this later,'' Kelly hissed. The movement at the door had materialized into a middle-aged woman who was taking notes.

''No, now,'' he insisted.

''We have company.''

Ryan grinned. ''Nice try. But the kids are all upstairs playing.''

''At the door. She's watching us and writing in a notebook.''

Ryan's dark eyes widened. He turned his head and froze. The gray-haired woman nodded and tapped on the storm door. He released Kelly with a jerk and strode over, snapping the door open with a flick of his wrist.

''Yes?'' His voice was curt and unwelcoming with its undertone of residual anger.

''I'd like a few moments of your time, Mr. Matthews. This is the Matthews residence, isn't it?''

Kelly sagged against the nearest wall, overcome with dread. She knew now without an introduction who the woman was. During the next few moments, Kelly's worst fears were confirmed as the social worker entered and explained that she had been assigned to take over the investigation for the custody case. A quick glance told Kelly the page was already filled. How long had she been standing there listening to Kelly and Ryan fight?

Kelly pasted on what she hoped was a friendly, unconcerned smile and offered to take the woman upstairs to see the children. The social worker played games with them for twenty minutes before breaking away to scribble still more in the ever-present notebook. Playing was just a cover for grilling the kids on everything from what they ate to who wiped their noses.

Kelly suffered through another grueling twenty minutes while the woman ran through a list of questions that would have made a CIA interrogator proud. Then finally it was over, and the woman was buttoning her coat.

"Just one more question," she said. "How does your fighting affect the children?"

Kelly's breath caught in her throat. Her eyes met Ryan's but as always he gave nothing away.

"It's difficult to tell," Ryan said. "We've never fought in front of them."

The social worker's sharp eyes darted between the two of them. "Children aren't stupid," she asserted. "And believe me, they heard you. They couldn't help it. I heard you as soon as I got out of my car."

This is it, Kelly thought. We blew it. We asked for another shot, and the blasted woman had to show up in the middle of the first real quarrel we had. "It won't happen again," Kelly said in a small voice.

"What was the fight about, Mrs. Matthews?"

Kelly gave a mental start, still unused to being addressed that way. Then she wondered what had caused the fight? It started with the newspaper. No before that. But she knew it really wasn't about the newspaper or the thesis.

"I don't know, really," Kelly answered. She did, though, but she'd never admit it to this woman. It was enough that she admitted it to herself.

"It's personal," Ryan interjected and ushered the woman out.

The social worker snorted. "Disagreements usually are."

"Wait," Kelly called. "How long before the final custody order?"

"You'll have to ask the judge that," was the only answer.

Together, Kelly and Ryan watched the social worker tuck the pad of notes into the car then get inside. Kelly leaned against him for comfort. His arm stole around her waist and pulled her closer.

"We didn't do very well," Kelly muttered.

"It was bad timing, that's all. The trouble is we can't very well tell the judge that and ask for a third chance." Ryan pushed the heavy wooden door closed, latching it firmly this time. "Let's check on the kids."

Not even waiting for Kelly's nod, he headed for the stairs, taking them two at a time and disappearing from sight before Kelly was halfway up. By the time she reached the top, Ryan was back at the stairs.

"They're fine," he said. "But I need a drink."

"I'll second that," Kelly said, then turned on her heel and started back down. "Milk or tea?"

"Let's really let go and have an ice cream soda," Ryan suggested.

Kelly grimaced. "And I thought it was only women who drowned their sorrows in calories."

"All right. Tea. Meet me in the study."

Groaning, Kelly turned the corner and entered the room, as ordered. She plopped into the chair and turned on the computer. When Ryan placed the steaming mug on the desk, she was staring at the message of rejection on the screen.

"Your computer doesn't even like me," she grumbled.

Without a word, Ryan reached around her and punched several buttons. Like magic, her thesis appeared on the screen, complete with her advisor's phone number.

Then he dialed the phone and handed the receiver to Kelly. A minute later, she had the satisfaction of handing it back. "No answer."

"You're off the hook for the moment," he said. "Why don't you work on your revisions while you're waiting for him to get back?"

Kelly shook her head and flipped the machine off.

"I'm too depressed. I wouldn't be able to concentrate." She spun the desk chair around to face him.

"Maybe it wasn't that bad," he suggested. Her only answer was a lifted brow. "You're right. It was. We were yelling."

"Everybody yells," Kelly said. "My parents yelled at one another all the time. I'll bet that social worker yells at her husband."

"I'll bet she yells at her kids, if she has any," Ryan added. "But nobody's going to take her kids away because of it."

"Ryan, she's old enough to be a great-grandmother, well a grandmother at least."

"You're not making me feel any better. I blew it. I had one last shot and I screwed up. And I've screwed up your life in the process. I'm sorry."

Kelly was kneeling in front of him within a heartbeat. "No. These last few weeks have been great."

Ryan clasped her hands, then trailed his fingers up her arms to rest lightly on her shoulders. "If we don't get custody of the children, I won't hold you to the marriage."

A dark emptiness filled Kelly at the thought. "We'll get them," she insisted.

Ryan cupped her face, forcing her to look him square in the eyes. "No. We might not. And if we don't there's nothing to keep you here."

There's you, her heart screamed. But pride wouldn't let her speak. Besides, she knew that no matter how much she loved him, it wasn't fair to keep him if the children were gone. He should be free to find someone else, to build his own family.

Slowly she nodded, unaware of the tears trickling down her face until Ryan kissed them away. "There's still a chance," she whispered shakily.

"There's always a chance," Ryan answered. "Maybe the judge should send someone to Grandmother Webster's house. I haven't heard anything about investigating her."

Kelly's eyes narrowed. "You've got a point there. A good one."

"I'll call the attorney." Ryan was already dialing the phone.

TEN

Kelly laughed as Rachel and Eric bounded out of the car and raced up the sidewalk behind the blue-suited mail carrier. She clutched the grocery bag to her side and fumbled with a slipping bag of apples while Eric accepted a handful of envelopes and Rachel banged repeatedly at the doorbell with her thumb.

Just as Kelly reached the porch, the front door swung open. "Here, let me help you," Mrs. Yates offered, then hoisted an escaping Sarah back inside. Taking the bag of apples, she held the door until Kelly and the children were all inside.

Kelly deposited the groceries in the kitchen, then followed the trail of dropped fliers and envelopes down the hall to the study, picking them up as she went. She dodged out of the children's way as they raced back out. Just outside the door lay a thick, official looking envelope. When Kelly picked it up, she saw the attorney's return address. Her heart clamored loudly in her throat as she carried it inside and set it on the desk beside the rest of the mail.

Seeing it, Ryan glanced quickly to her and then away again.

"Is that the custody order?" she asked.

Ryan studied the envelope, then pulled open a drawer and slipped it inside. "It's my copy of the book contract. I asked him to look it over before I signed it."

"It might be the custody order."

"He said he'd call me as soon as it arrived."

Kelly nodded, then reached for the remaining envelopes, flipping through them and extracting two with her name. "How long did he think it would take the judge to issue the final order?" She handed him the fliers and the electric bill, which she had found in the hallway.

Ryan gave a low whistle when he opened the latter, then tucked it into the desk drawer as well. Kelly hoped he'd take care of it soon. She had found during the past few weeks that he had an irritating habit of forgetting about the daily details of living.

"He didn't say," Ryan responded finally to her question. "Maybe after the first of the year we'll hear something. The judge is probably busy with all those grandchildren. Playing Santa Claus and letting them call him Jelly Belly."

Kelly grinned. "That reminds me. Grandmother Webster will be by later this afternoon. She's bringing Emily with her for protection. If you like, I'll tell her that you have a deadline to meet, and you can't be disturbed."

Ryan leaned back in his chair and shook his head.

"I might as well get used to her. She's not going to go away. And you won't be here much after next week to run interference."

Kelly propped herself against the doorjamb and sighed. "I wish I hadn't agreed to take Debbie's place this semester." She brightened as a sudden thought struck her. "I could postpone it a week or two. Maybe even a month. Debbie's baby isn't due until February."

"No way." Ryan shook his head. "You said yourself that anyone as pregnant as Debbie had no business wading through the snow half a dozen times a day or lifting all those kids. They need you there."

"I know. It's just wishful thinking, I guess. I've gotten kind of spoiled here."

"Lazy," Ryan insisted. "You still haven't finished the thesis."

Kelly groaned. "You're worse than my mother."

"I'll print out the last draft later this afternoon. You can take it with you and spend your evenings polishing it."

"I'll be back on weekends. I could work on it then."

Ryan frowned. "Not enough time. I'm going to have to make a few trips this winter to do research for the next Dirk Rambler book. I'll try to squeeze them in on weekends when you can be here with the kids."

Kelly nodded slowly and forced a smile. "Of course. I won't see much of you that way, though."

Ryan turned away. "It can't be helped. With this custody battle hanging over my head, I don't dare go while you're in Harrington. I don't think the judge would look too favorably on that.''

Kelly noticed the odd note in his voice and a shudder of apprehension swept through her. "I'm sure you're right," she said in a forced voice.

Ryan nodded at the screen, presumably occupied with the text there. Kelly stared quizzically at the back of his head. He was behaving strangely. It wasn't like him to shut her out like this, to turn his attention off as if she were a piece of furniture. Unless he was already bored with her, with their life together. He must be or he wouldn't be planning these trips. She'd been afraid this would happen, only she hadn't expected it to happen so quickly.

Irritated, she reached for the top drawer, intending to take the electric bill out and pay it before it was buried and forgotten. As she touched the knob, Ryan's hand grabbed hers. "What are you looking for?" he demanded.

Kelly extracted her hand, her eyes widening. "The electric bill. I thought I'd pay it. They almost shut the water off last week because you forgot to pay the bill.''

Ryan's jaw hardened. "I thought we settled all that a long time ago. I pay the bills. You buy groceries.''

Tears stung Kelly's eyes, but she refused to let them spill onto her cheeks. She wouldn't stand there and cry like a silly, hurt bride. She turned away and stalked silently from the room.

Ryan was apologetic at lunch, and even friendly to Mrs. Webster and Emily that afternoon. Later when they had a moment alone, he pulled her into his arms and squeezed her tight against his chest.

"I'll miss you," he whispered in her ear.

"Me, too." She hugged him back and planted a kiss below his ear before Eric interrupted them.

"Yuck."

Kelly grinned at Ryan, then turned and chased the little boy up to his room, threatening him all the way with yucky girl monster kisses.

Later when she passed Ryan's office, he was staring at the lawyer's envelope. She paused to tell him she was leaving for an early evening appointment, then noticed the tense set of his shoulders. He tapped the opened envelope indecisively on the desk. Then he snarled an epithet and slammed it back into the desk drawer. Puzzled, Kelly tiptoed on past the door, then retrieved her purse and bag of goodies from the living room. She peeked into the kitchen to tell Mrs. Yates when she'd be back, then quietly let herself out.

By the time she returned, the children were asleep. After putting her purse and bag away, she joined Ryan in the kitchen for a sandwich and a glass of milk.

Kelly devoured half her sandwich before she realized Ryan wasn't eating. She took another bite, then set the sandwich back on her plate. He watched her, his glance never wavering until Kelly had more and more difficulty swallowing, chewing, even thinking.

He was doing it again. He could unnerve her without a word, and he knew it.

"Something wrong with your sandwich?" Her voice was husky, but somehow that didn't bother her

as much as it used to. Her body was already responding to the thought of what was to come. Still, she
forced herself to take another bite.

"I'm not as hungry as I thought I was," Ryan
said.

The man never even blinked. Didn't his eyeballs
ever feel dry or his eyelids so heavy they eased
closed like hers were doing now? Her eyes popped
back open and she glared at him, but he didn't take
her mock anger seriously.

Instead, he pushed her plate aside and took her
hand. Grinning, she followed him upstairs, thinking
that he was probably the best diet she'd run across
yet. At this rate, she wouldn't have to worry about
middle-aged spread. But tonight he seemed different,
more intense. When he closed the door behind them,
she knew it wasn't her imagination. He made love
to her, coaxing her to a peak more quickly than ever
before, yet not quickly enough to keep pace with her
aching needs. He made love with an intensity that
bordered on desperation. And when it was over, he
held her tightly in his arms as if he were afraid she
would escape from him.

A long shuddering sigh escaped him. Kelly turned
in his arms and kissed him slowly, lingeringly. I love
you, she thought, and captured the words before they
could escape from her lips. She couldn't risk it. Not
until she was sure he was ready to hear it. Until she
was sure he loved her in return. And that might never
happen.

But this, she thought, could be enough for her. If
only it were enough for him. But it wasn't. He was
already restless.

"I was thinking," Ryan murmured into her ear.

"Hmmm?"

"Maybe we could adopt a baby."

Kelly pulled back, but his arms held her tight. "What?"

"You're so good with the kids. I was thinking maybe we should start from the beginning once just to see what it's like. You'd have the baby you always wanted." He nuzzled her neck, then pulled back when he realized she had gone rigid in his arms.

"What's wrong?"

"I think I hear something, one of the kids." She pressed a palm against his chest and pulled away. Wrapping a sheet around herself, she left the room.

Ryan dragged himself upright. He dragged his fingers through his hair, then sank his head into his hands. He hadn't heard a thing except their own voices. She hadn't run to the children. She had run away from him, and he couldn't figure out why. During the last few weeks, everything had been great, so much better than he had ever imagined.

The children had accepted her from the beginning, even Rachel. Except for the occasional play for attention, they had behaved better than before the marriage. And the nights? The nights in this bed had been beyond anything he'd believed possible. It was beyond sex, beyond anything in his experience. It was Kelly.

He wanted more than anything to make her happy, to erase the wistful yearning he sometimes saw in her expression before she turned away and hid her feelings. He saw it sometimes when they were alone, but mostly when she was with the children, watching them play. He thought he'd found the answer—a child of her own.

His attorney already knew of such a child—or at least knew the parents of the young woman who would give birth in a few months. A private adoption might be the best option for them all. The idea frightened him—frankly scared him half to death. But it made sense. Kelly was warm and motherly, with so much love to give. Her chosen profession was helping young children. It was only natural that she'd yearn for one of her own. So why had she run away when he suggested it?

No matter how he looked at it, he couldn't find the answer. He would have asked her, but she didn't return. When he finally went looking for her, he found her asleep in the nursery rocker. Sarah was snuggled against her, clutching at the sheet that covered Kelly's body.

So she had heard something after all. But before the wave of relief could take hold, Ryan noticed the dark stains down her cheek. Mascara. Tear stains. When he brushed at them, she nuzzled his hand and her eyelids fluttered open.

He gently lifted Sarah from her lap and tucked the child back into her crib. Then he led Kelly back to their bed and held her close, the wound sheet between them. Long after her body relaxed and her breath touched his chest, soft and even in sleep, he lay awake wondering. Finally he fell asleep, only to dream of Kelly dancing just beyond his reach, coming closer then darting away, then turning to stare at him with that wistful yearning he didn't know how to answer.

Kelly awoke that morning to a silent house. Glancing at the clock, she knew that silence at that hour was unnatural. She and Ryan had overslept. She untangled herself from Ryan's arms and the twisted sheet, then hunted for a robe. Locating it, she slipped it on and headed out into the hallway. Following the sounds of scuttling and the occasional spoken word, she located Eric and Rachel in Ryan's study.

Both jerked to attention when they spotted her in the doorway. Kelly meted out punishments for disturbing their uncle's papers, quieted the ensuing tantrums, located Sarah and fed them breakfast. Then she headed back to the study to repair as much of the damage as she could.

A crumpled page caught her eye. *Chapter 17: The Child*, the heading read. She skimmed down the lines until she realized that the story was far different from the one she'd first heard Ryan reading to the children that first afternoon. The characters were different, more normal, more real. Even Bambi seemed to have developed some intelligence. She'd also developed something else. Kelly read on.

As the sun's angle rose, Bambi stirred, awakened by the bright light in her face. Dirk watched her struggle to rise, burdened by the awkward weight of the growing child inside her. He held out his hand and helped her to her feet, kissing her full on the lips before releasing her.

"Have you checked the charts yet or shall I?" she asked. Her eyes were anxious, shadowed from the strain of the past few months.

"You can read them better than I. I'll let you plot our course. I'll catch our dinner."

Bambi wrinkled her nose and touched her mounded abdomen. "I'll take a ribeye, medium rare. And a glass of milk for junior."

Dirk stared off into the horizon. "How many more days before we reach the caves?"

"Two, maybe three."

"Six days with nothing but fish and bottled water." He shook his head. "The baby—"

Bambi's fingers on his lips stopped him. "If it weren't for you, neither the baby nor I would be here. Six days without vegetables is the least of our troubles. When we get to the caves we'll do better. Did you get a message to—

Kelly stared at the bottom of the crumpled page and wondered where it belonged. The wastebasket was her first guess. But maybe not. The kids might have done the crumpling. And she had to admit that Bambi wasn't such a bimbo anymore. Ryan had given her depth, grace under pressure. Kelly set the page on the desk and started on the rest of the mess.

She sorted the papers into stacks, put pens and paper clips back in the drawer and retrieved the stapler from the wastebasket. Then she got down on her hands and knees to look under the desk for anything she might have missed. She stretched and grasped a stapled bunch of papers, then sat upright.

Scanning the top few lines to determine which stack they belonged in, she gasped. Then she turned cold all over and started to tremble.

The top sheet was a letter from the attorney. But it wasn't about the custody suit like she expected. It was about adoption—about a specific mother in search of a family for her child. The following pages were a draft of an adoption agreement, followed by several photocopied sheets from legal journals.

She stared at them in perplexed curiosity, then began reading, turning the pages slowly, one by one.

She glanced up when she heard a noise in the hallway. She went from cold to hot in a single instant as Ryan's figure blocked the doorway.

"What are you doing?" Ryan asked as he knotted the tie of the blue bathrobe.

Feeling suddenly as if she was invading his privacy, Kelly almost dropped the papers to the floor. But she steeled her nerveless fingers. She hadn't been snooping. For that matter, he'd given her free run of his study the day he'd introduced her to his word processor. So why did she feel like the cat with the canary in its mouth?

"I'm picking up," Kelly said, irritated at herself for feeling defensive. There was no reason why she should be. She wasn't the one who was hiding something. "Actually, I was reading something I found under your desk. What is this?"

Nonplussed, Ryan looked around the room. "What happened here?"

"The little cyclones came through." Her eyes narrowed and she turned, hands on her hips, still clutching the sheaf of papers. "And you're changing the subject. In fact, you've been acting strangely for several days now, particularly since the envelope arrived from the lawyer yesterday."

Ryan eyed the papers in Kelly's hand with an expression of obvious regret. He probably wished he'd hidden them better, someplace the kids couldn't reach, Kelly thought bitterly.

The peal of the doorbell split the charged silence between them.

"Ignore it," Ryan ordered.

"I can't. Mrs. Yates isn't here yet." Kelly slapped the papers down onto the desk top, oblivious to the neat piles she scattered in the process. "It's probably Grandmother Webster, and you know how she is when you keep her waiting."

"She's not coming until Tuesday."

Kelly shook her head and pushed her way past him. "It is Tuesday," she muttered.

She caught a glimpse of herself in the mirror of the hall tree and halted. She stared at the deathly pale reflection of herself with shock-widened eyes. Remembering who was probably at the door, she rubbed some color into her cheeks. Then she squared her shoulders and marshalled her courage for the subtle battle of wills that was a side effect of Grandmother Webster's presence.

As she let the older woman in, Kelly noticed the deepening lines around her mouth. Mrs. Webster's penetrating eyes didn't miss a thing about Kelly's appearance either, but for once she didn't comment. She didn't have to. Her lingering gaze registered Kelly's edginess.

"Are the children ready?"

Kelly nodded. "They're playing upstairs. I'll get them."

"Why don't you let that Yates woman get them? I need to talk to you for a moment."

"She's not here yet."

Mrs. Webster's lines deepened. "Not here? I

thought she was coming along to help with the children.''

"Her niece had twins last night," Kelly explained. "She was at the hospital until late and then again this morning. I'll see if her car is back."

She looked up as Ryan entered the room, half expecting him to still be wearing the blue robe. He had changed into a burgundy sweater and a pair of jeans, and his shadowed eyes might have belonged to the devil himself.

"She's on her way across the yard," Ryan said, avoiding Kelly's gaze.

Mrs. Webster looked relieved. "Good. The children will feel more secure with her around."

"I'm sure you'll feel more secure knowing someone else will change the diapers," Ryan interjected in a wry tone. When Kelly laid a restraining hand on his arm, his only reaction was a lifted brow.

Mrs. Webster stiffened, holding herself in firm check. "Before you bring the children in, I must tell you that I've made a very difficult decision," she began. "A few minutes ago, I instructed my attorney to drop the custody suit."

Kelly's jaw dropped. She quickly clamped it and glanced up at Ryan. His surprise was tinged with a certain wariness.

"Why?" he asked.

Mrs. Webster shrugged. "I don't have the energy that I had when John was a child. I believe now they would be better off with someone younger to attend to their daily needs. I insist, however, on frequent visits and a voice in their upbringing. Whether you like it or not, those three children will be quite well-to-do, perhaps even wealthy someday if the company continues to do as well as it has. That wealth brings responsibilities they must be prepared for."

Ryan nodded then spoke slowly in an emotion strained voice. "I have to admit that I'm surprised. I never thought you'd give up on them."

"I'm not," she snapped back. "I'm only doing what I think is best for them. That has been my intention from the beginning."

"I know that," Ryan said. "But I don't understand what made you change your mind about me."

Mrs. Webster hesitated uncomfortably. "I didn't. But Kelly is a very responsible and capable young woman. I'm sure she'll be able to balance your rather lax approach to childrearing. I've seen a great change in this household since your marriage."

Before Ryan could speak again, Kelly squeezed his arm forcefully. "Why don't I get the kids now?"

"I will." Ryan said. "Why don't you get the car seats, Kelly?"

"Car seats?" Mrs. Webster questioned. "That won't be necessary."

"It's the law," Ryan insisted, his stance challenging. "They go in car seats or they don't go at all."

"I already have child safety seats in the car. I bought them yesterday, and they installed them at the store."

Kelly blinked. "Installed?"

"Of course. I've been a Webster long enough to know when to do something myself and when to consult an expert."

"If you like, I could show you how to take them in and out of the car," Kelly offered. "You might not want to leave the seats in there when you don't need them. They tend to get in the way.''

"They showed me at the store. But it really doesn't matter. I can always take the other car on bridge days. That's really the only time I have many passengers.''

Hearing Mrs. Yates at the back door, Ryan excused himself. A moment later, Kelly heard the two of them on the stairs. A glance at Mrs. Webster told her that the older woman was as uncomfortable as Kelly. "How is your job?" Mrs. Webster finally asked.

"It's fine,'' Kelly answered, equally polite.

"I assume you'll be leaving for that charming little town soon?''

"Harrington?'' Kelly had heard Harrington called many things, but charming wasn't one of them. Its bumpy streets and cracked sidewalks were home. But charming?

"When I was there for your wedding, I noticed it seemed to be a nice little town. You'll be doing the same work as you do here?''

"Yes. The staff educator will be on maternity leave.''

Mrs. Webster nodded. "This is a temporary post, isn't it?''

"Of course. Debbie plans to come back to work next fall.''

Some of the tension in Mrs. Webster's demeanor relaxed. "Good. I was afraid you might be considering moving back there permanently.''

Puzzled, Kelly watched the older woman twist the etched gold bracelet at her wrist. Kelly opened her mouth to ask why it mattered to the woman, then realized she was afraid they'd move the children away from her. But before she could reassure her, Eric burst through the door.

"I don't want to go," he shouted. "I don't like you. I want you to go away."

"Eric!" Kelly grabbed the child before he could execute the kick on his grandmother's shin.

Ryan's booming shout drowned anything further she said as he entered the room. He hoisted the child by the back of his pants and plopped him onto the sofa. The two girls stood wide-eyed in the doorway with Mrs. Yates.

Mrs. Webster shrank into herself, her pain at the child's rejection obvious. And Kelly felt sorry for her, whatever her faults. But she had to give the woman credit for poise. Within seconds, Mrs. Webster had schooled her face to hide that pain. She stepped to Ryan's side and bent at the waist.

"You are a rude little boy," she told Eric. "And if you continue to be such a nasty child, I'll leave you here."

Eric's lower lip protruded. "I don't want to go."

"Fine, then." Mrs. Webster stood up and rebuttoned her coat. "I'll give your piece of cake to the gardener."

Kelly held her breath, waiting for Ryan to say something. When he only grinned, she was surprised. But come to think of it, Mrs. Webster was handling Eric pretty well.

"Why don't you want to go to your grandmother's house?" Kelly asked.

"She's mean."

"She spanked him last time," Mrs. Yates explained. "He was sliding on the third floor banister."

Ryan blanched. "Why didn't anyone tell me? He could have killed himself."

Mrs. Webster nodded. "I haven't been that frightened since I spanked my own children for that."

"He'd already been punished," Mrs. Yates explained. "Besides, you have enough to worry about. I didn't think there was any reason to cause more trouble. I doubt he'll try it again."

"You, little boy," Ryan's index finger touched the middle of the child's chest with each word. "You had better behave. Mind your grandmother."

Subdued, but still angry, Eric allowed Kelly to help him with his coat, then strode silently out to the car. The new safety seats made him forget he was in trouble. After several minutes of adjusting straps and the inevitable fight over who sat where, the car backed out of the driveway.

"I wonder what he'll do this time," Ryan mused as he followed Kelly up the porch steps.

"I'm more worried about what'll happen when Mrs. Yates stops biting her tongue and being polite."

Ryan snorted. "I think Mrs. Webster can hold her own."

"Maybe. I'm not so sure. She's not as tough as she pretends to be."

Ryan fiddled with the magazines of the coffee table, hiding his expression. "None of us are. Some of us just conceal our emotions better."

Kelly sank into the sofa cushions and propped her feet on the edge of the table, ignoring Ryan's pointed look. "You're probably right. You should have seen her face. One minute she looked so hurt. And the next she'd covered it up and you'd think she didn't care at all that her grandson rejected her.''

Sitting down next to Kelly, Ryan slipped off his shoes and propped his feet alongside hers. Her limbs tightened with his nearness, and she struggled to hide how it was affecting her. She feared she was too transparent, though, to hide her emotions.

"Why were you—" She jumped when he rested a stroking hand on her thigh. "Why were you so nice to her today, even before she made her announcement? Usually you're at one another's throats.''

Ryan shrugged. "She didn't annoy me like she usually does. It seemed like she was actually trying to get along from the moment she walked in the door.''

"Maybe she knows something we don't. Maybe the judge has decided in our favor.''

Ryan's brows knit in perplexity for a moment, then straightened. "That makes sense. She'd rather do us the favor of dropping the suit than risk losing it.''

"She asked me whether I was moving to Harrington permanently. Why would she think that when you and the kids are here?''

Ryan crossed his legs at the ankles and leaned back into the cushions. His expression was nonchalant, but the gleam of mischief showed in his eyes no matter how he tried to disguise it.

"I can't imagine," he said. "Maybe she's afraid we'll all move there. After all, I can write anywhere.''

Something about his answer didn't quite ring true,

but Kelly wasn't sure what. She was less concerned about that than the fact that his hand was creeping higher up her thigh.

"Forget it," she ordered as she lifted the hand and dropped it into his lap.

She scooted down to the end of the couch, but he only followed her, trapping her between the arm and the warmth of his body. "You're not walking away this time," he said. "We need to talk things out."

Kelly stared at her hands. "I'm not sure I want to."

"I asked the lawyer to check into private adoption," Ryan finally said.

"When? Last year? The woman in that letter is six months pregnant. Now I know why it didn't bother you that I can't have children. You already had one on the way. One that'll be all yours. One you don't have to share with anyone." Her voice cracked with pain, and she turned her face away from him. "What kind of game are you playing with me? If she's expecting your child, why didn't you marry her instead?"

"She's not the woman I'm in love with," he said. "I didn't even know she existed until last week," Ryan said.

"Last week?" Kelly sniffed, and wiped at the lone tear streaming down her cheek.

"No. I wasn't even in the country when this child was conceived."

"So why is your attorney talking to her now? And why the adoption papers?"

"Isn't it obvious?" He pulled her stiff frame into his arms. "You wanted a child badly enough to marry me and take care of my three. If I lose custody, then you'll be cheated again.''

''I thought we settled that.''

''I thought I could do this for you, so that no matter what happened, you'd come out of this marriage with something, someone you value.''

Kelly's jaw dropped. She didn't know what to say even if she could have spoken.

''I didn't want to say anything,'' Ryan continued, ''until I knew more about the situation and about the adoption procedure itself.''

''So what were you going to do? Wait until everything was decided, until the baby was born, then hand it to me and say take care of this one, too. And who takes the baby when you so admirably release me from our agreement?''

''You do.''

''What?'' Her world spun as the whole scenario she had built up in her mind exploded. ''Why? How could you give up a child?''

Ryan groaned. ''I have no intention of giving up anyone. I've become very greedy over the past few months.''

''Then what are you talking about?''

Ryan pulled her across his lap, ignoring her weak protests. And they were weak. She couldn't really resist him, and he knew it. She knew she should just now, but it really wasn't possible. ''I'm talking about happiness,'' he almost whispered. ''About a family. One way or another, we'll have a family.''

She touched his cheek, and this time he leaned into the caress. ''Ryan, you don't have to find a baby to keep me happy.''

"If I thought it would keep you here with me, I'd find a hundred babies," he said. "When I heard about this woman, it seemed like the answer."

"I don't understand."

"She's really a remarkable young woman, from what I've heard," he said. Kelly bit down the surge of jealousy that flooded her and forced herself to listen. "An honor student. But she's still in school. She's considering putting the child up for adoption."

Kelly was ashamed. The "other woman" was no more than a teenager who found herself in a difficult situation. "And to think that I thought she and you—"

Ryan's kiss stopped her. Her lips responded of their own accord without any conscious thought on her part. All too quickly, though, he pulled away.

"I love you," he whispered. Then she stopped thinking altogether as his lips descended again.

It wasn't until eons later that she realized that Ryan still didn't know how much she loved him. Or maybe he did. She glanced around their bedroom, at the tangled bedcovers and widely strewn clothing.

"What are you thinking?" Ryan whispered in her ear, then ran a hand up her leg and tickled a very private part of her anatomy.

"I was thinking that Grandmother Webster would be shocked at how we're spending our free time."

"I doubt it. She was in love once."

Kelly stared into those warm, brown eyes in the dimness of the curtained room. "I do love you," she said. "I have for a long time now."

Ryan kissed her nose, then her swollen lips again,

long and lingeringly. "I'd give you anything," he whispered.

"I have everything I need here with you. Even if we don't get custody of the kids, I wouldn't want to leave."

"Good," he half growled, then rolled her over and trapped her beneath him. "Because I'd never let you go, not without a fight."

"There's nothing to fight," she insisted. "I knew I loved you when I married you. I couldn't have done it otherwise." She nuzzled his neck and felt the goose bumps that rose on his arms at the gesture. "I love you. I want you. And I don't need a baby to make me stay. All I need is you."

She laughed with delight at the fiery light in his eyes, then tweaked a firm buttock. But she sobered as his mouth descended slowly, deliberately teasing her to awareness.

"Maybe we should take your mother up on her offer," he whispered, his breath fanning the sensitive curve of her neck.

"What do you mean?"

"She called a couple of days ago about a house down the street. It's for rent."

"And?"

"And I told her I had to talk to you. I also figured I'd have to get permission from the court to move the children, even temporarily. I don't think that'll be necessary now."

Kelly ran her fingers lightly along his jaw line. With a quick turn of his head, Ryan captured her fingers between his teeth and nibbled gently before Kelly snatched her hand away.

"Don't," she said. "Not until I know what you and my mother are up to."

"Nothing much. I just asked her to keep an eye out for a place for us to live while you're working in Harrington. The occasional weekend together isn't enough for the kids," he explained. "And it definitely isn't enough for me."

"What about your research trips?"

"What about them? I can go during the week. Or we could talk one of your many relatives into baby-sitting and you could go with me," he said, as he dragged her across the mattress and held her tightly against him. She closed her eyes, enjoying the sensations until his head jerked up again at the sound of the jangling telephone on the bedside table.

"Ignore it," he said.

"The kids?"

"You're right." He rolled away and plucked up the receiver in a single fluid motion. His body snapped into alertness immediately.

Murmuring monosyllables between long jags of silence, he sat stiffly on the edge of the bed. Finally, he dropped the receiver back onto its cradle.

"That was the lawyer," he explained. "He just heard from Mrs. Webster's attorney. He confirmed what we already knew, that she's dropping the custody suit. But, there's bad news, too."

Kelly stilled. "What?"

"The unwed mother I told you about? Someone from the family has come forward and offered to take the child."

Kelly smiled. "That's not bad news."

"Well, not for her. But it means we'll probably have to wait a long time for a baby."

"It doesn't matter," Kelly insisted. "I have you. And we have Eric and Rachel and Sarah. That's enough for now."

Ryan nodded and pulled her back into his arms. "For now," he agreed.

JOANNE DOBSON

THE MALTESE
MANUSCRIPT

THE MALTESE MANUSCRIPT

JOANNE DOBSON

ibooks
new york
www.ibooks.net

DISTRIBUTED BY SIMON & SCHUSTER, INC.

To Nicholas Kohomban

Acknowledgments

Many thanks to:

John Hench, Priscilla Juvelis, and Anne Poe Lehr, for their expertise on rare books and libraries.

Diana Healy and Marie-Laure Degener, for the encouragement and the writing critiques.

Sandra Zagarell and Eve Sandberg, for the readings.

Nicholas Basbanes, for the vivid portraits in *A Gentle Madness: Bibliophiles, Bibliomanes, and the Eternal Passion for Books*.

Louis Cristantiello, for the loan of *The Maltese Falcon*.

Deborah Schneider, for her constant advocacy.

Barbara Peters and Rob Rosenwald, for their vision and daring.

Phyllis Spiegel, for being there.

Dave Dobson, for everything.

The detective novel does constitute escape…
not from life, but from literature.
—Marjorie Hope Nicholson
   "The Professor and the Detective" (1929)

Chapter One

The door to my office opened, and a dame walked in, bringing Trouble with her. The dame was Sunnye Hardcastle, celebrated crime novelist, and Trouble was her dog, a big Rottweiler with teeth like boning knives. I recognized them both from the author photo on the back cover of *Tough Times*, the latest novel in Hardcastle's edgy Kit Danger series. I'd purchased the book a week earlier at Smith's Bookshop, but hadn't had time to do more than look over the jacket.

My class notes went flying as I jumped up from the green vinyl chair. "Sunnye Hardcastle?" Ms. Hardcastle was tall with red hair in a modified poodle cut, tight curls trimmed close to the head. She was in her fifties and fit, with a runner's sinewy slenderness. She wore leggings and a black leather jacket cut close to the body, and Trouble dogged her heels, kept up short on a wide leather strap.

"Yes. And you're Professor Karen Pelletier." The writer's eyes were dark and opaque, her eyeliner a gunmetal grey. "Or so the secretary said." Monica Cassale, the Enfield College English Department secretary, hovered in the hallway, mouth agape. She was a big Hardcastle fan.

"Right. I mean, yes, I am." I pushed the door. It didn't quite shut. "Won't you sit down, Ms. Hardcastle?" I gestured toward the chair I had just vacated, and when she glanced at it and hesitated, I snatched up the scrawled-over class notes and deposited them in a clump on my desk. Sunnye Hardcastle graced the green chair with a visceral glamour the likes of which this office had never before seen. Her large leather shoulder bag rested next to the chair, within easy reach; rumor had it Hardcastle didn't go anywhere without carrying a weapon. Trouble lay at her feet. His muzzle rested on one heavy-soled leather boot. His vigilant brown eyes assessed me.

Good dog, I thought. *Stay.*

"I hope you don't mind me dropping in like this, without notice." The writer fixed me with her dark unsmiling gaze. It didn't much matter whether I minded or not; she was there. She let go of the Rottweiler's leash, laying it loosely across her lap. Trouble glared at me. A rumble emanated from a region deep in his throat. Vladimir Litvintsev, my linguistics colleague down the hall, would have called that sound a glottal rumble. The dog's owner didn't seem to hear it.

"Not at all." I ventured a sidelong glance at Trouble. *Stay!* "Sorry if I seemed rude, Ms. Hardcastle, but you're the last person I would have expected to see here." I made an all-encompassing sweep with my hand, signifying the plush encapsulated milieu of privilege that is Enfield College. She took my gesture as an invitation to scrutinize the room.

My office was spacious and professorial in the conventional manner, book-laden and a bit shabby. Floor-to-ceiling bookcases on two walls. A recessed seat beneath leaded casement windows. A large oak desk with an antique wooden swivel chair I avoided whenever possible. A matching conference table. Polished wood floors half-covered by a green needlepoint rug. All these glories had been bequeathed me by previous occupants going back to the 1830s when Dickinson Hall was erected. Nothing individual. Nothing mine—except for the life-sized black-and-white Humphrey Bogart poster plastered to the back of the door. Nonetheless, I inhabited the room comfortably. It was a Professor's office. I was a Professor. I was anything but complacent about that fact.

"I was in the area," Sunnye Hardcastle said, her gaze migrating back in my direction. "Book tour. I stopped by on an impulse because I wanted to talk to you." She glanced down at her fingernails. They were short and rounded, painted the bright red of heart's blood.

"To me?" What could this world-renowned crime novelist want with an English professor? From across the hallway I heard the English Department office door slam shut, then click as the key turned in the lock. Footsteps vanished down the hallway. I checked my watch. 2:07. Why was Monica leaving so early when her idol was within arm's reach?

The writer gave a short laugh. It was not what I would describe as a particularly joyous sound. "On my way to Boston I was looking over the preliminary program for a crime fiction conference I've been invited to appear at here in…when *is* it? March?"

"Oh," I said. "The Women's Studies conference."

"That's right—Women's Studies." The words did not roll off her tongue with the familiarity of use.

"Are you planning to attend?" Sunnye Hardcastle's participation would be a coup for the conference organizers.

"I'm thinking about it." As if it were of no import, she flicked away her possible appearance with the tips of her bright red nails. "But when I saw the topic of *your* talk, I told the driver to take a detour to Enfield."

The bell rang to announce the changing of classes. Ms. Hardcastle broke off and looked out the window.

It was mid-January, the first day of the spring semester. Students hurried by in noisy clumps on their way to classes: American Ethnic Literatures, Principles of a Pluralistic Polity, Great Books by Women. The weather was grey and mushy, and a girl in a red plaid jacket picked her way carefully around a big puddle just outside my window. L. L. Bean boots are expensive. No sense in getting them wet.

Then Peggy Briggs trudged by, plowing right through the center of the puddle in her K-Mart duck boots, weighed down by a canvas backpack that looked like Viet-Nam-era Army surplus. Peggy was a "mature student," the administration's designation for anyone over twenty-four. She was a stocky woman of about thirty, a single mother on welfare plucked from the graduation rolls of Greenfield Community College as part of Enfield's half-hearted efforts to diversify its student population. Among the sleek children of privilege, she stood out like an inflamed thumb.

"Obviously you're not teaching right now," Sunnye Hardcastle said. I had her attention again, and her confident tone set my teeth on edge. *You're not teaching right now.* As if I were simply sitting around on my duff waiting for celebrity writers to drop by.

"My American Popular Fiction seminar meets in an hour, Ms. Hardcastle. I'm free until then." To tell the truth, I wouldn't have minded something to distract me. It was an honors seminar, and I had a bad case of the first-day jitters.

"Popular fiction? You mean like crime fiction?"

I nodded.

"You're kidding. I didn't know they actually taught that stuff in colleges." Trouble nudged her leg. She scratched the big dog behind his ears. Her grey eyes assumed a distant expression, as if she were contemplating anything but the vagaries of college curriculum. Then, outside the window, a student yelled, "Hey, George, whatup?" and Sunnye Hardcastle snapped back to the moment.

"Professor Pelletier, I'll be brief." Her tone became brusque. "I'm just beginning a new book—a complete departure from the Kit Danger stories—"

A Hardcastle novel without Kit Danger? I couldn't imagine it.

"—and I could use some expert advice."

Expert advice? From me? The world of the Kit Danger novels was, as you might expect, a perilous place. Dysfunctional families destroyed their children. Corrupt civil servants bled communities dry. Corporations conducted massive cover-ups of deadly products. Brutal gang members terrorized neighborhoods. The wealthy preyed upon each other, and upon the poor. And Kit Danger, private eye, took under her wing the most vulnerable of the weak and needy, restoring a momentary justice at the end of each venture, most often in spite of the wiles of treacherous, alluring men. I certainly had no expert advice to offer her creator.

Unless, of course, she wanted to discuss the wiles of treacherous, alluring men.

"This is going to be an historical novel," the writer continued, "set in the New York City slums during the nineteenth century, and, to tell the truth, I'm feeling a bit overwhelmed by the research I'll have to do. The book needs to be as authentic as possible, but I'm no historian." Her dark eyes narrowed as she focused on me. "When I saw in the conference program that you were going to speak on the American working class, I thought maybe you could help me with some historical sources."

I was scheduled to give a talk on murder in American working-class literature. It had been listed in the program as Deconstructing Death: Class Binaries in the Representation of Murder in American Working-Class Discourse, 1845-1945. In spite of the quasi-lurid title, this was a fairly dry academic topic, and I was up to my ears in historical sources.

"Well, certainly," I said. "That would be no problem...."

Fifty minutes later, Sunnye and I were seated at the conference table, poring over bibliography printouts and old books. Someone knocked at the door, then, without waiting for a response, pushed it open. Monica entered, out of breath. A clump of short brown hair stood straight up where she had snatched off her baseball cap. "Mail delivery," she announced. *Mail delivery?* Our mail is never delivered any further than the pigeon-hole boxes two steps away from the secretary's desk.

Monica thrust a handful of envelopes in my general direction, but her eyes were glued to Sunnye Hardcastle, and she took an impulsive step toward her. Trouble growled. His mistress silenced him.

"Ms. Hardcastle," the secretary said, braving Trouble's tooth-baring snarl as she traversed the room, "I just wanted to make sure you didn't leave without signing my copy of *Tough Times.*" Her hand rose to her heaving chest. "I ran all the way home to get it. You're my favorite writer ever."

Sunnye smiled at her. I was surprised she possessed the appropriate facial muscles. "How nice of you to say so. I'd be happy to sign your book." She opened *Tough Times* to the title page, scrawled an inscription, and signed with a flourish.

"Thankyouthankyouthankyou," Monica gushed, hugging the book to her chest. "I'll treasure this forever." Then she turned to me, her eyebrows puckering. "Karen? Don't you have a class now?"

"Aaargh!" My watch informed me I had four and a half minutes to get across campus.

Sunnye stood up. "Professor Pelletier—Karen—I didn't mean to make you late." Then, very formally, she said. "I appreciate your help. If there's ever anything I can do…"

I was thrusting notes and books helter-skelter into my briefcase, but I paused. The class would wait for me. Ten minutes for an assistant professor. Twenty for an associate professor. A half-hour for a full professor. That was the common etiquette in any college I'd ever had anything to do with. I had no idea where these laws had come from in the first place, but they seemed to hold true at all times in all places.

I hefted the briefcase and gazed at Sunnye consideringly. My seminar was in popular fiction. She was a pop-fiction ground-breaker, the first of the hard-boiled female detective writers, the creator of that feminist icon, Kit Danger, the bad-ass sleuth from Detroit. The woman intimidated the hell out of me, but she had offered. "Well, maybe there *is* something…"

Sunnye Hardcastle was a smash hit with my seminar, twelve honors students seated around a battered mahogany conference table. The Emerson Hall seminar room was long and narrow, painted pale cream above blue-green wainscoting. The novelist sat at the head of the table and answered questions about writing and the writer's life for over an hour. Trouble brooded at her feet. She was gracious and charming, and, perversely, I was miffed by her congeniality. Why was she so damn pleasant with everyone else and so curt with me?

To cap off her appearance, the novelist read to the class from *Tough Times*.

> *Dead men don't tell tales, Kit Danger mused, as she peered from the catwalk high above the vast emptiness of the abandoned automotive plant. The two men sprawled on the fractured concrete floor were indisputably dead. She'd read that somewhere, that line about not telling tales; that was all just words, black ink etched on a white page. But the bodies were real. From where she balanced precariously on the catwalk, they looked like squashed white spiders oozing ragged trails of blood across a floor the color of lead shavings. These men were snitches. They were here to talk. They had arranged to meet her amidst the industrial detritus with the sole purpose of talking. Now they themselves were industrial detritus. The long impersonal forefinger of cold, hard power had reached out and pressed the discard button. There would be no more tales.*

> *At a soft sound from behind her, Kit spun
> around, the big Sig Sauer 226 ready in her hand....*

When Sunnye finished reading, my students heaved a collective sigh. The edgy glamour of Kit Danger—and her creator—had gotten to them. At that moment I would have bet fully one half had decided to become crime writers themselves, and the other half, private eyes. The impetuous career-plan switches would last all of twelve-and-a-half minutes; with more than thirty thousand dollars a year shelled out for their education, Enfield College students tend not to be risk-takers.

Only Peggy Briggs, my "mature student," seemed less than enthralled by Sunnye Hardcastle. Peggy watched the writer with hooded eyes, refraining from the general approbation. One hand clutched a blue ball-point pen, the other, clenched in a fist, lay taut on her thigh. As Sunnye Hardcastle signed bookmarks for the members of the class, Trouble raised his head from her boot and sniffed Peggy's clenched hand. Peggy flinched. Trouble's mistress yanked hard on his leash. The big dog sighed and lowered his muzzle to the floor.

Sunnye turned to Peggy and offered her an autographed bookmark featuring a lurid black-and-crimson image of a smoking gun. Peggy took one look at the bookmark, emitted a gasp, followed by a wail and a guttural sob. I turned to my student, concerned. Abruptly she leapt up from her seat and ran out of the classroom, leaving her books and backpack behind.

"My God," Sunnye Hardcastle said, "what the hell was that all about?"

Chapter Two

Late that night I headed to the parking lot. A college campus is never exactly dark, even at midnight: Security lights illuminate walkways, and eerie blue bulbs mark the location of safety call boxes. But offices were unlit, as were most of the dorm rooms, and the quad as I crossed it was a lonely place. Then, from Prescott House, where the freshmen lived, came a sudden series of drunken hoots, followed by the crash of a shattering window. I spun in the direction of the disturbance, then turned back again; rowdiness in the dorm is not a professor's business. A residential advisor would intervene. Or a security guard.

The night brooded in the tepid miasma of a January thaw. After the visit from Sunnye Hardcastle, the seminar, and the first full-college faculty meeting of the semester, featuring a nasty squabble over sexual-harassment policy, I'd gone back to my office to complete my opening lecture for the next day's freshman class. Now, exhausted, I had barely enough focus to keep my feet on the path. God only knew where I'd find the energy to fire up the Subaru and drive the back roads to my little country house.

The walkway to the parking lot passed the library quad, skirting Clark Memorial, the current Enfield College library building, and the construction site for the new, and as yet unnamed, Enfield College library center. When it happened, it happened so fast, I thought I was hallucinating. To my left, the library, dreaming in the darkness, flared suddenly to frantic life, alarms blaring, blinding white strobe lights flashing like a futuristic war zone. Then a figure sped out of the shadows with breathtaking velocity, slammed into me, knocked me to the pavement, staggered, recovered its equilibrium, and vanished into the night.

"A book thief?" Charlie Piotrowski repeated, incredulous. "You were knocked down by a *book* thief!"

It was Saturday morning, and we were taking a trip to the ocean, the last chance we'd have to relax together for the foreseeable future. On the way, we planned to stop at the nursing home in Leominster and visit Charlie's father. I wasn't particularly looking forward to the latter—Alzheimer's takes a pitiful toll. But the Maine coast has its own restorative beauty in winter, when the grey rocky skies match the grey rocky shores, and the only other people on the beaches are those strong-hearted souls who live on the rugged coast year round.

"Yes, a book thief," I said. "He triggered the alarm system, the entire library lit up like a disco dance floor, then—wham. God, was he strong! I went over like a bowling pin."

"You okay, babe?" He used to call me "Doctor," now he calls me "babe." Maybe as a feminist I'm not supposed to like that, but I do.

"Aside from a few bruises, yeah."

Charlie pulled the Jeep into the parking lot of a 7-Eleven and turned off the motor. "Unauthorized entry, huh?" Always thinking like a cop. "Did he get anything?"

I shook my head. "Thank God, no. But it was a close call. Nobody knows how the creep did it, but he got into the closed stacks where the rare books are, boxed up an entire set of Raymond Chandler first editions, and trucked them out to the library loading dock. Then it looks as though he tried to get into the vault where they keep manuscripts and inscribed volumes, and that's when he set off the alarm. Rachel Thompson says—"

"Helluva risk to take for a bunch of old books. Who's Rachel Thompson?"

"She's the Curator of Rare Books and Manuscripts."

"What's that?"

"The head of the library's Special Collections division. Security called her, and she came in to check it out. She thinks it's odd the intruder didn't go after something more valuable than mystery novels. Some of the incunabula, for instance—"

"What the hell is incunabula?"

"*Are* incunabula. It's a plural noun derived from the Latin." I hate it when he rolls his eyes. "Incunabula are the first printed books, from the second half of the fifteenth century. Some of them are priceless. The college library has a Gutenberg bible, for instance, donated by some hot-shot alumni book collector, oh maybe a hundred years ago. Compared with that and some of their other holdings—such as a Shakespeare first folio and their Bay Psalm Book—the Chandlers they have here aren't worth a lot. A few thousand dollars at the most."

Charlie whistled. "Thousands?"

"Oh, yeah. Rare books and manuscripts can get exorbitant, Rachel says, into the millions. And it surprised her that the thief didn't seem to target anything else. At least, she didn't see anything else missing. And Brady Hansell. He's—"

"—Head of College Security. Yeah, I remember him. Skinny guy in his forties. Dark hair. Shifty eyes."

"That's him all right. Brady says he's going to step up the library security patrols, but he has no idea how this guy could've got past the existing patrols, let alone bypass a state-of-the-art alarm system."

"But he didn't get past *you*, right? Of course not!" Charlie shook his head, clicked his tongue, then sighed, the full monty of Piotrowskian exasperation. "You were right there on the scene again to throw your body between a criminal and freedom—and get yourself trampled in the process. Karen—babe…What *is* it with you? It was bad enough when we were just acquaintances, but now…"

I smiled at him. "At least," I said, "it's not something *you* have to get involved with. At least…," and I laughed. "At least there was no body in that library."

"Body?" He had opened the car door. Now he halted, one foot on the asphalt, suddenly hyper-alert. "What do you mean, 'body'?"

"Miss Marple," I explained.

He gazed at me blankly.

"You know? Agatha Christie? *The Body in the Library*?"

"Oh." His expression relaxed. "A *book*."

"Yes, a book. Sorry, Lieutenant." I grinned at him. "I forgot that for you a body is more than simply a literary convention." I kissed his cheek. "Go get the coffee."

Charlie came out of the 7-Eleven five minutes later carrying two foil-wrapped bagels, two cardboard cups of coffee, and a copy of *People* magazine. We'd been lovers for months now, but for one split second as he pushed open the big glass door, I saw him as if he were a stranger: a tall, solid man with the shoulders of a linebacker, a broad, kind face, intelligent eyes, cropped beige hair, and extremely kissable lips. Then he was in the car and was simply Charlie again. I ran my index finger down his cheek, from his eyebrow to the corner of his mouth. He smiled at me. Then he laid the bagels on the dashboard, set the cups in the cup-holders, and handed me the magazine.

I gave him my *I'm-a-Ph.D.-in-English* look. "You know I only read *People* in the grocery store," I said.

"I thought you'd want to see this issue." Charlie winked, turned the key in the ignition, and checked the Jeep's rear-view mirror before backing out of the parking space. I took a closer look at the magazine.

"Whoa!" A full-page photograph of Sunnye Hardcastle wearing a black-leather motorcycle jacket and a tough-gal sneer graced the cover.

"I knew you'd be interested. You've been talking about this Hardcastle dame for days." He glanced over at me, and raised his beige eyebrows. "I thought you were never gonna put that book of hers down last night and turn off the light."

I grinned at him. "I did, though. Didn't I?".

He grinned back. "So…aren't you going to read me what *People* has to say about your favorite writer?" He unwrapped his bagel and bit into it.

"My favorite writer? Not really. And it's not as if I actually liked her. She was rude and self-centered. Although, I must say, she was very nice to my students—"

"P.R." Charlie said.

"Could be. It's just that…"

"Just that, *what*?"

We were driving through a strip of winter-denuded oaks and maples. An occasional clump of evergreens relieved the black-and-white monotony.

I was about to say something that I knew would sound stupid, so I phrased my thoughts carefully. "What appeals to me about Hardcastle's writing is the *restlessness*." I was having trouble peeling open the little sipping tab on the lid of the coffee container. "Her books make me want to live a life where I'd have some…adventure." I let it trail off lamely. Adventure is time-consuming and dangerous, not exactly what an assistant professor coming up for tenure really needs. "Anyhow, even though she's obnoxious, the books are good. You ought to read one." We hit a bump just as I got the tab open, and an ounce or two of coffee slopped over onto my new jeans. Yieeee! In the process of mopping at the burning fluid with a wad of paper napkins, I banged my bruised elbow against the door handle. Ouch!

"Detective novels? No thanks. They never get the facts right. When I want adventure stories, I'll stick to the seafaring stuff." Charlie had read every single one of Patrick O'Brian's tales of nautical life. "But she sounds like hot stuff—the Hardcastle woman." He glanced over at the magazine. "Foxy, too."

"Well," I said, "they must have taken an airbrush to the photograph." I couldn't believe I was being so catty. "But, yes, she is attractive—in a well-preserved sort of way."

Charlie laughed. "Read the article, babe. I want to hear what they have to say about her." He signaled for a right turn onto Route Two. The day was cold and bright, and we'd decided to take back roads. We had a two-hour drive ahead of us through the bleak winter landscape, and reading aloud sounded like as good a way as any to pass the time.

I opened the glossy magazine, paged through to the feature article, and read:

TOUGH BROAD FOR TOUGH TIMES

If the luscious Kit Danger of book, movie, and TV fame is anything like her creator, the mystery novelist Sunnye Hardcastle, she is one formidable woman. Hardcastle, 52, rides a Harley, is a crack shot with a pistol, raises Rottweilers, and holds a black belt in Tae Kwon Do. Further hobbies include "international adventures in exploration and infiltration," about which she is, appropriately, mysterious.

Brought up in Detroit's Cass Corridor, Hardcastle says she had to get tough at a young age or she wouldn't have survived her childhood. A full scholarship to the University of Michigan gave her the leg up she needed. In law school, the writer says, she was so bored, she spent her class time writing fiction. Then she dropped out of school to promote Rough Cut, *her first Kit Danger novel. That began a twenty-five-year writing career, during which Hardcastle added an enduring icon to the American imagination—the hard-boiled woman detective.*

Unmarried, but not, we would imagine, without romantic entanglements, Hardcastle lives in a starkly postmodern aerie on a rugged peak in the Colorado Rockies. Aside from her dogs and her horses, Hardcastle shares her retreat with ten thousand first-edition American novels, of which she is an avid collector.

Asked about her plans for the future, the novelist says she will "continue to write, write, write, write, write."

"Sounds like one tough cookie," Charlie said, when I closed the magazine.

I was lost in a daydream of living high above the world in a "starkly postmodern aerie" with my horses and my dogs, sighting down the barrel of a Sig Sauer 226 at a camouflage-garbed evildoer slithering through the underbrush.

"And is that supposed to be a bad thing?" I snapped.

"No." He wrinkled his broad forehead. "I like tough cookies. What's gotten into you, babe?"

I tossed my hair back. My feminist ire was aroused. "It just pisses me off when men mock a woman who steps outside the traditional gender roles."

"I wasn't mocking anyone!"

"And don't call me 'babe.' Now, if *I* could be more like her—"

"Like who? Sunnye Hardcastle? Or Kit Danger?"

"Either. And it's *whom*, not *who*."

He rolled his eyes. Again.

Why did I suddenly feel like provoking a fight? "If I could be more like her, I...I'd..." I wasn't certain what I'd do.

"Babe." Charlie placed his hand lightly on my thigh. "Don't even think about it. You get yourself in enough trouble as it is. If you were more like either of those…tough cookies… you'd probably be dead." He shuddered. "I can't bear to even think about that."

In Leominster we pulled into the circular drive in front of Pine Acres Nursing Home. "Karen," Charlie said, as I opened the door, "I don't want you to go in."

"You don't?"

"He was a great guy. I don't want you to think of him this way."

"Well…if you're sure…"

A half-hour later, I looked up from the student paper I'd just marked with a B+. Charlie got into the Jeep without meeting my eye.

"How is he?"

"Fine." He bit off the word.

"Fine?"

"Fine."

"That's good."

After ten minutes, his eyes intent on the road, Charlie spoke again. "I followed the nurse into the room. My father asked her who I was. I said, 'Dad, I'm Charlie.' Then he frowned and said, 'I used to have a son named Charlie.'"

Grown men don't cry, so I didn't even glance at him as I handed over the box of tissues.

Later that afternoon, with the cold sun slanting behind us, we sat on the rocks at Ogunquit, surveying the wind-driven waves.

"You know," I said, "somewhere I have a copy of Sunnye Hardcastle's first novel, *Rough Cut*. I picked it up maybe twenty years ago at a tag sale in North Adams. I think I paid twenty-five cents for it, which was about all I could afford in those days. I wonder if it's a first edition?"

"Would that make it valuable?"

"Couple of hundred bucks, I bet."

"Hmm," Charlie replied, and snuggled me closer to his warm chest.

"You just love me for my money," I said.

Chapter Three

In New England, February is the cruelest month, and we were right in the middle of it. Sleet drew a barely penetrable veil over the blocky red-brick buildings that surrounded the quad, grey, icy drops on the verge of becoming thick, wet flakes. I could see the fine scrolled carving at the base of the Dickinson Hall pillars directly in front of me, but on the edge of campus, the library, the scene of my collision with the book thief two weeks earlier, was merely an insubstantial image from some faded lithograph. Students and a few professors stomped by in heavy boots on walkways an inch and a half deep in gritty slush. I shivered, pulled my coat collar up, tightened my scarf, and headed cautiously toward Emerson Hall. My Freshman Humanities class awaited me.

On the bulletin board in front of the Student Commons, a brightly hued poster in acid-green and burgundy caught my eye.

CONFERENCE

MURDER: THE PEN/KNIFE AND THE PATRIARCHY

One Hundred and Fifty Years
of
American Crime Fiction

Distinguished Guest Speaker
The Feminist Mystery Novelist

Sunnye Hardcastle

Hellman Hall
March 7-10

A burgundy dagger skewered the word MURDER, whose final "R" oozed lurid drops of burgundy blood.

"Wow," I thought, "so Hardcastle's agreed to come." The tale of her surprise visit to my seminar had spread across campus like wildfire, granting me twenty-four hours of pedagogical fame. My colleagues, of course, were skeptical about having a pop writer in the classroom, but according to the students you'd have thought I'd lured William Shakespeare to Emerson Hall.

As I studied the poster, the date of the conference suddenly struck me: only a month from now. Little caterpillars of anxiety goose-stepped through my gut. In four weeks I was scheduled to deliver a scholarly paper during a panel called Murder in History. In the audience would be one hundred and fifty academic experts in the history and art of crime. I hadn't even begun to write it.

A breathy voice hailed me. "Karen. Hold up a minute."

Claudia Nestor glided through the slush, moving as effortlessly as if she were on skis. She was all in brown, and with her short dark hair slicked close to her head by the precipitation, she looked like a skinny seal. Claudia was the director of the upcoming conference, which the Women's Studies Program was sponsoring in an attempt to "reintegrate popular modes of expression with the Woman's Voice."

"Cool poster, Claudia."

"Thanks. I asked for something hard-edged, unsettling." She fluttered her eyelids nervously, caught herself, opened her eyes wide and fixed her gaze for two seconds, then fluttered again.

Unsettling? My colleague from Women's Studies must have led a far more sheltered life than I had. "Hardcastle's pretty unsettling all by herself," I responded. "How'd you get her to commit?"

"Money." The eye flutter again. The catch. The fixed stare.

"Yeah? How much money?" I'd tucked away tons of detective fiction in between megatons of abstruse scholarly volumes during my years of grad school and teaching, and most of it was by women writers. I wondered if "the Woman's Voice"—whatever *that* was—had ever actually been suppressed. But then I hadn't been granted a cartload of reparation dollars by an historically all-male college to run a conference based on the premise that it had.

"She held out for ten thousand dollars." Claudia glanced around furtively. "But that's in strictest confidence."

"Right," I agreed. If I knew the Enfield grapevine, it would be all over campus by tea-time tomorrow.

Enfield is a wealthy school, but not spendthrift. Last year they'd coughed up ten thou for an appearance by the film maker Spike Lee, then the same for a talk by comedian Sandra Bernhard. Now they were bringing in the hard-edged Hardcastle, whose Kit Danger unfailingly discovered vile corruption at the heart of that very same white-male power structure for which Enfield College kept churning out white-male power pups. But it was always a sure sign that a controversial artist was edging toward the mainstream when an elite college like Enfield shelled out cold, hard cash to lure her to campus.

"Thanks. I knew I could count on you." The eyelids fluttered. I found it impossible to talk to Claudia for more than five minutes at a stretch without becoming lightheaded, holding my breath, waiting for the next agitated twitch. Wiping slush from the lenses of my recently and reluctantly acquired eyeglasses, I put them back on, ready to resume the slippery trek to class. But Claudia didn't seem in any hurry to get in out of the sleet. "So, Karen, how's your conference paper coming along?"

"My paper?" The gut caterpillars clicked their heels and stomped into double-time. "Fine. It's going fine. Just fine." And, really, it *should* be fine. After all, how hard could it be to put together an authoritative study on class binaries in the representation of murder in American working class discourse? All I had to do was read through the college library's entire run of the *National Police Gazette* (1845-1936), then take a long look at their collection of nineteenth-century dime novels, and finish up with a review of mid-twentieth-century detective fiction paperbacks. That's all. And now I was going to be on the program with Sunnye Hardcastle, someone who really knew something about how murder scenes were constructed. I could feel my own eyelids begin to flutter.

After class, I checked in at the Enfield College English Department office to get my mail. Monica was standing by the fax machine, shamelessly reading her way through the latest private-and-confidential faculty fax transmission.

"This is for you, Karen," she said, without looking up. "You're invited to a high-school reunion, it says here." She gave me an appraising look. "Lowell High, huh? I woulda thought you'da gone somewhere a whole lot classier than Lowell. We used to play them in football, you know. You shoulda seen their cheerleaders. Talk about cheap! Those Lowell girls are *so* easy." Monica should talk. To my certain knowledge she had a bit of a history herself, and, like me, a fatherless child to prove it. A stocky woman in her early thirties, our secretary had chopped-off brown hair, a sallow complexion, and the shrewd black eyes of a witch. Which she was: a practicing witch and member in good standing of a local coven. A witch in orange stretch pants and a long rust-colored sweater hand-knit in a complicated cable stitch. Monica glanced at the fax again, then up at me. "You oughta be able to go, Karen. It's the end of February, and mid-term exams will be over by then. What's the matter? You okay, Karen? You look sick."

"I'll take my fax now, Monica," I said, plucking it from her hand. "Thank you very much."

Sleet had turned to steady snow by the time I left my office for the day. As I passed the library, I was warmed by the glow from the windows. A Gothic grey-stone mausoleum, the old library lacked the light, openness and electronic efficiency of the magnificent new edifice under construction. Nonetheless, it had served the college well for over a century, and the staff worked wonders in spite of the building's shortcomings.

Tomorrow, I told myself. Tomorrow I'll spend the entire day in Special Collections reading through the *National Police Gazette*.

But, of course, when tomorrow came, I found I'd forgotten about the ten a.m. emergency meeting of the English Department hiring committee. The committee wrangled until noon, then the final candidate for the African-American position showed up for an interview, and she turned out to be *white*, precipitating all manner of surreal discussion—and Tomorrow was swallowed up just as thoroughly as all my Yesterdays had been.

Not that I didn't find time to read Sunnye Hardcastle's latest, *Tough Times*. I closed each day in the company of Kit Danger, as if she were a fictional sister.

> *Power oozed from him like pus from a boil. Kit recognized the set of his shoulders, the cut of his suit. The black silk tee. The pants that fit where they were*

supposed to. The Italian shoes of leather too soft to be shiny.

She slapped a twenty on the table and slipped from her booth in the coffee shop window.

He was alone. So was she. She loitered at the pastry case as he passed. Kit was a mistress of disguise. A man like Jack Vecchio wouldn't even see the fiftyish shopper she'd become for the afternoon. She could tail him anywhere.

A man like Jack Vecchio. Muscle and money.

And murder.

By the end of that week, invitations to my high-school reunion had arrived in every conceivable form: fax, phone, U. S. Postal Service, and e-mail. It turned out my sister Connie had given my various numbers and addresses to Ruth Ann Bouchard, the biggest mouth in the Lowell High School class of 1978, and Ruth Ann was determined she was going to get me to attend. "How could you do that to me, Connie," I raged over the phone, after I'd hung up on Ruth Ann's interminable call. "You know how they screwed me at Lowell High."

I wanted nothing to do with Lowell High School ever again, not since a prudish administration had snatched away my prized valedictorianship twenty-some-odd-years earlier. In my senior year I'd disgraced myself by becoming pregnant, thus, in some incomprehensibly tortuous socio-economic-psycho-cultural manner, totally negating my thirteen-year unchallenged record as Class Brain. When word of my little problem leaked out in early June, pom-pom girls gloated and valedictorian-status slid greasily out of my hands and into the sweaty grasp of that suck-up dweeb, Ernie Conklin, with his measly 95.4. And—damn it—I let the school get away with it. I marched down the aisle, my barely discernible little belly concealed by a voluminous black graduation gown, as passively anonymous as any other mill-town kid, in spite of having the class's highest cumulative average, out-of-sight SAT scores, and a lifelong record of perfect attendance.

Of course, plenty of girls got knocked up by the end of senior year, but Karen Pelletier was supposed to be different. Karen Pelletier was supposed to provide evidence that Lowell's educators were not wasting their lives. Karen Pelletier was supposed to demonstrate that the American Dream is intact, that American education works, that even from the meanest homes in the meanest neighborhoods of the meanest towns a life can be salvaged through the proper teaching of Diligent Study Habits, Working Well With Others, and Proper Classroom Behavior.

And it's true. The American Education System has been good to me. Through the application of Diligent Study Habits, Working Well With Others, and Proper Classroom Behavior— plus a mind-boggling amount of dogged determination and a generous endowment of innate intelligence—I've earned myself a Ph.D. in English and a tenure-track position at one of the country's most prestigious colleges.

It's just that things would have been a hell of a lot easier if the purveyors of American Education had taught me a teensy leetle bit about Methods of Proper Birth Control.

"You know I don't want anything more to do with those people," I whined to Connie.

"Lighten up, Karen," my sister snapped. In the two years since my daughter Amanda forced me back into the bosom of my estranged family, Connie and I had seen each other only three times—old animosities die hard—and our relationship was still shaky. I could picture her standing at the kitchen phone in her tight jeans and tight red sweater, a doughnut in one hand, car keys in the other, impatient to be on her way. She worked as a department manager at the Wal-Mart, and she was ambitious. Store manager was the next rung up the ladder. When she hit it, she'd probably be making twice as much money as I was.

"I have to deal with 'those people' every time I go to work," Connie said. "Why should you be any different from the rest of us?"

I thought about it. Maybe she was right. Maybe it was time to forgive and forget. Maybe it was time to grow up. Hmm. When is this thing, anyway? In three weeks? Connie, have you ever gone to one of your class reunions?"

"You kidding?" she replied. "I see those people every day. I don't need to spend even a second more with them. But..." She paused, and when she spoke again, her usually abrasive tone had become reflective. "You know, after what they did to you, Karen, I'd say go. I mean—look at you, a professor and everything. I'd want to *show* them. You know? Now," her attitude defensive again, "you okay with this, Karen? I'm late for work."

I walked the cordless phone back to the kitchen, and set it on its base with exaggerated care. Connie was right. I felt warmed by her insight. I stood there with my hand still on the phone, chewing the inside of my lip. I could *show* those bastards. Show them *good*. Impulsively, right there at the kitchen table, I wrote out a check for fifty dollars, addressed an envelope to the reunion committee, and, before I could change my mind, licked the stamp. And, besides, it would be the mature thing to do, wouldn't it? Mend fences. Let bygones be bygones. Whatever. I was a grown-up now. Everything was under control. I headed to the doughnut shop.

Chapter Four

"Don't let this get around, Karen, but we've had another break-in." As I pushed through the double doors to the anteroom of the Special Collections Division the following Monday, Rachel Thompson, the curator, pulled me into her private office. "We're supposed to keep it quiet, but since you already know about the one last month..." Tall and full-bodied, with crisp dark hair styled medium-short and curly, Rachel was dressed, as usual, in flowing natural-fiber garments, today a cafe-au-lait tunic over a long pale rose skirt.

"When did it happen?" And I'd always thought libraries were such safe places.

"Last night, about two. I've got the alarm rigged to ring at my house as well as at Security, so I was here right behind the campus police, but—" She spread her hands. "Not a soul in sight."

"He get anything?"

"Not that we can tell. We've been doing inventory since the last intrusion, and it looks like nothing's missing."

"That must be a relief."

"You're telling me! Why the Gutenberg alone might be worth a couple of million at auction. If it was a legitimate sale, that is." In spite of twenty years in academe, Rachel still spoke with the twang of her native Texas. "Well, anyway,

I've been meaning to call you ever since the night of the first break-in, but as you can imagine, things have been insane here. How are you? That was quite a knock you took. I kept thinking you should go to the E.R."

"I must have been in shock. I didn't feel a thing until the next morning. Still have pain in my elbow, though."

Rachel gave me a down-home *tsk-tsk*, but she still had her mind on the intruder. "Avery wants both break-ins hushed up." Avery Mitchell is Enfield's president. "Bad for public relations, he says. And as long as we haven't lost anything…" She shrugged. "It's a mystery, the whole thing—how the thief gets in, why he tried to take the Chandlers last time, why he doesn't go after something worth mega bucks. Security didn't find any signs of an actual break-and-enter either time, Brady Hansell says. Brady thinks the thief must have a key, even though we had the locks changed after the last break-in. But Avery still doesn't want to go to the police."

She sat down at her desk, suddenly deflated, as if someone had let all the air out of her. Memos and book-order forms were strewn on top of dog-eared file folders. An ancient Styrofoam cup overflowed with paper clips. A stack of old library journals perched precariously by the phone. How anyone who had ever taken a course in library cataloging could live with such chaos was beyond me.

The fax machine clattered to life, capturing Rachel's attention instantly, as if she'd been waiting for it to ring. "Karen, I'll let you get to work. Glad you weren't hurt." She pulled a sheet from the fax machine, glanced at it, then vanished through a door marked Restricted Entry.

Pushing open the glass doors, I entered the reading room, a spacious chamber furnished with long golden-oak tables and an elevated librarian's desk. The walls were lined with built-in bookcases displaying priceless volumes locked behind glass doors with ornate metal grids. I glanced around me for possible book thieves. None in sight. A short, potato-faced man in a yellow sweater leafed through what seemed to be an early twentieth-century volume, taking notes on a laptop computer. A distinguished-looking woman with pewter-grey hair in a tight bun sifted impatiently through a folder of handwritten letters, obviously not finding anything that satisfied her. A few students reading old newspapers looked as if they might be doing research for a history course. The silence in the room was broken only by the occasional turning of a page or a sigh from the grey-haired woman.

I sat at one of the oak tables, filled out the request form for the first ten years of the *Police Gazette*, and handed it to the small, dry-as-dust desk librarian, Nellie Applegate. Where Rachel was vibrant and ruddy, Nellie was enervated and pale. Although only in her forties, she had salt-and-pepper hair, which was cropped off unimaginatively just below her ears. She wore a calf-length slate-grey shirtwaist dress and looked as if she had stepped out of an old photograph, not the sepia kind colored in earth tones, but a 1930s snapshot in washed-out greys and flat whites. She accepted the call forms hesitantly and said thank you apologetically, as if I were undertaking a job for her instead of vice versa.

Fortunately for me, with my specialization in the literature of the American working class, the Enfield College library boasts a world-class collection of popular fiction: newspapers, magazines, books and manuscripts. The *Gazette* is a nineteenth and early twentieth-century weekly magazine featuring every conceivable sensational variation on criminal activity. It's only one of many valuable crime-fiction resources available to researchers, thanks to the generosity of a wealthy alumni collector.

While I waited for the periodicals to be delivered, I slid the copy of *Tough Times* out of my book bag and began to read.

> *9:14 a.m. A Housemaid's Home Cleaning Services van pulled up to the luxurious Riverfront*

*Apartments. Two uniformed workers unloaded
cleaning supplies from the rear. The driver remained
in his seat as one woman lugged an industrial-sized
vacuum cleaner to the building's front doors and
pressed the entry buzzer.*

*"Yeah?" queried the doorman. Shiny name tag:
Raphael.*

*"Vecchio," said the tall blonde. "9-A." Her co-
worker came up behind her, a dark stocky woman
whose upper-arm muscle definition threatened to split
the seams of her uniform shirt.*

*The doorman shook his head. "Mr. Vecchio didn't
say nothing about no cleaning service."*

*The blonde widened her eyes. "He called last
night. It was like a real emergency. You sure he didn't
tell you? Heavy-duty work. Had to have it done by
dinnertime. Ain't that what you got in your book,
Gloria?"*

*The dark woman pulled a dog-eared appoint-
ment book from her cleaning caddy. "Yeah. Vecchio.
Nine a.m. Urgent."*

*The blonde spread her hands. "See? And we're
late already. Mr. V.'s gonna go ape-shit if we don't get
the job done on time."*

*Raphael was familiar with Mr. V.'s wrath.
"Awright. Awright. You got the key?"*

*"Oh, yeah." Kit Danger held up the key she'd
copied from Vecchio's. "We'll just let ourselves in."*

"Professor Pelletier?"

I jumped. The book skidded across the table.

"Sorry. I didn't mean to startle you." My student Peggy
Briggs stood by my chair with a dozen archival boxes on a
book cart.

"It's okay, Peggy. I guess I was just engrossed." I retrieved the book and turned it over so she could see the title.

She yawned.

Work-study, I thought, *probably on top of another part-time job. No wonder the poor woman is strung out. She must be exhausted.*

Peggy was an enigma to me. Following her departure in hysterics from my seminar the day of Sunnye Hardcastle's visit, she had waited for me after class and offered an apology, but no explanation. Since then she had attended classes, prepared her assignments, and taken dutiful notes. But she kept a very low profile, half-asleep most of the time, speaking only when called upon, never volunteering an opinion.

"Peggy," I asked, "how are things going?"

She gave me a wary glance. "I'm fine."

Pride. "I'm sure you are. It's just that I know how hard school can be for returning students. I was one myself. If you ever need someone to talk to, you know where my office is."

"Thanks," she replied. "Maybe I will…sometime." She eased the book cart up level with the table, cast me a wan smile and plodded away.

The newspapers were yellowing and smelled of the past. I lost myself immediately in the brute violence and lurid sensationalism that constituted much of what the nineteenth-century laboring classes read. Murder. Rape. Infanticide. Kidnapping. Theft. Fraud. Fraud. Fraud. All the stuff we never learned about in the sanitized history I was spoon-fed in college.

By noon I'd had enough of the *Gazette*. I filled out another request form, this time for three of the popular nineteenth-century Beadle's dime novels. Beadle's Dime Novel Series ran to 321 volumes, its pocket-size books, a mere hundred pages in length, featuring a distinctive burnt-orange cover and sufficient thrills, spills, and adventures to keep the American working-class reader occupied and out of trouble. It was nineteenth-century dime-detectives such as Old Cap Collier and Nick Carter who became the prototypes for the Sam Spades, Philip Marlowes, and Kit Dangers of the twentieth century. I submitted the request form to Nellie, who accepted it meekly. Then I headed out for lunch.

In the baronial hall that served as the library's foyer, a half-dozen display cases had been set up with mystery exhibits in anticipation of the crime-fiction conference. As I came up the stairs, a book jacket in the glass-topped case nearest to me caught my eye: 1970s hot-pink and chartreuse stylized design of a crouching woman aiming a shiny black revolver directly at the reader. I paused to look it over: a first edition of Sunnye Hardcastle's *Rough Cut*. Wow! That was it, the book I'd lugged around with me in various moves over the past twenty years. The one I'd mentioned to Charlie, and then forgotten again. Now I stared at the volume displayed like a jewel in its protective case: Was my twenty-five-cent copy a first edition? Had it become valuable over the years? And where was my copy, anyhow? In one of my cluttered bookcases? In a box in the attic? And, really, how much might it be worth? Then I brought myself back to the present. I had a conference paper to write, and I was in the library to do research, not to piss my time away with fantasies of unearned wealth.

When I returned from my hastily consumed tuna-fish-sandwich lunch, Rachel Thompson popped out of her office again and waylaid me before I entered the reading room. Her usually rubicund cheeks had gone pale. "Karen," she said, "I'm afraid there's going to be a delay in filling your request for the dime novels."

"Someone else has the books?"

Rachel hedged. "Not exactly." Her expression was somber. Through the glass doors behind her I could see Nellie Applegate at the reading-room desk, gazing abstractedly in the direction of the researchers at the long tables. Rachel reached up and fingered the filmy scarf at her throat. She beckoned me to follow her into her office, and then through the door marked "Restricted Entry." We entered an enormous room. I glanced around, curious. This must be what they called the closed stacks. Empty book carts lined the wall next to me. Book-laden shelves stretched from wall to wall, floor to ceiling, as far as I could see.

"What I'm going to show you has to be kept in strict confidence," Rachel said.

"Of course."

She led the way through a set of fireproof doors, then through a maze of corridors and book-filled rooms, around a sharp corner, and into a small annex. Twelve-foot-high shelves were squeezed between narrow aisles. Rachel motioned me down a remote row, then waved her hand in the direction of an empty shelf toward the top. "This is where the Beadle's Dime Book collection is supposed to be shelved." She looked completely baffled. "All three hundred and twenty-one volumes of it. Thirty linear feet of books. All gone. Not a single one left. Seems I was wrong when I said the book thief hadn't gotten anything."

Wednesday afternoon after class, I headed back to the library. As I passed the construction site for the new building, a crane was moving steel beams into place. Watery sun illuminated the winter-blasted campus. Two women students strolled by, the blonde wearing a short denim skirt. A worker acknowledged her passing with a long whistle. She froze in place for about five seconds, then pivoted and gave the wolf the finger. His face turned bright pink, convulsing his buddies in guffaws.

In the Special Collections reading room I filled out call cards for a half-dozen 1940s paperbacks. If I couldn't get the nineteenth-century dime books, I'd jump ahead a century. While I waited for them, I looked around for Rachel. Nowhere. Damn. I'd been silent as the grave all weekend about the stolen books, and was dying to ask her what was happening. And when—if ever—I'd be able to get my research done. I eyed Nellie hopefully, but couldn't imagine her doing anything as lively and life-affirming as passing on gossip. In any case, she was hardly aware I was in the room. Her eyes were fixed on the potato-faced guy with the laptop. As she gazed, and tapped on the polished oak of her desk with a pencil's pink eraser, I checked him out, to see what the attraction was. A short, sturdy man with straight dun-colored hair, thinning on top. Small nose and overly large jaw. Heavy five o'clock shadow. Not much to look at, but Nellie seemed mesmerized. She was hardly aware I was in the room. *De gustibus*, I thought.

I pulled *Tough Times* out of my book bag and opened it to the ATM receipt I was using for a bookmark.

> *Kit eased the apartment door shut behind her. So far, so good. Vecchio would be downtown for the day. She'd made sure of that. The coast was clear. She took a step forward.*
>
> *Heavy furniture cast dense shadows in a room decorated in homage to wealth. What wasn't leather was mahogany. Everything was oversize, and the walls were the color of money.*
>
> *Suddenly a bullet whistled past Kit's head. Beretta 9mm with silencer, she thought. Dropping to her belly, she slithered behind an ornately carved breakfront and slipped the big Sig Sauer from its holster—*

Plop: Peggy delivered the requested paperbacks to my table. I gave her a smile, closed *Tough Times* and addressed myself to the old novels. I ogled lurid covers, skimmed through two or three titles, settled down with *Dead Men Don't Love Blondes* (1952), and began to read in earnest. *The dame in the red dress was dead....*

What I learned from these books about perceptions of homicide in twentieth-century working-class literature was that hot babes look really good dead on the covers of paperback books. It was depressing as hell.

For most of the afternoon I was alone in the reading room with Nellie Applegate and the little researcher with the laptop. Today his sweater was salmon-pink instead of yellow, but I could have sworn that Potato-face hadn't moved from his seat at the table across from me since I'd seen him there the previous week. As the minute hand on the big, round clock over the door ticked jerkily to three minutes before the five o'clock closing time, he piled his books up, aligned their edges, set them on a book cart for return to the oblivion of the stacks. I followed suit. He pushed his chair away from the table, and stretched. Squeezing past him in the narrow aisle, I said, companionably, "Seems like you and I are closing the place tonight."

He gave me a blank look, processed my comment, recognized it as small talk, and responded with a stiff nod. "They say," he offered, "that precipitation is expected to hold off until well after midnight in our area. Then a band of snow squalls will cause hazardous driving conditions throughout the morning rush hour."

"Oh." I gave him a blank look of my own and shouldered my way through the double doors.

"Rachel around?" I asked Nellie, as she came out of the curator's office with a ring of keys in her hand.

"She took the day off." Nellie stood fidgeting with the keys, as if waiting for me to leave.

"Oh," I said. Pretty casual for a librarian whose library had just been plundered. "Will she be back tomorrow?"

She shrugged.

Perversely, I wanted to get something resembling a human reaction from this passive woman. "Who's the guy in the sweater?" I asked.

Involuntarily she turned her head to glance at him through the glass doors, then her gaze snapped back to me. "Th... that's Bob—Bob Tooey. From Lake Superior College in Michigan." The light wasn't all that great in the Special Collections anteroom, but I could have sworn a slight pink suffused her pallid face. Was Nellie blushing? I don't know why I was surprised. Even librarians fall in love.

"Lake Superior College," I responded, trying to draw her out. "Now that's one I haven't heard of."

"It's a community college. But he's very dedicated to his work," she said, with a defensive edge, as if I'd somehow maligned a stellar patron. She jingled her keys. "He's here every morning when we open the doors, and doesn't leave until we close them." More consecutive words than I'd ever heard from the little librarian.

Bob Tooey, dedicated researcher, exited the reading room with a curt nod. He jogged past me and up the stairs. I followed him, but we didn't engage in further social niceties.

I took a couple of minutes to peruse the exhibits in the lobby cases. Bob Tooey was also engrossed by the displays, studying one of the Enfield library's prizes, the only known manuscript of Dashiell Hammett's *The Maltese Falcon*, signed and inscribed with his handwritten revisions. Displayed next to the manuscript was a mint-condition first edition of the novel, its acid-yellow dust jacket featuring the falcon statuette and a hand dripping with jewels. In the more than fifty years since Hammett had published his hard-boiled, hyper-masculine private-eye fiction, his books had become highly collectible.

Collectable, I thought. I've really got to find the time to hunt down my twenty-five-cent copy of Hardcastle's *Rough Cut*. Who knows what it's worth by now?

On the narrow, twisting roads, a cotton wool fog obscured everything more than three feet in front of the car, and the twenty-minute drive home lengthened into thirty. As I turned into my driveway I spotted the big red Jeep backed up to the front door, then the smoke issuing from a newly kindled fire in the wood stove. A sudden flush of contentment suffused me, and I stopped thinking about anything at all other than a long cozy evening with Charlie Piotrowski.

Chapter Five

I still had my mind on murder as I met with my honors seminar the next week. They'd been assigned Edgar Allan Poe's "Murders in the Rue Morgue," and discussion centered on the grotesque nature of the killings: In a locked room, a mother and daughter are brutally slaughtered, then one is shoved up a chimney, the other thrown from a fourth-floor window. In their prurient focus on the heinous details of the crime, students ignored Poe's attempts to stress the analytical nature of the solution. At the far corner of the table an indistinct movement caught my eye; a hand attempted to rise, then faltered, then continued its shaky ascent. "Peggy," I called.

This was a first—Peggy Briggs actually volunteering an opinion.

"Murder isn't *fun*." Peggy glared at her fellow students. Mouse brown hair parted in the center and cut uncompromisingly straight just below her ears. Plump shoulders bulked out even further by a too-large hooded Red Sox sweatshirt in navy blue. Round face pink with indignation. "You people are getting off on this story. You're...*titillated* by it." She turned her glare to me. "Is that the right word? Titillated?"

I nodded.

"But there's nothing...*titillating*...about murder. Real murder is brutal and...sordid." She took a deep breath. "I *hate* this story. It exploits violent death simply to entertain people, just the way those Hardcastle novels do. I don't think this is a great piece of literature. I think it stinks."

The thick silence in the room was broken only by the laughing banter of students in the hallway. "Oh, that's so fun," a girl's voice exclaimed.

Peggy's diatribe was a shocking violation of the Enfield student culture of detachment. Almost as a religion, these young people practiced an outward show of languor and irony, a refusal to acknowledge themselves subject to the woes of the flesh. Also it was embarrassingly obvious to everyone in the room that Peggy's outbursts must be rooted in some traumatic personal experience, another no-no. In the Enfield classroom we deal with the life of the mind, clear and cold and pure, or the murkier political discourse of race, gender, and class, but never the painful, messy, merely *personal* clutter of individual lives.

This is a literature course, I thought. *Please, please, please, don't make me play therapist.* I zoomed into literary hyperdrive, evading the emotions behind the outburst. "Well, Peggy, you make an important point. Poe founded the genre of the murder mystery with this story and others, but the genre does operate on a fundamental disparity between its literary conventions and the realities of its subject matter. Violent death is terrible. Mystery novels are pleasurable. So, what can we make of a seeming contradiction like that?" Toss it back to the class. Diffuse the tension in the room.

I'd talk to Peggy later.

Stephanie Abrams, in appearance the polar opposite of Peggy—tall, model slim, with smooth, pale hair and a wardrobe of sleek pants and sweaters in muted autumn shades—leafed through her edition of Poe's works. She paused and studied a passage, then leaned forward, elbows on the table.

"If you notice, Poe says the same thing as Professor Pelletier—about pleasure, I mean—only he calls it amusement. He has his detective say, 'An inquiry will afford us amusement.'" She looked directly at Peggy as she spoke. "I think there is 'pleasure' in these stories. It stems from…what?…some kind of…existential damage control," she continued. "I mean, we're all going to die…."

Pretty Tiffany Milford gaped at Stephanie in blank incomprehension: *Die? Who? Me?*

Peggy nodded fiercely. She looked as if she were about to burst into tears.

Stephanie bit her lip, shrugged and fell silent.

I picked up the thread. "Stephanie's right. Given the randomness of life, each one of us is at risk of a violent death no matter how safe we think we are with our locked rooms. War. Insanity. Revenge. Anger. Greed. Simply being in the wrong place at the wrong time—the World Trade Center on September 11, 2001. It happens. Poe knew that. Telling stories about murder helps us feel in control when the world is so out of control. In mystery fiction, everything is tied up. Order is restored. There's justice in the end."

After class I took Peggy aside. "Listen, why don't you stop by my office sometime? We can talk about…ah…how the course is going for you."

Peggy's brown eyes grew skittish. "It's going fine," she said. "Isn't it?"

I wasn't going to let her evade me, as she had in the library. "Sure. But let's just set up an appointment—" But Peggy was out the door and into the hall, where Stephanie was waiting. Peggy handed the other girl a bulky bag. It was a common plastic bag from Stop 'N' Shop, but where it had once held groceries, it now bulged out with weightier fare. From a rip in the side of the flimsy bag, what looked like the corner of a thick manuscript poked out. Without exchanging a word, the two students separated and walked away in opposite directions.

You. Have. Four. New. Messages, the zombie lady on my voice mail informed me. *To. Hear. New. Messages. Press. One.* I pressed One and tucked the receiver between my ear and shoulder. With my hands free, I slid open the bottom desk drawer and inserted my class notes into the file folder with the rest of my teaching materials. If Dickinson Hall ever burns down, I'll be at a total loss for class preparation material.

Karen, it's Rachel, said the first message. *I want to apologize again for the missing Beadle's Dime Novels. I've been making some inquiries and have located a number of volumes at the Smith College library. They've got at least two you asked for, and their Special Collections operates on the same schedule as ours. Hope that helps.* Hmm, nice of Rachel to check into that for me when she had so much else on her mind. I made a note to get myself over to Smith as soon as possible.

Beep.

It's Claudia Nestor calling Tuesday afternoon. Karen, we need an escort to accompany Sunnye Hardcastle around campus during the conference. I assume, of course, you'll be only too happy to accept the honor. Thanks. The honor? Obviously Claudia hadn't met the arrogant novelist yet.

Beep.

Monica's voice said, *Karen, I'm forwarding a message. It's about your high-school reunion.* A couple of clicks, and Ruth Ann Bouchard, the voice from the past, said: *Karen, we're all so excited about Saturday night. Just wanted to let you know everyone's going to be dressed to the nines! See you later, alligator!*

God! Why had I let myself get sucked into this damn thing!

Beep.

Professor? Peggy Briggs' voice. *I'm sorry about how I acted in class today. Please don't hold it against me.* A long pause, then a sob. Then a hang up.

I sat with the receiver to my ear for a few seconds and listened to the silence.

"Something disturbing just happened," I said, as I pulled out the cane-and-chrome chair at Rudolph's Cafe and joined Earlene Johnson and Jill Greenberg. We meet there every other Tuesday for pasta, wine, and a good, long, grown-up-girl talk. "Earlene, you must know Peggy Briggs."

Earlene nodded. She's Enfield's Dean of Students. She knows everyone. And everything.

"I know her, too," Jill said. Today Jill looked every inch the transplanted Manhattanite. No one can wear black with quite the flair of a fairskinned redhead. "She's in my Soc 411 class. Conscientious student, but kind of weird…introverted." To an extravert like my pal, Jill, *introverted* was synonymous with *weird*.

"What's going on with Peggy?" Earlene was letting the grey grow into her close-cropped hair. A pair of hand-carved ebony tribal figures dangled from her ears.

I told them about my student's outburst in class and her message on my answering machine.

Earlene took a few seconds before responding. "I think I know where that's coming from, Karen. But it might be better if Peggy told you the story herself."

"The story?" Jill squealed. "Oooh! That sounds so…deliciously mysterious."

"Peggy's had a rough life." Earlene's expression was sober.

"Who hasn't?" Jill asked, her Park Avenue upbringing in abeyance.

Earlene shot me a side-of-the-eyes look: *Like she knows what rough is!* Then she glanced ostentatiously around the restaurant, crammed at 6:30 with Enfield students and faculty. "Want me to make you a list?"

Jill laughed. "No, thanks. I just want a bottomless glass of wine."

I beckoned to the waitress, then turned back to Earlene. "So, you're not about to enlighten me as to that scene in class?"

She adjusted one of her earrings. "I really can't. Let's just say that Peggy is not unacquainted with tragedy."

"Oh," I said, feeling chastised. "I of all people should know better than to pry into a student's past." I glanced around the restaurant. "Where's that waitress?"

Our server was on the other side of the room, uncorking a bottle of wine for Claudia Nestor. Claudia was seated alone at a table for two. I sincerely hoped someone was going to join her, if only to help consume what appeared to be a fine California red.

Jill noted Claudia's presence, then leaned over the table in a confiding posture: Good Gossip. Earlene and I instantly inclined toward her. "That woman just gets battier and battier," Jill said. Claudia was up for tenure this year in Sociology, Jill's department. "She does that thing with her eyes, you know?" We nodded. "She does it all the time. I heard one student call her 'The Blink.' And…" Jill leaned toward us so far her breasts brushed her plate. "One day last week, right smack in the middle of a department meeting, she pulled out a little flowered cosmetic bag, you know, the kind they give away in department stores. Then she proceeded to do a full-face makeup: foundation, blusher, mascara. Lip liner. The works. In a department meeting! In front of twenty colleagues! This from a woman who expects the Sociology Department to consider her a serious scholar."

Claudia glanced over at our table and waved. Jill gave her a flash of beautifully straightened teeth, then sat up primly. She raised her eyebrows at us. "Do you think she heard me?" she muttered through barely moving lips.

"Not possible over all the other gossip being mongered in this room," I assured her. Rudolph's clientele was almost exclusively composed of Enfield College faculty, staff, and students. A gabby bunch.

As I checked out the scene, a trio of students prepared to leave. Their table was littered with the remains of pricey food.

A kid in a retro wool-and-leather football jacket thrust a platinum credit card at the waiter. "Put it all on this," he said, waving his hand over the half-eaten steaks and melted parfaits. Big Man on Campus. Would Papa even notice the hefty charge?

"Anyhow," Jill said, "let's change the subject. So, Karen, how's that big gorgeous guy of yours?"

"Well, Charlie's big, all right, but I've never thought of him as *gorgeous*. Good-looking in a plain-brown-wrapper sort of way. Smart. Strong. Dependable. But *gorgeous*? I don't think so."

"Gorgeous," Jill pronounced, as if that settled it. "I could really go for all that muscle."

"We know," Earlene replied, dryly. "How's Kenny?" Kenny Halvorsen, the college soccer coach, was something more than merely Jill's next-door neighbor.

Jill shrugged. "He couldn't watch Eloise tonight. I had to get a babysitter." There was something wrong here. We waited, but our young friend had been struck by a rare case of discretion.

Earlene sat back and regarded me owlishly over the red rims of her glasses. "God, it's good to see you happy, Karen. You just about glow with it."

"Yeah, I am. But, if only..." I frowned, pulled the menu toward me.

"If only *what*?" Jill plucked the oversize parchment sheet from my hand.

"If only he would let well enough alone." I focused on the evening's specials printed on a blackboard in magenta chalk: linguine with chanterelles, shiitake risotto with smoked chicken, polenta with black bean sauce.

"What does that mean—*well enough alone*?" Earlene passed me the bread basket.

I snapped a bread stick in half and muttered, "He wants me to marry him."

"Hallelujah! We'll have the wedding this summer. I'll bake the cake. I make this fabulous Grand Marnier orange cake—"

Jill waved down the waitress. "Champagne, please. We're celebrating."

"I'm *not* getting married!"

The waitress was an Enfield student with short blond hair and a pewter stud in the center of her chin. Her brown eyes slid from me to Jill to Earlene, then back to me. Enfield is a fishbowl.

"Why not?" Jill seemed to have recovered from her discretion. She picked up Earlene's red-framed glasses, settled them on the tip of her nose, and adopted a shrinky expression most likely learned from her psychiatrist father. "Do I detect an inability to commit?"

I scowled at her, then turned to the waitress. "No champagne," I said. "I'll have a glass of the merlot."

"Me, too," Earlene said. "But bring us a bottle. We'll share." The waitress headed for the bar.

"Sorry about that," Jill apologized in lowered tones. "But it's just that I think Charlie's the perfect guy for you. You said it yourself. Smart. Strong. Dependable."

"You two," I allowed my voice to rise for emphasis, "I've told you before—I won't marry a cop. It's a terrible life. I don't know why we can't simply keep on as we are. You know, no entanglements. Just seeing each other, sleeping together. It's perfect."

Rudolph's service was unbelievably efficient that evening: The waitress stepped up from directly behind me with the wine.

I took a deep gulp of the California red and groaned. It would be all over the dorms before bedtime: Pelletier was sleeping with a cop.

Chapter Six

"Whaddaya know…it's Karen Pelletier. And all grown up." The handsome stranger materialized next to me at the Lowell High School Reunion buffet table. Ruth Ann Bouchard Napolitano, rhapsodizing about her three adolescent soccer-star sons, faltered in mid-paean.

Alumni were gathered at round tables in the large balloon-decorated banquet room of the Lowell Doubletree Hotel. The color motif was pink and purple. On the bandstand, a pianist, drummer, and guitarist launched into a rocking-chair version of "Motorcycle Mama" to the accompaniment of joyous shrieks from people who hadn't seen each other in decades—and hadn't wanted to. I didn't know what the hell I was doing there. The crime fiction conference was only a few days away, and I could have been at home, polishing my talk, comfortable in sweatshirt and jeans, feet up in front of a cherrywood fire.

Bored pie-eyed by Ruth Ann's heroic-soccer-mom tales, I'd been thinking about skipping out. The hell with the two hours it had taken me to drive here. The hell with the fifty dollars I'd plopped down for the ticket. I was still deep into *Tough Times* and had left Kit Danger teetering on the edge of a construction girder hundreds of feet up in a half-built skyscraper. Reading at home would be a lot more fun than this reunion.

But suddenly there was this intriguing man.

He was forty, gingery Irish, six feet tall, broad of shoulder, with eyes of such a light green they appeared empty. He wore a well-made brown suit and charcoal-grey dress shirt with a Jerry Garcia tie in deep reds and blues. He looked muscular, masculine, intelligent, capable of swift movement and decisive action—and oddly incongruous in this reunion crowd.

"Denny?" Ruth Ann queried. She was round-faced, pudgy, and fluttery, and the newcomer's unsmiling gaze seemed to fluster her.

The man had a stranger's face but vaguely familiar features. I squinted in the dim party light. Take one skinny, undersized Irish kid with bad acne and worse attitude; add three or four inches to the height, more to the shoulders, sandpaper the complexion, readjust the aesthetic scale of the facial features, once ludicrously outsized, now rough-cut and angular: come up with square jaw, thin lips, long nose, high cheekbones. And those cool green eyes.

"Dennis O'Hanlon? Is it really you?" The last I knew of this classmate, he was a cocky, red-headed runt, always in trouble, suspended during junior year for selling marijuana to the daughter of the local Episcopal priest.

"It's me." He shrugged. "I grew up, too."

"I'll say," I replied, trying not to stare. "You look great."

"Thanks. Same back atcha." He gave me a long, slow smile. "Can I buy you another one of whatever poison it is you're drinking. For old time's sake." I glanced around. Susie Leblanc was headed in our direction clutching a puffy pink photo album.

"Sure can," I said. "Scotch rocks." I followed him off to the bar. Ruth Ann, fortunately, had been struck immobile, as well as mute, by Dennis O'Hanlon's miraculous transformation.

When I was a kid, the O'Hanlons had lived down the hill one street over on an Irish block that abutted our French-

Canadian neighborhood. The only difference between our sagging frame row house and theirs was the number of people crammed into the five miserable rooms. Counting my grandmother, there were six of us, but Dennis was the youngest in a brood of thirteen. While we Pelletiers weren't exactly solid citizens, at least my father worked when he wasn't on a tearing drunk, and my mother somehow managed to put three squares a day on our chipped enamel kitchen table. Nobody knew what went on at Denny's house, but the O'Hanlon kids ate wherever they could grab a mouthful, and come five o'clock my mother more than once had set a place for the grubby little Denny. My dominant memory of the young Dennis O'Hanlon was that he was a troublemaker, always on the run from somebody—and always hungry.

Now here was once-scrawny Denny O'Hanlon bulking out the shoulders of what I could have sworn was a custom-made suit.

The Doubletree cocktail lounge bustled with highly made-up women wearing pastels. It was either an evangelical women's gathering, a convention of politician's wives, or a Mary Kay conference. Dennis and I bellied up, ordered two Dewar's, and took them to a glass-topped table in a back corner, out of the sight-line of any classmates who might decide to forgo the inferior libations available in the ballroom.

"To old times." Dennis raised his glass and touched it to mine. "May they never return."

"Skoal," I replied.

The green eyes studied me. They were clear, like arctic ice. "I always did like the way you wore your hair, Karen," he said, finally. "All loose and shiny like that. Unpretentious. And, tonight, that simple, flowing dress, not fussy like the rest of these girls." He motioned toward the ballroom with his drinking hand. "You know…" he gave me a cock-eyed grin, "all these years later, you still look damn good."

"Thanks." I swallowed hard. Graciousness in the face of praise does not come naturally.

That simple, flowing dress had cost me a full weekend's shopping time and three hundred dollars at an Enfield boutique whose doors I hadn't previously darkened in the entire four years I'd worked at the college, and most likely would never darken again. But once I'd made my impulsive decision to attend the Lowell High reunion, I'd been determined to appear naturally, and effortlessly, elegant. Dennis O'Hanlon's appreciative gaze confirmed that the effort had been worth it.

"You look like life has been kind to you," Dennis pronounced. He said it as if he were used to making complex evaluations given minimal evidence. And used to being right.

Poker-faced, I tipped my head in acknowledgment of the remark, if not necessarily of its truth. The grown-up Dennis O'Hanlon was an intriguing guy, and I was titillated by this serendipitous encounter.

He registered my demurral. "I didn't say life had been *easy*. Believe me, if anyone knows what your childhood was like, it's me. I said life had been *kind*. It's not the same thing."

I contemplated the distinction, shrugged, then nodded. Life had walloped me hard at the start, but now I had my wonderful daughter, Amanda. I had work I loved. I had Charlie Piotrowski, who wasn't with me tonight only because I'd refused to let him come. If I was going to face my teenage demons, I'd wanted to do it alone. Now, sitting here drinking with this adult version of Denny O'Hanlon, I was wickedly grateful not to have Charlie tagging along like a chaperone. Or like a husband. In my tame life this encounter felt deliciously—almost dangerously—like adventure.

"Do you remember the fish?" Dennis leaned back in his molded plastic chair and regarded me with a faint smile.

"Fish?" This wasn't what I expected from adventure—fish talk.

"Your father took us fishing one afternoon. Remember? First we got some frogs in the marsh." He said *maash*, like a good Lowellian. "God, those things were ugly little fuckers, freaked me out to touch them. Then we went down to the river. I caught an enormous bass. Your mother filleted the fish, battered the frog legs, cooked it all up and served it with French fries." He was smiling into his Dewar's. "You know, I don't think I've ever eaten anything I enjoyed as much as that meal, and, believe me, I've eaten in some classy restaurants over the years."

I remembered then. We must have been about seven, and we'd trekked along the Merrimack until we'd come to a marshy spot outside of town. My father wielded the net, and it was Denny's job to drop the frogs into the pail and slam the lid down. When my father flipped him the first huge warty bullfrog, Denny screeched and dropped it. My father curled his lip in derision, and called the panicked boy "Frogface." Denny burst into tears, and Daddy hooted in derisive laughter. Then Denny caught the bass, and my father taunted him for thinking he was a hot shot. Even now, thirty years later, I wanted to apologize to Dennis for my father's nastiness that afternoon—but all he seemed to recall was the good meal.

Before I could respond, Dennis abruptly changed the subject. "I see you're not wearing a wedding ring."

I glanced down at my left hand. He was right. I wasn't wearing a wedding ring. "Neither are you," I replied.

"Not anymore."

We looked each other over. It was a frank appraisal, on both sides. Then he asked, again abruptly, "So...what are you up to these days?"

Behind him, one of the pastel women glided by, clutching a Manhattan in a rocks glass. *Not* an evangelical gathering. From the ballroom came a mangled medley of John Denver tunes.

"I'm an English professor." I sipped my Dewar's.

"No kidding. A professor, huh? Impressive." There was a reflective pause while my companion processed the information. "Well, you always were a brain."

"Ha!" I sipped more Dewar's. "Among other things, you mean. What are *you* up to, Dennis?"

He paused again before he responded. "Oh, a little of this, a little of that." Cagey. I didn't let it go, tilting my head in inquiry. He tapped his fingers on the glass tabletop. "Nothing as fancy as a college professor, I'll tell you that."

"Give me a break, Dennis. I'm not about to buy the rube act. Look at you." I swept a hand in his direction. Fifty-dollar haircut. Hundred-dollar shirt. Million-dollar attitude. "Obviously you're doing well at something."

His broad shoulders moved up and down easily in the beautiful jacket. "I'm an investigator."

"Really? A cop?" I'd known a number of cops in my life, but they didn't run to bespoke suits.

"No. Private."

"Private!" I stared at him, then grinned. "Well, that makes sense, I guess. Once you hit high school, you became a hard-ass troublemaker."

He laughed. "That I did. But it's standing me in good stead these days. And you…" Dennis evaded the topic of himself as if he made a habit of it. "You're a professor," he repeated. "Where do you teach?"

"Enfield College."

"Enfield!" Pale lashes blinked over startled eyes. It was worth the entire fifty-dollar admission fee to see Dennis O'Hanlon's taken-aback reaction. Then he set his drink down on the table and sat up straight. "Enfield College. Well, I'll be damned." The eyes squinted, as if in speculation. He gave me a slow, thin smile. "Lowell High is doing itself proud. But, like I said, you always were a brain. Kind of a prig—but a brain."

"Ha!" He surprised another laugh out of me. *Prig* was the last label I'd ever have expected from one of my high-school classmates. He was right of course. I had been a prig. I'd read all those doom-laden nineteenth-century novels where the virtuous young woman is seduced by an experienced older man, becomes pregnant after a single act of sexual intercourse, gives birth to a virtuous daughter, and dies. But, in the end, the lesson hadn't taken. And I hadn't died, just submitted myself to marriage, in my particular case a fate worse than death, given birth to Amanda, and lived on to untangle myself from everything about the whole sordid mess. From everything, that is, but my wonderful daughter.

"And you always did have…" He eased into silence, as if his words were leading him into an unexpected train of thought. I had the impression of strong muscles under pale skin, and, oddly enough, a still-hungry expression in the cool-green eyes.

"Dennis?" I queried after a silent minute.

He shook his head. "Sorry, Karen. I was woolgathering. Hazard of the profession. I was about to say, you…always did have your nose in a book." He leaned toward me, elbows on table, chin on hands. "So. Karen. Here we are, twenty years later. Tell me about your life. Tell me about your job. Tell me about Enfield College…."

We chatted our way through another round of Dewar's, then I turned down an invitation for a post-reunion drink in his room. He walked me to the parking lot and saw me safe into the Subaru. "Be seein' ya, Karen," he said, smiling crookedly.

Be seeing me? I reflected as I drove away, and wondered just exactly what I'd do if the boy from Lowell ever called.

Chapter Seven

Avery Mitchell took my hand in both of his. "Karen, how are you?" His clear blue gaze gave me the usual flutter in the gut.

I detached my hand. "I'm fine, Avery." It was hothouse warm in the president's office, and a scent of roses wafted from the arrangement on the long table by the bookcase. "What's up?" I knew I sounded rude, but I wanted to get this— whatever it was—over with.

"What's up? Let's see…ah, what time is it, Karen? 4:13? Would you like a drink? Scotch, maybe?" He motioned me to a maroon leather chair and walked over to the liquor cabinet across from the fireplace. Avery was tall, sandy-haired, fine-boned, with the thin lips and long nose of the true New England WASP. Today must have been a dress-down day; he was wearing khakis and a bright green sweater over a blue chambray shirt. "I have Glenfiddich, Black Label…"

"Coffee," I said. "If you have any." I hadn't quite recovered from my overindulgence at the reunion Saturday night. Now, after an intense Pop Fiction seminar, I felt drained. It didn't help when I returned from class and found the message on my office voicemail from Lonnie, Avery's administrative assistant. President Mitchell would appreciate it if I could free up a few minutes in my busy day to speak with him in person—at my earliest convenience, of course—about a matter that must remain confidential.

"Lonnie," Avery called into the outer office, "coffee, please. For two." We talked about the Braque exhibit at the college art museum until Lonnie came in with a tray holding an insulated carafe and a monogrammed bone china coffee service. A fire crackled in the fireplace, its light reflected in the gold rims of the cups. I could have sat there for hours in that elegant room with its jewel-toned Persian rugs and its muted Hudson River landscapes, discussing art with Avery, but that wasn't the purpose of the summons, and it wouldn't have been a good idea, anyhow. Again I asked, "What's up?"

"What's up?" he echoed, and tightened his fine lips. "Well, Karen, we find ourselves in a situation…by *we*, I mean the college, of course…we find ourselves in an unanticipated difficulty into the midst of which I understand you have been inadvertently interjected." He measured sugar into his cup.

I translated from administratese: *The college has gotten itself into some kind of shit, and I'm involved.* "Ah," I said.

He waited for more, then smiled. "Never one to waste words, are you, Karen?"

"Well…" I replied, playing for time. Next year I would petition Enfield College for tenure. If I had been "inadvertently interjected" into something so serious the president had to handle it personally, I'd just keep my mouth shut until I found out what it was.

"I heard, of course," Avery said, "about your unfortunate encounter with that intruder in the library last month, and now I understand Rachel Thompson has acquainted you with our recent loss of an entire set of nineteenth-century books. Baffling! Absolutely baffling!"

I nodded, and replaced my cup in its saucer. He was finally getting to the point.

"But there have been further developments I don't believe you know about." A phone rang in the outer office. Through the heavy mahogany door Lonnie's greeting was nothing more than a murmur. Avery slid his gaze toward the door and waited. When it was clear that Lonnie wasn't about to put the call through to him, he turned back to me and let out his breath in a big huff. "Rough day," he said. "But I'm going to try to relax. Listen, Karen, there's more stuff missing from the library, but right now I'm not in a position to tell you precisely what. After Rachel found out that the entire dime-book collection had been stolen, the library staff conducted an in-depth inventory. They discovered additional losses." He looked very sober. "Over the past few months the library has lost at least five hundred thousand dollars in rare books and manuscripts."

"My God, that's…"

"A half million. And we have no idea where—or who—the leak is. Very distressing." He raised his eyebrows, inclined his head for emphasis, offered me more coffee. I accepted. He poured more for himself, added milk and sugar. "We've got to investigate these losses closely in the next few weeks, and that will require the utmost discretion." He gave me a direct and meaningful look. "Now here's the tricky part. According to the guidelines of something called the ACRL—"

"What's that?"

"The Association of College and Research Libraries. They mandate prompt and full disclosure of stolen rare books and manuscripts, in part to prevent them from being purchased by unwary dealers and collectors. Now, I know this isn't strictly kosher, but I need to buy a little time here. We're talking to an alum about donating a major book collection. If word of these thefts got out right now…"

I got it. "Rachel asked me to keep the loss of the dime novels to myself, and I'll keep quiet about this as well."

"Good." Avery sat back in his chair. "As you can imagine, anything concerning our collections, which, as you know, are exceptional, involves extremely delicate issues of public relations, such as donor confidence and perceptions of campus safety. Most likely I'm going to have to take a drastic step, a step not everyone will be comfortable with. And, oddly enough, as it turns out, I may have to request that you…" He sat immobile for a second or two, then jumped up and strode over to the fireplace to poke at the glowing logs. The iron poker had an Enfield crest wrought into the handle. He spoke with his back to me. "Anyhow, everything has to be done on the q.t. If I might ask you, for the good of the college, and as a personal favor to me—"

I held up a hand. I didn't think I needed to hear the rest of it. "Silent as the grave," I said. "I promise." *Personal favor to you. You slick piece of work.…* A two-year-ago kiss hung heavy in the air between us. I could still feel its ghost on my lips. Then I thought about Charlie and rose from my chair. "Well, if that's all—"

He turned and gave me a long, blue, hooded look, then sighed. "Yes, Karen, that's all. For now."

I pulled into the driveway later than evening, and my headlights raked over a battered grey Jetta. Amanda! What the hell? What was my daughter doing home on a weeknight in the middle of her final semester at Georgetown?

"Amanda?" I called, as I twisted the key in the kitchen door. "Honey?"

She came out of her bedroom in black leggings and a navy sweatshirt, frowsy with sleep although it was only eight o'clock. "Hey, Mom, I was worried about you. Where've you been?"

"Hey, Kid," I mimicked, throwing my arms around her and squeezing. "I'm a grown-up. I stay out late."

"Yeah. I guess." Her short hair was sticking straight up on top. "But I was looking forward to one of your beef stews."

I smoothed down the cowlick. "What say I throw together some bacon and eggs? I'll tell you what I was doing at school, and you can tell me what you're doing home."

My daughter was uncharacteristically subdued. "I'm tired, is all. It's been a rough semester, what with my thesis, and the course work, and the waitressing." Amanda had worked part-time throughout her college years to help me patch together her tuition, room and board. In spite of generous scholarships, the fees for her top-of-the-line university were more than an assistant professor's salary could handle. "I just had to take a break, Mom. Called in sick at Giorgio's, and I'll cut a couple of days' classes." She gave me a defensive look. "I haven't missed a class yet this semester, and I'm beat."

"You don't have to convince me, Sweetie," I said, giving her another hug. "A little hooky never hurt anyone. But are you sure you're okay?"

I was worried. Amanda was pale and quiet. She picked at her eggs, and almost fell asleep at the table. And then my usually up-half-the-night daughter went to bed again at nine and immediately fell asleep.

The next morning Charlie and I sat on the living room floor pulling books out of the old glass-front bookcases I'd picked up years ago in a North Adams junk shop. The sun cast blocky shadows on the faded rag rug. A fire glowed in the wood stove. It was a cozy domestic scene. Although we weren't officially living together, Charlie and I spent as much time with each other as we possibly could. We'd talked about me moving into Charlie's small frame house on a side street in Northampton. Or, rather, Charlie had talked about it. What he really wanted, of course, was The Big Commitment, but the mere idea of another marriage freaked me out at some deep, dark level I couldn't bear to probe.

Maybe Jill was right; maybe I did suffer from a congenital inability to commit. After our conversation at Rudolph's, Earlene had called to apologize for being so pushy about me and Charlie.

"I'll tell you what," I'd said to her, "I'll take the wedding cake. But no wedding."

"But, really, isn't your relationship with that beautiful cop already the same thing as being married?" Earlene had queried. "Don't tell me you don't worry about him all the time, anyhow." She laughed. "Only this way, if he dies in the line of duty, you don't get the pension and the insurance."

I shivered, my blood suddenly frozen. "Jee-zus, Earlene," I'd snapped at her. "I thought you were going to butt out of my personal life."

"Hey, is this the book you've been looking for?" Charlie had discovered a copy of a brightly covered Hardcastle novel shoved behind other books. "*Bad Attitude*?" He held it up. The lime-green and jonquil jacket featured the Hardcastle motif, a stylized woman aiming a huge hand gun at the reader.

"No. The one I'm looking for is titled *Rough Cut*. But put that one aside, too."

"Sure thing." He placed the book on the coffee table, lowered his hand and ran it slowly down my leg, then cuffed my ankle. Umm.

"What're you guys doing?" Amanda wandered out from her bedroom, still in her leggings and sweatshirt. Awkward with Charlie in his Mom's-boyfriend role, she gave him a high five instead of a hug, then plopped down on the couch and picked up the TV remote.

I sat up straighter. "We're looking for a book called *Rough Cut*. You remember it, Hon? Hardcover. Hot pink with a gun."

"One of those Kit Danger books?"

"Yeah."

"I read them all when I was—oh—maybe, thirteen." Her voice grew reminiscent, as if that were decades in the past, instead of a scant nine years. "Decided right then and there I was gonna be a hot-shot private eye when I grew up."

Charlie grinned. "You'd be a natural."

I cast him an evil look. "Over my dead body. I didn't raise this girl so she could put herself in harm's way."

Amanda squinted at me. I changed the subject before we could take the discussion any further. "So, you have any idea where my copy of *Rough Cut* went?"

After a short beat of silence, she said, "You kidding, right? We've moved twice, no, three times, since then. What do you want it for?"

"Sunnye Hardcastle's going to be on campus for a conference next weekend. I'm her escort."

"Cool! Wish I was gonna be around. I've never met an author."

I raised an eyebrow. "Yeah, well, I've met this one. You're not missing much. She's a pain in the ass, even if she is a terrific writer. *Rough Cut* was her first novel. I want to ask her to sign it."

Charlie had a flannel rag I'd cut from one of my old pajamas and was dusting each book so carefully you'd think he was checking for fingerprints. "Your mother's convinced she's got a gold mine hidden away somewhere," he said, "a rare first edition. She's gonna sell it and put you through grad school."

Amanda's dark eyes momentarily became opaque; she dropped her gaze. "Grad school? I don't think I—" My daughter paused for a few seconds. Then she shook her head as if to clear it, and recovered her usual aplomb.

Charlie stacked the dusted books in piles by author. By the time he was done, I'd have the cleanest and best organized library in the Commonwealth of Massachusetts.

"I hate to say this, Mom," Amanda nonetheless said, "but when we moved up here from the city, didn't you donate, oh, maybe, seven or eight boxes of books to the Salvation Army?"

"Ouch! I think you're right. But would I have put the Hardcastle book in with them?"

"Who knows? She shrugged and clicked on the TV. "You were in a real slash-and-burn mood." She began channel surfing.

I took a closer look at my daughter: Was she losing weight? "How about some oatmeal, Amanda? I'll make it the old way, with butter and brown sugar."

"Oatmeal with butter and brown sugar," Charlie repeated. "And raisins? I haven't had that since I was a kid."

"You got it now," I said, grinning at him.

"Maybe later for me," Amanda replied. "I don't have much appetite." She clicked through another half-dozen channels. "Oh, look, a rerun of Cagney and Lacey. Cool!"

That afternoon, Charlie watched the football game, Amanda dozed, and I picked up *Tough Times.*

> "So, you think you can play with the big boys, Danger. Well, you got another think coming."
>
> "I'm no hard guy like you, Vecchio, but I've got what it takes. And more."
>
> "Oh, yeah. Like you're gonna pull that trigger. Little girl like you. Anything happens to me, and my boys'll be all over you like shit on toilet paper."
>
> Kit gave him the steely glance she reserved for heartless thugs. "Bang, bang," she said. Then she pulled the trigger. The bullet whipped just past his left ear, as she intended. It zipped across the vast empty factory space and embedded itself with a thunk in a discarded wooden packing case. Jack Vecchio made his final move—a recoil that sent him back against the catwalk's low steel rail. Coolly, Kit watched him stumble, overbalance, and fall headfirst, a long, fatal drop, to spatter like a squashed white spider on the unforgiving concrete floor.
>
> The End

The End? Already? I sighed. Okay, so it was a little over the top. Quite a bit over the top, actually. But, oh, to be Kit Danger, bold, and brave, and strong.

I rose from the chair and went into the kitchen to start the chili for supper. I wondered how much of Kit Danger there was in Sunnye Hardcastle. I wondered if there was any in me.

Chapter Eight

I worried about Amanda, but she rallied after a few days at home and returned to school on Sunday. Wednesday, opening day, I was free to slip into conference mode. I drove to campus under a lowering sky experiencing the usual pre-conference combination of excitement and dread. An academic gathering is something like a carnival. A participant steps outside of her daily identity, for one brief shining moment divorced from her daily self: appearance, personal history, even course load. She is "Woman Thinking," as Ralph Waldo Emerson might have phrased it, would he not have considered such a statement to be a contradiction in terms.

In the coffee shop Claudia Nestor passed me carrying a tray with two chocolate glazed doughnuts and a mug of milky-white coffee. "So the big day is finally here," I said. "How're things going?"

"Diversionary modes of occluding the class binaries," she muttered.

"Claudia?"

"Held hostage to fashionable political and theoretical agendas," she hissed.

"Claudia?" She neither saw nor heard me. *Dear God*, I pleaded, *just let her make it through the conference with her sanity at least semi-intact.*

And mine, too, after God knows how many hours as Sunnye Hardcastle's escort.

Miles Jewell, English Department chair since God was a boy, stopped me as I approached Dickinson Hall juggling my briefcase, a large coffee, and an egg-and-bacon sandwich in a white paper bag. He was well protected from the frigid weather in a grey wool overcoat, a crimson scarf with the Harvard insignia in white, and the kind of brimmed felt hat I think is still called a fedora.

"Karen, what's this I hear about you canceling a class today?" His thick white hair flopped over his thick white eyebrows.

A chill ran down my spine that had nothing to do with the weather. I'd deep-sixed my freshman class that afternoon because of the conference. "The opening reception is at four o'clock."

He frowned. "Opening reception of *what?*"

"Of the crime fiction conference. I'm serving as escort for our guest of honor, Sunnye Hardcastle."

"Oh, Women's Studies. I suppose…Well, just don't make a habit of it, Karen. Teaching comes first. And remember," he said vaguely, as he wandered off, "your tenure decision comes up next year…."

The chill migrated to the pit of my stomach: *Bastard! "Remember your tenure decision," indeed! As if I could forget it! Asshole! Pompous son of a bitch!*

My conference paper was completely drafted but needed fine-tuning. I thought I'd take the morning to slash clichés that had weaseled their way in despite my vigilance: *gender binaries; cultural construction of identity; patriarchal power structures.* I assumed that by four o'clock I'd have this sucker honed to a razor point, ready for a knock-em-dead delivery first thing tomorrow morning.

Peggy Briggs was seated on the floor outside my door. *No, Peggy*, I thought. *Not now!* She saw me and slapped shut her dog-eared paperback, sliding it into her canvas backpack. "I know you don't have office hours today, Professor," she ventured, levering herself up. "But I hope it's okay for me to talk to you."

I swallowed my sigh; there went a prime chunk of revision time. "It's fine, Peggy. Come on in."

She shifted her backpack from one hand to the other. "I work in the library every day until just before my classes. It's hard to make your regular hours."

"It's all right. Really." I dumped bag, briefcase, and coffee cup and hung my coat on the rack. Peggy sat down on the green chair, on the very edge of the seat, as if she felt she had no right to occupy the entire space. She wore a royal-blue ski jacket, the down kind with rows of horizontal stitching every three inches, and the puffy strips bulked out her already stocky body.

"I want to apologize for missing class yesterday, Professor," she said. "You see…I fell asleep in the closed stacks." That was as honest an excuse as I'd ever gotten from a student: *I fell asleep in the closed stacks*. No dead grandmothers. No life-threatening gynecological symptoms. And, indeed, as always, Peggy did appear exhausted, her skin pasty, dark circles beneath her eyes.

"Don't worry about it," I said. I'm a patsy for a student's hard-luck tale. "It could happen to anyone."

Peggy began to say something further, hesitated, then gathered up her courage. "I don't know what you know about me?"

I couldn't imagine an opening like that leading to anything I wanted to hear. I tried to swallow yet another sigh. "Why don't you tell me what I need to know."

The plastic coffee-cup lid resisted my fingertips. I cast a yearning glance at my briefcase.

Peggy balanced on the six inches of chair she had allowed herself. "Five years ago my twin sister Megan was murdered by her boyfriend."

"Oh, Peggy!" The top popped off the cup. I forgot about Miles' vague threat. I forgot about the speech.

My student's eyes brimmed with tears. "He was abusing her. One week she'd have a split lip, the next, a black eye. Once he even broke her arm. I kept trying to get her to leave, but she was so afraid of him. Said he'd kill her if she left. Finally I found a battered-women's center and talked Megan into going to their safe house. He tracked her down. He shot my sister right in front of her four-year-old daughter. She died on the spot."

"I'm so sorry!" Suddenly Peggy's outbursts in class began to make sense. Of course the literary exploitation of violence would disgust her.

She was practically whispering now. "I keep thinking that if Megan hadn't listened to me, she'd be alive today."

"Peggy, there was no way you could have known."

That seemed to be what she wanted to hear. She slid back in the chair and let her body slump. "It changed my life, Megan's death—working with the Women's Center, talking to the cops, testifying at the trial. I was so angry. I missed Megan so damn much, and…what was worse, I was terrified I'd go down the same road myself one day. So I…I got some help. Then I decided to become a social worker. Things haven't been easy, but I got through Greenfield Community College, and I'm going to make it here at Enfield."

"Of course you are." At that moment I identified so strongly with my student that I had her already graduated—with an M.S.W. to boot.

"It's just that, you know, the bit about missing class…I was never in one of your courses before, and I don't want you to think I…well…have a problem with it or anything. Especially after I…well, you know." Yes, it made sense now: the hysteria during Sunnye Hardcastle's visit, the strange eruption of anger in seminar. All were Peggy's response to what she must perceive as trivialization of tragedy. What had she said in class? Something about murder in real life not being entertaining or amusing, but "brutal and sordid."

She sighed, looked down at her intertwined fingers. "I'm tired, is all. I carry a full load of courses. I have custody of Megan's daughter, Triste. I have a work-study job fifteen hours a week in the library. On weekends I tend bar at Moccio's. To top it all off, we live with my mother in Durham Mills. In her house. With her husband." She tightened her lips. Something wasn't being said. "It's not easy, Professor, but I'm going to make it. For Megan's sake—and for Triste."

She rose from the chair and hefted her bulging backpack. A small stuffed animal was attached to one strap, a grungy old Pink Panther. It had been a while since I'd seen one of those. She caught me looking at it. "It was Megan's," she said.

"Oh," I replied. Here was someone who faced serious life challenges, not simply a department chairman's absent-minded admonitions. Sexual harassment guidelines prohibit us from touching students, but I gave her a squeeze on the arm. "Don't worry about missing the class, Peggy. And try to get some rest."

When I realized that I'd read *patriarchal power structure* twice in contiguous sentences without deleting either, I knew I had to pay closer attention to my revision. But I couldn't help brooding about Peggy Briggs and her quest for a better life. I'd have to find some way to let my student know she could count on me. But for what? To give her advice? To cut her some slack? To listen when she needed a sympathetic ear?

Soon I had the talk in decent shape, except for one publication date about which I was uncertain. I trudged over to Special Collections to check it at the source. Bob Tooey was at his usual place in a baby-blue sweater that seemed to have shrunk in the wash, pulling tight across his shoulders and upper arms. As Nellie placed the requested book in front of me, with a sidelong glance at the little researcher, my eyes adjusted. It wasn't that Tooey's sweater had shrunk, it was that the little man was really built. I hadn't noticed that before: a short, plain-looking guy, but with the upper-body definition of an Olympic gymnast. Surprisingly powerful looking. I stared at him for a few seconds, then caught myself. I checked the date I was looking for, and went back to the office.

"I told you I'd be seeing you." I glanced up from the computer monitor, startled. Dennis O'Hanlon stood in my office doorway. He was wearing an olive drab trench coat of some fashionable crinkly fabric, and looked just as out of place in the Enfield English Department as he had at the Lowell High reunion.

"Dennis? What the hell are you doing here?"

"Don't get up," he ordered, closing the door quietly. He pulled over one of the captain's chairs and sat down, practically knee-to-knee with me. He looked me in the eye, straight on. In the light coming from the tall window I could see what the dim illumination of the Lowell Doubletree bar hadn't revealed, a straight white scar running from the corner of his right eye across his temple and disappearing in the curly ginger hair. "Karen, I need a favor," my visitor said.

"A favor? What kind of favor?"

He reached in his coat pocket, removed a cigar case, tipped out a fat brown cigar. "I need you not to know me."

"What are you talking about? *Not to know you?*" This was just a little too much like a TV police drama. "And what are you doing at Enfield anyhow? And what the hell—"

"I told Mitchell this wasn't gonna be easy." He clipped off the end of the cigar, returned the case to his pocket, and retrieved a silver lighter.

"Mitchell?" That stopped me cold. "You mean Avery?"

"Avery Mitchell. President of Enfield College. Right. *That* Mitchell. Your boss. My client. I told you I was a P.I., didn't

I." He tilted the unlit cigar in my direction. "You don't mind, do you?" The flame flicked to the cigar's tip before I could respond. He took a drag, then studied the incipient coal. "You see, Karen, I'm on a case, and in pursuit of the investigation I'm attending your crime-fiction conference. Undercover."

I gaped at him. "An undercover scholar! You've got to be kidding!"

"Undercover *as* a scholar," he corrected me. "There'll be so many professors on campus for the conference, no one will notice one more new face. That gives me a perfect opportunity to hang out, talk to people, get the lay of the land. Only, I need you…not to know me." He leaned back, took another deep drag, let out a slow, thin stream of smoke. In spite of myself I inhaled deeply. The smoke smelled warm and strong and masculine. The smoker exuded an air of sensuality powerful enough to make my skin tingle. *God!* What was the matter with me? This was grungy little Denny O'Hanlon.

I looked out the window, away from Dennis. The campus was at its most dismal: bare branches, denuded lawns, cold, hard sky. Students on their way to classes hurried by, hands in pockets, heads bowed against the invisible wind. *Snow before lunchtime*, I thought. *Late March, and this winter refuses to end.*

Dennis sat very still, watching me with sea-glass eyes. His red-blond hair sprang into sleek waves in spite of the ruthlessly short cut. He looked like a street-bred tabby cat.

"Avery, you say?" I recalled the conversation in the President's office. Avery had talked about stolen books. He had mentioned taking *drastic steps*. For a classy institution such as Enfield, engaging a private investigator would indeed constitute a drastic step. Despite nods in the direction of social equality, Enfield College represented the entrenched values, interests, and institutions of the rich. Dennis was a Lowell street kid. I could easily imagine him, like Raymond

Chandler's Marlowe, snarling, "To hell with the rich!" I was intrigued by the paradox. "Avery?" I repeated.

"Yep." Dennis puffed at his smoke.

"Tell me about it."

Chapter Nine

My glamorous-sounding job as Sunnye Hardcastle's escort came down to finding a secure closet for her ankle-length leather coat, locating her conference badge, bringing her a glass of champagne and a plateful of tiny smoked-salmon sandwiches, and making introductions.

"So, you're supposed to be my bodyguard?" Sunnye said, when I met her in the library.

"Escort. From what I've heard, you should have no need of a bodyguard." I looked closely, but couldn't see anywhere Sunnye could possibly be packing heat beneath her shimmering grey silk sheath. Must be in the soft leather shoulder bag.

The novelist gave me a Cheshire-Cat grin. Then she stuck on her conference badge, took a hefty slug of wine, slipped Trouble a sandwich, and flashed an automatic smile at the first admirer to approach her.

The reception was being held in the library's large foyer, the area temporarily closed to students and other patrons by discreet green plush-covered chains on upright brass poles. And permanently closed to dogs, as a vigilant security guard explained to Sunnye. "I'm a public figure with a need for protection from deranged fans," she informed him. "He's a trained guard dog—goes with me everywhere." My eyes widened as I watched a crisp fifty-dollar bill change hands, and Trouble entered the library without further challenge.

Long tables laden with succulent tidbits had replaced the foyer's book and manuscript display cases. A bar anchored the far end of the room. Among the attendees, only Rachel Thompson and I—and one pseudo-scholar, undercover— knew that sometime in the early morning hours of the previous day a locked and alarmed library display case had somehow—impossibly—been opened, and an invaluable manuscript had been stolen.

"What do you know about bibliomania?" Dennis had asked me in my office earlier that day.

"Bibliomania?" I broke the word down into its constituent parts. Latin derivation. *Biblio. Mania.* "You mean biblio-philes? People who are crazy about books? I think you'd have to put me into that category."

"But *you're* sane—at least I assume so." He gave me an Irish grin. "What I'm talking about is something more like *bibliokleptomania.* People who are so obsessed with books that they'll go to any lengths to possess them. *Biblioklepts,* I think they'd be called."

"So," I mused, "you *are* working on the library thefts. I thought so. Avery told me about them, you know. He said a half million dollars...."

Dennis rolled the fat cigar in his fingers. "Karen, when you and I were kids back in Lowell living on beans and potatoes and Merrimack River fish," he flashed his feline smile, "did you think we'd ever be sitting in a room like this one talking about a *half million dollars*?"

I shrugged. "It's still someone else's half million. Why you, Denny? How'd you get involved in this?"

"I did some work for UMass Lowell. Word got around. I'm...damn good."

"But…rare books? You know about them?"

"I'm a fast learner." He waggled his cigar like Groucho Marx. "Anyhow, Karen, let me bring you up to date. Last night the s.o.b. who's been heisting the books got into the library again. Took something big-time—a manuscript worth maybe $100,000—from a locked display case in the foyer."

"You're kidding!" I visualized the contents of the cases. "Oh, no! Not *The Maltese Falcon!*"

"Yeah, that's it. A scrawled-over stack of old pages. An annotated typescript, Mitchell called it. A hundred grand! Tell me, Karen, why the hell would that thing bring such big bucks?"

I pondered for a moment. "The *Falcon*'s…seminal, I guess you'd say—an apt term, if not p. c. at the moment. It established a transformative myth in the American imagination, the loner private eye—an incorruptible man in a crooked universe. An icon of American crime novels, films, even TV police dramas. And the manuscript? I saw it there, in that case. It had Hammett's revisions all over it, in his own hand. Jeez…only $100,000? I'm surprised. The thing must be priceless."

"Priceless, huh? Nothing's priceless." Dennis brooded for a long moment. Then he stubbed his cigar out in an empty coffee mug and dumped it in the trash. I knew the sweet brown aroma would linger in the air for days. "Well, back to the theft: No signs of forced entry to the building. Even weirder, the showcase was still locked—like the manuscript had just been vaporized right through the glass. No signs of forced entry: no broken glass, dents, scratches. Just *poof!* Gone."

"Someone must have had a key…."

Dennis shrugged. "If they did, it's an inside job, but I'm not convinced…" He let it trail off, and fell silent again.

"Dennis?"

He shook his head, as if to clear his thinking. "So, anyhow, Mitchell's been talking to me for almost a month about an investigation—since before I met you at the reunion." Another ginger-cat grin. "You could have knocked me over with a first edition of a Dick Tracy comic when you told me you taught at Enfield."

I thought back. "You did look flabbergasted."

He nodded. "Mitchell was…" Dennis waffled his hand back and forth to indicate Avery's indecision. "But this morning, when they found that manuscript missing, he called, told me to get my ass over here right away."

"He didn't say 'ass.'" I knew Avery. He was anything but crude.

"He might as well have. He wanted me here pronto. Karen, I'm building a top-notch reputation as an investigator, and this is a big case for me. I need your help. And, the first thing I need is for you not to know me."

Now, at the reception, I abandoned Sunnye to her fans and wandered over to a tray of fat red strawberries imported, no doubt at hideous expense, from God-knows-which despot-ridden equatorial nation. "Lose the glasses," I muttered to the ginger-haired conferee dipping a berry into a pot of melted chocolate. "Horn-rims went out with Professor Henry Higgins." The strawberry-eater was six feet tall and lithe like a tiger. The white scar stretching from his eye to his hairline was only partially obscured by the clunky glasses. His name tag read *Prof. Mark Slade, Mount Helen College*. "And," I added, "do you see a single other person here under the age of seventy wearing tweed? With suede elbow patches, no less?"

"So nice to meet you, Professor Pelletier," Professor Slade said. "I've read all your work, of course. And with great admiration. Although I must say I do believe you've over-estimated the role of class binaries in the cultural construction of a robust national identity."

"Slade's" critique was lifted verbatim from a hostile *American Literary History* review of my scholarly book. "You really do your homework, don't you?" I simpered at Dennis, moved on to the seafood bar, and nabbed a plateful of shrimp.

Paul Henshaw, an Enfield rare-book dealer, had backed Sunnye into a paneled alcove. Paul was in his sixties, attractive and grey-haired, and Sunnye seemed to be enjoying the encounter. Trouble was asleep at her feet. In spite of the neat ponytail, Paul was a tough guy, broad-shouldered, heavily muscled, and virile, with a pushed-in nose that at one time had been broken, then poorly set. His shop, Henshaw's Rare and Antiquarian Books, was an Enfield institution. I knew his tales of fabulous book discoveries and heartbreaking misses could be engrossing, but right now he was monopolizing the novelist. I gave him a cordial brush-off, found a small table upon which Sunnye could sign books, brought her a chair, and bullied people into an orderly line. In spite of the purported academic indifference to the commercialized products of popular culture, a number of attendees carried luridly colored copies of *Tough Times*.

My post at Sunnye's side gave me a prime view of the crowd. In the crush around the writer I spotted familiar faces. Claudia Nestor flitted from person to person, greeting newcomers with a high shrill laugh, refilling her wine glass, scowling at the selection of hors d'oeuvres. Nellie Applegate, in a too-long grey dress made from some nubby fabric manufactured exclusively to be sold in second-hand shops, sipped at something colorless and gazed vaguely around the room. Bob Tooey, the little potato-faced researcher from Special Collections, was all dressed up now in a baggy blue suit, waiting in line for Sunnye to sign a bright new copy of *Tough Times*.

Behind Tooey, Rachel Thompson drank red wine in big gulps. She appeared pale and stressed, her dark eyes nervous, her thin lips tight. And no wonder. She had primary responsibility for the library's collection of rare books and manuscripts. The loss of *The Maltese Falcon* manuscript, not to mention all the stolen books, did not place her in a favorable light. To say the least. Her job might even be at risk. And where, after all these thefts from the Enfield holdings, would Rachel find a new job? The academic world is small and news travels fast. Who would hire a librarian who couldn't keep the books on her shelves?

Rachel introduced herself to Sunnye and handed the novelist two copies of *Tough Times*. One for herself, I assumed, and one for the library. I remembered the signed first edition of *Rough Cut* I'd seen in the display case. Had that been stolen along with the *Falcon* manuscript?

Dennis, in the guise of Professor Slade, sidled up to me. "Karen, who's that?" He tilted his wineglass in the direction of a half-open door sequestered in the foyer's paneling. Peggy Briggs stood in the shadow of the door, a bulky manila envelope hugged to her chest. It was an internal mail envelope, the kind with the twist closure and the little viewing holes.

"That's Peggy Briggs, one of my students. Why?"

He didn't answer my question. "Where does that door go?"

"God knows. This old building is riddled with odd doors. It can be like a bad dream. Strange winding corridors. Staircases that lead to walled-off hallways. I've gotten hopelessly lost more than once. But that particular door? To tell the truth, I never even noticed it before."

"Looks like it was designed as a concealed entry." Dennis took a step in Peggy's direction. "Wonder what she's got there?"

"Don't!" I grabbed his sleeve. My student was under enough pressure already.

He pulled away, then turned to me, his expression suddenly so menacing I shivered. "I'm here on an investigation, Karen. Don't get in my way."

I was momentarily stunned. "You're the one who brought me into this."

"Yeah, I did. But I didn't expect you to be obstructive." His scowl brought on a second shiver. He pivoted to stare over at the door where Peggy had stood. It was closed now, outline barely visible in the intricate paneling. My student was nowhere in sight. "Shit!" he said, and strode over to Rachel Thompson. I couldn't hear what he said to her, but I didn't need to. She immediately glanced over at the sequestered door, then they took off together in the direction of the main staircase.

I stood alone and stared after Dennis. Nobody gets away with talking to me like that! No way was I going to cooperate any further with that son-of-a-bitch. He could go back to Lowell and choke to death on Merrimack River fish bones for all I cared.

And, where *did* that door lead, anyhow? Had Peggy gone through it? If so, Rachel and Dennis would surely find her. I sighed; I couldn't mother all my students all the time. Peggy would be fine, and her comings and goings were none of my business anyhow.

The room was stuffy. A few English Department colleagues huddled by the bar. In pursuit of a fresh drink I joined them and stumbled into the middle of a wrangle over the value and purpose of crime fiction. Ned Hilton insisted that Kit Danger's significance lay in the manner in which the character destabilized the subtexts of performative femininity.

Miles Jewell's irate tones cut through Ned's tentative assertion. "Blatant social constructivism, Hilton. Where's the *literary* value? That's what I want to know."

Ned squared his slender shoulders. "Literary aesthetics do not account for the recuperation of heterogeneity from hegemony. What more valuable function can you assign to a text than the inscription of personal agency within repressive social circumstances?"

Miles didn't seem to know the answer to Ned's question. Neither did I.

It was stifling in the crowded foyer. I gave up the wait for a drink, and pushed my way through the crowd to the front door for a breath of air. The big door had an iron frame, inset with thick glass, criss-crossed with hammered grids, and embossed with brass lions. It weighed a zillion tons; not a door that was ever meant to be opened by a woman. I opened it anyhow. Outside, two smokers puffed silently in snow that thickened with the gathering night. Claudia Nestor found me on the threshold. She was wearing black silk, and the eye tic was on automatic pilot.

"Now, Karen, you do remember that at six o'clock promptly you are to escort our guest to dinner at the president's house?"

"Yes, Claudia."

"And make certain that she arrives at the Emerson Hall auditorium at 7:50 precisely...."

"Yes, Claudia." At eight Sunnye was to speak to the conference on the topic of Crime Writing and the Moral Health of the Nation.

"And, you do recall, don't you, that after Sunnye's speech, a few distinguished guests will gather for drinks at Rudolph's."

"Yes, Claudia."

"You may, of course, feel free to join us."

I bit my lip. "Thank you, Claudia."

The evening threatened to go on forever. If the snow kept up, my trip home would be late and long and hellish. Then I would have to scurry back to campus first thing in the morning to give my own talk.

"See you at dinner, Claudia."

I rejoined Sunnye. The crowd around her was thinning. The novelist seemed to be holding her own in a contest of wits with Professor Sally Chenille. Sally was loquacious. No, *loquacious* was too generous a word; Sally suffered from terminal logorrhea. She was blathering on about Kit Danger's "incrimination of patriarchal social practices." The encounter was good for at least ten more minutes.

I still needed a drink. Slipping away to the bar once again, I waited patiently in line. "Vodka and tonic," I told the pony-tailed bartender. "Better make it a double."

"That kind of day?" he asked.

"That kind of day," I agreed. When I turned back, libation in hand, to resume my post at Sunnye Hardcastle's side, the writer and her dog were nowhere in sight.

"Sally, where's Sunnye Hardcastle?" A sudden irrational burst of alarm at Sunnye's disappearance had caused my heart to speed up.

Sally Chenille pivoted toward me, always a tricky move when you're wearing purple suede stiletto heels. "Why ask me?" As usual she was made up in the hues of domestic violence, eyes shadowed in contusion plum, cheeks blushed in blister brown, her stubble of hair a rich infection green. She wore a short skirt and tight jersey in tones of black and blue. The clothes hugged a bone-thin body; I'd once over-heard the custodians complaining that the bathroom next to Sally's office "reeked of puke."

"I'm asking you because you're the last person I saw talking to her," I replied. Then I couldn't resist a dig. "You were, I believe, encouraging her to persevere in her decades-long interrogation of patriarchal social practices."

"That woman!" Sally twisted her bruise-colored lips into what she seemed to think of as seductive petulance. "She's impossible. She just stood there like a lump. No political consciousness. No conversation. You'd think a writer of her sophistication—"

"I need to find Sunnye right away. Do you have any idea where she went?" In my experience, it was difficult for *anyone* to have any conversation when Professor Sally Chenille was in the room.

"Probably off somewhere to take a leak." She pouted at me. "How should I know?" Her gaze slid away from me, and fixed on a spot over my shoulder. I turned, curious about the object of Sally's sudden raptor-like attention. Dennis O'Hanlon, a.k.a. Professor Slade, stood in the corner of the foyer by the concealed door, a wine glass in one hand, the fingers of the other idly tracing the joins in the paneling. Even in his academic-nerd getup, Dennis was all man, and Sally had taken note of that.

"Thanks, Sally," I said. *For nothing.* "I'll look for Sunnye in the bathroom." Of course, that's where she must be. My momentary panic was for nothing. But now it was time to get the conference star on her way to Avery's dinner party.

"Wait! I remember now." My colleague's attention had returned to me. Dennis must have vanished in the crowd. "She went off with some little prick I never saw before. Face like a potato. Body like a toad. What a hot-looking chick like Hardcastle would want with a limp-dick like that…" She let it trail off, predator eyes scanning the room. For Sally, everything was about sex. My colleague was a talk-show-famous advocate of what she called "unplugged" sexuality: indiscriminate erotic activity without regard to genders or numbers. In public. The "public pubic," she famously explained. Professor Chenille fancied herself to be a naughty girl, the Mae West of postmodernist literary criticism. At a recent gathering of the Modern Literature Association, Sally had renounced feminism as sexually repressive and had allied herself with "material fetishism." Her next book would be a study of the garter as it formally normalizes a discourse of invagination in twentieth-century world literature and film.

Hmm. *Face like a potato? Body like a toad?* Sounded like someone I'd met. "Was Potato-face wearing a bad suit?"

"Seventies polyester, big lapels. Must have been from the Goodwill. He was too young to have worn something that god-awful first time round—"

"Thanks for the fashion note, Sally. I'm sure I'll recognize him when I see him."

My gaze swept the library's foyer. Bob Tooey was nowhere to be seen. Nor was Sunnye. No sign of Trouble. It would be easy to overlook either human in this crowd, but you'd think there'd be a visible empty space around the trained attack dog.

I edged past the green-plush chains into the main part of the library. A line of conferees extended out the door of the first-floor women's room, but no one had seen the novelist. I checked the reading room with its twenty-foot ceilings, high, wide windows and massive tables laid out in parallel rows. Sunnye wasn't there. The periodicals room held periodicals and a half-dozen sleepy-eyed readers. I peered into the reference room. Students hunched over computer monitors. No Sunnye.

Claudia jumped me when I re-entered the foyer. She seemed close to hysterics. "Karen, for God's sake, what are you doing here? Sunnye's supposed to be at the president's house in five minutes, and it's way the hell across campus!" The twitch in her right eye had gone into hyperdrive.

I held up a hand. "Take it easy, Claudia. I'll find her."

"You'll *find* her? She's *lost*?" People were getting ready to leave the reception now, shrugging into coats, tugging on gloves, pulling wool scarves tight against the cold and snow. "Sunnye Hardcastle's *lost*?" Claudia's wail brought a momentary halt to all activity.

I smiled reassuringly at colleagues and conferees, clasped Claudia by the elbow, and pushed through double glass doors into a darkened library office, turning on the overhead lights at the switch. "For God's sake, Claudia, settle down!" My hand still on her arm, I could feel my charge begin to quiver. The quiver turned into a full-blown shaking.

"Lost," Claudia whimpered. "Sunnye Hardcastle is lost. Our guest speaker—"

"Claudia, stop that!" I had to resist the urge to shake her. I'd never seen anyone in quite this shape. She needed help, but could I leave her alone while I went to get it?

Rachel Thompson shoved open the door. "Karen? Claudia? How'd you get in here? This room is supposed to be locked."

"Rachel," I said, thrilled to see her, "Claudia is a little… ah…stressed. Could you get a glass of water?"

Rachel took in the situation at a glance. "Water's not gonna do it." She leaned over the conference director. "Claudia," she said, sharply.

Claudia looked at her blankly. "Lost…." Her breaths had begun to come in thick, short gasps.

Rachel slid her gaze over to me. I spread my hands. She turned back, speaking in slow, distinct tones. "Claudia, do you have any medication for this…this…er…stress?"

The empty look again. The flutter, catch, fixed stare.

Rachel shrugged, reached into the macramé bag she carried slung across her chest, pulled out a prescription bottle, and shook out a couple of salmon-colored pills. "Xanax," she said. "Don't leave home without it."

It was a full twenty minutes before Claudia stopped shaking. Then Rachel took her to the librarian's lounge to lie down. Under a cloud of doom, I resumed my search for Sunnye. A missing novelist, a colleague with a panic attack. What next?

The reception was all but over. A few conferees—most likely grad students on limited budgets—lingered at the hors d'oeuvres table, making a full meal out of the remnants of the feast. As I passed, a tall young woman in a fringed black silk shawl, her dark gold hair clasped back with a scarlet clip, systematically worked her way through the remaining spanakopita as she lectured her rib-chewing male companion on the feminist politics of meat. A skinny guy in black munching contentedly on a chicken wing fingered the speaker's silk wrap slyly. "What about this shawl, Dara? Wouldn't you say it implicates you in a particularly egregious form of species-ism, the imperialist appropriation of silkworm production?"

Then I heard Sunnye Hardcastle's voice. "Karen," she called.

I turned sharply. Sunnye entered through the sequestered door in the foyer's paneling, Trouble at her heels.

"Sunnye, where have you been?" I inquired. "I've been looking everywhere for you."

"Oh, I had to...to use the bathroom," she said, with an un-Hardcastle-like delicacy. "There was a line at the one on this floor, so I...looked around."

I checked my watch. It had been over a half hour since I'd last seen her.

She raised her chin, tightened her lips. "Something didn't agree with me."

"Ah," I said, light dawning. "Too bad." Must have been the mussels. "I hope you're all right now. We're more than fashionably late for the president's dinner."

Chapter Ten

All through the rack of lamb, polenta, and asparagus, which we ate off gold-monogrammed china in the president's dining room, I kept checking the door for Claudia, but she remained absent. Under ordinary circumstances even an angry mob couldn't have kept Claudia Nestor away from dinner at the president's house. Where was she? Who would run the conference if she had a total breakdown?

The room was elegant, as befitted the occupant of the house: high-ceilinged, wallpapered in a vaguely colonial print, furnished with Chippendale table and chairs. An arrangement of iris and white forsythia defied the wintry message of the snowstorm that raged outside. Neither the elegant decor nor the bright flowers served to salve the uneasiness Claudia's continued absence caused me.

At the head of the table, Avery, as usual, was charming, but tonight he hosted the party alone. According to the college buzz, his wife Liz hadn't been seen around town for a couple of weeks. For eleven days, to be precise, but who's counting? She may simply have been indulging herself in a solo winter cruise; I know nothing about the vacation practices of the rich.

Sunnye, at his side, laughed at Avery's witticisms and ate heartily, which surprised me, given her usual dour demeanor and her earlier indisposition. Trouble gnawed on a lamb rib. Once or twice Avery glanced down at the big animal by his feet, concerned either about his ankles or his antique Persian rug.

Aside from Sunnye, the literary guests included Amelia Smith, who wrote cozy murder mysteries with embroidery themes—the Stitch in Crime series—and Eloise Pickwick, who composed academic novels so arch and erudite I was amazed she had more than a dozen readers to her name.

Women's Studies was represented by Harriet Person, the Chair, and Rex Hunter, newest member of the department. Rex was qualified for the women's studies position because he was a lesbian trapped in a male body. At least so he'd informed us during his job interview. I'd laughed, thinking he was joking, then quickly had to turn the guffaw into a hacking cough when I realized he was dead serious. Since Rex's unique sexual orientation mandated that he sleep with women, I had difficulty thinking of him as anything other than heterosexual. Or, perhaps, opportunistic, since Sally Chenille, who had chaired the hiring committee, was a noted theorist of male lesbianism.

Harriet sat next to Avery, on the other side from Sunnye. She was tall, slender and austere, her thick dark hair with its widening silver streak cut in a severe, almost geometric wedge. Tonight she wore a black leather suit with a straight short skirt, black stockings and black-laced pumps with clunky heels. Heavy silver parrots dangled from her earlobes. She sipped her pinot noir and addressed Sunnye. "As a woman author suppressed by the cultural strictures of patriarchal capitalism, do you find murder provides you with a transgressive symbol system for an anti-essentialist social critique?"

Sunnye stared at her. "Murder?" she queried. "Are you asking me if I condone *murder*?"

"Only as a mode of hermeneutical rhetoric."

The novelist turned abruptly to me. "What's she talking about?"

I translated. "I believe she's asking if you write about murder in order to protest the male-dominated power structures of modern life."

She pursed her lips, annoyed. "Why doesn't she say that?"

I shrugged.

"No," she said to the Women's Studies chair. "I write about murder in order to tell a good story. Oh, and to make some money. Patriarchal capitalism has been very generous to me."

Harriet, ever-vigilant in ferreting out political deviance, narrowed her eyes. "Are you claiming complicity in oppressive social practices?"

Sunnye's dark eyes glinted in the light from the chandelier. "I'm claiming that I tell stories people want to hear, and they pay me well for it."

You go, girl, I thought, then glanced over at Avery. He was sitting back in his chair with a half-smile on his patrician face, enjoying the skirmish.

To diffuse the escalating antagonism, I turned to Amelia Smith, our "cozy" author. "And you, Ms. Smith? Why do you write murder mysteries?"

Amelia Smith was in her sixties and pretty, with grey hair frizzed out in a wild halo around her cherubic face. "Do call me Amelia, Karen. Oh, my. Now let's see? Why do I write mysteries? I guess I'd have to agree with Sunnye. I write mysteries in order to tell a good story and make some money." She glanced across the table at Eloise Pickwick. "How about you, Eloise?"

Eloise frowned, professorially. She was tall, thin, and precise, and accentuated her remarks with emphatic hand gestures. "The narrative momentum of the mystery genre with its focus on moral violation, secrecy, disclosure, and ultimate justice provides a compelling readerly experience that demands repetitive satisfaction."

"In other words," Avery said, blue eyes crinkled with amusement, "you write to tell a good story and make some money."

"Precisely," Eloise Pickwick agreed, making a neat little tent with her fingertips.

Harriet Person devoted herself to deconstructing her rack of lamb.

Dinner had been served efficiently by Stephanie Abrams, who proved as capable a waitress as she was a student. Seated facing the kitchen, I half consciously followed her movements. Briefly my attention was captured by a tableau in the kitchen doorway: Stephanie in her server's whites, about to enter the dining room with a tray of crème brulée, was halted by a hand grasping her arm. She disappeared back into the kitchen with the tray, but not before I caught a glimpse of Peggy Briggs speaking to her urgently. How'd Peggy get there? She must have come in through the back door. Then a phone rang, and in a moment Stephanie returned, bent over me, and whispered.

"Professor Pelletier, you have a call. It's from Ms. Thompson. You know, that librarian."

I followed Stephanie into the large yellow kitchen with its restaurant-size gas and wood-burning stove and huge Sub-Zero refrigerator, and picked up the cordless phone on the counter. No sign of Peggy.

"Karen," Rachel's voice said, broken up on what must have been a cell phone, "Claudia went home. She wanted me to ask you to make her apologies to Sunnye and Avery."

"How was she?"

A brief silence. "Not good."

"Should we expect her in the morning?"

Another silence. "I couldn't say, Karen. But I wouldn't count on it."

I left most of my dessert on the plate, and got Sunnye to Emerson Hall with seconds to spare. She spoke well, as I knew she would. The audience's response was enthusiastic. Afterwards the distinguished company at Rudolph's was witty and articulate. The drinks were potent. Time flew by. Claudia did not show up. Neither did she answer her phone the four times I called.

Halfway through the party I felt a hand on my arm, and Dennis slid onto the barstool beside me as smoothly as if he hadn't just bullied me in the library. His ginger-blond curls were damp with melting snowflakes. "Karen, sweetheart, can we get out of here? Go someplace where we can talk?"

I gave him slit eyes. "Sweetheart?"

He smiled like a repentant Satan. "My way of apologizing, Karen. I was rude, but I had my reasons. Listen, we can't talk here. These people have gotta keep thinking I'm just another conference-goer."

I took a ten from my wallet and slid it over the bar. All right. He wanted to get away from academic conferees. I'd take him to Moccio's, where the hardcore student boozers drink. The scumbag should feel right at home there.

"Listen, Karen, I understand you're pissed, and I don't blame you," Dennis said, as we walked down Field Street, deserted now in the falling snow. "Let me explain. I'm used to working on my own. Sometimes my...my people skills are a little lacking. When I saw that girl with that thick envelope, I thought immediately about the stolen manuscript. I had to go after her. I *had* to. Never did find her, but it turns out she was a library worker. Student aide or something like that. So, no big deal after all."

"She's my student. She has it rough. I didn't want you to...hassle her."

"Sorry about that. And sorry about growling at you before. Just write it off to me being a crude mill-town kinda guy." There was the fallen-angel smile again. *Crude mill-town guy,* my foot. But my irritation was waning. Dennis's charm was irresistible. I began looking forward to our tête-à-tête, even at the lowest dive in town.

It was only a three-minute walk from Rudolph's, but Moccio's was a different world. The place stank of cigarettes and stale beer. Neon signs threw ghastly hues on already ghastly faces. While Dennis ordered drinks at the bar, I sat at a table as far away from it as I could get. The stained-oak surface was sticky with the residue of last week's drinks. I swiped at it with a napkin. The thin paper bonded to the gunk.

Dennis carried over two sweating bottles, dangling them by the necks. No glasses. I watched him approach: In spite of the academic garb, he really did look right at home in Moccio's. It had something to do with the white scar knife-straight across his temple, the easy way he walked, on the balls of his feet, as if ready to spring. You can take the boy off the street, but you can never get the street out of the boy. You can dress up a jungle cat, but he never really leaves the jungle.

Dennis told me about his evening. Rachel had given him a brief tour of Special Collections: the reading room, the librarians' offices, the stacks. "It's a maze down there—corridors, cul-de-sacs, huge, open rooms crammed with books. A vault that must have been manufactured in 1892. Oh, yeah, the place is alarmed, but it's a security nightmare, anyhow. A shitload of potential access points. I'll have to ask Mitchell for a diagram—electrical wiring, heating systems, book elevators." Dennis drank beer.

"You mean this is your first look at the place?"

"Yeah, well…" The Lowell accent became more pronounced. "Yaw distinguished president couldn't make up his mind about whethah or not The College should do anything as crass as dealing with a common shamus." The acid in his words could have eaten through a junkyard fence. "Especially one from the othah side of the tracks."

"Avery's not so bad."

He glared at me from under furrowed eyebrows. "Give me a break. The man's a platinum-plated snob. But so's the college's money—platinum-plated, I mean. So, on my own I put in a few hours on the Internet."

"Doing what?"

"Oh," he said, vaguely, "there are data bases, if you know where to look. I knew Mitchell would call back. I was ready for him."

I laughed. "Dennis O'Hanlon, a Sam Spade for the twenty-first century. How'd you get into this business anyhow?"

He shrugged. "Tried a little of this, a little of that. Couple of years as a Boston cop...."

"Really."

"Didn't work."

"You never were any good at taking orders."

"Right."

"Ninth-grade English. Mr. Mulford. You told him he could take his sentence diagram and shove it up his ass with a razor blade."

"Is that what I said?"

"He slugged you. The guy must have been twice your size."

"I hit him back, though. Right? Puny as I was."

"That was smart. Got you kicked out of school, didn't it?"

"Sure did." He laughed ruefully. "After that I was more cautious. It was cold out and the only place I had to go was home."

"Ouch."

"Yeah." He tipped the bottle back, drank the last of his brew. "But, you know, thinking back, it was all good training. Life handed me a habit of looking out for myself."

"A habit of...observation," I agreed. "Wariness. Very useful in the academic world, too."

"A habit of observation,'" he repeated slowly, as if trying the words on his tongue. "And a certain set of suspicions, too. Nothing is ever what it seems to be."

"Well," I said, only partially agreeing, "*sometimes* things are not what they seem to be."

"*Never*. More beer, Karen?"

"Sure." He went and got it, plopped mine in front of me. I picked it up, then set the bottle back on the table without sipping from it. "You know, I shouldn't do this, Dennis. I've got to drive home. One more drink, and I'll be over the limit."

"Give it here," he said. I edged the bottle across the sticky table toward him. He guzzled his own beer, then started on mine. His eyes began to develop the meditative inward gaze of the mildly sloshed. "You know, Karen, I can't forgive myself for going off on you the way I did earlier. By nature I'm pretty much a loner, and I do a loner's job. It gets me away from trusting people. But the last thing I want to do is put you off."

"It's okay, Denny. I understand." The air in Moccio's was one part oxygen to three parts beer fumes. Distilled with Dennis's liquid-green gaze, it was intoxicating. Three hours earlier I had been ready to clobber this guy. But, now…those eyes. And here was someone with whom I had shared twin traumas: a deprived childhood and an American public high school. I reached over and patted the back of his hand. "After all, what are old friends for."

He caught my hand and held it. My breath tightened in my ribs. A thrill ran through my body. "Karen," he said, gazing into my eyes, "Listen, sweetheart, tell me, are you… seeing anyone?"

For a millisecond I couldn't remember whether I was or not. Then Charlie's plain honest face swam to the front of my addled consciousness. "I…am."

Although I didn't pull my hand away, Dennis gave it a squeeze, then slowly, and reluctantly, I thought, he let it go. "Sometimes I feel such a weight of loneliness," he said, smiling wistfully, "and you're so…I think we could…But I wouldn't want to screw up anything for you."

"No, of course not," I replied, thinking, not for the first time, what an unnatural thing monogamy is. "Of course not," I repeated. "But," I sighed, "you know, it's getting late. Maybe we better go."

He held my coat like the Victorian gentleman civilized manners demanded, and we left the bar. Six inches of snowfall had turned the town into a pristine fairyland, and the storm showed no signs of abating. The chill air eased in at my collar despite the wool scarf. I shivered. We parted at the corner, Dennis turning toward the Enfield Inn, me toward campus and my no-doubt snow-buried car. I thought about having to dig it out. I thought about the long drive home—and the long drive back to Enfield again in the morning. I thought about Dennis, warm and snug at the Enfield Inn. I thought…. Then I remembered. "What about that door?" I called after him.

He turned back. "What door?"

"The one Peggy used."

"Oh, that. Just a service stairs. Goes into the stacks."

Chapter Eleven

I forgot to set the alarm clock, overslept, then hustled through a shower and into a grey wool pant suit. The snow had stopped sometime before dawn, and the roads were passable. On campus snow blowers roared and shovels scraped against concrete as the grounds crew cleared the walkways. A massive snowball battle on the quad pitted female students against male. The men occupied a lopsided snow fort in the center of the snowy quad. The women, led by a small, fierce black girl in a red parka, had launched a major offensive. I watched, amused, as I climbed the wide granite stairs to Emerson Hall behind two other conference stragglers.

Suddenly, without a word of warning, a blow on the back of my head slammed me straight into the closing door. What the hell? Hard-packed snow shattered around my shoulders and fell with a soft whomp to the newly shoveled stairs. Stunned, then angry, I spun around. Claudia Nestor was packing another hardball, ready for a second assault. I glared at her. She paused, stared at me blankly, then, unexpectedly, giggled and whipped the missile directly into the center of the student melee. Someone yelped as the snowball hit home; the conference director had a powerful arm.

At least Claudia had shown up in time to introduce the morning's panelists. Last night she'd been in meltdown; this morning she was high as a kite. On their own, the little pink pills Rachel had given her couldn't possibly account for this euphoria. She made her opening remarks with a manic flippancy that set a bizarre tone for the scholarly presentations.

The lecture hall was tiered, with half-circle rows of seats. My hand gave a slight tremor as I bent the microphone toward me. The hundred scholars didn't faze me, but Sunnye Hardcastle did. She was seated in the third-row center-aisle seat, with Dennis O'Hanlon one seat over behind her. Both Sunnye and Dennis were pros when it came to dealing with crime— more specifically, the P.I. writer, and the P.I. Their presence made me feel like a fraud. Who was I to speculate about murder in history? But then, in my own way, teasing life from the dry bones of historical texts, I was a pro, too. *A habit of observation*, I recalled. *A certain set of suspicions.* I took a deep breath, cleared my throat, and opened my mouth. Words came out. They seemed to make sense. At least people weren't squirming in their seats. Greg Samoorian gave me a thumbs-up from front-row center where he sat next to Jill Greenberg. Earlene Johnson smiled encouragingly from the fourth row. Rex Hunter watched me inscrutably from his seat next to Harriet Person. A dozen or so students clumped together toward the back, listening intently. Avery Mitchell wandered in late.

I settled into the rhythm of my talk. Sunnye took notes, much to my surprise. Even Dennis seemed interested, although it was hard to tell just exactly what he was interested in. Halfway through, I realized I was enjoying myself.

As I glanced up from the final page and out over the audience, I noted a face staring at me from the back of the auditorium, a face that didn't belong in this academic setting. A familiar face, but set on an unfamiliar body. Who was it? I squinted; I'd left my glasses in my jacket pocket. Could it be Charlie's partner, Felicity Schultz? I concluded my talk: "Thus nineteenth-century working-class discourse on homicide

re-envisions the class hierarchies of patriarchal power structures, but, given cultural biases, leaves intact the oppressive
hermeneutics of race and sex. With such characters as Ned
Buntline and 'Old Sleuth,' the iconic tough-guy sleuth was
born in nineteenth-century American fiction for the masses.
But it wasn't until the late twentieth century that racial and
gender barriers became sufficiently permeable for characters
such as Walter Mosley's Easy Rawlins and Sunnye Hardcastle's
Kit Danger to flourish in the popular imagination.

"Thank you."

The applause seemed genuine, but I wasn't paying much
attention. The familiar face in the back of the room was giving
me the familiar eye. *What the heck?* Then a hand rose in a
peremptory gesture: *Come.* Sergeant Felicity Schultz of the
Massachusetts State Police wanted me, and wanted me *now*.
Schultz was eight months pregnant with what from the size
of her looked to be quintuplets, but was, I knew, just a single
boy. She was so big, it was a wonder she could still walk. But
what was this homicide cop doing here in the middle of a
very tame scholarly panel at the beginning of an equally tame
academic conference?

Suddenly, my heart stopped. Had something happened
to Charlie? Was Schultz here to break the news? Abruptly
nodding my apologies to the other members of the Murder
in History panel, I descended the steps from the podium
and hurried down the narrow side aisle to where she waited.
The sergeant gripped me by the elbow and hustled me out
into the hall. Shultz was wearing a green gabardine pup tent,
and her fingers, normally short and stubby, had swollen to
the size of kumquats.

"Charlie?" I queried, anxiously.

"Not here yet," she replied.

Huh? What would Charlie be doing here? "He's okay?"

"Of course, he's okay. It's just that he was way the hell
down in Springfield when the call came in."

"The call? What call?"

Schultz shot a narrow cop look at a student who was kicking a lobby vending machine, trying to get it to release his soda. Then she turned back to me. "The call about the body in the library."

I stared down at the pale figure sprawled awkwardly between the PR and the PS sections of the closed stacks. There was no blood, no particular sign of violence. Just the twisted body in that awful blue suit lying snug against the rows of shelves, its head bent at an unnatural angle against PS / 3515 /.A34. A half-dozen volumes lay toppled open around him.

Long aisles stretched across the cavernous, windowless room. From twelve-foot ceilings, fluorescent tubes cast anemic light on ecru walls and scarred oak shelves. Countless books in the brown leather bindings of bygone centuries were lined up in rows, spines straight. A set of library steps on wheels blocked the aisle at an oblique angle to the shelves. It looked as if it had skittered there under some propulsive force. Had the dead man fallen? Had he been shoved?

Two town cops stood near the body, shifting from one foot to another. The heavy bald man gripped the butt of his gun, as if a killer might materialize at any second, weapon drawn. The short, young guy bit his thumbnail, then jammed his hands deep in his uniform pockets. A uniformed trooper interviewed two college security guards while his partner strung yellow crime-scene tape.

"His name is Bob Tooey," I said, after a moment of shocked silence. "What happened to him?"

"That's what they said—Tooey. What do you know about Mr. Tooey?" Schultz was good at evasion.

"Not much. He's a researcher here, on leave from some community college…someplace out in the mid-west. How did this happen?" I was in that blank state of emotional denial that follows any horrific event. Even my tongue was numb.

"Lake Superior College?"

"I think that's it. How'd he die?"

"Too soon to tell. So, you ever talk to him, this…Tooey?" She took a notebook from the pocket of her voluminous green dress.

"No.…well, yes. Once. Was he…murdered?" I couldn't take my eyes off the sprawling body. By the time I'd arrived at the coffee hour in the Emerson Hall lobby earlier that morning, the only pastries left were prune Danish. Now I felt the sour bile of half-digested prune rise into my throat.

"Can't say yet. What'd you talk about?"

I swallowed. "For God's sake, Schultz, we talked about the weather! He told me it was going to snow! What the hell happened to the man?"

Schultz gazed at me, her eyes narrowed. "You're looking kind of punky, Karen. Let's get you away from this…Mr. Tooey." Her kumquats gripped my elbow, and she steered me toward a door in the wall.

"Get *me* away?" I shook her hand off my arm. Then I relented, took her hand and held it for a minute. "What about you? You're the one who's about to go into labor any second. What're you doing here, anyhow?" I cast a sidelong glance at the pathetic corpse. "This can't be good for the baby."

"The baby doesn't know anything about it." She opened the door and we walked directly from the stacks into Rachel Thompson's empty office. Where was Rachel anyhow with all this excitement happening on her turf? She should be right here in the center of it. Schultz lowered her bulk into the desk chair. Then she untied the laces of her brown leather boots and eased them off. Her feet in green socks had the shape and definition of over-ripe zucchini. "And if you think I'd give those boys in there," she tilted her head toward the big room behind the door, "the satisfaction of having to leave the job one second before I pop with this kid, you're not the feminist I thought you were. Ooof!" Her hand flew to her swollen belly.

"Felicity? Are you—"

"It's nothing. He kicked me, is all." She laughed. "He's gonna be a soccer player, the little bruiser."

A voice outside said, "It's right in here, Lieutenant." The office door opened. Charlie Piotrowski walked in. He stopped short at the sight of me and frowned. "Karen! What the hell are you doing here?"

I opened my mouth to respond, but Felicity Schultz stuffed her feet back into her boots and intervened.

"My call, boss," she said, pushing herself up from the chair. "Karen's the only one we really know here, and there's some question about the I.D. on this victim."

I furrowed my forehead at her. First I'd heard of it.

"Thought she might be able to tell us for sure who he is." She placed both hands on the small of her back and stretched to ease the strain. "Now, what I'm thinking is this isn't necessarily a homicide. Guy fell off a…" she glanced at me, "whatyacallit?"

I shrugged. "A set of rolling library steps—you know, with the little wheels."

Intent on Schultz's report, Charlie nodded without glancing over at me.

"So, I'm thinking suspicious death. Could be it's an accident, but there's a couple of odd things we gotta look into, just in case."

"Yeah?"

"I mean, number one, what was the guy doing here in the first place? He's been dead, oh, I'd say maybe five, six hours. That puts it in the middle of the night."

I broke in. "And how'd he get in, anyhow? It's a restricted area, and he's not a library employee. No way he had permission, let alone a key."

"Hmm." Charlie finally looked at me.

"Plus, number two," Schultz continued, "there's some question about his identity."

"He's—he was—Bob Tooey," I interjected. "I told you that."

She ignored me. "So, maybe the steps did just slip out from under him, or maybe—"

"Not likely," I said. "Library steps are made to be stable. Look…." I could see a set of steps out in the reading room. I pulled them toward us, and they rolled smoothly on their little wheels. Then I climbed onto the first step. We heard a click as my weight activated a locking device and the steps became immobile.

Schultz gave a little push; the steps held firm under me.

"No way these babies are going to skitter across the floor with anyone on them," Charlie said. "You're right, Sergeant. We've gotta treat this as a suspicious death, possible homicide, until we find evidence otherwise."

My heart sank. Was there a killer among us, here, in the library? A place I considered to be sacred space.

"So, Schultz, who've you talked to so far?"

"No one, really. We haven't located the head librarian for this department, yet…the, ah, curator. And the woman at the desk…" She glanced down at her notebook. "Ah, Nellie Applegate…I gotta say it, she's useless. Just whimpers on and on about not being in charge. A student worker found the body first thing this morning and came running out to this Applegate woman, who went into some kind of meltdown, so the student called Security and waited around—"

"A student? What student?" I queried.

Schultz checked her notebook again. "Briggs, Margaret."

"Oh, God, no, not Peggy! Not after all she's been through!" I was beginning to get a truly sick feeling.

"Peggy…Briggs?" Charlie's eyes slid toward me. "You know a Peggy Briggs?"

"She's my student."

"Kinda plain? Brown hair? Heavy set? About…let's see… she'd be about thirty now?" He stared at me, quizzically.

I nodded.

"Peggy's a student here?" He beamed. "Well…good for her!"

"*You* know Peggy Briggs?"

"She was involved in a case…." He let it trail off.

"Her sister."

"She told you about it, huh? She must really trust you. You know, I always thought Peggy had what it took. I'm glad she got her act together—"

"Ahem," Schultz interjected. "We have a possible homicide just the other side of this door."

"Right, Schultz." He turned to her, expression vanishing from his face like a drawing from an Etch-a-Sketch. "So, give me the whole story."

Peggy had found the body shortly after nine and had identified it as that of a regular researcher in Special Collections. The name in the sign-in book was Bob Tooey, just as Nellie had told me weeks before. Schultz had retrieved his wallet, a cheap imitation alligator trifold with curling edges. The picture on the Lake Superior Community College faculty identification card verified that he was Professor Bob Tooey of the English Department. He also had a Boston Public Library card in the name of Bob Tooey. But according to his driver's license, he was Elwood Munro of Chesterfield, Massachusetts, and the photo on his license confirmed that. He had credit cards as both Bob Tooey and Elwood Munro. A man with two names: odd.

"Get someone on the Internet, *toot sweet*," Charlie ordered Schultz, "and see if we can pin this bird down. And get…her…"

he cocked his thumb at me and scowled at his sergeant, "the hell out of here. I gotta take a look at the body."

"Don't worry about me, Lieutenant," I replied, stung that I had suddenly become a *her*, not *Karen*, who just night before last had been his *hot little*—er, his significant other. "The last thing I want…Lieutenant…" I said, haughtily, "is to go back in there." I shuddered. "I'll get myself out of here, thank you both. If you want me, I'll be…" And then I paused, because I didn't know where I would be. Back at the conference fielding questions about murder in history with that poor, pale corpse so fresh in my mind?

Charlie stopped short, registered the brusqueness of my tone, winced, then came over to me and squeezed my shoulder with his big hand. "Sorry, Karen. Don't get pissed, okay? I get carried away. It's just that I don't want you anywhere near this ugliness. I mean…" He glanced over at Schultz, who was conspicuously absorbed in tying her leather bootlaces. This was not an easy task, given the size of the belly over which she had to bend. "You gave us some useful stuff. But, you didn't know this guy, right? You don't have any involvement here, right? I really want you out of it. You do understand, don't you? I worry about you." He looked so anxious that I had to smile at him. He let out his breath in a relieved huff. "We okay?"

I nodded.

"Good." He glanced over at his sergeant again, then patted my shoulder. "Now you go back to your conference—that's where you are, right? At that conference? And just behave as if nothing had happened."

"But people will know something's wrong. There are police cars—"

"We'll make an announcement as soon as things get sorted out over here and we talk to the college authorities. You—just—go." He gave me a gentle push in the direction of the door. "And I'll see you later. Okay?"

"But—" I suddenly remembered that I'd seen the victim in the library the previous evening at the Hardcastle reception.

"Schultz, can I give you a hand with that?" Charlie bent and tackled one of Schultz's bootlaces with the aplomb of a professional shoe salesman. He was dismissing me.

Oh, well, I'd tell him later. He'd hear about Tooey's presence from a hundred other reception attendees, anyhow.

I climbed the stairs and pushed through the glass-and-iron front doors, making my way through a cluster of students gawking from the library steps. "Sweet Jesus, look at that!" gasped a tall thin blond guy in a red-and-blue parka. A crime scene van had pulled up in front of the building, joining an ambulance, a half-dozen police patrol cars, Charlie's red Jeep, and two other haphazardly parked unmarked cars. "You think somebody's dead in there?" Technicians, a man and a woman in grey coveralls, began unloading ominous-looking steel cases from the rear of the van. A buzz of speculation spread through the crowd of students. It wouldn't be long before the news whizzed across the snowy campus and reached the conferees. Then an actual homicide investigation would intrude into the world of academic make-believe.

Chapter Twelve

Back in Emerson, I peered into lecture halls. The Postmodern Detective and the Demise of Evidence had attracted a serious, middle-aged audience. The group at Death and Deviance: The Aesthetics of Sexual Violence was young and stylish. A handful of aging feminists attended Mommy and Me: Domestic Ideology and the Rise of the Housewife Sleuth. None of the topics appealed to me. I headed for the women's room.

It was a nineteen-thirties bathroom, immaculately maintained. The taps were chrome with white ceramic hot-and-cold buttons centered in four-prong handles. Miniature black-and-white tiles formed an octagonal pattern on the floor. Hospital-green blocks topped by a black border mounted the wall beneath a long beveled mirror. A faint scent of face powder and cashmere sweaters lingered ghost-like in the air. In front of the mirror, Sunnye Hardcastle was applying bright-red lipstick. Trouble skulked under a pedestal sink. As the door slammed behind me, the big dog raised a lip, displaying efficient teeth.

The novelist must have had built-in radar for crime. "Did you hear sirens, Karen? Sounds like something's going on out there."

I closed the door to the stall and spoke from behind it. "There were a couple of police cars over by the library." I was stunned and disoriented by what I'd seen, and mindful of Charlie's charge to keep it to myself.

"What? Some kid have an overdue book?" The words were tight, as if she still had her lips stretched for cosmetic application.

It didn't require a response, and I didn't give one. The click of the lipstick closing announced the completion of Sunnye's toilette. When I came out of the stall, she was standing with her hand on the doorknob, deep in thought. Trouble bared an eloquent fang. The snarl came with a deep, low rumble. Sunnye jerked at his leash, and he subsided.

"You particularly interested in Death and Deviance, Karen? If not, I'd like to buy you a cup of coffee somewhere away from…this scene." She gestured toward the hallway and the lecture halls beyond. "Most of what I heard this morning was total crap, but I really liked your talk. I have a paying proposition for you."

In light of Amanda's upcoming grad-school expenses, the word *paying* rang with a bell-like resonance. "Bread & Roses," I said. "It's right across the street." For at least thirty seconds, I forgot poor Mr. Tooey-Munro and all the shock and suspicion his death was about to let loose on an unsuspecting campus community.

"Let's go," Sunnye replied. She opened the door. Trouble led the way.

The town roads were not as well plowed as those on campus, and, having jaywalked across Field Street, we clambered over a three-foot heap of snow to get onto the sidewalk. In wool-and-down-garbed Enfield, my black-leather-clad companion with her big Rottweiler drew immediate glances, then recognition. We were stopped twice for autographs on campus and once on the sidewalk in front of the coffee shop. "Let's get a table in back, so people will leave us alone," she said, once we'd purchased coffee in tall white mugs. On the bentwood ice-cream chair, she positioned herself with her back to the room. Trouble prostrated himself at her feet. Through plate glass I had a view of the campus entrance gate. A convoy of three state-police patrol cars entered, lights flashing, sirens doused. Two coffee-drinkers with Banana Republic shopping bags abruptly ceased talking and stared out the window, gaping at the patrol cars as they turned up the library road.

Then Sophia Warzek, the Bread & Roses baker and my former student, came out from behind the counter and approached us. She smelled of vanilla and almonds. Her pale hair was pulled back with a thin black ribbon, her blue eyes alight with curiosity. "What's going on over there?"

Sunnye snatched up black-framed glasses and twisted in her chair, just in time to glimpse the last of the police cars. "Whoa," she said, "I knew something was coming down."

I told Sunnye and Sophia about Tooey's death; the news would be all over town in an hour or two anyhow. The name meant nothing to either of them. But, then, suddenly, I recalled Sally Chenille's account of Sunnye's conversation with "Potato Face." I paused, undecided about whether or not to inform the writer she'd actually been talking to the victim.

But Sunnye was in full novelistic mode, fascinated by the story of murder in the stacks. "Good God," she said, "I have a homicidal imagination, as you know, but I couldn't have dreamed this one up." She tipped her glasses down on her nose and gazed at me over the rims. "This is out of my ball-park—it's so damn Agatha Christie. But…" Her eyes narrowed. Her right forefinger twitched on the ceramic cup handle. Trouble growled. For one brief moment I thought I was taking a mid-morning coffee break with Kit Danger.

"Hey, Sophie," came a whoop from behind the counter. "The oven!"

"Yikes!" Sophia hastened back to the kitchen. The acrid smell of burnt scones wafted through the air.

I was thinking about how, at least according to Sally Chenille, Sunnye had gone off somewhere on her own last night with the victim, Bob Tooey.

News of a death in the stacks began circulating during the conference lunch hour. Conferees were shocked, then titillated, by the delicious irony of a homicide (because what else could it be with all those cop cars—and a crime-scene van!) during a crime fiction conference. Much nervous repartee was bandied back and forth over the Faculty Commons' grilled chicken and Caesar salad.

Claudia Nestor joined me at a corner table, her tray loaded with a mish-mosh of vegetarian selections. "Did you hear anything about a death in the library?" she asked. Her eyes were wide and scatty.

I nodded, solemnly.

"It's just terrible. Terrible." The stress was back in her face again, muscles tight, lips thin. "Why do these things always happen to me?" The left eye twitched.

"To you?"

"Do you think they might cancel the conference? I've been trying to get Avery Mitchell for over an hour, but he's not taking calls."

I sighed. Yes, of course, it was all directed at her. "I don't know why they would, Claudia," I replied. "It's not as if the death had anything to do with the conference. The...er...victim wasn't a participant, was he?"

"What was his name? I've been working on this thing so long, I think I've got the registration list memorized."

I told her.

"Bob Tooey? Robert Tooey? No, doesn't ring a bell. So, Karen, you think we should just plan on going ahead?"

I shrugged. "It isn't even certain that it's homicide. He looked as if—"

Her fork halted, a cube of tofu halfway to her mouth. "How do you know what he looked like?"

"Ah, someone told me," I said. "It looks as if he might simply have fallen—"

"Oh, well, in that case—"

A deep voice interrupted us. "May I join you?" Dennis O'Hanlon was still in undercover-scholar garb, only today he had taken some fashion tips from fellow conferees: grey jacket, black sweater, black jeans. A hot-looking Young Turk of a professor. He wasn't wearing his nametag, however, and I couldn't recall his scholarly alias. "Oh, hello, Professor, er…"

"Mark Slade," he replied, sliding his tray onto the table, retrieving his tag from a breast pocket, and sticking it to his lapel. "We spoke last evening at the reception." He'd chosen the blackened Cajun catfish special with rice and beans. It smelled…fishy. I pushed away my turkey on white, the least offensive lunch available. After what I'd seen that morning, I wouldn't be able to eat for a while.

"Yes, I recall our conversation, Professor…Slade." Dennis had the kind of eyes that saw everything and expressed very little. "And you work on…?" I couldn't resist baiting him.

"The public execution as performance art," he replied, without missing a beat.

Claudia leaned across the table, hand extended. "I'm Claudia Nestor, conference director. It's nice to meet you, Professor Slade, but…" she puckered her brow, "…I don't recall the name—or your topic—from the registration list."

"On-site registration." The ersatz professor shook her hand and grinned. "Didn't know until the last minute if I could get away or not." His green eyes crinkled. "These four-course teaching loads are hell."

"Mount Helen College?" Claudia persisted, studying his name tag. "Do you know June Landow in Women's Studies?"

"Vaguely," he replied. "I'm a newcomer." He inclined toward her. "And, by the way, terrific conference, Professor Nestor. Too bad it has to be marred by the sad event in the library this a.m." His smile was meant to distract. Not that he needed to use it for that purpose. Dennis was so damn plausible as a scholar, I almost believed in him myself.

Then I was struck by a totally off-the-wall idea. If Dennis could so convincingly create a false academic persona, why couldn't Bob Tooey have done the same? I could easily check on that. I had to get to my office, and my computer, right away. I pushed back my chair. "Listen, suddenly I'm not feeling so well. Think I'll take a bit of a break before the next session."

"But Kar—" Dennis halted. "—Ah, Professor Pelletier, that is. Although I do hope first names are okay with you. I'd love to have a chat about your work." His gaze was direct and meaningful. "Seriously."

"Later," I said. I wanted to get on the Internet right away, and, in the face of a possible murder, Dennis' investigation into book theft didn't seem quite so pressing. "We'll talk later."

The sun pouring in the high windows of the Faculty Commons was strong and springlike, in spite of the eight inches of new snow. The large room was packed with conference goers, swelling out the usual ranks of faculty members. Each of the round tables held eight diners, and mouths were busy with more than turkey sandwiches and blackened Cajun catfish. As I rushed toward the French doors leading to the Commons foyer, I caught snatches of gossip about the "library murder," along with speculation on whether or not the conference would continue, given this shocking event. Passing a group of administrators, most likely working on damage control, I heard Harvey O'Hara's voice ring out in what I supposed must be the official line.

"After all," the Director of Public Affairs announced, during an unanticipated lull in the babble, "it isn't as if he were really one of ours." Then he glanced around, embarrassed by his own callousness.

I stopped dead in a shaft of light from a window by the door, and delayed synapses connected in my brain. *Stolen books. A body in the library.* I almost turned back to Dennis, but more synapses hooked up, and I thought again. He was investigating the book thefts for the college, but murder was the more pressing crime. If the stolen books, and the manuscript, of course, had anything to do with the death in the library, Charlie Piotrowski, not Dennis O'Hanlon, was the person to talk to. I'd told Charlie weeks ago about my collision with the book thief, so the idea of a…what had Dennis called it?…a *biblioklept*…wouldn't exactly be news to him.

I hesitated. It was all pretty wild speculation, a link between book theft and murder. One of my brainstorms. Charlie would probably tease me about my habit of fictionalizing. I should do some investigating first before I talked to him.

In my office I turned on the computer and clicked on the Internet. Up popped an e-mail from the president. In a campus-wide broadcast Avery announced the death of the researcher.

The identity of the deceased, he wrote, carefully not calling him a victim, *remains undetermined. Although we are shocked and saddened by this occurrence in our midst, we can take at least a pittance of comfort in the fact that the deceased is not a member of the Enfield College community. Every possible effort is being made by police and college officials to verify his identity. Meanwhile, students, faculty, and staff may remain assured of the safety and security of the Enfield campus.*

I sighed. Had Avery seen Bob Tooey's poor, pale body? The man had been a human being. Very much "one of ours."

I deleted the president's e-mail, called up the computer search engine, accessed the Lake Superior College website, and clicked on the link for the English Department. Professor Bob Tooey's office phone number was listed along with other contact information. I dialed it and let it ring four, five, six times. Just as I was about to hang up, a male voice answered. "Professor Bob Tooey, English. May I help you?" He sounded out of breath, but healthy, and very much alive.

Chapter Thirteen

I called Charlie on his cell phone. He wasn't at all surprised by my news about the real Bob Tooey. "We left a couple of messages at that number ourselves," he said, "but he didn't get back to us."

"He was in class all morning," I said. "Poor guy teaches three sections of Intro to Lit back to back." I shuddered. "Can you imagine discussing 'I heard a Fly buzz—when I died' with three groups of eighteen-year-olds, then coming back to your office to be faced with the news of your own demise? And then," I mused, "what if there were a fly in the room?"

"You're babbling, babe." Charlie was in a car: I could hear the motor, then there was the irritated blare of a tractor-trailer horn.

"I know. But, good Lord, Charlie, the man practically went into shock when I told him someone with his name was lying dead in the closed stacks at Enfield College."

There was a long moment when all I could hear was the burr of cars passing at a high rate of speed. Then Charlie said, "Do me a favor, please?"

"Anything. I want to help all I can."

More road hum. Then, "That's what I was afraid of. But, look, babe, keep out of this. Okay? We were on to this Tooey—same way as you were, most likely. The Internet, right?"

"Right."

"He would have called as soon as he got our message. Now you've given him time to think about what he's gonna tell us. Not a good move."

I winced at the reproach in Charlie's voice. "Sorry."

"So…" with infinite patience, "since you've talked to him already, what did Mr. Tooey say?"

"Two or three years ago he lost his faculty I.D. card. He thinks someone swiped it in the library. He had a new one made up, of course, but strange things started happening, mostly overdue notices from libraries he'd never been to for books he'd never heard of. He even got billed a hundred and fifty dollars by Bennington College for a copy of the *Encyclopedia of Mystery Fiction*."

"Identity theft."

"What?"

A voice spoke in the background. Schultz. Charlie listened for a few seconds, then said, "Hey, Karen, Tooey's on the cell. Talk to you later—"

"But I wanted to tell you—" I wanted to tell him about the book thefts.

"Later—"

"Wait! Where are you?"

"Mass Pike. Gotta go."

Mass Pike? That could be anywhere from Boston to the Berkshires. The Massachusetts Turnpike runs straight through the state like the backbone of a great whale.

As I sat in my office with the phone still in my hand and speculation about murder and book theft still on my mind, the college carillon rang two o'clock. Time for the first afternoon conference session. What were my choices? I leafed through the program. "Hard-boiled Dicks and Soft-boiled Janes." "The Epistemology of the Pen: Writing about Prison Life." "Yo' Mamma: Ethnicity and Ageism in Blacksploitation Film." I knew I had to show my face at one of these panels;

literary study was my chosen profession, after all. But, perversely, what I really wanted was to be out on the road with the cops. Piotrowski, Schultz, and Pelletier: intrepid crime fighters on the move for justice in the Massachusetts Commonwealth.

I was surprised to find Sunnye Hardcastle in Emerson Hall, just outside the door to the panel on "Hard-boiled Dicks." I thought she'd have been well on her way back to her Colorado aerie by now, but here she was, with a small notebook in her hand, gazing around. She was so intent on the scene in the lobby, I paused to see what interested her. Sally Chenille strolled by, in putrescent green today. Sunnye watched her, eyes narrowed, then scribbled on her pad. A white girl crossed the lobby on her way to class, dreadlocks poking out from under a Rastafarian wool hat. Sunnye scribbled. An impossibly thin girl with a shaved head and tattooed skull passed. Sunnye scribbled. Why did I get the feeling some future book would be set on the Enfield College campus?

Earlier that day at Bread & Roses, I'd come down on the side of discretion and had said nothing to Sunnye about her conversation with the murder victim. As far as I knew, she had not yet put the face together with the name. The death of the library researcher was to her an anonymous crime, simply a curious event to occur at such an unlikely place as an elite college, nothing to do with her. It had been about her own work that she'd wanted to speak to me. The writer needed a researcher to help with historical background for her next book, the one she planned to set in nineteenth-century New York City. She was willing to pay top dollar, she said, to someone who would delve into the slums and saloons of old Manhattan and bring back the details of the grime and squalor. Was I interested?

Was I interested! But, then, there was my own work to take into consideration, not to mention next year's petition for tenure. And besides, in all good conscience, I couldn't take on the job. Sunnye didn't need a full-fledged scholar to do the actual research, just to supervise. I'd be more than happy to outline the work, and oversee the researcher. But what she needed for the hands-on research, I told her, was a young person with a good education, an agile brain, and an interest in the past—plus a cast-iron butt for all that sitting around in hard library chairs. A young person with a crying need for some of that "top-dollar" income.

Peggy Briggs.

Now, in Emerson, Sunnye was waiting for me; she figured, she said, I'd show up sooner or later. "Listen, I decided that as long as I'm out here on the East Coast, anyhow, I'd like to meet that student you recommended to do the research." She stowed her notebook in a pocket of her bag. "Can you put me in touch with her?"

"Peggy? Sure. Come back to the office with me, and I'll look up her number in the college directory."

We sloshed across campus through the fast melting snow. In front of the library we paused and gawked with the other gawkers. State Police cars and vans were still parked on the sidewalk, but the ambulance was gone. "They'll have taken the body to the M.E. by now," my companion said with dispassionate professionalism. "But the SOC guys must still be here, and I'm sure they'll have a truckload of investigators interviewing everyone in the building. When do they think the homicide occurred?"

"Sometime in the night."

She stopped walking and slewed me an enigmatic glance. "During the evening, you mean?"

"No."

"You mean *late*? The *night* night?"

I shrugged. "The library closes at midnight. He must have been hiding away somewhere."

"Huh," she said. "That's odd. Why would someone want to spend a whole night in a library? I mean, no one likes books more than I do, but..." She let it trail off, and we completed the trek to my office in silence.

No one answered the phone at Peggy's house, and no answering machine kicked in. The Dean of Students' office had Peggy's class schedule. Sunnye and I waited outside Sociology 411 in Loeb Hall.

"Maybe she was so traumatized by finding that body that she had to go home," I suggested when Peggy failed to exit with the rest of the class.

"Maybe she's still being interviewed by the police," Sunnye said.

We followed two girls in maroon basketball jackets out the Loeb Hall door. Rachel Thompson came up behind us, said "hi," and reached down casually to stroke Trouble on the head as she strolled past.

"No!" I warned. But Trouble made no move to snap Rachel's hand off, just placidly allowed himself to be patted.

"Whew!" I said, as Rachel passed safely by.

"You afraid of Trouble?" Sunnye asked, squinting at me.

"Shouldn't I be?"

She gave me a "you kidding?" look.

Okay, I'm a wimp where vicious-looking trained attack dogs are concerned. So, shoot me. "How long are you planning to hang around here?" I asked.

"I think I'll stay in town for another day or two. This conference is strictly for the birds, but I hear there's some terrific antiquarian bookstores around here. You know a place called Henshaw's? Specializes in Americana."

"Yeah, Paul Henshaw. You met him, remember? At the cocktail party in the library, tall guy, grey ponytail, good-looking. He had you backed in a corner—"

"Oh, yeah. Quite a talker, right? And for a man his age, he's built."

"That's the guy."

"Point me in his direction. And," she paused, "Karen, when you get in touch with Peggy Briggs, I'll talk to her."

When I get in touch with her? Who'd made me Sunnye Hardcastle's secretary? But Sunnye's query about bookstores had jogged something in my memory. "By the way, I've been looking all over for a book of yours I bought years ago. *Rough Cut.* I know I've got it somewhere. I wanted to ask you—"

"If I'd sign it? Sure. Is it a first edition, by any chance?"

"I don't know. Could be, I suppose." We strolled past a kid in a blue knit hat with ear flaps. He was listening to his cell phone right through one of the flaps.

"If it is, and it's in good shape," Sunnye said, "you've got something special there. Mint copies of *Rough Cut* are going for about three grand. More if they're signed."

"Three thousand dollars? Jeez! I hope I didn't donate mine to the Salvation Army!"

"Ha! That puts me in my place." The first glimmer of humor from Ms. Hardcastle, and it had an edge.

"No. I'm sure I would have kept it." Damage control. "I just can't put my hands on it right now."

I pointed Sunnye in the direction of the P. R. office, where I was certain they would find a car for her, and went back to my office. It was well after three. From the window I could see conferees smoking cigarettes on the Emerson steps. Before the second afternoon session there would be coffee and muffins in the lobby. My stomach reminded me that I had forgone lunch. Pumpkin muffins, I hoped. And that nice Colombian brew Food Services did for special occasions.

In the English Department office, Monica was treating Dennis O'Hanlon to coffee, the special hazelnut blend, and a plateful of the little chocolate-covered wafers Miles doles out one apiece when distinguished visitors descend on the English department. Monica was behind her desk, and Dennis was seated in the upholstered side chair. They were laughing at something that could only be an off-color joke, that down-deep-in-the-belly guffaw that bonds us in our common smutty humanity.

"Dennis!" I stopped short in the doorway. They swiveled toward me.

He recovered before I did. "Professor Pelletier," he said, "just the person I wanted to see. Monica here didn't think you were in."

"His name is Mark," Monica informed me. "Not Dennis." She leaned toward him, her hand a mere half-inch from his arm. "Isn't that right, Mark?" It was finders keepers, and she wasn't about to let me snatch him away.

"Monica was just telling me all about you," Dennis said.

"She was?" I frowned at her.

"I was going to leave a note, but here you are. Hey, Monica, sweetheart, looks like I'm gonna have to go. A little idea I want to run by the good professor while I'm on campus. Thanks for the coffee."

She scowled at me all the way out the door.

Dennis took my arm as we crossed the quad in the misty afternoon air. "Listen, Karen, I'm gonna make this quick. Looks like I have to suspend my investigation. Mitchell called me in. He thought we should nudge the book-theft case onto the back burner, given that it might possibly be connected to that homicide last night in the library."

"Oh, too bad," I said, stupidly. I'd had a couple of intriguing dreams about Dennis during my fitful night's sleep. Oh, man. I could feel my face heat up just remembering them.

"Yeah, toooo bad." He grinned, then winked at me. "But, he's right. I mean, this dead guy's a wild card nobody counted on. Who knows? Maybe the book thief killed him. Or, maybe he *is* the book thief. Anyhow, I don't want to touch anything that's got murder written all over it. Leave that to the cops. I'm going back to Lowell." He squeezed my arm. "For now. I've got a feeling I'll be back. And, Karen, Mitchell still wants this kept on the q.t. He asked me especially to tell you. Ya got that?"

"Got it."

"See ya, Karen."

"Yeah," I said. "See ya." Then, thank God, he turned toward the parking lot, before I could ask *when*.

In the Emerson lobby a long table was set up with stainless-steel coffee urns against the marble wall. Between the doors to the main auditorium, another table held trays of muffins—no pumpkin—and platters of sliced melon and pineapple. I had my coffee halfway to my lips when Claudia homed in on me as if I were electronically programmed to attract crazies. Her eyes were fluttering up a storm. She seemed to have forgotten the snowball she'd lobbed at my head earlier.

"Karen, what am I going to do? They want to talk to everyone who was at the reception last night. This mean-looking S.O.B. of a cop yanked me out of the Hard-boiled panel. I almost lost my lunch, I was so terrified. Then he bullied me into giving him the conference registration and housing lists."

"Bullied you? I'm surprised. They're usually so polite." Well, maybe not Schultz; I'd hardly ever known Felicity Schultz to be polite.

"He didn't exactly *bully* me, but he made it clear I had no alternative but to give him the information." Flutter, catch, stare. "'What about invasion of privacy?' I told him. 'What about police harassment? What about fascist oppression of helpless people?' Plus, I have ethical obligations to my conferees!"

Aiiee! "Claudia, it's a homicide investigation. A man has been killed. We have ethical obligations to help find out who killed him."

The four-o'clock panel options were: "Good Cops in Bad Times"; "Gay Cops in Straight Times"; "Black Cops in White Times." I'd just settled into the back row of the "Black Cops" panel when I felt a firm hand on my shoulder.

"Professor Pelletier?" It was a tall, thin uniformed trooper. I couldn't tell if he was a good cop or a gay cop, but he was definitely black. "Come with me, please."

At the sight of a conferee being led out the room by a state trooper, a pale, weedy guy across the aisle almost popped his eyes out. Thank God I hadn't sat up front where I'd have provided a spectacle for dozens of thrill-deprived academics.

The cop opened the door to an empty classroom and handed me a cell phone. "You'll have some privacy in here. The lieutenant wants to talk to you."

"Karen," Charlie said. "You know where Chesterfield is?"

"West on the Mass Pike," I replied, "then way the hell up in the mountains. Why do you ask?" I'd been there once, years before, checking out a summer arts-and-crafts camp for Amanda. The isolation of the camp had put Amanda off; the fee schedule had done the same for me.

"Yeah. Can you get yourself out here? There's something we need you to see."

"Now?" Then I paused. Chesterfield was where Bob Tooey's alter ego lived—at least according to the driver's license on the dead man's body. What the hell was that name? Munro: Elwood Munro. "This has to do with the body in the library, doesn't it? I thought you didn't want me involved."

"Well, yeah." His tone said, *that was then, this is now.* "It's just that Schultz and I have stumbled across something real odd, and we don't know what to think about it. And seeing as it's right up your alley…" Charlie wouldn't give me more details. "I'm not gonna say another word," he said. "I want you to get the full impact."

"Jeez, Charlie, this isn't some grisly shoot-'em-up massacre scene, is it?"

"What? You think I'd subject you to that?"

"I guess not. But you've got me so damn curious. Just give me a hint."

"Curious, huh? Well, believe me, babe, it gets curiouser and curiouser."

"You've read *Alice in Wonderland*?"

"I raised kids, didn't I?"

I flashed on an image of a younger Charlie Piotrowski sitting between two tow-headed little boys reading about the Mad Hatter's tea party. For a brief, yearning moment I wished they'd been my little boys, too. Then the good lieutenant brought me back to the moment.

"I'm sending a car for you. Meet it out front at five."

Chapter Fourteen

The patrol car exited the Mass Pike at Lee, turned right, and began to follow a tortuous route through the Berkshires, first a commercial strip, then a country road past derelict farms, then a hard-pan dirt road snaking through snowbanks alongside a mountain stream and up a steep incline. The higher we went, the deeper the snowbanks got. After a three-mile climb, the headlights picked out a rusty road sign with an arrow pointing to CHESTERFIELD. We turned in at a country lane and pulled to a halt at a barrier of reflective cones and yellow crime scene tape. Charlie's Jeep was parked next to a state police SUV in front of a small red-shingled farmhouse with a wide porch. Charlie was waiting for me by the door. "Don't walk on the driveway," he called. "Tire tracks."

I followed a footpath in the snow and climbed four sagging steps to the porch. "What's going on?" I asked.

He gave me a long, level look, then threw open the farmhouse door. "This."

A narrow hall ran through the center of the house. I peered into it, squinting in the dim light of the single bulb hanging from a ceiling fixture. Charlie flipped on an industrial-strength flashlight and trained it down the hallway.

"Books," I said, after a minute. "Books. Lots of them."

"Thanks," Charlie replied. He was grinning at me. "Just what we needed, the testimony of a trained specialist."

The hall was jam-packed floor-to-ceiling down its entire length with bookshelves. Their ranks were broken only by two doorways on one side and a simple arch leading to the back of the house. The staircase as far up as I could see was crammed with books, its treads serving as de-facto shelves, with only enough space for a thin person to pass. Sideways.

"What the heck *is* this?" I asked, after a moment's stunned amazement.

Charlie shrugged. "According to town records, this house belongs to an Elwood Munro. I believe you knew the man as Bob Tooey. The entire house is stuffed with books, basement to attic. Thousands of books."

"My God!" I peeked through a door into what must have once been a living room: fully loaded bookshelves here, too, arranged in parallel rows with no room for furniture. Old-fashioned cloth blinds were rolled down over tall windows, and the air was thick with the faintly musty smell of old paper. "I've never seen anything like this. It looks like some kind of a demented library. It even smells like a library."

I walked over and reached out to pluck a volume off the staircase's fifth riser. Then before I touched it I hesitated and glanced at Charlie.

"Go ahead," he said.

I took down the book. It was a mystery novel, *The Leavenworth Case*, by Anna Katharine Green, a late nineteenth-century American writer. Crossed keys were embossed in red on the green binding. On the title page the seal of the Oberlin College library was impressed into the paper.

"This is a copy of Anna Katharine Green's first novel," I reported. "It seems to have belonged at one time to Oberlin College."

"Uh huh. Now take a gander at the one next to it."

I pulled the book out. It was another copy of *The Leavenworth Case*, only this one was in a much finer binding, black cloth, with red leather spine and corners.

"Open it," Charlie directed. I did. On the title page was imprinted the seal of the Smith College Library.

"Another library book," I said, something gnawing at my consciousness. Something I hadn't had a chance to tell him earlier. Then, "Oh, my God!" I grabbed another book from the staircase, then another. All early copies of novels by Green. All of them with library ownership clearly indicated in the volume. I pivoted around and yanked a book off another shelf: *The Glass Key* by Dashiell Hammett, seal of Indiana University Library. Another: *The Lady in the Lake*, by Raymond Chandler, no seal, but a New York University Library Special Collections card poking out with the book's archival call number inked in black. I opened to the publication data on the back of the title page: 1943. A first edition?

"The book thief!" I exclaimed. "Tooey—or Elwood—or Potato Face—or whatever the hell the guy's name is—was the goddamned book thief! I've got to tell Dennis O'Hanlon!"

"Book thief? Dennis O'Hanlon?" Charlie wrinkled his brow in puzzlement. He looked just a little bit like a boxer dog. Then he remembered. "Oh, book thief. You mean the guy who knocked you down that night by the library?"

"Yes," I said. Impatiently. That was old news. "And the guy who's relieved said library of a half-million dollars in rare books. And the guy who just this week stole the only extant manuscript of *The Maltese Falcon* from the Enfield College library." I ran my eyes over the shelves until I spotted a solid line of matching burnt-orange paper bindings: "And, whatd'ya know, here's the goddamned Beadle's dime novels I was looking for! All three hundred twenty-one volumes of them, I bet."

"*Dime* novels? A *half-million dollars*? That doesn't compute. What the hell are you talking about, Karen?"

I looked around for a chair. "This is going to be a long story."

Charlie pushed a set of library steps in my direction. "The guy didn't go in for furniture," he said. "So, tell me your long story." He leaned against the living-room doorway prepared to listen until doomsday, if that's what it took. "And who's this Dennis O'Hanlon?"

I could hear footsteps upstairs, at least two sets. "Your officers?"

"Yeah." His size thirteen boot tapped impatiently against the wide pine floor boards. "Come on, babe, talk!"

Babe? I narrowed my eyes at him. "'Talk?' You mean, as in 'Spill the beans'? 'Cough it up'? 'Spill your guts'? So, tell me, where's the other cop, the good one? Where's the bright lights? The rubber hoses?"

"Very funny, babe," he said. "Just tell me, will you? Please?"

"Well—"

"Wait!" He raised a hand. "Schultz," he called, "come here. I want you to hear this."

Felicity Schultz came waddling out from what I assumed was the kitchen, looking for all the world like a pale eggplant. I stood up and offered her my seat on the rolling steps. She sighed and—to my surprise—sat down without protest. She even thanked me.

I told them about the books that had been stolen from the library. I told them about my talk with Avery. I told them about Dennis O'Hanlon and his investigation.

"Christ," Charlie grumbled. "What the hell was Mitchell thinking? That kind of money, he should have reported it to us. Just what we need, some private bozo snooping around, screwing up the evidence."

"It wasn't a murder investigation then," I said, reasonably. "And, besides, he's not like that."

"Who? This private guy? You've met him?"

"Well, yes. Avery sent him to talk to me. And, actually…"

"Actually, *what?*"

"Actually…I knew him in high school."

"You *what?*"

"Remember that class reunion I went to a couple of weeks ago?"

"Yeah, I remember. You didn't want me along."

"I never said that."

"You made it clear."

"I did not!"

Schultz's head was swiveling from side to side, as if she were watching the U.S. Open.

"So," Charlie said, his face devoid of expression, "you went to the reunion to meet this…O'Hanlon."

"It wasn't like that. I simply ran into him—"

"You *ran into* him—"

"Ahem," Schultz said, looking at us with weary eyes, "about these book thefts? A lot of money involved here?"

Grateful for the change of subject, I surveyed the shelves, recalled Avery's estimate of Enfield's losses alone. "God, yes. Millions, maybe."

"Millions!" Schultz's eyes met Charlie's. "You know what that means."

Charlie was all business again. "Yeah. We've gotta definitely treat Munro's death as a possible homicide. What could have been a simple fatal accident, now has major criminal factors— false identity, evidence of grand theft…."

Unconsciously Schultz rubbed her belly. "Possible motives for murder: Might be an accomplice wants to cover up complicity. Might be murder for gain. Lots of money on the hoof here."

"Millions of dollars worth of stolen books…" Charlie mused. "It complicates everything." He turned to me abruptly. "And you," he ordered, "are not to say word one about any of this to that O'Hanlon guy."

I was sobered by what I was seeing here. Biblio-larceny on a vast scale. And, now, the death of the book thief. "Okay," I agreed. "Mum's the word."

Trooper Deirdre Flynn, a slight woman with straight blond hair, pale eyes, and a long thin nose, provided a deluxe guided tour, from basement to attic, of what I'd come to think of as the Book House. My initial impression of chaos was quickly dispelled. What had at first seemed to be disorder on a gargantuan scale was nothing of the sort, merely an attempt to house a multitude of books in a tight space, three floors of the old farmhouse and a finished basement. Everything was surprisingly clean and orderly, even the bathroom, which was stacked with comic books on both sides of the toilet. Trooper Flynn first took me down a narrow set of stairs leading from the kitchen into the basement. The cleanliness of this make-shift library was explained by a big boxy climate-control and air-filtration system worthy of a professional archive. Whoever Elwood Munro was, he certainly had cared about books, not only enough to take the risk of stealing them, but also enough to take good care of them once he had.

"Equipment like this doesn't come cheap," I told the young officer. "This climate-control setup alone must have cost a bundle."

"That's what the lieutenant said," she replied. "Only he phrased it differently."

"I'll bet he said it 'cost a shitload.'"

She gave me a sideways glance. She knew I was the boss's girlfriend: She must have been thinking she'd better watch her words.

The first floor was the real treasure trove. Mystery fiction, which seemed to be Munro's larcenous specialization, filled the place: hallway, living room, and dining room. All three rooms now glared with light. Someone must have sent out for two-hundred-watt bulbs to replace Munro's deliberately dim illumination. Bright light is not good for books, and he would have known that. I stifled the impulse to protest.

Following instructions to touch as little as possible, I scanned the spines of shelved books. Munro's collection was wide-ranging and impressive: not only the classic hard-boiled American writers—Chandler, Hammett, Spillane—but also the newer authors—Sue Grafton, Sara Paretsky, Tony Hillerman. There was something thrilling about seeing all these books together, many of them in their original dust jackets. A familiar volume caught my eye, and I eased a copy of Sunnye Hardcastle's *Rough Cut* from its niche. The bright jacket with its hot-pink, chartreuse, and black design was identical to the one on my own misplaced copy. I opened the book to the back of the title page. Yep, first edition. What had Sunnye said this could go for? Three thousand dollars? A single book out of this huge collection, I mused, three thousand dollars. Suddenly it struck me, the full extent of what I was looking at. This whole bizarre scene—the remote farmhouse, the expensive equipment, the thousands of purloined volumes— represented possibly one of the world's major collections of American mystery fiction. The bright lights, the police officers, my own intrusive presence, were merely tangential to the massive controlling obsession that had gone into planning and carrying out the acquisition of these books. This unique collection had been built risk by risk by risk.

What was it Dennis O'Hanlon had called the perpetrator of the Enfield book thefts? A *biblioklept*? *Bibliopath* would be more like it: a crazed intelligence focused on books—not necessarily on the knowledge or stories they contained, but on the books themselves as objects of desire. Literary archives are locked, guarded, and alarmed, but Elwood Munro had somehow found his way into the stacks. Now he was dead, and his collection remained as a perverse testimony to one man's tastes, interests, and knowledge. Was that what he was looking for as he gathered these books together, a kind of bibliographic immortality?

Expecting more book stacks in the kitchen, I stood surprised in the doorway: no shelves at all. A long room with speckled grey linoleum on the floor and makeshift counters of some weird prehistoric Formica. Two long metal folding tables were stacked with volumes of various sizes, seemingly in the process of being sorted and classified. An old-fashioned oak card-catalog cabinet stood incongruously next to a 1930s gas stove with curved chrome legs. I leafed through cards. "Not Library of Congress classification," I told Flynn, who wrote everything down as if I knew what I was talking about, "and not Dewey Decimal System." Munro had gone in for some eccentric, seemingly self-invented classification system. Using his cards, I wouldn't have been able to locate a single thing in the collection, but the books themselves on the shelves had seemed logically enough organized.

In a large pantry off the kitchen, there awaited another surprise: a worktable stocked with the tools of book repair—Exacto knives, glue, large needles, binding thread, tape, a book press. If any of Elwood Munro's stolen books were sick, he knew how to heal them.

The trooper and I climbed the steep back stairs from the kitchen. Two bedrooms housed a collection of books on American politics that seemed sketchy compared to what I'd seen downstairs; another was devoted to nineteenth-century cookbooks and domestic advice manuals. The attic featured Civil War history, and memorabilia such as uniform buttons, regiment insignias, confederate currency, and letters from the front. A small cabinet tucked under the eaves provided a refuge for nineteenth-century erotica.

"Whoa!" Trooper Flynn said, as she opened the covers of a pop-up book picturing a couple in sexual congress. The man was on top, and flipping the pages revealed rather energetic activity on the part of a rather large male member. "I didn't know the Victorians went in for pornography."

The stairs creaked loudly, and Charlie's head appeared in the stairwell. Deirdre Flynn slapped the smutty book shut without regard for its moving parts. As she slid it back into the unlocked case, Charlie asked, "What've you got there?"

The trooper's fair skin turned strawberry pink. "Just m-more of the same," she stuttered. In spite of the uniform, the gun belt, the badge, she was still very young.

Charlie wrinkled his forehead at her quizzically, then turned to me. "You about done here, Karen? There's sandwiches and fresh coffee outside in the van."

"I've given it all a once over, but, Jeez, Charlie, I don't know.... This is big time—an absolutely extraordinary collection. Way over my head. We're dealing with a highly esoteric collector here. Obviously, he specialized in American books, and from a populist perspective."

"What's that mean?"

"He collected books published for the masses, not for the literati. Look, detective fiction here. Upstairs, military stuff, cookbooks, erotica." Trooper Flynn was still transcribing my every word.

"Erotica? Really?"

"I'm not versed in book-collecting, per se, you know, just literature. You need to get specialists—rare-book dealers and curators. People with a comprehensive overview of this field. They'll be able to tell you what you're looking at here."

"I thought we'd start tomorrow with your Ms. Thompson from the library. She could identify the books that were stolen from Enfield College."

"Rachel? Hmm. That's a good idea. She knows this stuff."

"But we've got to get a crime scene team in here first, before the evidence gets completely screwed. Munro may be dead, but, who knows, maybe he wasn't working alone. Maybe he had an accomplice."

"Ah!" I said, "that's why you wanted to preserve those tire tracks, in case someone else is in on this."

"Hmm," he replied. He grinned at me. "That's a good idea." Then he got serious again. "Now, anything else you notice about this place that you haven't mentioned?"

"Aside from its isolation out here in the boonies?" I checked around. "No. Nothing in particular."

Charlie chewed his lip. "Think about it. Nothing here but books. No food in the fridge. No toiletries. No clothing. Where did the guy actually live?"

I sat on one of the folding chairs the cops had brought in and ate a dried-up roast-beef sandwich while Deirdre Flynn sealed the doors with crime-scene tape, and Charlie gave orders: Schultz was to wait for him in the Jeep. Try to get a little rest while he finished up here. Flynn and her partner were to keep watch on the house until the SOC technicians arrived.

Before we left, I took one last stroll through the downstairs. Once the experts were called in, and the business of cataloging the collection and finding the true owners of the books began, I wouldn't be let anywhere near the place. I stood in the living-room doorway: With its tightly pulled window shades and tightly packed shelves, the room, and the dining room beyond, seemed, in the hallucinatory forensic light, like some bookworm's phantasmagoric wonderland: *Red Harvest*; *Devil in a Blue Dress*; *Edwin of the Iron Shoes*; *The Big Sleep*; *"A" is for Alibi*; *Some Buried Caesar*; *Bitter Medicine*.

In the kitchen, I perused the piles of books awaiting Munro's classification. Christ! From under a mint-condition Nancy Drew I plucked a worn copy of Edgar Allan Poe's *Tales*. Eureka! 1845: a first edition. Poe is the father of detective fiction. If I remembered correctly, this was the first book to contain all three of his C. Auguste Dupin stories. Yes, here they were, listed in the table of contents: "The Murders in the Rue Morgue," "The Mystery of Marie Roget," "The Purloined Letter." I handled the book reverently. Better tell the cops we had a piece of the American canon here. But, then, would that make any difference to them? Just another stolen book.

Then, turning to leave, I was stopped cold by the sight of a vaguely familiar object tucked between the card-catalog cabinet and the chrome-legged stove. It was a beat-up canvas backpack with a grungy little Pink Panther doll attached to its army-green strap. I stared at it in disbelief. Unless I was badly mistaken, the last time I'd seen that bag was yesterday morning when Peggy Briggs had visited me in my office.

Chapter Fifteen

The classic teacher's nightmare: wandering through institutional corridors, searching for the right classroom. Haven't prepared. Don't have my books. Don't even know what the course is. I open a door. Twenty-five heads turn in my direction. Twenty-five hands reach for pens. This must be it. I stride to the front of the room with as much authority as I can muster wearing a pajama jacket that doesn't quite cover my nether regions. I open my mouth to begin the lecture.

Then I'm awake. It's eight a.m., and the phone is ringing.

"Uhhh?"

"Babe? You get home okay?"

"Umm."

"Listen, you were a big help last night. Did I tell you that?"

"Uggh."

"You got us on the right track with all that book-collecting stuff. Otherwise we wouldn't have known what the hell we were looking at."

"Ufff."

"So, listen, babe. I'm gonna be tied up all day with the Munro case. And you've got that conference thing. So maybe I'll see ya around campus." A little chortle, like water over smooth stones; he seemed to think that was funny.

"Unhuh."

"You okay, babe? You sound wasted. Oh, shit—there's the other phone. Gotta go."

God, I hate a morning person.

It was Friday, the second full day of the crime fiction conference. I was scheduled to teach my freshman class at four p.m. I wasn't prepared, but at least I knew what the course was. With any luck, I could cobble together a discussion outline during office hours this morning. Then I'd be free to attend an early afternoon conference session. The choices were: "Dead Blondes in Red Dresses: Whiteness Studies in American Crime Fiction" and "Beowulf to Nero Wolfe: The Curriculum and the Crime Novel." After a shower and coffee I donned a teal jacket and black skirt, more appropriate classroom wear than a butt-baring pj jacket. By 9:12 I was in the car and on the road. A spring sun was shining, and the Subaru's wheels splashed through puddles of melting snow.

All the way into campus I worried about Peggy Briggs. The poor kid: Her sister had been killed, what, four, five years ago. The last thing she needed now was to be dragged into another homicide. Short of stealing her backpack, thus tampering with evidence, there was nothing I could have done to help her last night except what I actually did do, and that was to keep my mouth shut and buy her some time. In that cluttered house, the backpack was only one item among thousands, but the police would look at it early in the investigation. They'd think it was Elwood Munro's; perhaps they'd even conjecture that he'd used it to spirit books away from libraries. But they'd soon identify the pack as Peggy's. And, since she was still living at her mother's house, Charlie would know precisely where to find her.

On campus the snow was heavy and wet, the walkways a half-inch deep in murky water. Remnants of yesterday's towering snow fort sagged on the quad. This morning the scene around the library seemed normal: no crime-scene tape, no police vehicles. Three tall students I recognized from the basketball floor lounged on the steps, basking in the sun's rays. From an open dorm window came the voice of Lucinda Williams singing about this sweet old world.

I called Peggy from the office, but the man who answered the phone at her house said he didn't know where the hell she was, and, no, he wouldn't take a message, he wasn't no goddamned secretary.

I looked up her e-mail address in the directory and sent a message: *Peggy, get in touch. It's important.*

Not that I was about to clue her in on the location of her missing backpack; she'd get that bad news soon enough. My good news—Sunnye Hardcastle's research proposition— wouldn't really counteract it, but, then, an offer of money never comes amiss to a scholarship student.

Or to anyone.

I was deep into preparing a spontaneous class discussion on liberty and self-determination in *Jane Eyre* when I sensed a scrutinizing presence. I looked up. Harriet Person, in a black pantsuit under a navy wool coat, loomed in the open doorway. In her short dark hair, the white blaze had widened strikingly.

"Karen, the a.m. sessions have already started. If we leave now we'll make the end of the first paper."

I laid down the green pen and pushed the desk chair back. "Sorry, Harriet, I can't go this morning. I have a class to prepare."

"Can't go?" Over her narrow features came an expression of consternation. "Karen, this conference is a Women's Studies highlight. It's the apex of the year's events."

"But I have to teach at four, and I've already canceled one class because of the conference." *And have been thoroughly chastised by my department chair.* I stood up and walked around the desk.

From the hallway came a young woman's voice, "And then I go, but Kevin, that is so wrong...."

My senior colleague entered the office, closed the door behind her, and shot me the slit-eyed glare of a sixth-grade teaching nun. "You do realize, Karen, don't you, that your tenure decision is scheduled for next fall?"

I went icy cold. First Miles, now Harriet. "Of course I do."

Her thin lips pressed together. "What I'm going to say to you now is for your own good. It is not in your best interests for colleagues in Women's Studies to receive the impression that your feminist commitment does not extend to supporting our collective endeavors."

In spite of her elliptical wording, this was a direct threat, far more serious than Miles's vague maunderings. The ice in my veins turned to fire. "Harriet," I said, hearing my voice rise with each word, "if my colleagues in Women's Studies don't know by now that I'm a feminist to the very marrow of my bones—"

A staccato rap on the door interrupted me. I scowled at Harriet, stomped over to the door and threw it open. Charlie Piotrowski stood there, his muscular bulk filling the doorway: Superman to the rescue.

"Hi!" I said, with a big, false, smile.

Charlie's attitude was curt and professional; you might have thought we'd only met once or twice, and that in fully clothed situations. "Sorry, Professor Pelletier, I didn't realize you were in the middle of something."

Right. They could hear my outraged bellow as far away as Boston. "Professor Person was just leaving." I cast her a good-riddance look.

Charlie watched Harriet stalk away down the corridor, her back ramrod straight. Then he turned to me. "What was that all about? I heard you clear down the hall."

I told him what she'd said. "I'm doomed, Charlie. Not only have I been insufficiently supportive of Women's Studies,

I've also smarted off to Harriet. To *Harriet*, a full professor!" I placed the back of my hand to my forehead and tilted my head like a Victorian heroine, but I wasn't really playing it for laughs. "I'll never get tenure now!"

And Charlie didn't think it was funny. "Shit! Can she get away with treating you like that?"

Suddenly I was shaky. "As I said, she's a full professor. She can get away with anything."

"I suppose you could apologize...." He sounded dubious.

"No, I damn well couldn't!"

Charlie placed a comforting hand on my shoulder. "It'll be all right, babe. You'll see."

"Umm. What're you gonna do? Arrest her?"

He pushed the door shut, pulled me to him, and held me till I stopped shaking. When I felt composed again, I sat in the green chair.

"Now, listen," he said, sitting down across from me. He suddenly seemed hesitant, even nervous. "I'm sorry about the timing, Karen, but some new evidence has come up, and I'm afraid I have to ask you a few questions." His gaze was straight and sober.

"Me?" A new terror arose: *Oh, God—he found Peggy's backpack!* "Charlie, suddenly you're talking like a cop."

"Yeah, I am." He gave me a sidelong look. "I need to know a few things about Ms. Hardcastle."

I could feel my eyes widen with astonishment. "Sunnye Hardcastle?"

"Wednesday evening. The reception in the library. Were you with her the entire time?"

"Yes," I replied, without thinking. "But why are you asking questions about Sunnye?"

"Why didn't you tell us about Hardcastle and Munro?"

"Huh? Hardcastle and Munro?" It sounded like a high-end funeral home.

"You must have known that Sunnye Hardcastle went off somewhere with Elwood Munro. We have a witness who saw them together."

"Oh—yeah…" I remembered now. "Sally Chenille."

"The weirdo with the green hair," he agreed.

"Is it green today?"

He gave my arm a gentle squeeze. "Don't try to sidetrack me, Karen. This has become an…er…issue in the investigation. Why didn't you tell us?"

"I didn't actually see them together. Sally mentioned it." I shrugged. "Then I forgot."

"You forgot?"

I'd deliberately evaded telling Charlie about Peggy's backpack—and that was something like outright prevarication—but I'd merely forgotten to mention Sunnye's talk with Tooey, er, Munro. "That crazy scene last night at Munro's house just about drove everything else out of my mind."

He sighed. "I don't know what to do," he said, shaking his head. For several long seconds he pondered his immaculate fingernails. Then he looked up at me. "I'm really uncomfortable about this. I shouldn't have called you up to Chesterfield yesterday."

I frowned at him. "But you said I was a big help."

"And that's true. We wouldn't have had a clue about all those books without you. But now you're involved in this investigation, and it's just not a good idea…"

"So, you think you can turn me on and off like a light bulb?"

He rolled his eyes. "See what I mean. You just won't…"

He chewed on his upper lip and tried again. "So, Karen, you, personally, didn't see the subject in conversation with Munro?"

"The subject? Jesus, Charlie, why are you talking to me like a cop?"

"I am a cop. Don't forget that."

"Don't worry, I never do."

He gave me a sharp look. "Where did *that* come from?"

"Sorry. Knee-jerk reaction." I ran a hand through my hair. "But why are you calling Sunnye Hardcastle *the subject*? She's an internationally respected crime novelist—"

He held up a hand. "Just answer the question." This was a far cry from the light-hearted man who had called me earlier that morning—and from the gentle man who had just moments ago comforted me.

"I want to know why you're asking me these things about Sunnye. Lieutenant."

"I can't tell you." Charlie leaned forward, an elbow on one knee, a hand splayed on the other. He sighed again. "Look, babe, I'm in a bad position here. Can't you understand that? Something unexpected has come up, and I need your cooperation. And I need you to back out of this case and stay out. Believe me, the last thing I want to do is piss you off, but there's stuff I've got to keep to myself. Can't you trust me? Can't you just answer the question?"

He was so sincere I gave in. "Well...I was with Sunnye Hardcastle all evening except when she..." I paused, recalling the period of time—about a half hour—when I hadn't been able to find Sunnye. Then she and Trouble had reappeared through the hidden door in the library's foyer. The hidden door...the library foyer.... The pieces fitted together: The police suspected Sunnye Hardcastle of murder! I stared at Charlie in horror. Would my statement that Sunnye had vanished for a half hour incriminate the novelist even further?

"Except when she what?" Charlie asked. I could tell by the control in his voice that he was doing his best to placate me.

I eyed him narrowly. "Oh, except when she went off to the bathroom. I didn't find it necessary to accompany her there. After all, she had Trouble."

"Yes," he said slowly, "she had Trouble. That dog."

Forty minutes later I'd completed my class prep. If it hadn't been for Harriet's attempt at intimidation, I would then have gone to hear the last paper of the morning session. But I wasn't about to give her the satisfaction of showing up. Monica eyed me snidely when I stopped by the office to pick up my mail. At first I thought she must have heard my altercation with Harriet, but, no, it was Dennis O'Hanlon she wanted to talk about.

"So, where'd you end up going with my hot guy yesterday?"

"We didn't go anywhere. Just walked across the campus."

"Yeah, right." She took her nasty grin right to the precipice of a leer. I had to remind myself that Monica didn't single me out for insults; she dissed everyone. "Man, first time I saw that stud, I thought, *I could go for that.* Then, when he showed up again yesterday—"

"What? He's been here before?"

"Yeah. Couple of weeks ago. I saw him in the library. There's no mistaking him, he's so sexy. Sure doesn't look like a professor though. More like one of those tough TV cops. You know—kind of a hard guy."

I didn't respond right away. I was trying to recall; hadn't Dennis told me that yesterday was his first day ever on the Enfield campus? When I did speak, it was absently. "Yeah, I do know—kind of a hard guy."

Forgetting to pick up my mail, I went to the Dean of Students' office to look at Peggy's class schedule again. I needed to talk to that girl. No classes on Friday. I trekked over to Special Collections, assuming she would be at her library work/study job. When Nellie Applegate saw me walk through the reading-room doors, she plucked a number-two pencil from a cup and began to tap the eraser end against the desk. Pallid by nature, today Nellie seemed even whiter than usual. She was also disheveled, her chopped-off salt-and-pepper hair in need of a good brushing, a button on her white cotton blouse dangling by a thread.

"Hi, Nellie. Is Peggy Briggs here?"

"No." Her voice was so muted, I didn't quite catch the response.

"No?"

"Peggy didn't show up this morning," she whispered.

"Oh, is she upset because of…yesterday?" There was something about Nellie that made a person resort to evasions and euphemisms.

No response. Her complexion bleached even further. She was the whitest person I'd ever seen.

"When she stumbled over…well, you know," I blundered on. "In the stacks. You must all be…upset to have something like that happen in a place like this." *Upset. Something like that. A place like this.*

By response, Nellie sniffed into a crumpled tissue.

Belatedly, I recalled her interest in the little researcher, or at least that's how I had interpreted the few surreptitious glances I'd noticed.

"Poor Mr. Tooey," she choked, and dropped the pencil. It rolled off the high desk, hit a half-loaded book truck, fell to the floor of the quiet room with a sharp *click-clack*. I bent over to pick it up.

"Munro," I corrected her and held out the long, yellow pencil. It was dumb, but that was all I could think of to say. "His name was Elwood Munro."

"Munro." She swallowed visibly. "Rachel told me that. But he called himself Bob Tooey." She took the pencil from my outstretched hand and sniffed again.

"Did you know Mr. Munro well?"

"Know him? What do you mean, *know* him?" Tap, tap, tap with the pencil.

"I meant—"

She gazed at me with a flat look in her mouse-brown eyes. "I didn't *know* Mr. Tooey at all outside the venue of the library." *Venue of the library?* "Now he's dead." Her tone was oddly devoid of affect.

I bumbled on. "Is Rachel around?" Nellie had made it clear I was bothering her, but I felt compelled to find out how Munro had smuggled all those books out of the library.

"She got a phone call first thing..." She pulled another tissue from the box. Maybe she was broken-hearted; maybe she just suffered from an allergy to book dust. "And left without even letting me know how to reach her."

Probably a call from the state police, I thought. Rachel's most likely in Chesterfield right now, identifying stolen books.

"And now," Nellie continued in the same flat tone, "Peggy hasn't shown up. I've got all this reshelving to do." She gestured at the cart with its modest load of books. "And no help. I don't know how Rachel expects me to do it. Someone's got to watch the desk, and these returns just keep piling up. I can't do everything by myself." Suddenly there was an undercurrent of feeling in her voice. She wiped her red eyes with the tissue. "It's just not humanly possible," she concluded and blew her nose. At first I'd thought it was quiet grief that had caused Nellie's sniffling, but, perhaps it was simply the arduous business of reshelving.

I said good-bye to the pathetic little librarian and left without having learned anything more about my worrisome student.

On the library steps, I hesitated, squinting in the glare of sun on snow. *Peggy Briggs. Peggy Briggs. Where the hell was Peggy Briggs?*

Chapter Sixteen

I was still assigned to escort Sunnye through the mean streets of Enfield. On this final evening before the conference broke up at noon on Saturday, Women's Studies was treating its guests to a farewell dinner at the Mai Thai restaurant on Varsity Street. When I called the novelist to confirm that she was planning to attend, she asked if I'd gotten in touch with Peggy yet about doing research for her. My negative response goaded her into a plan of action. "You said she lives near here. Why don't we take a ride over to her house? How far is it, anyhow?"

"About ten miles. But we've got this dinner..." I'd thought about that, too, tracking Peggy down at home. But between teaching, the conference, and incidentals such as murder and a house full of stolen books, I hadn't had a moment to do anything more about my student than simply worry.

"A Women's Studies dinner. Oh, joy," Sunnye intoned. "The things I do for money. So? What time is it now, five o'clock? The dinner's at seven, right? We'll be back in time. We can't just let this student of yours vanish."

Sunnye's take-charge attitude began to rankle. "I don't know that Peggy's *vanished*. It's just that no one at the college seems to have seen her in a couple of days. And the man who answers the phone at her house is a real jerk. He won't talk to me."

"When did you call?"

"I've been trying off and on all day. The last time was a few minutes ago, right after class. He recognized my voice and slammed the phone down."

"He'll talk to *me*," Sunnye said. "Pick me up in front of the Inn."

"When?" I replied automatically. Once again Sunnye was barking out orders, and I was obeying. Who did she think she was? Kit Danger?

"How about right now?" Yeah, she did. And I was her sidekick, Karen the Wimp.

I sighed. She was right. We could whip over to Durham Mills, talk to Peggy if she was home, and be back in town in time for the Women's Studies dinner. And I had a compelling reason to control my irritation with Sunnye. It wouldn't hurt to have Trouble at my back when I talked to Peggy's nasty stepfather.

Any other student's absence from school wouldn't have concerned me so much, but Peggy Briggs was compulsively conscientious in a manner known only to those who were studying, like her, to change the course of lives otherwise predestined to poverty. She was as motivated as hell. It made me extremely uneasy that she wasn't where she was supposed to be when she was supposed to be there. It also alarmed me that she was leaving personal belongings, her backpack, with her books and notebooks, I assumed, in places where she had no reason to be.

"Right now is fine," I agreed.

It was rush hour in Enfield, as much as Enfield ever has a rush hour: As I edged along Field Street, I passed professors on their way home from office hours, parents car-pooling eight-year-olds from ballet lessons to soccer practice, students out for pizza prior to the weekend booze fest. A faint mist hung in the dusk, diffusing the illumination from headlights and street lamps, glamorizing storefronts and purifying piled-up mounds of filthy snow. It all seemed picturesque and exceedingly quaint, yet down the street, at the red-brick college drowsing in its Friday-evening lassitude, a man had just met his death, and a student seemed to have mysteriously vanished.

At Field and Main, the traffic signal turned red, and I braked the Subaru. Making a left turn, a sleek pea-green BMW passed me, its driver hunched over the wheel, oblivious to the world outside the trajectory of her vehicle. I did a double-take as I recognized Rachel Thompson. For as long as I'd known her, the librarian had been driving a super-annuated white Nissan. What was she doing tooling around in such an expensive car?

Sunnye waited by the cut-granite curb in front of the Enfield Inn, Trouble at her side. *Christ, she looks tough*, I thought, struck once again by how closely the novelist resembled her own protagonist. In jeans, leather jacket, and thick-soled boots, she was stripped down, ready for action. In my own teaching clothes and long wool coat I felt encumbered, and—god help me—more than a little bourgeois. *I'm going to get a dog*, I thought, though I've never wanted one. *Not a Rottweiler like Trouble, but something just as edgy, just as fierce. A canine fashion statement. A Great Dane, maybe. Maybe a Doberman.* Then I pondered feeding such an animal on an assistant professor's salary. *A miniature Bulldog? A Schnauzer? Maybe a scrawny little mutt from the pound?*

We headed out of town to the address in Durham Mills I'd found in the college directory. Trouble slobbered over a dried pig's ear in the back seat. Leaving the village and its precious little shops behind, we plunged into the miracle-mile chaos just outside of town where the primary commercial activity of the area occurs. Home Depot, Wal-Mart, Super Stop 'N' Shop, McDonalds: where anything you could ever possibly desire to purchase was available except for the truly unique, lovely, and delectable.

"Tell me about Peggy," Sunnye demanded.

I took my eyes off the road to glance over at her. I'd had just about enough of Sunnye Hardcastle, Alpha female. I shook my head slowly. "I don't get it, Sunnye."

"You don't get *what*?" She scrabbled in her bag and came out with a couple of foil-wrapped bars.

"I don't get *you*." I pulled into the left lane and passed a Volvo station wagon carrying a half-dozen thirteen-year-olds and their hockey sticks. "I don't get what we're doing here: you, me, and Trouble on our way to Peggy Briggs' house. Yeah, she's my student, and I should be—I am—concerned about her. But what is she to you that you should bother? You've never even met this girl…woman."

She tipped one of the foil-wrapped rectangles in my direction. "Want a nutrition bar?"

A nutrition bar? Yuck. "No, thank you."

She peeled a wrapper and held the sesame-seed-studded concoction back over her shoulder. Trouble mouthed it gently from her hand, then wolfed it down as if people food was a familiar treat. "But I think I have met Peggy. Isn't she the one who freaked out the day I came to your class?"

"Oh…" I recalled the first day of the semester. "I'm surprised you remember that." We stopped at a red light, and the Volvo pulled up next to us. I recognized a harried colleague behind the wheel. In the back seat one of the adolescent passengers, a girl with a blond pony tail, flashed us a rude hand sign. Without seeming to have noticed, Sunnye flipped an infinitely more obscene gesture. The wide-eyed girls consulted but couldn't come up with anything to top it. Then they noticed Trouble glowering at them from the back seat, still chomping toothily on his goody, and their eyes swerved forward, suddenly intent on the back of the driver's head.

"But, Sunnye," I said, "that doesn't tell me what you're doing out here on a Friday evening." I slid another glance at her, and couldn't resist a dig. "Especially when you've got a dozen adoring Women's Studies scholars waiting for you back in Enfield."

She gave a short laugh. It sounded like one of Trouble's barks. "Karen, I've gotten used to getting what I want when I want it and *doing* what I want when I want to. Right now I want to talk to Peggy Briggs about undertaking that research for me."

"Uh huh," I replied. "And finding a research assistant is urgent enough to warrant facing down a hostile stepfather, in a strange town, before dinner?"

She concentrated on peeling the foil wrapper off the second bar. "Well, I have to admit it, Karen, I'm curious. I'm a mystery writer, and it's a bit of a mystery, isn't it, Peggy's disappearance?"

I consulted my years of teaching experience. "It is, and it isn't."

"What's that supposed to mean?" She took a bite.

"It's a stressful and unsettled period, the college years. Every once in a while a student self-destructs and goes AWOL. Professors tend not to get involved—the deans handle it. But I wouldn't expect that kind of behavior from Peggy. She's older than the typical student, and more motivated. She knows this is her big chance. And…there's Triste…." Concern for my student nagged at me.

Sunnye seemed to be more involved with her own thoughts than with my apprehensions. We cruised by the massive blue-grey facade of the Wal-Mart. "Besides, I'm ready for some action," she mused.

Ah! That was it. Kit Danger, girl detective. I was worried sick that something horrific had happened to Peggy, but Sunnye was simply bored. Ready for some action.

"That back there at the college…that conference…" She waved a strong, slim dismissive hand. "That's just…*words*. Nothing is really *happening*."

"My colleagues would disagree with you, of course. The current mantra of literary studies is that *discourse makes things happen*. But I agree, what we've heard so far at this conference is largely derivative, mediated not only through language but through codified politico-linguistic theories."

She gave me a condescending look. "Just when I start to think you might be a stand-up kind of gal, you go ahead and blather out bullshit like that. You sound *just* like a professor, you know."

"I *am* a professor. That doesn't make me a mushy-headed pedant, you know. That doesn't make me an effete intellectual snob. That doesn't make me a…wimp."

"Of course not," she replied, without conviction. "But I'm interested in the real world—not in 'codified politico-linguistic' theories about the real world. I might even get a *story* out of this visit to Peggy. God knows, I won't at a dinner with English scholars."

"Women's Studies scholars," I said. "Not English."

The look she cast me made it clear that one set of academics was just as bad as the other.

I glared at her. "And are you saying that a story—a fiction—is *real*? Isn't that a contradiction in terms?"

Abruptly Sunnye Hardcastle laughed. This time it was less like a growl and more like a genuine expression of amusement. "You *are* a fighter, aren't you, Karen? I do like that in a person." She scarfed down the final bite of her nutrition bar and winked at me. "Even if she is an effete intellectual snob."

A half-dozen miles later, I turned west on Federal Road, past a row of abandoned brick mills, into a neighborhood of aging frame duplexes. Peggy's mother's house was shingled in green with two cream-painted front doors set off to one side on a narrow green-scalloped porch. A hot-pink child's bicycle leaned against the railing. I parked in front of the house. Sunny and I got out of the car, leaving open a window for Trouble.

It was supper time and various cooking odors competed for our attention. "Liver and bacon," Sunnye said, as we strode up the concrete walk to the front steps. "God, I haven't had that in thirty years—maybe forty." She pressed the doorbell, but I didn't hear a ring. Sunny sniffed the air again. "And haven't wanted it, either. What's that other smell?"

I took a deep discerning whiff. "Meatloaf," I replied. "The kind made with Campbell's tomato soup." The conversation in the car had altered something between us. Now we were a couple of working-class girls talking about dinner.

"Oh, yeah," Sunnye said, "I remember that. You serve it with canned peas and instant mashed potatoes."

I laughed. "And chocolate pudding made from a box."

When no one answered the bell, my companion pressed it again. No discernible ding-a-ling. She pounded on the door. It opened immediately. "Yeah?"

He wasn't particularly tall, and what was left of his hair had gone grey, but he was a powerful man, broad through the shoulders, thick rather than flabby in the gut, and fit in the way a middle-aged man gets only when he works at it.

"Hi," I said, "we're looking for—"

But Sunnye overrode me. "Officers of the court." She flashed her wallet open, then shut. "We're here for a Ms. Briggs."

He narrowed his eyes. "What's this about?"

She gave him an enigmatic look. "That's between us and Ms. Briggs, sir. Tell her we're here, please."

"I won't tell that bitch nothing."

"Sir," Sunnye barked, "ask Ms. Briggs to come to the door."

"Fuck you," he snarled, and gave the door a vicious shove, but Sunnye's heavy boot kept it from slamming shut.

"Sir, that kind of attitude will only get you trouble—"

From somewhere behind the man came a woman's querulous voice. "Are they here about Peggy?"

Without turning to look at her, he ordered, "Stay out of this, Cath."

"But it's been almost two days—"

"Shaddup!" He raised a threatening fist.

"Watch out!" I shouted. "Here comes Trouble."

Sunnye must have signaled to the dog. Suddenly he was bounding down the walk toward us.

The man's eyes widened. His fist unclenched, transformed itself into a hand outstretched to ward off the dog's attack.

"Please stand aside, sir," Sunnye ordered, "and let us talk to the lady."

The muscles in his face tightened, as if he considered resisting, but then, abruptly, he pivoted, shoved past the woman, and disappeared into the rear of the house.

Peggy's mother was a smaller, plumper, more harried version of her daughter. Not only was she willing to talk, she was eager to talk. Someone had picked up Peggy and Triste the previous morning for school. Who? Some friend; she didn't know who. Why? Something wrong with Peggy's car; she wasn't sure what. Neither of the girls had come home last night. She'd called Triste's school. They told her that Peggy had come to get the child before bus time. That was it. No phone call. No nothing. She was worried half out of her skin.

Now I was worried half out of my skin. This was more than simply a student's weekend escapade. She had her child with her as well.

Missing student aside, we still had to show up at the god-damned Women's Studies dinner. At 7:25 Mai Thai was packed with students, townspeople, and conferees. Trouble followed us in the door. When Claudia saw us, she waved frantically from the long crowded table in the corner. "I was afraid you weren't going to show," she muttered as I pushed my way past her to the almost inaccessible seat to which she motioned me. I shrugged, and the conference director turned to Sunnye, for whom she had saved a prime outside seat. I squeezed into my chair, nodded at my neighbors, and tried to relax. The lights were dim, candles flickered, bead curtains clattered as waiters pushed through with loaded trays. The enticing odors of Asian cuisine whetted my appetite.

As my main course I ordered a double vodka martini, with coconut soup and Shrimp Pad Thai to follow.

At a corner table, a group of graduate students from the conference were on their second round of Tsing Tao. "Then I said to him," a young man with straw-colored hair exulted, "put that in your pipe and deconstruct it!" A howl of laughter went up from the young diners. I sipped my drink and smiled. This was the post-theory generation of grad students, and their irreverence toward the intellectual pieties that bound their elders was refreshing.

All went well until we left the restaurant at 9:05. As Sunnye and I walked out the door, we were suddenly blinded by the glare of television lights. A heavily made-up woman I recognized as a local-news reporter stuck a microphone in Sunnye's face. The novelist flinched. "Ms. Hardcastle, how does it feel," the reporter blared, "to be a suspect in a real-life murder mystery?"

Chapter Seventeen

"I don't know what the hell you're talking about. Buzz off!" Sunnye grabbed my arm and pulled me out onto the sidewalk.

"What's going on?" I queried, dazed by the lights, the camera, the action. Trouble skidded to a halt. His ears went back.

"I don't have a clue, but these people are jackals. Let's get out of here."

"Ms. Hardcastle," jabbered the pursuing reporter, "is there any truth to the rumors that you were seen with the Library Victim just moments before his death?" The Library Victim. Obviously those words had been media-mutated until they now boasted permanent initial caps.

Trouble bared his teeth. The reporter took a prudent step backwards. Sunnye straight-armed her way past the TV crew.

We hoofed it down Division Street, Trouble at our heels. I snatched a glance at my companion. She looked as bewildered as I was. I yanked Sunnye down an alley to where the Subaru was parked in the municipal lot behind Scoops Ice Cream Parlor. When we came within electronic range, I clicked the unlock button on the remote, we slammed into the car, and I threw it into reverse. The news crew halted at the end of the alley. We sped off.

"Whew! Close one." Sunnye mimed wiping her forehead. "What the fuck was that about?"

"You really don't know?" The reporter's words were echoing in my mind: *You were seen with the library victim.*

"Not a glimmer. What did that bitch say? Something about a murder victim?"

"Yes, the guy in the library," I mused. "Elwood Munro."

Sunnye's face went bloodless in the green dashboard light. "Munro? Did you say *Munro?*"

"Yeah. That's the name of the guy who was killed in the library stacks."

She stared at me. "That's not what you told me yesterday. You said *Tutu* or something."

"Tooey. Turns out that was an alias. His real name was Elwood Munro."

"Elly? Shit!" she took a deep breath and held it for longer than seemed possible. Then she huffed it out. "Then I *was* talking to the victim. Elly? Dead? I can't believe it!" Sunnye slapped the dashboard with the flat of her hand. "Oh, shit! I must have seen him just before…Oh, *holy* shit!" At our backs, Trouble rose, made uneasy by Sunnye's distress. She turned around to soothe him. "It's all right, good dog. It's okay, sweet pup. Lie down again, you excellent boy." Trouble subsided.

Traffic was scant at this time of night. I made the left at Field and Main without stopping—without even slowing. Suddenly maximum speed seemed like a good idea. "Sunnye, if you were with the victim that close to the time of his death, the cops must know—especially if the press does. Look, you've gotta go to the police, before they come after you. I'll take you to the station."

"No! I'm deathly allergic to cop shops. I'll call them from the Inn."

We cruised down Field Street, and I slowed to turn into the Enfield Inn's circular drive. A male duo staked out the canopied doorway. The short heavy guy puffed on a cigarette. The tall one in the baseball cap checked the film in his camera.

"Shit! More reporters. Keep going."

"Duck down so they don't see you." I accelerated past the sprawling white building, slamming my right arm protectively across her body, as if she were the toddler Amanda.

"What should I do?" she moaned, from her crouched position. For once, Kit Danger seemed to be at a loss.

"Come home with me," I said. "You can call the police from there."

Except for a minor skid on black ice, the drive home was uneventful. Sunnye told me about Elwood Munro. I'd never known her to be so talkative. "We belong to this group... Urban Explorers, we call ourselves. It's a kind of a global network of...recreational infiltrators. We get together once a month, always in a different major city—New York, London, Paris, and we...explore."

"Explore *what*?" I didn't understand the evasiveness in Sunnye's tone. Exploring sounded harmless enough. "And isn't it prohibitively expensive if you have to hop between London and Paris to do it?"

"We're all moneyed people."

Moneyed people? "Elwood Munro was rich?"

"He had generous trust funds, or so everyone said." But money was the least of Sunnye's concerns. "I couldn't believe it when I saw Elly in that library. A *library*, of all places. I couldn't understand it—we always have backup, but he was on his own. He was...startled...to see me, too. We talked for a few minutes, then he...showed me around."

"Showed you around?" I echoed.

"Around...the library. I left him in the closed stacks—"

"But they're restricted to everyone but library personnel."

"Yes, they are. Forbidden spaces—that's the whole point. Infiltration. Incursion. Criminal trespass. It's a kick. I've been everywhere. Kayaking storm drains in Minneapolis. Picnicking in a Bronx subway tunnel. Wandering through Paris catacombs—"

"But that's—"

"Illegal. I just said, that's the point. What's the problem? We don't do any harm. But if the press gets hold of this..."

"I was going to say—that's *dangerous*."

"That, too. I *love* it. And you can get in anywhere if you try. Think about it—windows, manholes, elevator shafts, ventilation ducts."

"Christ, Sunnye, are you out of your mind?"

"It's a hobby. And, besides, I learn a lot. I write it off as research expenses."

Criminal trespass? Incursions? Cheap thrills for rich people. "So that's how Kit Danger—"

"Knows how to get around, say, an abandoned industrial site. Deserted factories have a beauty all their own, stark and ruinous."

"Abandoned factories? Storm drains? You sure don't like to play it safe, do you?"

She laughed. "You got it."

"And that's how you came to know Elwood Munro? Through this...hobby?"

"The guy's a master. He's got...he *had*...more balls.... One time he got into a closed tunnel in Grand Central Station by crawling down an active elevator shaft." She shook her head. "I just can't believe he's gone."

"Hmm." *Balls.* I thought about all those stolen books—and all the risks he must have taken in heisting them. Elevator shafts? Hmm.

"That's why I couldn't believe he was infiltrating something as tame as a library. What for?"

"Books." I was starting to put two and two together: A secure library. A master infiltrator. Ventilation ducts. Elevator shafts.

Stolen books.

"Like I said, I left Elly in the closed stacks and came back up to the reception. He was fine, but he didn't have any *books*. He said he was just going to…to poke around a little more."

Poke around. Trespass. Break and enter. Steal books.

Fun and games.

"Sunnye, how well did you know Elwood Munro?" An early skunk waddled across the road. I slowed to give him plenty of space.

"Not what you'd call *well*. It's not as if we were friends, or anything. He was simply an…associate in…extra-curricular adventure. And a damn good one, too."

I weighed telling the novelist about Munro's *extra*-extra-curricular adventures, but was overcome by a sudden attack of discretion. Elwood Munro stole books. Sunnye Hardcastle collected books. Was it possible their association had something more to it than mere *adventure*?

It was after ten when we turned into my driveway, and dark in the way it gets in the deep country, thick and plush like black velvet. I braked at the kitchen door. At the sight of my little house, warm and safe, I felt the final dregs of the day's energy evaporate. Home at last. "God, I'm beat," I said, extracting the keys from the ignition.

"Me, too," my companion replied. For a change the glamorous Sunnye Hardcastle looked every bit her fifty-some-odd years. Confrontation with Peggy's angry stepfather. Escape from the jackal press. News of a friend's murder. And, to top it all off, dinner with Women's Studies faculty. Kit Danger had had a stressful day.

"I'll make a pot of chamomile," I said. "You call the police. Then we'll turn in. You can have my daughter Amanda's room. You'll be safe. Those reporters will never think to look for you here." I switched off the headlights and opened the door.

An intensely bright light flared, trained on the car. I squinted and raised my arm to shade my eyes. Sunnye blurted out, "What the hell?"

"I *thought* you might bring her here," said Lieutenant Charlie Piotrowski, frowning at me from behind an industrial-strength flashlight. Then he looked over at Sunnye. "Massachusetts State Police, Ms. Hardcastle. We need you to come into headquarters with us. We have a few questions for you."

Sunnye seemed shocked into silence. The only response was a low growling sound from somewhere deep inside the car. Charlie swept his light into the back seat of the Subaru just as Trouble reared his ugly head.

The following morning Charlie and I met for breakfast at the Blue Dolphin Diner. He'd spent the night interviewing Sunnye Hardcastle. After the sharp words we'd exchanged as his officers had loaded Sunnye and her dog into a patrol car, I wasn't at all certain he'd ever again spend the night with me.

Charlie was on his way to some official function, wearing full-dress uniform. When I saw him waiting for me in a back booth, I was unexpectedly thrown off balance by the authority of the man: insignias, medals, gun belt, gun. All right, so I knew just exactly what lay underneath that dark blue wool; nonetheless, in uniform, at six-foot-three and close to two hundred and fifty pounds, Lieutenant Charlie Piotrowski of the Massachusetts State Police Department of Criminal Investigation, Homicide Division, was all cop. Intimidating as hell.

I slid in across from him and attacked before I lost my nerve. "I'm really angry at you."

"I could tell." He smoothed out the *Globe* he'd been reading and folded it. "I'm pissed at you myself. Like I said last night, you had no business aiding and abetting a homicide suspect, especially after I explicitly told you to stay away from the investigation."

"You think I've forgotten that?" I looked him straight in the eye. "What I want to know is, where the hell do you get off *telling* me anything?"

He hesitated, gave me a sober look. Then he reached across the table and took both of my hands in his. "Let's not do this, Karen. I don't want to screw up what we—"

But I was in full spate. "You explicitly told me not to have dinner with a distinguished conference guest? You explicitly told me not to help a celebrated author escape persecution by the press?" A waitress approached, coffee pot in one hand, orange-banded decaf pot in the other. Hearing the tone of my voice, she halted. I pulled my hands away, and snatched up a menu. "Cheddar omelet and sausage," I informed her, without opening it. "Rye toast. Marmalade, if you have it."

She poured coffee, set the pots on the table, and wrote my order down, her expression blank. Then she turned to Charlie and granted him a slow, appreciative smile. "And for you, Captain?" There was a quarrel going on here, and she knew whose side she was on.

"It's Lieutenant, and I'll have the same, only give me the ham steak instead of sausage."

I took advantage of the interruption to cool down. "Sorry, Charlie," I said, when he turned back to me. "I didn't mean to go after you like that, now, or last night either. I know you're the cop here, but, as you said yesterday, you got me into this when you called me up to Chesterfield. Plus I have professional obligations, too. While Sunnye's here, she's my responsibility. I'm concerned about her."

"I understand that. And you're concerned with good reason."

Damn! It must be worse than I thought. "You still have her in custody?"

"Yes."

"But—"

"Karen, you must be aware that we wouldn't proceed in questioning Ms. Hardcastle without probable cause. You know what concerns *me*? Whether or not you *trust* me. Isn't that the issue? Trust."

"Of course I trust you."

"Then why are you giving me such a hard time?"

"*I'm* giving *you* a hard time? After the way you spoke to me last night in front of Sunnye and Felicity Schultz—telling me, and I think I've got it verbatim, that I should *keep my nose out of police business.*"

"I regret the tone, but I worry about you. I worry." He paused a moment, then sighed, long and deep and slow. "And when I asked you about Sunnye Hardcastle yesterday morning, why didn't you tell me that the night of the murder she was out of your sight for over half an hour?"

I winced. "I didn't think it was relevant." I'd deliberately evaded giving him that information to keep Sunnye from what I'd thought of then as an inconvenient complication.

"Uh huh. And why did you impersonate a law-enforcement officer at Peggy Briggs' home?"

Oh, hell, how had he heard about that? "*I* didn't impersonate anyone. That was Sunnye."

"You went along with it."

"We needed to find Peggy."

"So you interfered in a police investigation? That's one of the reasons I'm concerned about you. You're not a trained investigator. You just don't think things through. Not only could you endanger yourself, you could also muddy the waters for us. This is official business." He glared at me. I glared back.

There was a momentary pause. Then he spoke in softened tones. "Besides…you're distracting me from my work. Do you realize that? I'm charged with determining what happened in the college library that resulted in the death of Elwood Munro, and you're running around playing cops and robbers with a primary suspect. How can I concentrate?"

I shrugged, but didn't trust myself to say anything.

"And, this I really need to know," he went on, brusque again, "whose idea was it to go searching for Peggy Briggs in the first place? Yours? Or Ms. Hardcastle's?"

I sat back and considered him from as far a distance as the narrow diner booth allowed. "Charlie, I think you've made up your mind a priori that Sunnye is guilty of homicide—"

The waitress delivered platters heaped with the kind of breakfast delicacies unavailable in any other eatery in health-conscious Enfield. I immediately forked down a bite of omelet. I hadn't gotten much sleep, and needed the Blue Dolphin's cholesterol and caffeine to jump start me on what had already become a rotten day.

Charlie ignored his meal. He leaned toward me. "Karen, you know that only a jury determines guilt or innocence. In my job I'm charged with gathering evidence, and proceeding according to the rules of evidence. And, believe me, in this case, there's plenty."

"What kind?"

"Physical evidence, evidence that places Hardcastle at the scene. And that's more than I should be telling you."

"But she must have explained why she was in the library stacks."

"Oh, yeah. Urban Explorers. Quite a tale." He attacked his ham steak with the dull-edged table knife.

"Are you going to charge her?"

He evaded a direct response. "Trust me," and the words were freighted, "given that Hardcastle's involvement turns this into a high-profile case, you can damn well believe we'll have secured good, solid, incontrovertible physical evidence before we proceed with any charges. But, if the evidence we've gathered pans out, we may well *have* to charge her. And I'm not saying another word about it, Karen."

I opened my mouth to respond, but he went on, "And, besides, how can *you* assume her innocence—*a priori*, to quote you—given that she freely admitted to you her involvement with the victim in systematic, planned illicit activities?"

"I don't know," I replied, pushing my plate away after half a dozen bites. "She may be a bit of a renegade when it comes to some things, but I'm damn sure Sunnye Hardcastle had nothing to do with Elwood Munro's death. It just doesn't make sense."

We were seated at a rear booth, as usual, with Charlie's back against the wall, again as usual. I could take comfort in the fact that if anyone should ever attempt to assault me at the Blue Dolphin, say with an overcooked ham steak, I'd be well-and-truly protected.

There was a long period of silence, which he finally broke. "Maybe we shouldn't see each other until this is over," he said. "I need to concentrate on the investigation without having to worry about you."

He was probably right, but his words felt like a knife in my heart. They hurt so much, I retaliated like a spoiled adolescent. "Maybe we shouldn't see each other—period."

"Karen, no…" When I raised my eyes from my coffee, Charlie was as white as the sugar in the bowl in front of him. He grabbed my arm to keep me from leaving. "Don't go, Karen. Listen, I care about you so much. This is really hard for me. I know I got you into this. I called you up to Chesterfield the other night because you're smart, you know about books, and I knew you could help us." He had my hands again. "And, I gotta admit, it was such a weird scene, I just wanted to share it with you. I knew you'd love it. But, this job of mine can be so damn shitty, there's just no leeway. Look what I've done, I've dropped you right smack in the middle of a stinking mess." His tone shifted from apologetic to worried. "And you just won't keep out of it."

I sighed. "Don't beat up on yourself." I freed my hands. "I would have been smack in the middle of the mess anyhow. I'm Sunnye's assigned liaison with the college." Tentatively I reached out to stroke his cheek. Before I could make contact, his eyes widened and he jumped up from his seat. At first I thought he was recoiling from my caress, then I realized he must have noticed the time on the round diner clock: 9:32.

"Damn, I gotta go. Now, listen, Karen...I've got Trouble." He paused for a last slurp of coffee.

"You've got trouble?" It sounded so dire my breath tightened.

"Yeah. He's out in the car. Ms. Hardcastle didn't want us to put him in the kennel. She requested that I ask you to take him."

"Oh, God, no," I moaned. "Not Trouble. Not that dog. Not now."

Chapter Eighteen

I drove to campus for the final conference session. Trouble rode shotgun. The big dog balked as I led him into my office. His upper lip began a slow, sinuous ripple. Fangs appeared. I shivered, then breathed in deeply. Survival instinct took over. I visualized myself in a classroom: *Never let them smell fear*. I assumed the scowl and bark of a hardened teacher. "Trouble. Come! Sit! Stay!" He came, sat, and stayed. I breathed again. I closed Trouble in behind the door.

As I passed the president's office on my way to the session in Emerson Hall, Avery Mitchell called me in. He wore grey wool pants and a starched blue broadcloth shirt open at the collar. He must have dressed in a hurry; his belt had missed one of the belt loops. "Aiiee, Karen," he groaned theatrically, closing the door behind him and leaning against it. "Who would have thought it? Another murder on this peaceful little campus."

"There's been another murder? When? Who?" I stared around, as if he might have a corpse concealed behind the maroon leather furniture.

"I mean that guy in the library. Elwood Munro, the police say his name was."

"Oh." Two days ago. Old news now. "Yes, of course."

"The book thief. I'm glad I ran into you—for a couple of reasons. Listen, we're going to be taking some heat here for not having promptly reported the book and manuscript thefts." He raised an elegant eyebrow.

"Hmm," I said. "Did you get your donor?" I hoped it didn't sound snide.

"Oh, yeah," he replied. "A substantial addition to our collections." He leaned toward me. "All the more reason to keep mum about any conversation we might have had." He sat back and grinned disarmingly.

"Hmm," I repeated. I seemed to recall having talked to Charlie about all this.

"And, also…now this is awkward…O'Hanlon, the investigator we hired to look into the…er…library situation…the book thefts, I mean, not the murder. He says he knows you."

"Yeah. High school."

"After Munro was found dead, he, O'Hanlon, that is, seemed to lose his enthusiasm for the job. Thought he should back out until the homicide investigation was completed."

In the outer office a phone rang. Lonnie pushed open Avery's door. "Sorry to interrupt, but I've got his secretary on the line."

"I'll be right there." He headed to the phone on his desk.

"But he said, you—"

"Told me he didn't want to mess around in anything that involved murder. Can't say as I blame him." He sat at his desk and pulled the phone toward him.

"I thought you were the one who—"

His hand was on the receiver, but he wanted to finish his thought. "And now that the police have discovered all those books at Munro's place, it's pretty clear he was the thief. So, we probably won't need O'Hanlon again. Nonetheless, Karen, I'd also like to ask you to keep quiet about the college having hired an investigator. Still the same PR reasons."

"Of course, if you want me to, but—"

"Okay, Lonnie, I'm on." Hand covering the mouthpiece. "Bye, Karen. And thanks." Turning from me. "Hey, George, good buddy, how's the golf game?" His eyes were still on me as I went out the door.

Claudia gave the closing speech in the main auditorium, Emerson 101. "Historically," she began, "American crime fiction testifies to a fatally compromised position on female agency…."

I tried to listen. Truly I did. But I had Trouble on my mind. How did Sunnye expect me to take care of a big, potentially vicious dog like that? Would he continue to obey me? Or would he tear my throat out?

Then there was Sunnye to worry about: What evidence did investigators have on the novelist that they would take the risk of detaining such a high-profile celebrity overnight? It must be something damning. She could really set my teeth on edge, but despite her abrasiveness, I'd come to like the novelist. So she was rich and arrogant—and a criminal trespasser, to boot—but the creator of Kit Danger was no killer. Kit Danger was an icon of humane values, of honor. For Hardcastle's errant sleuth, it didn't always come down to obeying the law, but it did always come down to justice and morality.

Sunnye was a book collector, and Elwood Munro's murder had to do with the theft of rare books. But the novelist was no thief. She could well afford to buy anything she wanted, and not from some larcenous bibliomaniac. As to killing him, the thought was absurd. I'd promised Charlie that I'd keep quiet about Munro's cache of stolen books, and so far I had. But, Goddamnit, I intended to do whatever I could in order to prove Sunnye Hardcastle innocent of murder.

I hoped I could manage to do that without pissing the hell out of Lieutenant Charlie Piotrowski.

The scene with Avery was troubling, too. I thought Dennis had told me that Avery himself sidelined the library investigation, but maybe I was wrong. Avery had definitely said it was Dennis's idea.

And where, oh, where was Peggy Briggs?

I slipped a yellow pad out of my bag and printed Elwood Munro's name in the center of the page. Then I circled it. Claudia's microphone squealed: "ideological assaults on the female subject position." I shook my head to clear my ears, then wrote Sunnye's name in the upper left hand corner. I circled it and connected it to Munro's with a line labeled *Urban Explorers*. I chewed on the top of the pen for a moment, then added another line, this one labeled *Collectible Books*. Then I wrote on the bottom of the page: *To Do: 1.) Find Urban Explorers. 2.) Talk to Book Dealer.*

I tuned into the conference briefly: Claudia was blathering on about the essential instability of evidence in postmodern epistemology. I tuned out. I wrote Peggy's name in the upper right-hand corner of the page, circled it, and connected it to Munro's with a line on which I wrote *Backpack*. Now I really had to locate Peggy, so I could find out how her backpack had gotten into Elwood Munro's kitchen. On my *To Do* list I scribbled: *3.) Find Peggy*.

Claudia built to a crescendo: "A hermeneutics of equality charges feminist scholars to interrogate the subtext of the ideological bunko scheme that constitutes modernist and postmodernist literary strategies. Thank you." *Applause*. Hastily I scrawled Dennis O'Hanlon's name and connected it to Munro's with a line labeled *Library Investigation*. In the *To Do* column I wrote: *4.) Call Denny*. I'd ask the private investigator what he'd found out about the book thefts before Avery took him off the library case.

Or, before he'd dropped out of it himself. I was still confused about that.

People began to leave the auditorium. I stood up. Two men in denim and a woman in black edged past me. The woman said something to the shorter man about "the necessity in any neofeminist model of self-agented subject position to address the implicit cultural inscription of essentialized female culpability." I sat down again and settled into my seat. I wrote *Rachel Thompson* on the sheet and labeled her connection: *Stolen Books*. What did the librarian know about how the book thefts were carried out? Then I went back to my *To Do* list: *5.) Talk to Rachel*.

The room was now empty except for me and my busy little pencil. I sighed. Was all this frenetic investigative planning truly necessary? Or was it related to my need to convince myself that Charlie Piotrowski had no right to call the shots about whether or not I could "aid and abet" Sunnye Hardcastle? Or was it perhaps a way of forgetting what had just happened between us in the diner. All Charlie had said was that maybe we should take a break until the investigation was completed. Then I had to go and blurt out that maybe we shouldn't see each other again, period. Should I call him and tell him I didn't mean it. That my remark was nothing but knee-jerk pigheadedness? That I loved him and didn't want to risk losing what we had together?

Someone lowered the lights in the auditorium and closed the door. I jumped up; the last thing I needed was to spend the weekend locked in Emerson 101. I slid the pad into my bag and headed for the exit. It was Saturday morning. I had to teach again on Monday. When was I going to get any of this Goddamned sleuthing done?

In the lobby, coffee and bagels provided traveling sustenance to departing conferees. I decanted coffee from an urn and looked around. Anyone here from my *To Do* list? Rachel Thompson was off in a corner deep in conversation with

Paul Henshaw, the antiquarian book dealer. I headed toward them. The librarian's complexion was even more rubicund than usual; her plump hands were flying. She was excited about something. And so was Paul. He was leaning forward, listening hard. As I approached them, I was struck by his intensity, the knowledgeable passion of the connoisseur oddly out of sync with the rugged features, the once-broken nose.

When she saw me coming, Rachel exclaimed, "Ohmigod, it's you, Karen!" She grabbed my arm and pulled me into their conversation. "You saw that house! That cop told me you were there." So Charlie had followed up on our conversation and called Rachel out to look at the books. "Wasn't it the most extraordinary experience?" In Rachel's excitement, her Texas twang had intensified. "I thought I'd fallen down a rabbit hole! Book theft on such a massive scale, they've actually called in the FBI."

"Really?" Charlie hadn't mentioned that to me at the diner, but, then, he had other things on his mind. "The FBI? Why?"

"Illicit interstate commerce—or something like that."

Paul turned to me, eyes avid. "You were there? In Chesterfield? Why, Karen? You're not in the book trade."

"No, but I…I know the police working on the case. I helped them out before…." I left it vague.

"Oh." He studied me as if I were a volume being priced: collectible but slightly chipped. "And you think Rachel's right, that the contents of that house are priceless?" He ran his tongue over his lips, as if anticipating something tasty.

"Well, yes. But, of course, nothing's for sale," I continued. "It's all got to go back to where it came from."

"Of course," he said, "but what an amazing collection. I'd give anything to see it before they break it up." He showed teeth, a wolf's grin. "You say you know the investigators? Could you get me in there?"

"Well, they are going to need a rare-book expert. Why don't you call and mention your credentials?"

"Hmm," he said, "I'll do just that. Thanks."

Rachel turned to me. "Paul knows about the theft of *The Maltese Falcon* manuscript. I told him."

"Oh."

He laughed. "That'll be a hot item. In more ways than one. Not the kind of thing you could tout on the Internet, but word'll get around among the cognoscenti if it's put up for sale. It's unique, to say the least. And with Hammett's corrections, in his own hand? Invaluable. An irresistible lure to just the right person."

"Who would that be?"

He shrugged. "Some mega-wealthy collector, who'd horde it for his own private delectation."

"Delectation?"

"His own private pleasure. Word of this gets around, they'll be coming out of the woodwork, oil sheiks, media moguls, Internet billionaires."

"How much do you think?"

He smiled with an insider's secret knowledge. "Might start out at a hundred thou, but something like this, there's no telling where the ceiling is. You get a bidding war going, and it all depends on how badly someone wants it."

This entire exchange had taken place in lowered tones. We must have looked like huddled conspirators planning a political coup. As far as I could tell from the conference buzz as I'd passed through it on my way to Rachel and Paul, news of the cache of stolen books was not yet circulating. But, given the rumor dynamics of Enfield College, it would be common knowledge before the day was out.

As it happened, we didn't have to wait that long.

The TV local-news crew was setting up on the wide steps as I exited Emerson with Rachel and Paul. "Professor Karen Pelletier," yammered the same blow-dried blonde who had waylaid Sunnye outside Mai Thai, "we have information that you've been helping the cops solve the college homicide. Is that true?" She thrust the microphone at me.

I was stunned. Academics are hardly newsworthy; I'd never before had a TV camera pointed directly at my face. It was a moment before I could respond. "N…no comment," I said. Brilliantly.

"And how did you feel when you saw all those stolen books at that house in Chesterfield? Can you tell our viewers what it was like to actually be in that house, surrounded by a fortune in rare books?"

I gathered my wits and took a deep breath. "You shouldn't split infinitives on the air," I said. Pivoting on my heel, I slammed back into the building. Claudia Nestor passed me on her way out. Before the heavy door closed behind her, I heard Claudia say to the reporter, "Oh, how wonderful! You've come to do a piece on the conference? What can I tell you?"

I knew Earlene was often on campus on the weekend, so I hotfooted it upstairs to the Dean of Students' office. The door to the outer office was open. The light was on in the inner room. "Earlene," I wailed, "help. The vultures are after me."

Earlene took me home with her. Her house is a small yellow colonial four blocks from campus in the center of the faculty residential district, otherwise known as the faculty ghetto. The houses are mostly nineteenth-century neoclassical, colonial, and Gothic revival, built on small lots shaded by hundred-year-old oaks and maples. Earlene lived next door to Rachel Thompson, back-to-back with Claudia Nestor, one down from Sally Chenille, and across the street from Miles Jewell. I didn't envy her the lack of privacy and the gossip-ridden neighborhood, but today the near refuge was more than welcome. Earlene had gutted the original cramped rooms and rebuilt the house on an open plan, with kitchen and bathroom in the rear and sleeping lofts reached by a spiral staircase. The result was a generous light-filled space, which she had furnished in black and golden brown and hung with vivid African weavings.

"Catch me up on what's been happening," she said, as she measured freshly ground coffee into a filter pot.

I sat on a high wooden stool at her butcher-block kitchen counter and brought her up to date. When I got to the part about my visit to the Briggs house with Sunnye, Earlene paused in the middle of pouring boiling water into the pot. "You mean not even her family knows where Peggy is?"

"Not unless she came home last night, they don't."

"That's not good; not at all. You know, I think it's time for the Dean's office to look into this."

I slumped in one of her comfortable armchairs with a mug of black coffee while she called Peggy's home number. When she didn't get an answer, Earlene said, "Usually at this point I would talk to the roommate, but Peggy doesn't have one. What about friends? You have any idea who she hangs with?"

"I've seen her with Stephanie Abrams a few times. They seem tight."

"Really? Hmm. That's an odd couple."

"Why do you say that?"

"Stephanie comes from such an illustrious family. Her father's the novelist, C. Lawrence Abrams. Her mother's also literary, something in the book business, can't remember exactly what. And Peggy…she's so…rough around the edges."

"Yeah? Well, education's the great leveler."

"I thought *death* was supposed to be the great leveler."

"That, too."

Earlene called the dorm and left a message on Stephanie's voice mail. Then she sat by the phone with the college directory still open, tapping the oak desk with slim brown fingers. It seemed to me that she had something more on her mind than she was admitting.

"How about her car?" I asked. "We could keep an eye out for that. Do you know what she drives?"

She snapped back from wherever her thoughts had taken her. "No, but Security will. They get that info for the parking permit." Earlene called the Security office. It took her a while to get through to someone who knew something. I glanced around. It was so comfortable here, I could stay forever. Earlene's living room, dining area, and study nook flowed together without disruptive barriers, and in the sun-flooded space with its wide-board floors and exposed beams, ordinary objects such as plates and vases became almost luminous.

Earlene hung up the phone. "Peggy got a parking permit in September for an orange 1984 Chevrolet Citation."

"Oh, that's hers, huh? It's hard to miss. It's got 'I'd Rather Be Reading' bumper stickers plastered all over it. Not many of those around anymore."

"Or many Citations. It's a wonder the thing still runs." She went back into the kitchen and returned with a platter of black bread, Jarlsberg cheese, and Granny Smith apples.

The food looked good, but I was worried about Peggy. Why hadn't I told Charlie that the backpack in Munro's kitchen was hers? Okay, so I wanted to shield her from being hassled, but that was before I knew she'd dropped out of sight. Her disappearance threw a whole new light on everything.

"Listen, Earlene, I need some advice. There's something I haven't told you about Peggy."

She nodded, attentive.

"That guy who died in the library? Elwood Munro?"

"Yeah? This is about *Peggy*?"

I hesitated. Charlie had sworn me to silence on Munro's stolen book collection, but obviously someone else had leaked it to the press. "Yes. I was up at Munro's house night before last—"

"His house? Did you *know* him?"

"Of course not." I told her about my visit to the Book House.

"Oh…I see. Charlie."

"Yeah. Charlie." Earlene raised an eyebrow at the tremor in my voice. "And the very last thing I saw before I left that house was Peggy's backpack. It was just sitting there on the kitchen floor."

"Her backpack? In the victim's house?"

"Uh huh."

"How'd you know it was hers?"

"The stuffed Pink Panther hanging from the strap."

"Oh. Yeah, I've seen that. You pointed it out to Charlie, of course."

"No."

"My God, Karen, why not?"

"It was stupid. I realize that now. At the time I was certain there must be a logical reason for it being there. Peggy's had it so rough, I didn't want any suspicion to fall on her. But, surely the police must have looked at it by now. And those kids carry so much junk in their bags—her name would be on everything." I let my head drop into my hands. "Charlie's going to be pissed I didn't tell him at the scene."

"Uh oh." She gave me her Wise Woman of Enfield look. "Trouble in paradise?"

Her words galvanized me. My mouth fell open. I leapt up from the deep chair. "No, in my office!"

"Huh?" Earlene placed a hand on my arm.

"I've got Trouble in my office," I explained, grabbing for my coat.

"Karen?" Her grip tightened.

"He's a dog."

She frowned. "What's that? A metaphor, or something?"

"No, he's just a dog. He belongs to Sunnye Hardcastle. I'm taking care of him."

She released my arm. "Oh, *that* dog."

I gathered up my bag. "I've got to get back. He doesn't want to be with me in the first place, and now I've left him alone for hours. Poor thing, he'll be frantic."

She snatched the cordless phone from her desk and thrust it at me. "I'm not letting you out of here until you call Charlie about Peggy."

"Okay, okay." I called him and told him about the backpack.

He was not a happy man. "And now she's disappeared? Shit." A long silence ensued. "Why didn't you tell me this on the scene? Or last night? Or this morning? We would've examined it right away."

"Listen, Charlie, I know I did the wrong thing. I don't blame you for being angry. If I'd been aware then that she was missing, I'd have mentioned it immediately. And now I'm worried sick about her."

"Good. You should be. We could have been on her from the start."

That was when I remembered it was Peggy who had stumbled across Elwood Munro's dead body in the closed stacks.

"And Karen..." Charlie continued, his words slow and distinct, "I am so damn upset by what you said earlier about us not seeing each other, *period*. If that's the way you feel, then I don't know..." A long, deep sigh. Before I could reply, he hung up.

Chapter Nineteen

I stopped at a deli on the way back to campus and purchased three roast beef sandwiches, one for me, two for my new companion. Trouble had come with a handwritten list of instructions for care and feeding. Roast beef hadn't been on the menu. In the hall outside my office, I unwrapped a sandwich, then eased my way into the room. The big Rottweiler met me at the door. He didn't growl. He didn't lunge for my throat. He did look enormously disappointed. The poor animal was yearning for his mistress. "Good boy," I said, and got close enough to hand him the sandwich. He accepted it with dignity, his big jaws chomping through the bread and meat until his teeth met with a click.

I sat in the green chair and unwrapped my own lunch. Trouble watched every move of my sandwich from the impromptu plate of deli paper on my lap to my mouth. He still looked hungry. A strand of drool hung from his chops. How much roast beef should a fully grown Rottweiler eat in one sitting? More than I'd offered him, obviously. I gave him his second sandwich.

On Saturday afternoon the campus slips into low gear, faculty avoiding their offices, students sleeping off hangovers or catching up on assigned readings. This was the first quiet moment I'd had to process the calamitous events of the past two days: a researcher murdered, a new friend under suspicion, a vulnerable student missing. And now, Charlie. He'd sounded so angry on the phone. I was worried and exhausted, and the food tasted like Styrofoam. I gave my sandwich to Trouble. His third. He wolfed it down. That was more like it. Then he began pacing back and forth by the door. Time for…walksies. Then—home.

Rachel Thompson waylaid me in the parking lot. "Kar-ren! What are you doing with Sunnye Hardcastle's dog?" Her eyes grew wide. "Has Sunnye been…arrested? Last night, the eleven o'clock news—"

I cut her off. "She's just tied up for a few hours." I assumed that wasn't literally true. "She asked me to keep Trouble for her. Rachel, listen, can I buy you a coffee? I'd like to talk to you about…well…you know…Elwood Munro, the book thefts, that crazy Book House."

"You bet. I'd be thrilled to talk. I haven't been able to think about anything other than stolen books for weeks. Avery imposed an absolute moratorium on the subject. I've been so damn uneasy about that. Professional guidelines mandate that we inform police, the press, and the rare-book and manuscript trade anytime something's stolen from our collections. But when Avery says 'jump,' I've got to ask 'how high?' And, I guess, now…" Then, in an abrupt change of demeanor, she bent over to rub Trouble's ears. "Who's a good boy? Huh, who's a good boy?" She slapped his big flanks playfully. I flinched. If I took such a liberty, he'd rip my arm off. "Who's the best boy?" Rachel crooned. Trouble wagged his stub of a tail. This big scary dog seemed to like the librarian.

As Rachel and I crossed Field Street on our way to Bread & Roses, Trouble at our heels, a CNN van turned onto campus, followed by a satellite truck with its otherworldly protuberances. We groaned simultaneously. "I'm afraid

Enfield College is about to hit prime time," my companion said. "How about we get a little further away?"

The BMW was a sporty model, with just enough room in the back for Trouble. "You don't mind a dog in this fabulous car?" I asked.

"What kind of damage could he possibly do? It's all leather. Isn't that right, big boy? Nothing wrong with a little dog hair, right?"

I ran my hand over the shiny pea-green exterior. "Is it new?"

"Yeah." No explanation.

I pushed it. "Sure doesn't look like a librarian's car."

"No, it sure doesn't." That was all I was going to get.

"Nice." I stroked the cherry-wood dashboard. We headed through town, past outlying pizza parlors and video rental stores, then skirted a new subdivision of huge, featureless houses situated on a former onion field. The sky was blue, the sun was warm, the brown winter grass was beginning to poke through what was left of the now-filthy snow.

Rachel seemed to have no particular destination in mind. "Do you really want coffee?"

"No. I'm already saturated with caffeine. I want to talk."

"Then let's just drive. And talk." She turned left on Route Two, and we drove west through evergreen woods and the occasional hamlet, picking up speed, listening to the powerful engine growl like a crouching lion.

"How are you doing?" I asked. "It must have been a nasty shock to have a man die in your library."

"God, yes." But Elwood Munro's death wasn't the librarian's primary concern. "On the other hand, it's been an enormous relief to have the book thief identified." She gave a short laugh. "And, selfishly, it's good to know that it wasn't only *my* library he hit. From what I saw yesterday, he's looted dozens of colleges and universities. Even major institutions. I saw books from the Houghton at Harvard, the Beinecke at Yale, the Perkins at Duke." She shook her head. "He must have been at it for years." She glanced over at me. "When I saw those Beadle's dime novels in that house I immediately thought of you. Let me tell you, they were a welcome sight. Not many of those left around."

A yearling deer edged out of the trees, paused by the road. Rachel slowed and sounded the horn. The young buck turned and vaulted back into the woods.

"What about the *Maltese Falcon* manuscript?" I asked. "Any sign of that?"

"No. And believe me, I kept my eye open for it. I was in that place for hours, but only scratched the surface of Munro's…er…collection. And I wasn't allowed to recover any of our holdings. I think I told you that the state cops are turning the whole thing over to the FBI."

"Unbelievable. Books!"

"This is big time, Karen. Transporting stolen goods over state lines gets the attention of the Feds, especially when it's to the tune of millions of dollars."

We turned left onto a country road and wound through the main street of a small town and past a farm with crumbling barns. The Berkshire mountains, tinged red with early spring buds, loomed to the right. I'd lived in Massachusetts most of my life, but this little pocket of country wasn't familiar to me.

"What do you know about this guy—this Munro?" I asked. "Did the police tell you anything?"

"That lieutenant…Piotrowski?…I think you know him?"

"Yeah, I know him." My throat constricted. Just how angry was he?

"He was close-mouthed about the whole thing. Didn't impart any info. Only asked questions. He was pretty brusque."

Hmm. "What kind of questions?"

"Like how the hell did Munro get into the vaults? How did he get all that stuff past the alarm system? How did he evade the guards? All the questions we've been asking ourselves since books started to go missing."

I recalled Sunnye's tales of Elwood Munro's derring-do, slithering through sewer systems and ventilation ducts, scaling elevator shafts. It made a great story, and I was itching to tell it, but didn't. That information was between Sunnye and the investigators. "Did you have any answers for the...the good lieutenant?"

"No. To get through our alarm system, the guy must have been a magician."

"Why would he do it? What kind of twisted thinking compels someone like Elwood Munro to take such risks?"

"Who knows? There's a kind of mystical aura about books. They represent learning. Maybe for someone who felt...oh, say...insecure about his education, stealing all those books from colleges could serve as a substitute."

"Pretty far-fetched, don't you think?"

She shrugged. "Can you think of a reason that isn't?"

The BMW passed a dilapidated grey church next to a grange hall with a For Sale notice. At a crossroad, a rusty white sign with black letters pointed the way to Chesterfield. *Chesterfield!* "Turn right!" I ordered impulsively. "I want to see that house again."

Rachel glanced over at me, a half-smile flickering. Then she shifted smoothly, and the car took the quick corner without hesitation. The road narrowed and began to climb. We climbed with it. Eyes on the road, she said, "They won't let us in, you know. Piotrowski made it clear that once the FBI took it over, that place would be locked up tighter than Walpole Correctional."

I shrugged. "Let's drive by, anyhow. See what's going on."

She grinned. "Sure thing. I'm curious, too."

The blue-and-greys in Munro's driveway were out-numbered and outranked by government SUVs and a sinister black van. The latter must have been packing some heavy-duty crime-scene equipment; it had sunk to its hubcaps in the muddy drive. The old red farmhouse brooded in the brown earth as it had for over a century, its latest crop not the traditional New England corn or hay or Macintosh apples, but a more enduring harvest of print on paper: American villains and heroes; American violence and redemption; American myths and nightmares.

Rachel slowed as we passed the house. At the sound of the sports car's downshift, a tall woman in a sensible blue suit turned in the doorway to check us out. About a half-mile down the road from Munro's property, the cause of her vigilance became clear. The local-news van and a network satellite truck lurked at the entrance to an abandoned farm lane just outside a keep-clear zone marked by police traffic cones. The House of Stolen Books would provide a whimsical story for Local News at Five.

"Jeesh! They were after me all morning. We're not safe anywhere. Let's get out of here." Rachel stepped on the gas. We sped through a stand of native pine. Abruptly she took the first right, onto an even narrower road.

"Where are you going?"

"I'm looking for a place to turn around so we can head back the way we came." She raised a thick eyebrow at me. "I haven't got the slightest idea how to get out of here otherwise. A person could get so lost in these mountains that she'd never be found."

I shuddered. Is that what had happened to Peggy Briggs?

Rachel pulled into a rutted lane, stopped, and began to back into her turn.

"Stop!" In the drab landscape, a swatch of orange caught my eye.

"Why?" She frowned, but braked the car.

"There's something back in that field I want to take a look at." I was already gripping the door handle.

"Huh?" The field in question looked like a hundred others we'd passed: Overgrown bushes poked through granulated snow cover, at this altitude still inches deep.

"Just bear with me, will you?"

Seasoned in New England ways, we were both suitably shod for a trek through the March muck. I led Rachel over a collapsed stone wall, into a scrawny woods growing up on what must have been a short ten years earlier an active farm. With Trouble straining at his leash we trudged straight back through the young evergreens and birch, then circled around and came out at the edge of a spongy field. At the far end of the abandoned farm lane, half-hidden by a tangle of wild raspberry bushes, sat an old orange Chevrolet Citation plastered with "I'd Rather Be Reading" stickers.

"That's Peggy Briggs' car!" Rachel exclaimed. "What the hell is it doing here?"

"I don't know, but I'm going to find out." I took a step in the direction of the vehicle.

She grabbed my arm. "No, Karen, don't!"

"Why not?" I knew very well why not. We were thinking the same thing: If this was Peggy's car, was Peggy still in it? If she was, was she dead?

"Because…because it's not safe. And…because of footprints." An unbroken expanse of snow lay between me and the car. When had it last snowed? The opening night of the conference? The Citation must have been here since then.

I hesitated, half-persuaded by the footprint argument. Trouble changed my mind. He suddenly pulled loose and loped over to the car, trailing his chain-link leash. He sniffed at the driver's door, then jumped up and looked in the window. I ran after him and snatched up the leash. I took a deep breath, then peered inside the car. I couldn't help it; I had to know if Peggy and Triste were in there. Tattered cloth upholstery. An empty Burger King kid's-meal carton in the back seat. School books scattered around. No dead bodies. I exhaled.

Somewhere in a tall oak, a crow cawed. I started and screeched.

"Karen! What?" Rachel remained in the cover of the woods. "Is she there?"

"No, she isn't." I reached for the door handle, then halted just before touching it. Better not. Fingerprints. I'd tampered with evidence enough already.

Trouble continued his olfactory investigation. When he paused at the rear of the car, Rachel gasped. "What if she's in the trunk?"

"I think we'd…know." But I pivoted and followed my footprints back to the librarian. "You have a cell phone?" My hands were still shaking as I pressed the buttons.

"Piotrowski."

"It's me." I sucked in a deep breath. "Look, Charlie, I know you're pissed at me, but this is very important." Heavy silence. I waded through it. "I'm really worried. I found Peggy Briggs' car—"

"Huh?"

"It's in the woods near Elwood Munro's house. It's an old Citation. Orange. I've seen her in it a hundred times, but she's not in it now." I swallowed. "At least I don't think so." I gave him details of the location.

"Okay. We're on our way." There was a long pause, and then a heartfelt, "Thank you." Another pause, and again, "Thank you for letting me know. And, Karen, I'm not even going to ask what the hell you're doing up there."

A person savvy about her health shouldn't eat General Tso's Chicken. And she shouldn't feed it to a fine pedigreed dog.

But it was Saturday evening, and we were both alone. Trouble lay on my living-room rug with his muzzle on his paws. Every five minutes he gave vent to a mighty sigh, longing for Sunnye. I sat in the old recliner, dipping chopsticks into my cardboard carton long after Trouble had gobbled the contents of his. I was longing for…God knows what.

Within minutes, a patrol car had arrived at the field where Rachel and I had found Peggy's car, and I told my story to a hefty red-faced trooper who looked uncomfortable in a too-tight winter uniform. After a lengthy phone call, he returned to where we sat in the BMW. "The lieutenant says you can go now. He knows where to find you."

Now, back at home, when I pushed the power button on the TV remote, the Six O'clock News flashed on the screen with as much urgency as if it actually had something crucial to impart to viewers. Voices and images flashed by in an impressionistic montage. My full attention was triggered only when the camera focused on Ms. Blow-Dry standing on the steps of Enfield College's Emerson Hall. "Professor Karen Pelletier, is it true that you have been assisting investigators in the bizarre case of the murdered book thief?"

The screen switched to the image of a startled dark-haired woman in a long wool coat. "N…no comment," she stammered. She looked guilty as hell.

I groaned. Any minute now the phone would start ringing, friends and colleagues on the scandal alert, making sure I didn't miss my fifteen seconds of infamy.

The phone rang. I grabbed the cordless by my chair. "I know. I saw it."

"Mom? *What* did you see?" Amanda sounded disconcerted.

"Sweetie! Nothing! Nothing at all. How *are* you?"

"Not so great."

My heart sank. "Baby! What's wrong?"

"I just got back from the infirmary. I have mononucleosis." She dragged the word out to eight syllables. "That's why I've been feeling so lousy this past couple of weeks."

"Honey! I'll come and get you! I'll leave right this minute!"

"No, Mom. You don't have to. Luke is gonna drive me home. He's already gone to get the car."

"Luke? Who's Luke."

"Just a guy." I heard the call-waiting signal click. I ignored it.

"Just a guy? Or just a *guy*?"

"Mom, don't start. I feel like shit." The signal clicked again.

Another maternal failure. "I bet you do. I'm sorry. So, okay, you'll be here by, what, midnight?"

"Around then. Oh, and Mom?"

"Yeah?" *Click.*

"Can Luke sleep on the couch?" *The couch. Whew!* "I'll get everything ready," I assured her. "I love you, Sweetie."

"Yeah, me too. You."

I hung up, and the phone rang. I ignored it. Claudia Nestor was on the TV screen. Ms. Blow-Dry asked, "Can you tell our viewers how you feel about the detention for questioning by state police investigators of the crime novelist, Sunnye Hardcastle?" I thumbed the set off in the middle of some old footage of Sunnye doing an interview on Book TV.

Chapter Twenty

The Stop 'N' Shop was semi-deserted, and I sped through aisles, throwing food into the cart. Ginger ale, sherbet, crackers, noodles. Chicken: mother-love in plastic wrap. What was the recommended diet for mononucleosis, anyhow? I added chocolate-frosted cupcakes with cream filling to the cart. Those were for me; my daughter doesn't eat junk food. I stopped at the mall and bought Amanda a Gap sleep shirt, then, when I got to the car, turned around, went back, and bought two more; it takes *weeks* to recover from mono. I went to Video Heaven and picked up her three favorite films, even popped into Bed, Bath, and Beyond for two new pillows. Still it was only nine o'clock when I arrived home.

What to do? Put the groceries away? Make up Amanda's bed with fresh sheets? Run the vacuum? Clean the bathroom?

Mononucleosis? Mononucleosis? I didn't know a damn thing about mononucleosis. Why hadn't I become an M.D. instead of a useless Ph.D.?

Trouble met me at the door. He allowed me to pat him on the head. "Good dog," I told him. What else can you say to one hundred and twenty pounds of tooth and muscle? I dumped the bags on the kitchen table and headed for the computer: Maybe I could learn something about mono on the Internet.

The phone rang before I could log on. I snatched it up. "Amanda?"

"No. It's Sunnye." The novelist was uncharacteristically subdued. "Where have you been? I've been trying to call you all evening."

My daughter's illness had driven Sunnye Hardcastle from my mind. "Where are *you*?"

"I'm back at the Enfield Inn, but I've got to get out of here. Can you come get me? Those damn journalists are swarming the place."

"The police let you go?"

"For now. But, Karen…" She paused. I could hear her swallow. "I'm in deep shit. They really do think I killed Elly. They told me not to leave the county."

"God, Sunnye, I'm sorry." Charlie and his team don't make unfounded accusations. Was I crazy, helping her out? "Do you have a lawyer?"

"He's on his way out from L.A. right now. And Merry will be up from New York in the morning."

"Who's Merry?"

"She's my publicist. I'm gonna need big-time damage control. Can't you see the headlines? *Hardcastle Gets Hard Time*."

"Hmm." The police suspect this woman of homicide, and she worries about P.R. What's wrong with this picture? Then, all of a sudden, over the telephone line, I could hear the tough cookie crumble. "But for tonight…you said I could use your daughter's room?…" She sounded like a homeless waif.

The silence on my side of the line must have gone on too long. Charlie's admonition to stay out of his case was all too fresh in my mind.

The waif-like voice faltered. "Look, I can go to a motel."

Her plaintive tones melted my resolve. "Actually, Sunnye, Amanda's coming home, but I can put you up anyhow." My house has three small bedrooms, and I'd converted one into a study. It has a lumpy futon. I could put Sunnye and her dog in my room, make up the futon for myself. Amanda could sleep in her own room, Luke—whoever he was—on the couch. What had been earlier this evening an empty shell of a house was quickly being transformed into Home Central.

I suppressed any qualms I might have about harboring a suspected murderer. Charlie doesn't know everything. He's skilled at what he does, but he's not infallible. Sunnye might be abrasive, even obnoxious, but she was a good person. I'd read all her books. The creator of Kit Danger was no killer.

Right?

"Don't worry, Sunnye. I'll be there in twenty minutes."

"Thanks. You're a pal." Her voice seemed to creak, as if she hadn't said "thank you" in a long time. "When you get to the Inn, come around to the kitchen door. The staff's going to smuggle me out that way."

"Okay," I said, "see you there."

But Sunnye wasn't ready to hang up. "And, oh, Karen... how's my big boy?"

Huh? Her big boy? "Trouble's fine. He's right here." The Rottweiler was panting at my elbow.

"Let me talk to him."

"Talk to Trouble?"

"Yes. Please."

I put the phone to the big dog's ear. I could hear Sunnye's voice echo faintly through the receiver: "Hey, sweet boy. Mommy's coming home. See you soon."

The dog's muscular body quivered. "Ruff! RUFF!"

When I spoke into the phone again, Sunnye was gone.

The rescue operation went without a hitch. I drove my nondescript Subaru down the Enfield Inn's rear drive, picked up a nondescript individual in dark-green work clothes toting a nondescript black plastic garbage bag. Trouble almost wriggled out of his skin greeting Sunnye. We exited the service road under the blind surveillance of the press.

"Thank God!" Sunnye exclaimed, as we turned north out of town. "And thank *you*, Karen. I won't forget this. What can I do to repay you?" Sunnye looked exhausted, her fine features drawn and haggard. I wondered if she'd had any sleep at all since she'd left my house in police custody the night before.

"You can tell me what's going on." I flicked the turn indicator for a left onto Route 138.

She closed her eyes and sighed. "The police have physical evidence that places me at the scene of the crime."

"But they know why you were there. I heard you tell them."

"Why should they believe me? I don't make a very credible witness, do I? Hardened scofflaw that I am. Unrepentant criminal trespasser."

"Oh, Sunnye, speaking of trespass?" I recalled the notes I'd made about looking into her association with Munro. How could I ask her about other members of the Urban Explorers without letting her know what I was up to? I made the question as casual as possible. "Who else was in that explorer group?"

She didn't bite. "Confidential. We take an oath."

Dead end there.

She was still musing over her encounter with Massachusetts' finest. "One of those cops asked me if I thought I was above the law. Like Kit Danger, he said." She pulled down the visor, checked herself in the lighted mirror, then slapped it back up. Nope—not Kit Danger. "It didn't help any when I said Kit wasn't *above* the law, she was simply *outside* the law. That the law to her was a set of fictional constraints by which she chose not to imagine herself bound."

"Jesus! Who'd you say that to? Piotrowski?"

"Yeah. The big guy that was at your house. The lieutenant. You know him, don't you?"

"Oh, yes. You could say that. We've been...together...for a while."

She regarded me soberly. "Karen, if you're involved with this guy, I don't want to get you in hot water with him. Just drop me off at some motel. I'll register as Jane Doe."

"No, for Chrissake! I do what I want to. You're coming home with me."

We drove through the Enfield outskirts. Smoke rose from chimneys. TV screens flickered in windows. Porch lights glowed. A peaceful evening in the New England countryside. Then I blurted out, "But, Sunnye, what on earth possessed you to smart off to Charlie Piotrowski about the law being a fiction!"

She grinned at me, sheepishly. "Well...I was quoting verbatim from one of the talks I heard at the conference—something about the *cultural imaginary*. The author said the law was a complex set of agreed-upon conventions by which we choose to imagine ourselves safe."

"Ah, social constructivism."

"Yeah? Well, the idea took my fancy, and, I thought, what the hell, it's just scholarly claptrap, how much trouble could it get me in?" She checked herself in the mirror again. The lighted frame lent her tired features a greenish cast. She was not now Kit Danger, nor had she ever been. "Stupid, I know."

I could picture Charlie's reaction to her banter: The intelligent brown eyes widen for a mere second. The full lips purse. Then the official mask falls: The strong face negates all response. I sighed. A tidal wave of longing almost knocked me over.

"Well, Sunnye, you *are* a bit of a renegade."

She took it as praise. "Damn right, I am." She slapped her thigh in emphasis. In the confines of the small car, the impact sounded like a gun shot. Trouble jumped up and poked his dark muzzle into the front seat uneasily. She patted him. "And, Goddamn it, Karen, you should be, too. What good is life if you have to follow every fucking rule?"

I thought about it for a minute. Given where I come from, simply doing what I'm doing is a renegade act. If moving from the squalid row houses of Lowell to the ivory towers of Enfield College isn't social trespass, I don't know what is. I don't need to kayak the storm sewers of Minneapolis to get my jollies. "Well, Sunnye, there's this to say about it, a strictly law-abiding person doesn't often get picked up and questioned about involvement in a homicide case."

She relaxed back into the seat. "That's true. There is that to be said about a law-abiding life. It's *safe*. Boring, but safe."

My…difficulty…with Charlie Piotrowski came to mind, then my upcoming tenure decision. *Yeah. Safe.* I changed the subject. "Did they say what kind of evidence they have against you?"

"Dog hair in the closed stacks. Trouble sheds a lot."

I clicked my tongue.

"And fingerprints on books, of course. They've got some fabulous editions there. I couldn't keep my hands off them. Elly must have been killed shortly after Trouble and I left him. So, according to the investigators, I've got means and method. *Means*: I was there and I've admitted it. *Method*: I could easily have shoved those steps out from under him. Anyone could have. What they don't have is a *motive*." She leaned her head back against the headrest. "But they're looking into it."

Sunnye was silent as we drove deeper into the countryside. Just when I thought she'd fallen asleep, she sighed again. "In case you're wondering, Karen, I do know the difference between right and wrong, between fiction and reality. I didn't kill Elwood Munro. I *write* about murder—I don't *commit* it. And, while I can't exactly say I liked Elly, I did admire the little weasel. God, did he have balls! And, damn it, it looks like I'm going to have to find out who killed him, if only to save my own neck. But, first..." She fell into another silence.

"But, first?" I prompted.

"First I'm going to sleep. And then I'm going to sleep some more."

Sunnye looked around my living room. "This is cozy," she said. Then she went to bed in my bedroom without waiting for me to change the sheets. Trouble flopped down on the mat beside her. I could hear his ecstatic sigh as, toting pajamas, bathrobe, and a change of clothes for the morning, I closed the door behind me.

In the kitchen the sherbet had melted in the paper grocery bag, slopping all over the other provisions I'd forgotten to put away in my rush to rescue Sunnye. I dumped the sticky carton in the sink and mopped up the mess. Then I pulled a big soup pot out from the shelf under the counter. The chicken went in the pot, covered with cold water and accompanied by carrots, celery, onion, and peppercorns. It was ten thirty. I could let the soup cook until Amanda got home at midnight and finish it tomorrow.

By midnight the house smelled of simmering chicken. No Amanda. At one o'clock, I put rice on to steam. No Amanda. I lifted the chicken and vegetables out of the pot, then mashed the vegetables into the broth. I let the chicken cool while I flavored the soup with sea salt, bay leaf, and parsley. Then I shredded the tender meat into the broth and added the rice. One thirty-seven. Soup was done. No Amanda.

Automobile accident? Arrested for speeding through some small town in Delaware? What did I know about this Luke, anyhow? What if he was a boozer with a DWI record? Or, oh my God, what if Amanda had suddenly collapsed and was lying dangerously ill in some hick hospital?

I had my medical manual out now. *Infectious Mononucleosis: fever, nausea, exhaustion.* Okay, okay, okay: we could live with that. But there was more: *Chest pain, difficulty breathing, tachycardia.* Yikes! *Rupture of the spleen!* My God!

I began pacing.

At one fifty-three Amanda's Jetta pulled into the driveway. A skinny kid slid out from behind the wheel. "Hi, Mrs. Pelletier. I'm Luke. I drove Amanda home." He added, "I'm pre-med," as if that explained something.

Amanda got her door open. She was pale, shaky, and thin. I rushed around the car so she could lean on me. "How are you, Sweetie? And what took you so long? I've been worried to death."

"Mom," she said, ignoring my words. "What's going on around here? We just passed two TV news vans pulled over with their parking lights on."

I groaned. "Oh, no! They've found her!"

"Found *who*?"

"Sunnye Hardcastle. She's spending the night in my bed."

Luke's eyes widened. Amanda hadn't told him her Mom was such hot stuff. But my daughter took the news in her stride. "Sunnye Hardcastle, the novelist? At our house? Cool!"

When Sunnye and Trouble came padding into the kitchen at seven-thirty the next morning, I was mixing waffle batter. Sunnye sniffed the air. "Coffee," she said. She held out a mug. I filled it. "Thanks. And thanks for the good bed. By the way, did you know someone's asleep on your couch?"

"That's Luke. He drove Amanda home last night. Sunnye, sorry to have to tell you this, but the vultures have tracked you down. They're hovering outside even as we speak."

"Shit!" She lowered herself onto a kitchen chair. "What am I going to do?" It was a genuine plea for direction. The resourceful Kit Danger seemed to have deserted her creator.

"Eat some breakfast, and we'll think about it." I slid a thick waffle onto a plate and handed it to her.

"Yum," she said. "Do you have one of these things for Trouble?"

I pondered the options. It was Sunday morning in a college town; there were possibilities. I got on the phone and issued some invitations. Then I started cooking. Quiche. Donuts. More waffle batter. Quarts of coffee. By eleven o'clock people began to arrive. Jill came first in the mammoth Ford Excursion her parents had given Eloise for her first birthday. She pulled up to the kitchen door, lugged the toddler in, and went back for two quarts of strawberries. Then came Greg and Irena with their twins, Jane and Sally; Earlene with Lou, her man of the moment; George Gilman with his foster son, six-year-old Shawn. We gabbed and ate for a couple of hours. Sunnye seemed to enjoy herself. Trouble tolerated being mauled by toddlers. Luke told hilarious stories about his summer job in a morgue. Even Amanda, wan as she was, joined in the conversation.

Then it was one o'clock, and everyone prepared to leave—simultaneously. Jill was taking Luke to the bus station in Springfield so he could get back to school for Monday classes. While Jill tucked Eloise into her car seat, Luke, with many effusive good-byes to Amanda, climbed into the front passenger seat of the Excursion. Everyone else got into their cars. In the hubbub of the mass departure, the lurking journalists didn't notice the two blanket-covered figures huddled on the floor of the Excursion's cargo area. The convoy pulled out of the driveway. Sunnye Hardcastle and Trouble were on their way to meet Sunnye's entourage of publicist and lawyer in a luxury suite at the Springfield Marriott.

Under assumed names, of course.

Chapter Twenty-One

Monday morning, sitting at my desk during office hours, I realized I had no idea how to get in touch with Dennis O'Hanlon: no street address, no phone number, no e-mail. Dennis had been investigating the thefts from the library, and, as much as I hated to admit it, her backpack in Elwood Munro's kitchen linked Peggy Briggs to them. The more I knew about where she had been before she disappeared, the more likely it was I would locate her. Maybe Dennis had a line on her. Besides, I thought it would be fun to talk to him again; that combination of childhood memories and jungle-cat masculinity was so damn enticing. I called Information for Lowell. Tons of O'Hanlons—after all, it was an Irish-Catholic family—but no Dennis.

I knew Avery Mitchell would have the investigator's address, but it would be impolitic, downright stupid, actually, to let the president of the college know I was particularly interested in the private eye he'd hired. Or in the college library book thefts. Or in the death of Elwood Munro. If I wanted to be tenured at Enfield next year, I had to keep my head down and my forensic curiosity to myself.

Anyhow, it was the new millennium; the Internet was the way to find Dennis. I logged on, went to the White Pages, keyed in his name, and clicked. Fourteen Dennis O'Hanlons popped up, but *Dennis O'Hanlon, Investigative Services* headed the list.

The O'Hanlon website advertised Investigations: Background, Fraud, Undercover. I clicked on the e-mail link and composed a brief note. Five minutes later the phone rang. Dennis. "Hey, Karen, what's up?"

"Hey, Dennis. Listen, I need some info on what was happening in that library. Can I ask you a few questions?"

A hesitation, then, "Shoot."

"A student of mine seems in some strange way to be connected to the book thief. Peggy Briggs? The young woman you were looking for in the library. The girl with the overstuffed envelope? Now she's missing. No one has seen her in three or four days. I thought if I knew more about what was stolen and how, I might be able to help find her."

"In that case I guess it won't hurt to divulge a few facts."

Divulge? "Did you run across her at all?" I asked.

"No. But you've got to remember I was only on this investigation for a couple weeks, and only those two days on site."

"Uh huh." Hadn't Monica mentioned that she'd seen him around before that?

"My preliminary inquiries made it clear that the Enfield situation was not an isolated case. As I informed Mitchell and that librarian, Ms. Thompson, the thefts in your library seem to be part of a widespread pattern of rare books and manuscripts stolen from colleges and universities all over the country."

"Yes, I know. I saw hundreds—thousands—of them." I bit my tongue; he was the one person in particular I'd promised Charlie I wouldn't tell about the Book House.

"You *saw* them? Where? How?"

It was my turn. "I really can't divulge that."

"No fair." He was the boyish Denny again, almost flirtatious. "I gave you what I had."

Not really. But I told him about the farmhouse on Chesterfield Mountain anyhow. "The story was all over the news. You must have seen it."

"I did, of course. That Munro was a smart little bastard, wasn't he? To look at him you wouldn't have thought…" He went into one of his silences.

"When did you ever see Elwood Munro?"

He ignored my question. "I had no idea *you* were up there in Chesterfield." He was quiet for a second or two. "Interesting."

"Well, it's just that I know a couple of the investigators—"

"Do you, now? There's more to you, Karen, than meets the eye. What do you say we get together, have a long talk? Wednesday. Dinner. Say, seven o'clock. I'll pick you up at your house."

Spending actual time with Dennis was more than I had bargained for. I hoped he didn't have expectations of anything other than a good talk. "But I live way the hell out—"

He bulled right through my evasion. "Don't worry. I'll find it. See you then." He hung up.

There was a tentative knock on my office door. I should call Dennis back and cancel, but this was office hours, and my students came first. I took a deep breath and pushed the chair back from the desk. Stephanie Abrams was standing at the door. Obviously she'd been waiting for me to get off the phone. Had she heard any of the conversation?

The student hugged books to her chest. "Dean Johnson said you wanted to see me."

"Hi, Stephanie. How are you?" I seated her in the green vinyl chair. "Listen, I'll get right to the point. I've been looking for your friend, Peggy Briggs. Do you know where she is?"

"Dean Johnson asked me that. And there was a message from the police when I got back on campus this morning. They want to talk to her, too. But—no. No, I haven't seen Peggy since Wednesday evening. I don't have any idea where she is. Really." She flipped her sleek, pale hair back over her shoulder.

She was lying. There's a certain straightforward earnestness in a student's eyes when she fibs to a professor. Stephanie Abrams was so goddamned earnest I could have cut it with a knife and spread apple butter on it.

"Stephanie, this is important. Tell me where she is."

"I don't know, Professor. Really. If I did, I'd tell you."

"She lies like a rug," I said to Earlene. We had met at Rudolph's for lunch. "And she didn't seem at all worried about her good friend's whereabouts, so I assume she thinks Peggy's okay."

"Students! Sometimes they drive me bonkers. I called Rachel Thompson in the library this morning. Peggy didn't show up for work again. Her schedule shows two classes this afternoon. What d'ya want to bet she doesn't show for them either?"

The waiter approached, a skinny student whose entire head was shaved except for a flop of bleached hair at the crown. Earlene asked for a Caesar salad.

I opened the tall menu, stared mindlessly, then slapped it shut. None of this stylish food appealed. "Earlene, what would you say if I ordered a double martini?"

She pursed her lips. "You're teaching this afternoon, aren't you?"

I nodded.

"Then I'd say you're out of your mind." She turned to the waiter. "She'll have a Caesar salad, too. No martini." He scribbled on his pad and slouched away.

I shook out the linen napkin and spread it on my lap. "Earlene, I am getting such a sick feeling about Peggy. You know a lot more about her than you've told me. You really have to help me out here."

"Hmm." She waved at Avery Mitchell, just entering with two white-haired men, both in navy blazers with gold buttons.

Tweedledee and Tweedledum. They had to be either college trustees or wealthy alumni ripe for the fleecing.

The waiter delivered a basket of bread, what Amanda calls "holy bread," presented with such a reverential air it feels like worship to bite into it. I chose a chunk of Russian black bread and lavished it with pale sweet butter. Earlene went for the cornbread with jalapeno.

"So...give," I demanded.

"Well, okay...since we definitely need to find out what's going on with her. This is all confidential, Karen...."

"Of course."

She sighed. "Earlier this spring Peggy had a problem at home that almost caused her to drop out of school. I can't be more specific about it than that. We were looking into the possibility of college housing for her and her little girl—her niece really—"

"Triste. She told me."

"Peggy is devoted to her. But it was difficult. You can't house a child in a dorm, and there were no openings in faculty housing. To tell the truth, I was about to take them in with me until I could work something out. Then Peggy changed her mind, said she had to stay at home—her mother needed her."

"Poor kid, she must be torn between her two lives." I watched the waiter deliver my martinis to Avery's table. Checkbook lubrication, I thought, and took a sip of Perrier.

"She's not a kid—we've got to remember that about Peggy. She's a fully grown woman. I've never known a student so mature, so aware of her responsibilities. When I think of some of the spoiled cry-babies at this school...Anyhow, that's what makes me so uneasy about her missing classes and not showing up for her job in the library. It's just not like her. And, in addition to everything else, Peggy's been working on a book—"

"She has?" This was news to me. "What kind of book?"

"The story of her sister's life and death. She's just about finished it. She practically made me take a blood oath of silence. That's why I didn't say anything when you were at my house the other day. But now...You *have* talked to Charlie about Peggy, haven't you?"

"Yes."

My brusque response merited a raised eyebrow.

"Why didn't Peggy want anyone to know about the book?" I asked.

"I think she was...embarrassed."

"You mean it's no good?" The waiter placed the salads in front of us with a flourish, then produced a high-tech stainless-steel pepper-mill from a holster on his hip. Earlene waved him away before he could press the trigger. I had to grab him by the sleeve to get him back.

"No. Not that at all. It's more like she feels she doesn't have the *right* to be an author, that she's encroaching on forbidden territory. She actually said, 'People like me don't write books.'"

"Trespass..." I thought about Sunnye Hardcastle, also from a deprived background, but with no compunctions at all about trespassing.

Earlene laughed. "That's actually very apt. Literary trespass."

"As if," I mused, "the world of print was a reserve for the privileged." I took a bite of salad. It was perfect, just the right touch of anchovy in the dressing. I wished I were eating a hamburger. "So...she wants to get it published?"

"Yes. She's adamant that her sister's story be told, and precisely as it happened, with no embellishments."

"Hmm. True Crime—there's a market for that. Have you read the manuscript?"

"No. She said she wanted to show it to a friend first. She didn't say who, someone who knew about those things. Someone who was taking a creative writing major."

"Must be Stephanie," I said. "She's a poet." Then I recalled Stephanie waiting for Peggy after class the day of Peggy's outburst. Peggy had handed her a bulky bag. I tried to re-visualize the scene. A plastic grocery bag, Stop 'N' Shop, with pages poking out of a rip in the bottom. And Peggy had been almost furtive about the exchange. It could have been her book manuscript in that bag.

"Stephanie definitely knows more than she's letting on," I said to Earlene. "How can we encourage her to tell us?"

My companion sighed. "She'll talk if and when she wants to talk. Until then all we can do is make ourselves available."

The sound and scent of sizzling steak caught my attention. I glanced over at Avery's table where fajitas were being delivered. I beckoned to the waiter and requested the dessert menu.

Chapter Twenty-Two

My class went well, and I called Amanda before I left for home. "Hey, Sweetie, how you doing?"

"I'm tired, Mom. I'm just really tired."

"Can I bring you anything?"

"Videos. I've been watching *Key Largo* on HBO, and I want more, more, more—black-and-white, moody Humphrey Bogart."

"I'll see what I can find, kid. We'll have a Bogie festival."

When I pulled up to the house an hour later, a black Lincoln Town Car was parked at a skewed angle in my driveway, one wheel mired in the tulip bed. I stared at it hard but couldn't make it belong to anyone I knew. My skin crawled: Amanda, alone, sick, helpless in the hands of a sinister intruder. The afternoon was just edging into evening. A wind had sprung up, tossing the bare tree branches. No one was anywhere around. Across the street, the only house in sight was long abandoned. The road was empty of vehicles. I checked my car for a weapon, and grabbed the plastic bag of videos—sharp edges, good heft. I swung it for practice, then crept toward the house. The kitchen door was ajar. I edged it fully open and tiptoed in.

A fire blazed in the wood stove. The smell of buttered popcorn hung in the air. Amanda was curled up in one corner of the couch, Sunnye Hardcastle in the other. Trouble sprawled between them. They were watching the end of *Key Largo*.

"Sunnye! What the—" She'd torn up my flower bed, left my kitchen door open, and scared the hell out of me. Now here she sat, cool as a cucumber, eating my popcorn and watching videos with my daughter.

The novelist held up an imperious hand. "Give us a minute, Karen. This is almost over." No light in the room other than the glow of the fire and the flickering grey of the TV screen. Without removing my coat, I sank into the black Naugahyde chair. The theme music swelled and the film credits began to roll. No one spoke until the screen resolved into visual static. Amanda sighed, then looked intently at the video bag. "What else did you get me?" She was wearing one of the sleep shirts I'd bought her, over grey sweatpants. Her short hair stuck straight up on one side.

"You're going to love these." I tossed her the bag of videos. "Hello, Sunnye."

"Hi, Karen." She dipped her hand into the big green popcorn bowl. She wore dark jeans and a rose-red sweater. Next to poor, pallid Amanda she seemed to glow with health.

"Did we have a date, or something? Did I forget you were coming?" I levered myself up from the chair and unbuttoned my coat.

She shrugged. "I got bored at the hotel, so I thought I'd rent a car and come up to hit the antiquarian bookstores again. Then I decided to drive out here to see if you knew anything more about what's going on with the library case." She was talking too fast. "Got here just in time to catch Bacall tell Bogey to pucker up his lips and blow. What a knock-out film!"

Amanda stacked up the videos. "*The Maltese Falcon!* Co-oo-l! Sunnye, can you stay for dinner? We'll watch this one afterwards." Without waiting for a response, my daughter looked over at me with her beautiful hazel eyes. "You know, Mom, I should probably tell you something. Sunnye and I have been talking about—"

I broke in. I didn't want to hear it. To tell the truth, I was envious of my daughter's admiration for the mystery novelist. "She's probably seen *The Maltese Falcon* a thousand times," I told Amanda. Anyhow, I didn't have time for company. I had tons of reading to do before class tomorrow.

"But it's always fun. You want to watch it again, don't you, Sunnye?"

"I'd like to…" Sunnye seemed hesitant. She slid her eyes over at Amanda. What *had* they been talking about, anyhow? Trouble fixed me in his enigmatic gaze.

Suddenly the writer's uncharacteristic diffidence struck me. *Sunnye's lonely*, I realized. *Sunnye Hardcastle, celebrity author, world traveler, urban explorer wants to be friends. She needs a refuge.*

And her little dog, too.

"Great," I said, my jealousy dissipating. I could prep my class in the morning. "I picked up a roast chicken on the way home, potato salad, some other stuff. We'll eat, then have an evening of film noir."

Sunnye grinned at me, and hefted her leather bag, which had been leaning against the couch. "Isn't that odd—I just happen to have a nice bottle of pinot noir in my bag."

I was too tired to attempt anything complicated like carving the chicken. I slid it whole from the plastic container onto a platter, slapped down silverware and plates, took out wine glasses and rinsed them. We sat, and Sunnye poured the wine.

From the road, headlights raked the dining-room window, then vanished. Then another car passed slowly, its motor loud in the country quiet. Two cars in a row on my deserted road.

Hmm. I rose from the table and drew the curtains shut. Another car crawled by, this time in the opposite direction. I shuddered: What had happened to my safe, sane, predictable life? I hacked a thigh off the chicken, then flopped the bird over to fork out the two succulent pieces at the base of the backbone. Trouble eyed me lovingly. He laid his head in my lap. I hesitated, then slipped him one of the tender back morsels. He accepted it gingerly, leaving my fingers intact.

"You should assume you're being watched," I told Sunnye.

She paused as she spooned potato salad from the plastic tub onto her plate, then glanced nervously at the window. "You think there are reporters out there?"

"Well, maybe. But I meant, by the police. As far as I know, they don't have any other suspects, and they'll want to know where you are, who you're with, what you're up to."

"Surveillance," Amanda said. Her eyes were slitted, like those of a street-savvy television cop.

"Oh, the police." Sunnye shrugged, and returned her attention to the food: *No problem*.

I wondered just exactly what had transpired that morning with her high-powered L.A. lawyer.

"Then I hope they had fun lurking outside Henshaw's Rare and Antiquarian Books for over three hours," she continued. "I know *I* enjoyed being there. Paul's got terrific stuff." She tore a wing off the chicken and winked at us. "In more ways than one."

Amanda grinned. At least my poor, ailing daughter wasn't being freaked out by the prowling cars.

"Henshaw's? Isn't that the shop you went to last week?" I asked.

"Yeah. Any law says I can't go back?" Sunnye nibbled on a wing. "He is a bit of a hunk, don't you think? Not bad for a…a mature guy."

"Not bad at all, for any guy. So, you two hit it off?"

"Sure. He's smart, knows everything there is to know about American first editions. He's got a sense of humor. Great conversationalist, too. He showed me his stock. I signed some books. We had coffee. Talked for a long time. I bought a couple of books, even found a copy of—" She stopped abruptly.

"You found a copy of *what?*" I asked.

"Oh, just something I was looking for. Nothing particularly interesting." I could almost hear the gears grind as she changed the subject. "Listen, Karen, you ever get in touch with Peggy Briggs?"

"No."

"Hmm. That's not good. Maybe we should take another swing by her house—"

"No!"

"Why not?" She laughed. "You afraid of that muscle-bound goon?"

"Goon?" Amanda's head swiveled back and forth, trying to follow the conversation.

"Of course not. It's just that I'll...I'll catch hell if I go there again."

"Catch hell from who?" Sunnye wrinkled her brow.

"From *whom*."

"Mom, what are you talking about?" my daughter demanded.

"The correct pronoun relative to the direct object is *whom*, not *who*," I lectured.

"Don't evade the question," Sunnye said.

"Yeah, Mom, who'll give you hell? And for what?"

I set my fork down. The chicken was still warm and juicy, but my mouth was dry, and I had lost my appetite. "Lieutenant Charles Piotrowski of the Massachusetts State Police is displeased that I meddled in his investigation."

Amanda: "Charlie! So that's why—"

Sunnye: "That big cop? You gonna let him—"

Me: "Shut up, both of you." I slapped my hand down on the table, and the fork clattered on my plate.

Amanda stared at me, wide-eyed. "Mom, it's not like you to lose your cool. Are you guys—"

"I'd rather talk about the bookshop," I said. "Sunnye, tell us more about your visit to Henshaw's."

She and my daughter exchanged knowing glances. Amanda, exasperated, spread her hands wide.

Sunnye tore a chunk off the wholemeal baguette and buttered it. "The bookshop? Well, okay. Paul's got a great crime fiction collection. I couldn't resist a first of *The Dain Curse*, signed, with jacket. He's shipping it home for me." She took a bite. "And, then—"

Another slow car with powerful headlights. Sunnye glanced at me. If it was the cops, they must have some particular reason for being so obvious. Was this plain and simple police harassment? If so, what role was Charlie Piotrowski playing in it?

After we'd watched the video, Sunnye slipped into her leather jacket and clipped Trouble's leash onto his collar. She had her hand on the doorknob when she remembered something. "Paul Henshaw said he knew Elly Munro."

"He did?"

"Yeah, but he knew him by the name of Bob Tooey. Tooey used to come into the store to schmooze. Never bought anything, though—a real Lookey Lou." She wrapped the leash around her wrist, and turned the knob. "Over the weekend the FBI asked Paul to go up to the house in Chesterfield, give them a preliminary idea of the value of the stolen books. He was there all day yesterday. He told them five, six million dollars."

Amanda gasped. "Millions!"

"And he said Munro's collection is so knowledgeable and comprehensive he hated to see it broken up. Funny, isn't it. A genius book collector, but a thief."

I watched Sunnye's Town Car turn—there went the rest of my tulips—then pull onto the road. A minute later another set of headlights raked the kitchen window, following the rental car.

I sat up until after midnight reviewing my underlinings in *The Long Goodbye*. Then I went to bed and fell asleep with the book in my hand.

> *I was with Sunnye Hardcastle at the Book House. Trouble had turned into a cat and was winding in and out between my feet as I stepped my way past precarious piles of leather-bound tomes. "This beast is trying to kill me," I said.*
>
> *"Don't be absurd," she replied. "He's simply committed to intertextuality."*
>
> *"Oh. Well then." I reached down to stroke the silky animal. He sank his teeth into my hand.*

Paul was just placing the CLOSED sign in the shop window when I arrived at Henshaw's Rare and Antiquarian Books after class on Tuesday afternoon. "Karen Pelletier? What a surprise."

"Hi, Paul. Glad I caught you. Could I buy you a drink?"

"Now I have younger women after me." He raised an amused eyebrow. "Life is good."

"I have an ulterior motive." I wanted to find out if he knew anything about Elwood Munro and Peggy Briggs.

"That's what I hoped."

"Flirt." I grinned at him. Paul was of the generation just previous to the rise of politically correct male-female social interaction. We walked over to Rudolph's, and sat at the bar. I ordered Cosmopolitans. Spring was on its way, and the fruity drink made me think of carefree days ahead, however delusional that thought might be.

"Salut," Paul said.

I tipped my glass toward him, then drank.

Across from us Claudia Nestor sat alone, drinking beer from a green bottle. Her gaze was riveted to a local news program on the TV above the bar.

"Here's what I want to ask you, Paul. I understand you knew Elwood Munro—"

"Bob Tooey, the little bum." He twisted his lips. "Yeah, I knew him. Used to come into the shop, handle the books. Smell them, even. Never bought anything." He gave an ironic laugh. "And I always had this feeling in my gut, you know, like I shouldn't turn my back."

"Good instincts."

"Yeah. Why are you asking about him?"

"A student of mine is missing," I said, "and I'm looking for her. I think she may have known Munro." I told Paul about Peggy and her backpack. "And today she missed class for the second time in a row. That's totally out of character for her."

He shook his head. "You say this Briggs girl works in the library? Do you think she could have been Tooey's—er, Munro's—accomplice in crime? Given the guy's obsession with books, I wouldn't put anything past him. But if she started giving him problems, he'd have gotten rid of her in a New York minute."

"He couldn't have 'gotten rid of her,'" I said. "She's the one who found his body."

"Oh." He raised his eyebrows. "Then maybe *she* killed *him*." He spread his hands. "It wouldn't be the first time murder's been committed in the pursuit of books. There was this guy in Spain sometime in the nineteenth century, a man named Don Vincente, who killed at least eight people in order to get their books. And he started out as a good guy— a librarian in a monastery."

"Not Peggy," I said. "She's too…well, not Peggy. Do you really think that's why Munro was murdered? For his books?"

Paul turned his glass slowly by its stem. "What better reason could there be?"

When I got home with burgers and fries from Rudolph's, Amanda was deep into *The Lady Vanishes*. I set a tray on the coffee table in front of her. I came back into the living room a half hour later, and the untouched meal was still in its Styrofoam take-out case. The video had ended, and Amanda was asleep in front of the staticky TV screen.

Chapter Twenty-Three

Thirteen women and Rex Hunter sat around the pine conference table in the Women's Studies office Wednesday morning holding a post-mortem of the crime fiction conference. The consensus was that if it weren't for the actual murder that had kicked it off, the murder-mystery conference would have been an unqualified triumph.

After the meeting I followed Rachel Thompson out of the building. I had more questions for the librarian.

An early spring sun had evaporated all traces of the recent snow. Crocuses poked tentative shoots though the raked earth of flower beds. Although March in New England could hardly be called tropical, students strolled by dressed in shorts and T-shirts. I foresaw a pneumonia epidemic within the week.

"Any word from Peggy?" I asked Rachel.

"Nothing." Her ruddy complexion was deepened by the crisp air. "I've been querying the library staff. Nobody has seen her since last Thursday when she stumbled across Munro's body. Poor thing."

"I know the cops talked to her after that," I mused.

"And then she vanished—kaput." Rachel spotted a discarded Pepsi bottle, plucked it off the sidewalk, and marched it over to the blue recycling bin. "This may sound heartless, but I don't know what to do about Peggy's job.

She's supposed to do the reshelving and the stacks are in a mess. Lately Nellie doesn't even seem capable of something as simple as getting the books back where they belong." She let her breath out with a frustrated *whoof.* "I don't know what's gotten into her. It seems to be all she can do to show up and park her butt at the desk. And mope. I find it very difficult to keep from letting her see just how annoyed I am with her. She needs help." She paused and thought for a moment. "Help with reshelving, I meant, but…" She shrugged. "Listen, I know Peggy is desperate for the income, but if she doesn't return soon, I'm going to have to hire a replacement."

A job was the least of Peggy's problems, I thought. I shifted my book bag from one hand to the other; it was loaded with course anthologies and felt as if it were packed with lead. "What about the book thefts? Any news there?"

Rachel gestured toward an ornate marble bench. "Can you sit for a minute?" The bench sported a brass plaque commemorating the class of 1934. When we sat, I could feel the stone's chill through the light wool of my skirt.

Before Rachel could answer my question, Claudia Nestor came bounding up. "Rachel. Karen. You left the meeting before I could ask if you'd caught my interview on WENF-TV." Her purple wool coat was unbuttoned, her striped wool scarf askew.

"I saw a bit of it," I replied.

Rachel said nothing. Reaching into the capacious pocket of her light wool jacket, she pulled out a handy-wipe packet, tore it open, and proceeded to clean her hands with the towelette.

"And did you know that the *Boston Globe* picked it up? They sent out a reporter and photographer. There was a shot of me on the front page Monday. Did you see it?" She took a swig from the water bottle that was all she carried.

I shook my head. Rachel studied her fingernails.

"It was right next to a photo of Sunnye Hardcastle. I looked great." She sighed blissfully.

The blankness of our expressions must have registered. She had the grace to look momentarily abashed. "Of course I know the murder coverage isn't exactly good publicity for the college. That's why I didn't mention the interview during the Women's Studies meeting. But everyone who saw me said I really handled myself like a pro."

"Your Warhol moment," Rachel muttered.

"What's that?"

"Your fifteen minutes of fame."

"Yes. And isn't it wonderful. I'm hoping the face time will lead to new opportunities—who knows, maybe even as a television cultural commentator. That's what it's all about these days, isn't it? Image. Exposure. Visibility. If it worked for Mark Fuhrman it can work for me."

Mark Fuhrman? Her role model was Mark Fuhrman?

Claudia brushed her hair back with such an exaggerated gesture that I couldn't help but notice the blond highlights that surely hadn't been there last week. She guzzled more water. Her face glowed with what might have been a new vision for her life—or might just as easily have been a professional make-up job.

Or might have been the contents of the clear plastic bottle.

As Claudia floated away on her cloud of anticipated celebrity, Rachel gave a disgusted snort. "Cultural commentator, my ass. Can't you just see Claudia as a talking head?"

"Well, if anything good is to be snatched out of that poor, obsessed little man's death, Claudia will be the one to snatch it. And, hey, if she doesn't get tenure, she'll have a backup career."

"Yeah, superstar conference director. Whoop-di-doo. Did you notice something odd about Claudia?"

"You mean, aside from the fact that she's Claudia?"

"That's just it. She's not herself. The whole time we were talking to her just now, her eye didn't twitch once."

I laughed. "She certainly seems to be…happier than she was last week."

"*Happy*? Is that what you call it?"

"I did get a distinct whiff of…what was it? Gin? Anyhow, Rachel, you were going to tell me about the book thefts."

"Let's see. What don't you already know? The FBI agents warned Avery to expect a lengthy investigation. And we're not going to get any books back until the Feds are done. Can you imagine? They're going to have to inventory all those volumes."

"What would you call that? *Forensic bibliography*?" I quipped.

She laughed at the absurd-sounding expression. "I suppose. Then academic librarians are going to have to schlep in from all over the country to identify their books. It could take years."

"It must have taken years for Munro to steal them in the first place. What did he want with all those books?"

"I think he just *wanted* them," Rachel said, "the way some men want all the women they can get. Or all the money. He *lusted* for them."

A red Frisbee whizzed out of the air and landed at our feet. Rachel scooped it up, glanced around, and whipped it back to a black kid with blond hair and a stringy blond goatee. He plucked it out of the air, held it to his heart, and gave her a bow.

"The other day when I was looking for Peggy, Nellie told me Munro did research in Special Collections all day, every day. What was he looking at?" I phrased the question carefully; I knew I was on shaky ethical ground in asking it.

She pursed her lips and gave me a Marion-the-Librarian look. "Professional protocol prohibits me from releasing that information."

"Okay. I understand."

She deliberated for a moment, then relented. "Oh, God, Karen, the cops asked me that, too." She sighed. "Library borrowing information is supposed to remain strictly confidential. When I refused to let them look at our records, they got a warrant and did it anyhow." A shrug. "He's dead now, what harm can it do? At least I can tell you that Tooey—er, Munro—began using our collections in mid-January—"

"Jeez, that's just about when I was knocked down in front of the library."

"That's right." She raised her eyebrows. "Well, there's one mystery solved."

"Are you allowed to say what he was researching?"

"Not really." She glanced around, then lowered her voice. "He was not a particularly noticeable person—probably on purpose—and so I didn't notice him. But Nellie did."

"I could tell."

"She's freaking out about…something. Munro's death, maybe? Who knows? Maybe she's just overwhelmed with the increased workload now that we're missing a student aide. But she did pull herself together long enough to tell the police he was doing descriptive bibliography. He called up a large number of books—I'm not allowed to divulge precisely which ones—and paid close attention to individual volumes. A couple of hours on each one. I can't give you more details than that."

"Descriptive bibliography?"

"You know, describing books as material objects. The bibliographer details the particularities of each existing volume of a certain text. Not only the usual author, title, publisher, but also type face, quality of paper, binding, signs of prior ownership—book plates, library markings, marginalia. It can tell you a whole lot about books and who uses them. For instance, if a volume of sermons had a great many annotations in the margin, that would reflect close attention to religious issues by the reading public. If a novel had library markings, the binding was worn, and the pages were coming loose, that could indicate an active readership and wide popularity."

"Uh huh." My eyes had begun to glaze over. I prefer to read my books, not transcribe their marginalia.

"Munro entered whatever data he was interested in into a laptop computer. I asked that pregnant detective if they'd found it with his things, and she just gave me a cryptic smile. I think she's seen too many Jack Nicholson movies."

Peggy's friend Stephanie Abrams crossed the quad in front of us, deep in conversation with Greg Samoorian. I jumped up from the bench. "Rachel," I said, "there's someone I've been trying to get hold of. Can we continue this later?" I'd meant to talk to Stephanie again after class yesterday, but, like her friend Peggy, she hadn't shown up.

"Hey, Pelletier," Greg greeted me. "Haven't seen you in a dog's age." His dark hair needed a trim, but he was still good to look at.

"You were at my house Sunday, Samoorian."

"That didn't count. The kids were there. We couldn't carry on an adult conversation."

"As if we ever do." I grinned at him, and turned to my student. "Hello, Stephanie. I need to see you."

The girl gave me a straight, serious look. But, then, she was always serious. At twenty, she already had faint etchings of worry between her eyes. When time had completed sculpting Stephanie' face, she'd have multiple deep lines bracketing her narrow lips.

Greg glanced from me to Stephanie, then back to me. "Karen, are you brushing me off?"

"'Fraid so, buddy." I squeezed his arm. "But just this once. Give me a call, will you?"

"You should be so lucky." He winked at me and ambled away. Fatherhood had been good to Greg. He seemed settled and happy, tied to the earth in a way he hadn't been when I'd first known him.

Stephanie looked wary. Slender and blond, with a pale, almost bloodless complexion, she appeared cold in her thin Indian wrap skirt and Madonna tee.

I buttoned the neck of my quilted jacket. "It chills me just to look at you, Steph. Can I buy you a hot drink?"

"Okay." She was a typical Enfield student, far too polite to tell a professor to butt out. "But I've only got a few minutes before class."

Most of the bustle in the coffee shop at this late morning hour was behind the counter, as workers prepared for the lunch onslaught. I set the tray with my coffee and her hot chocolate on a table in a window nook. "You know what I want, Stephanie, so tell me—have you heard anything from Peggy?"

"No." She picked up her cup, sipped, and winced as steaming liquid burned her mouth. Then she concentrated on stirring the pillow of melting marshmallow into the hot chocolate. She had no intention of making this conversation easy.

I sighed. "Look, I know you and Peggy are friends, so I'll be brutally frank with you if that's what it takes to get you to tell me where she is. Peggy's in trouble, and not simply because she's missing work and classes. You remember that... suspicious death that occurred in the library last week?"

"Of course." Stephanie nodded solemnly. Her voice was low. "Peggy found the...the man when she went into the closed stacks Thursday morning. She was so freaked." So Stephanie *had* seen Peggy on Thursday, and after the police had questioned her. I wondered whether she'd told the investigators that.

"Well, there's more, I'm afraid," I said. And I told her about the backpack found in the victim's house.

Stephanie slapped a thin hand on the table. "So that's where it went!"

"What do you mean?"

"Somebody stole Peggy's backpack. Let's see, when was that? The day of the reception in the library."

"Wednesday..." Peggy had been in my office Wednesday morning. And her pack with her.

"Yeah. Someone snatched it right out of the library. When Peggy came in to work at noon, she stuck it in her cubbyhole in the staff room, like she always does. When she went to get it that evening, it was gone. Her books, wallet, car keys—everything. I had to drive her home after the president's dinner."

"You mean Peggy's wandering around out there without even her wallet."

"Well, she's not exactly wandering around—"

I'd had it with her evasions. "Steph, look, you've got to understand, there's been criminal activity involving the library. And a man has been killed. Peggy could be a suspect. And she may even be in danger. I, personally, am very concerned about her."

The student jumped up, leaving her drink unfinished. "Can't be late for class, Professor. Bye."

With narrowed eyes, I watched Stephanie disappear through the door. Distrust authority: the code of the young. I sighed. It was my code too.

The smell of tomato sauce and pepperoni began to clamor for my attention. It was almost noon. At the pizza counter, I ordered a slice to go. The pie wasn't quite ready. While I waited, I checked out the large room. Students, staff, a few professors. Rachel sat at a table by the window with Nellie Applegate. The light shone on Rachel's crisp, dark curls. Over her broad shoulder I could see that even the white had drained from Nellie's complexion, leaving her face a pasty grey. On my way to the door, I caught a snatch of Rachel's voice, oddly flat: "...must see a marked improvement in job performance. Just one more lapse in professional standards and we will have no choice but to..." I sped up. It was too pathetic; I didn't want to hear any more.

I ate the pizza at my desk, dripping oil on the lined notepad in front of me. I'd known from the start that the presence of Peggy's backpack at Munro's house could make her a suspect in the eyes of the police. Now, I planned to call Charlie and tell him that Peggy hadn't left it there herself, that it had been stolen from the library. But first I needed to think about how to approach him. Everything between us was up in the air. Charlie had said we shouldn't see each other until the investigation was over, and he'd followed through. I hadn't spoken to him since Saturday when I'd called about finding Peggy's car.

Life can be so damn hard.

Okay. Back to work. No matter how things stood between Charlie and me, I had to organize my thoughts before I spoke to him about Peggy. I'd seen how he put together investigation notes, and I tried to follow suit. It wasn't unlike outlining my thoughts for a lecture or an essay. *Peggy Briggs*, I wrote, *missing from home, work, and classes.*

Then I made two columns: *Guilty*, and *Not Guilty*.

Under *Guilty* I listed:

> *—Discovered Munro's body.*
> *—Vanished immediately thereafter.*
> *—Works in the library. Would have had opportunity to become acquainted with Elwood Munro.*
> *—Needed money. (Badly enough to collude in book theft?)*
> *—Backpack found in victim's house.*
> *—Car located nearby.*

Under *Not Guilty* I wrote:

> *—Backpack stolen from library on day of murder. (By Munro?)*
> *—Best friend may know where she is.*
> *—Friend seems not to be worried about her.*
> *—Car keys stolen with backpack. How could she have gotten her car out to Chesterfield?*

Chewing on pizza crust, I sat back and regarded the two columns for a full minute. Hmm. Heavy on the *Guilty* side—at least circumstantially. I sighed, picked up my pen and scratched out the entire *Guilty* list. I didn't want to be able to read it myself, let alone have anyone else stumble across it.

Charlie answered his cell phone on the third ring. I told him what Stephanie had said about Peggy's backpack having been stolen. He grunted, taking in the information.

A long, heavy silence ensued. I broke it. "We have to talk, Charlie."

"Yes, we do. You free?"

"I have a class later."

"How about lunch?"

"I've already eaten, but, sure, I'll meet you. Rudolph's is closest."

"I'll be there in half an hour."

I never drink before teaching, but at Rudolph's I asked for a glass of the house white anyhow. Fidgeting with the wine glass would give me something to do with my hands. Charlie ordered a burger. His fingers were laced together as if permanently locked.

"How's your father?" I asked.

"Fine," he said. "How's your daughter?"

"Fine." Although she wasn't, not completely.

More silence. The waiter delivered our drinks, and I took a long sip of the cool wine.

Charlie pushed himself back in his chair and gazed over at me somberly. His broad face was half-illuminated in the bright noon light from the window. "Now, here's what's bugging me, Karen. As to your support of Sunnye Hardcastle, I just don't get it. The woman's a suspect in a murder investigation, an investigation I'm responsible for. And you continue to hang out with her. You invite her to your home, even after I advise you she's a primary suspect. How stupid is that? Or…is it just a slap in the face for me?"

I opened my mouth and found I had no voice, so I began to fold my cocktail napkin lengthwise in fanlike pleats. Construction of the flimsy paper fan required all my attention.

"I don't know where you are," he went on. "Are you with me or with some total stranger—a half-baked thrill-seeker like Sunnye Hardcastle?"

My voice came back. "She's not a stranger. I've read all her books." I carefully tore a strip off the fan. "I feel as if I've known her for years."

He shook his head and leaned toward me. "Karen, I truly don't know what to think. I want you so much, but I don't know where I am with you."

"Oh, Charlie," I said. My hands were shaking. He was a policeman—an officer of the law. He was dedicated to his job. At times he was overbearing and overprotective. Those were all things I couldn't stand. Then there was the other Charlie…. I swallowed hard, afraid I might choke on my words. "The last thing in the world I want is to risk losing you." I ripped another strip off the paper fan. "But I have to be my own person, and I don't believe Sunnye's guilty. I can't abandon her. As tough and outrageous as she seems to be, she's at a loss about all this. When I first met her, she bugged me, too. But now I'd go so far as to say we've become friends. You have to respect that. You have to respect my maturity and judgment."

He reached across the table and plucked the half-shredded napkin from my hand. "Okay, I can do that. I can respect you. But here's my position. What I said the other day. I don't think we should see each other until this case is over. It compromises the investigation if I…fraternize with associates of a suspect."

"Fraternize!" I choked down a nervous laugh. "Is that what you call it?"

But Charlie didn't see the humor. "Besides, like I said, you distract me." He sighed enormously, then dropped his gaze. "It makes me wonder...you know, in the middle of the night...if I really have room in my life for...someone like you. You've made it clear ever since I first knew you that you would have a problem living with a cop. Now I'm beginning to wonder if maybe you're not the kind of woman a cop can live with."

My heart must have stopped, because the blood ceased flowing through my veins. With chilled lips, I retorted defensively, "What kind of woman is that? A saint? Mother Teresa?"

"Nobody's a saint." He leaned forward and ran a finger across my lips. "I'm crazy for you. You know that. I don't want to hurt you. But if I have to worry all the time...."

I swallowed. "I'm sorry, Charlie. Don't pay any attention to my smart mouth. Just listen to what I'm saying now. I love you. I need you."

His brown eyes were full of pain. "Do you?" He sat back, to distance himself from me. "Listen, when this case is resolved, we'll talk about us. We'll see where we are. Does that make sense to you? Can we do it that way?"

"Yes," I breathed, "we can do it that way."

"Until then it'll just be hands off. Got it?"

"Hands off? Okay. Got it. Hands off."

Chapter Twenty-Four

Sunnye Hardcastle came to my house for dinner that evening. The police insisted that she remain in the area, and her big-time L.A. lawyer had advised her to cooperate. That marvelous mountain aerie in Colorado, I mused, and here she was, stuck with a suite at the Springfield Marriott. She seemed to prefer my little house in the woods to the hotel, and since Amanda was at loose ends and beginning to get restless, they were killing time with a mini film festival. My daughter and the novelist seemed to have become great pals. I'd become chief cook and bottle washer. My visit with Sunnye to Peggy Briggs' house had revived our appetites for childhood foods. I was cooking a modified retro meal: no condensed tomato soup in the meatloaf, the mashed potatoes were real, the peas were frozen, not canned, and I'd purchased the chocolate cream pie at Bread & Roses rather than make one from pudding mix and graham cracker crumbs. For a few moments I even forgot my worries about Charlie.

The phone rang as I closed the oven door. Sunnye and Amanda were watching *The Thin Man* and had *The Thirty-Nine Steps* scheduled for later. I was planning to spend the evening grading papers for my Freshman Humanities course. Eighteen five-page essays on Emerson's "Self-Reliance." I'd rather be watching movies with Sunnye and Amanda.

The phone gave its second shrill. Must be a telemarketer, I thought; after all, it's dinnertime.

"Hello." I still had the oven mitts on, and the receiver slid out of my hands.

A man's deep voice said, "Karen, I'm on my way. Just passed through Enfield."

Huh? Oh, shit! Dennis O'Hanlon! I'd forgotten to cancel with him.

"Oh, Denny, I—" I juggled the receiver to keep from dropping it.

"See you in fifteen minutes." He ended the call.

"Oh, shit. Oh, *shit!*" The phone hit the floor. I took off the mitts and retrieved it.

Sunnye came into the kitchen carrying two empty beer bottles. "What's wrong, Karen?"

I slammed the receiver down. "Nothing. I'm just so stupid."

"What?" She dumped the bottles in the recycling bin and plucked another from the refrigerator.

"Oh, this guy said he was coming over. I meant to brush him off, but I forgot. Now he's on his way, and it's too late to—"

"Leave it to me. I'll get rid of him."

For a split second I entertained the thought of Sunnye giving Dennis O'Hanlon the old heave-ho, but then I said, "No, thanks. He came all the way from Lowell." I might as well take advantage of Dennis being here. On the phone Monday I'd asked him if he knew anything about Peggy, and he didn't. By now he might.

"Lowell? That's north of Boston, right? On a rainy Wednesday night? Whatever it is you're cooking with there, Karen, it's hot stuff. You ought to bottle and sell it."

"It's not like that, Sunnye."

"It's always like that." She ran a slow finger around the sweating beer bottle, then carried it into the living room.

Dennis was wearing black denim and leather, and his ginger hair had been freshly cropped. I met the P.I. at the door, coat on, ready to go, but he slipped past me into the living room. "So this is where you live, Karen?" His cat's gaze darted over the modest room with its Naughahyde recliner, faded green couch, rag rug, and my one good possession, a glowing Scandinavian cast-iron wood stove. "Comfy." The comment was uninflected.

"Yes," I replied. "We like it."

Dennis's pale eyes scrutinized Amanda recumbent on the couch, took in the black-and-white film on the TV. Just then, Sunnye came in from the kitchen with a second helping of meatloaf. Trouble eyeballed the newcomer.

He jerked to attention. "You're Sunnye Hardcastle!" Dennis usually flaunted the Alpha-male attitude of being surprised by nothing, but the novelist's presence here tonight took him aback. His eyes appraised her—silver earrings, old jeans, sweater: nothing much. But the boots: yes. His eyes lingered on the boots. They were alligator, hand-tooled in a traditional western pattern. He approved of the boots.

"That's right," Sunnye said. How else was she going to respond: "I am?"

Dennis strode over to the novelist, ignoring Amanda's presence. It was a small room; two strides did the job. He thrust his hand out. "I heard you speak at the conference last week. Impressive."

"Thank you." Her handshake appeared as unenthusiastic as had Dennis's response to my home. Was it simply that she knew I didn't want him there?

"It's an honor to meet you, Ms. Hardcastle. We're in the same business, you know."

She raised her thin dark eyebrows. "You're a crime writer?"

"I'm a crime *fighter*." Every muscle in his body was suddenly on steroids. "Investigator. Private."

A long, cool stare. "'Zat so?" Nope. It had nothing to do with me. She'd taken against Dennis all on her own. She turned back to the screen. William Powell lit a cigarette. A moment of silence ensued. Trouble shifted on his haunches.

Dennis wanted more from Sunnye, but she wasn't giving. William Powell claimed her full attention.

"See you guys later," I said. He had no choice but to follow me out the door.

My companion wanted "serious" food, so we drove to Rudolph's in his big black Dodge Ram. The restaurant was crowded. We sat at the horseshoe bar, waiting for a table. Across from us, Claudia Nestor nursed something amber in a rocks glass. As we'd entered, her eyes snagged on Dennis the way his had snagged on Sunnye Hardcastle. He was a babe magnet, dressed to attract any woman's eyes in black jeans and a soft black leather blazer, a close-fitting plum-colored shirt. Unlike most men, Dennis knew how to put his clothes together. Charlie just wore guy clothes, disappearing into his guyness as if he were permanently undercover, but Dennis *dressed*, and the effect was all shoulders and muscle and strength and height. I did enjoy showing off this tall, blond, mysterious stranger in Rudolph's, but, oddly enough, I'd rather have been at home eating meatloaf with Sunnye and Amanda.

The bartender was a former student of mine, so skinny she had no breasts. She wore a red sweater, and her hair was cut like a little boy's. She looked poignantly like the French cartoon character Tin Tin, and seemed barely old enough to drink liquor, let alone serve it. Dennis ordered Chivas, straight up. I asked for an Absolut martini with an olive, also straight up. I really prefer the drink on ice, but then you don't get the debonair stemmed glass.

"That Hardcastle broad's a cold bitch, isn't she?" Dennis said. "What's she doing at your place, anyhow? I heard the cops fingered her for the library murder."

"Where'd you hear that? Nobody's 'fingered' her for anything." I gave him a wide stare, then picked up my glass. The martini was cold and smooth. I drank it slowly.

"Hey, take it easy, Sweetheart." He held up an elegant hand. No rings, but the fingernails were manicured. Just like a funeral director, I thought.

I drained the martini and stared at him for a long minute. "Look, buddy. You're starting to piss me off. First you insist on this get-together, even when I make it clear I'm not interested, and now you insult my friend. And what are you doing here, anyhow? What do you want from me?"

"Karen, honey, I don't 'want' anything from you. We're old pals, aren't we? This is just a get-together for old time's sake." He sat back and smiled. "And, besides, you're one hell of an attractive woman. Why wouldn't I want to spend an evening with you?"

Tapping my fingers on the golden-oak bar, I thought back to the phone conversation where he'd made the date, tried to reconstruct the dialogue. "You know, you showed very little interest in me until…until I said I was acquainted with the police officers working on the Elwood Munro case." I snapped my fingers. "That's it! Then you started to press it. You want to pump me for what I know about the…" His eyes went still, but I plowed on. "About the…the book thefts! Damn it, Denny! You're still working on the stolen-books case, aren't you?"

He let his breath out in a huff, sat back and gave me a rueful Irish-boy grin, little Denny O'Hanlon again. "It's not every lady college professor hangs out with cops. That's intriguing all by itself. You're still one tough cookie, aren't you? And then they turn out to be homicide cops investigating the death of a book thief I've been hunting down. Oh, yeah,

I'm interested. On a couple of levels. So, shoot me. Here," he gestured to the bartender, "let me buy you another drink."

"No." I waved the young barkeep away, and took a deep breath. Restraint, girl, restraint. If Dennis was still on the library case, it was all the more possible he knew where Peggy was. If he had learned anything about her, I wanted to find out before I bad-assed him. I rubbed the back of my neck to ease the tension, and tried to relax on the high chrome-and-wicker barstool.

"Listen, Kar," he said, "you've gotta see my point of view. I told you before, this is a big case. Mitchell's paying serious money. I know the Feds are involved…" he was talking fast, "…but the college still needs to know where its security failed. That's what I'm working on, security. And that manuscript's still missing. So, don't get uptight. We're all on the same side here."

"Are we? Looks to me like you're working *your* side." I plucked the olive out of my beautiful, empty glass and nibbled on it.

"Karen, you know where I come from, how hard it was. Sure, I'll admit I'm in it for the bucks. But, hey, what better motivation? There isn't a lot I wouldn't do for money. And why not? Look at you, for instance." He paused, then spoke super-casually. "All that education, Ph.D., prestigious job, and, really, you're no better off than your old man was, rented house, five-year-old car, secondhand furniture. And on top of that, you've got all those education loans."

I choked on the olive. "How do you know that?"

"Know what?" It was warm in the bar. My companion reached up and loosened his silk necktie. Its purple-on-grey zigzag design suddenly resolved itself into a stylized pattern of squared-off hand guns.

"About my house and car. And the loans."

He sat back complacently. "You have to ask? It's what I do. What I can't get on the Internet, I find out over coffee or drinks. People like to talk." Another casual pause. "That's how I found out that you and Mitchell got it on a couple of years ago. It's my business to learn what I need to know about people."

I recoiled from him. "Avery and me! That never happened!" I was suddenly aware that Claudia was staring at us across the bar. How loudly had Dennis and I been talking? And, oh, God, if gossip about Avery and me hadn't been flying around before, it surely would be now. Oh, God, oh, God, oh, God: my tenure petition! It was only a single kiss in a country driveway, and three or four years earlier, but rumors of a romantic involvement with Enfield's president, no matter how misguided, could lose me my job.

Rachel Thompson and Paul Henshaw entered the bar hand in hand. At any other time I would have been goggle-eyed at the pairing, but now I was too embarrassed to pay any attention. And too angry.

"Whatever you heard, it was nothing but rumors. And, damn it, you investigated my finances? You creep!" I gathered up my bag and slid off the stool. "You've turned out to be a total sleezeball, Denny O'Hanlon." I turned away from him, then snapped back over my shoulder, "Don't call me again."

"Suit yourself," he replied, raising his voice. "But, remember, *you* got in touch with *me*. And, by the way, Karen, how do you think you're going to get home?"

"No. Trouble." And where was that dog when I really needed him? The door closed behind me with a pneumatic hiss, but not before I noticed Rachel nudge Paul and raise her eyebrows. Then I took in the fascinated eyes of students, colleagues and townspeople. Everyone in the whole damn bar had been listening in on the nasty spat with my former childhood pal. Had they all heard what he'd said about Avery and me? I was doomed. I was truly doomed.

I called home from my office, betting that Sunnye was still there with her big rented Lincoln. Fifteen minutes later she and Amanda picked me up outside Dickinson Hall. I didn't want to think about how they'd gotten to the college that fast. I opened the passenger door of the Town Car. My daughter didn't even wait until I'd gotten my butt on the seat before she started hassling me from the back. "Mom, the minute he walked in the door, I wanted to tell you to watch out. That Dennis O'Hangman has trouble written all over him. How could you not have seen it?"

"Hanlon. It's Dennis O'Hanlon. And, anyhow, what are you doing out of bed?"

"I'm freaking out from being stuck in the house. Must be getting better." She reached over the back of the seat and squeezed my shoulder. "Hey, Mom, you're shaking. Just exactly what did O'Hangman do to you?"

"Yeah," Sunnye echoed, glancing over at me. "What went down with you two?"

I told them what he'd said about my finances. "It was like some kind of a threat, an *I know where you live* kind of thing. He even knew about my Goddamn college loans! He deliberately let me know that he's taken the trouble to learn my business. I feel so...violated." I kept the bit about Avery to myself.

"What a jerk!" Sunnye said. "The guy's a problem, Karen. You can't just let him get away with this. Let's get a drink at Rudolph's and talk it over."

"No!"

"Why not? It's a great bar, and, besides, I think Amanda's in desperate need of a change of scene."

"That asshole O'Hanlon might still be there." And the entire nosy audience of colleagues. "How about Moccio's?"

"Point the way."

For most Enfield students the weekend begins on Thursday evening. This was Wednesday, but half the football team was drinking at the bar as if classes were already over for the week. I slipped in next to a guy with a full mug in each hand, and asked the bartender for bottled beer. My daughter ordered Jack Daniels, straight up.

"Amanda!"

"Mother!" she snipped back. "I'm twenty-two!"

"But you're *sick*."

"So…this is medicine."

"Give her a break, Karen." Sunnye turned to the bartender. "Same for me," she said.

"Yeah, Mom, give me a break." My daughter grinned at me. It was the first spontaneous smile I'd seen since Amanda had come home. "Look at that dude," she whispered, tilting her head toward the kid with two beers. "He's pounding."

"Pounding?"

"Yeah, if he had another hand, he'd be drinking three beers."

We took a table in the back of the room, the same table at which I'd sat with Dennis. I shuddered and took a sip from the room-temperature bottle. The warm brew left a sudsy trace on my tongue. "How's the bourbon?" I asked.

Sunnye shrugged. "It might even really *be* Jack Daniels."

The tepid beer was awful. I lifted my hand to get the bartender's attention, then pointed to my companions' drinks. "The same for me," I mouthed, then strolled to the bar to pick up the whiskey. The angry beat of rap throbbed from the jukebox.

"Puff Daddy," I said, as I returned to the table. I tossed it off: *the things I know.*

Amanda cast me an amused look. "Jay-Z," she corrected me. *The things I think I know.*

On top of the martini I'd already had that evening, the bourbon put me in a garrulous mood. I spilled it out: How I'd first run into Dennis at the reunion; how he'd approached me about his investigation into the stolen books; how I'd asked him what he knew about Peggy.

"He's still working for the college?" Sunnye asked, with narrowed eyes.

"So he said tonight. Investigating the flaws in the library's security systems. But, it's funny, Avery told me—"

"He a security specialist?"

"How would I know? Before I ran into him at the reunion, I hadn't seen the guy in twenty-five years. Why?"

"It's just that usually they specialize in one or the other—investigation is a whole nother animal than security." She finished her drink. "Seems to me there's something more than a little *off* about this O'Hanlon. I'm with Amanda on this one. The minute he walked in I said *uh, oh. A little too smooth.* You're a smart cookie, Karen. I don't know why you didn't see it."

I shrugged and sipped at the bourbon. "I went to high school with him."

"Well, duh," Amanda said. We went back for seconds on the bourbon. My brain began to feel extremely…concentrated. The mention of libraries reminded me of overhearing Rachel's warning to Nellie to shape up or ship out. So I told my companions about that, even though it had nothing to do with anything. I felt so foolish about Denny, I wanted to change the subject.

Sunnye went up to the bar to order a third round. A husky guy in jeans and a muscle shirt draped an arm around her shoulder. She flashed him a killer smile and snapped her fingers. Trouble bared his fangs. Muscle shirt wimped off. When she returned with the drinks I told them about Peggy Briggs, and how I'd found her car in the field near Elwood

Munro's house. It felt good to get all this stuff off my chest. I drank more bourbon.

"I don't understand why I worry so much about Peggy. College students do stupid things all the time. If I let them all get to me, I couldn't do my job. But Peggy…"

"I think you over-identify with her, Mom," Amanda said. "She's like you were. All that crap you had to go through just to get an education."

I frowned at her. Was I so transparent even my daughter could psychoanalyze me?

"And then," I continued, evading her remarks, "Paul Henshaw—you know, the bookseller—asked me if I thought Peggy was Munro's accomplice. She had access to keys, maybe even security codes. But I don't think—"

Sunnye jumped in. "Yeah, working at the library does link Peggy to Elwood Munro. But, he's connected to a lot of people, including those librarians you were just talking about. Even to Dennis O'Hanlon."

"Even to you."

She gave me a funny look. "Even to me."

My mind clouded up even more. *Elwood Munro and his bibliomania*, I thought, *Elwood Munro—his books, his house, his death.* Oh, the man did love his books, especially the mystery novels. All those Ross Macdonalds, Mary Roberts Rineharts, S.S. Van Dines. Strange, though, you'd think he would have had some Brits in his collection. Where was Sir Arthur Conan Doyle? Where was Dorothy L. Sayers? Ruth Rendell? P.D. James? Colin Dexter? My brain was surfing on waves of inebriated brilliance. Where was Miss Marple when you needed her? When you had a body in your own library?

One of the football players barfed his evening's beer into a corner. "Damn you," the bartender bawled. "If you can't hold it like a man, don't drink it in my bar."

Phew! Time to go.

We donned our coats. The bartender slammed open a closet door, yanked out a pail and a mop.

Definitely time to go.

Halfway out the door, I turned back to Sunnye. There was something I urgently needed to know. "Sunnye? You know what the real question is here?"

"What?"

"The real question is—what would Kit Danger do now?"

Chapter Twenty-Five

We returned to the scene of the crime.

It was eleven thirty p.m. when I ushered my companions into the building. With the bug-eyed gape of the celebrity spotter, the student worker on the desk recognized Sunnye and her dog. Trouble entered the library with no trouble. In the reference room, a few students more diligent than those we'd run into at Moccio's hunched over computers. A half-dozen leafed through scholarly journals in Periodicals. Through the glass door of Reference I spotted a trio of students from my FroshHum class passing around a book. Hmm, it looked like a volume from the *Masterplots* series.

"Excuse me just a moment," I said to Sunnye and Amanda. I pushed open the door and headed for the one occupied table. Keith Burrell glanced up and choked on the cold Pop-Tart it was illicit to consume on library premises.

"Hey, guys," I greeted my students. "You're working late." I plucked the volume from Samantha McCarthy's hand. "*Masterplots*, huh? The *S* volume? This wouldn't be in lieu of actually reading *The Scarlet Letter*, now, would it?"

Frankie Rodriquez was the quickest, and the most glib. "Of course, not, Professor. Simply a preliminary survey of themes and motifs. We wish to approach the text as informed readers." He could hardly keep the smirk off his face.

Preliminary survey. Informed readers. Right. The neatly penned words on the open notebook page in front of him read, *prison & cemetery = sin & death.*

"You know," I said, closing the book and setting it on a handy book cart, "I'd really prefer you think for yourselves."

Frankie grinned at me. "Sure thing, Professor. If that's what you think we should do."

The green velvet rope was stretched across the top of the stairs that lead down to the Special Collections division. I walked my fellow sleuths past it and into the deserted corner of Periodicals by the literary theory journals.

"Okay," I whispered, "what now?" All that booze had rendered me just a little bit reckless.

Sunnye sat at the table, made a tent from her fingers, and turned to me with narrowed eyes. She looked as if she were settling in for a prolonged planning session. God help me, I realized with a momentary spurt of clarity, I'd been reduced to functioning as a sidekick to Kit Danger. "Where was the body?" she asked.

"In the Special Collections closed stacks, but we can't get there. Special Collections shuts down at five."

"Hmm," she mused. "There *might* be a way. And the library itself? How late does it stay open?" Sunnye asked.

"Midnight, except during finals, when students have access round the clock."

"Are there finals this week?"

"No."

"Good." She checked her watch. "Twenty minutes until midnight. Where can we hide?"

I started, shocked into sobriety. "Hide! My God, Sunnye, what are you up to? You want to get me fired?"

Trouble was at her side. She reached down and ran a hand over his muscular neck. "I thought you asked me what Kit

Danger would do, Karen. I'll tell you what she'd do. She'd hang around this place until she had an opportunity to investigate the murder scene. She'd search through whatever library records she could get her hands on, especially in Special Collections. And—"

"We can't do that! It's against the law!"

"Of course it is. Criminal trespass. And I'm good at it." Sunnye crossed her arms over her chest and chewed her upper lip. She had strong, white, efficient-looking teeth. "You really don't have a choice, Karen, because now that you've got me in here, I'm going to investigate. I'm under suspicion of murder, and I have a right to exonerate myself." Her hard dark eyes looked straight into mine. "Unless, of course, you're planning to turn me in."

"Sunnye!" I hissed the word. "Don't do this to me! I could lose my job!"

But Amanda was wide-eyed. "We're going in, aren't we?" She practically buzzed with excitement.

I swiveled my head toward her. "*You're* not going anywhere, young lady!"

Her face went blank. "Mother, you keep forgetting that I'm an adult now. If we can help Sunnye clear herself, we have a moral obligation. And, Mom…this may not be the best time to tell you…but…I want to work in criminal investigation." She glanced down at her interlaced fingers. "I've signed up to take the state police entrance exam. I want to do what Charlie does, Mom. I want to do what Sunnye—well, what Kit Danger—does. And…tonight…this would give me some hands-on experience with a pro."

"Amanda, no!" I stared at her in horror. I'd sensed a growing distance between us lately as I'd blithely blabbered on and on about graduate school applications, and she'd become increasingly close-mouthed about her future. I should have picked up on it sooner. My worst fears had been realized; my daughter wanted to be a cop. That's what I got for sleeping with police investigators. That's what I got for consorting with crime writers. I'd put Amanda in harm's way.

For one wild moment I wished fervently that she were a toddler again. Then I could shake a finger at her: *no, no, no, no, no.* Instead, powerlessly, I snipped, "Besides, Sunnye's not a pro. She's a novelist."

"Whatever," Amanda said. Her lips were straight, her clear hazel eyes focused on mine. She'd left her third bourbon untouched on Moccio's gunky table. "I am very serious about this. I'm not going back to school after graduation. Not now. Maybe not ever. Why does everything have to be about education, education, education? Isn't there a real world out there?"

My chest was so tight, I could hardly breathe. If my daughter insisted on joining Sunnye in this investigation, I had no choice but to stay with her. To hang with her, as the kids would put it.

And, besides, if I was at her side during this madcap scheme, at least I could protect her—if it came to that. Ridiculous, I knew; what danger could threaten anyone in a library, even after midnight?

But then, as if it were spoken aloud in an actual voice, the thought came to me: *Look what happened to Elwood Munro.*

I took a sidelong glance at my daughter's adamant expression and sighed. "Follow me," I said.

We climbed the worn marble staircase that led to the literature stacks on the third floor. "Cool," Amanda said, as we turned a corner into the shadowy, vaulted chamber in which American literature is housed. "This is like the best part of a bad movie. But where's the gibbering scholar? Where's his hunchback henchman?"

"The gibbering scholars are all safely tucked into their tenured little beds with volumes of Foucault where they belong," I retorted. The clanking of a security implement belt caused me to gasp. "Not dodging security guards in libraries. Watch out, here he comes!"

We ducked into a darkened study alcove. The guard strode by us, flicking off light switches as he passed each rank of books. In his wake, the room's dim illumination assumed an eerie red glow from the EXIT signs.

"He's getting ready to close the place down," I whispered. My head was spinning.

"Good," Sunnye replied. She placed a hand on my arm. "Now, don't worry, Karen. I know what I'm doing. Trust me. I can get us in and out of the closed stacks without tipping anyone off. Compared to the Paris sewers, this is a piece of cake."

"Yeah?" I pondered the thought for a moment. In for a penny, in for a pound. "And the Special Collections office, too?"

"No problem. Now, tell me, you said you stumbled across a bad scene between two librarians…?"

"Rachel and Nellie. Rachel's the professional librarian. Nellie works the desk."

Sunnye waved the distinction away. "What if one of them committed this homicide?"

"Couldn't be," I objected automatically. "They're *librarians*." Then I thought about it: Librarians work very hard; they're poorly paid. It was possible, I supposed, that one of them might have at least colluded with Elwood Munro.

Suddenly Rachel's BMW came to mind. And all those valuable editions passing through her hands, day after day.

Books are designed for maximum portability, easy to slip into a briefcase—or even a pocket—at the end of a day. Easy to pass on to an obsessed collector for a monetary consideration.

Easy, in Rachel's position, to leave a door unlocked, keys in full view, the alarm system turned off. Easy.

"Rachel has a new BMW," I said.

"So do I," Sunnye replied. "What's your point?"

"Her salary's probably not much more than fifty thousand a year, and the cost of living around here is astronomical."

"Oh. Point taken. Let's search her office first."

"I like Rachel," I protested. But Sunnye was already leading the way to a remote corner of the AmLit stacks and through a short corridor to a narrow arched doorway I'd never even known was there.

"Aha! I thought I'd find a door here. These are the stairs Elly took when we went into the restricted area. It's some kind of service staircase from before elevators. They're closed to the general public, but library workers use them all the time. Elly said the doors were alarmed if you opened them from the outside, but not from the inside. Sooo…"

"We're on the outside," I said. Not unreasonably, I thought.

"But maybe not for long. Look around. See any heating vents?"

"Here." Amanda pointed to a large vent at floor level. It was covered with medieval-looking black grille work.

"Hmm," Sunnye said. "I could probably squeeze in there."

"Jesus, Sunnye!" That was me.

"Let me do it." That was Amanda.

"No!" Me again.

"Well, you're skinnier than I am. You feel up to it?" Sunnye.

"Sure." Amanda was grinning like a lunatic.

"Please, Amanda, don't," I pleaded. "You've been so sick."

"It's not going to hurt her, Karen. We'll unscrew this grate from the wall and she'll go in. I've got the tools. I've even got a dust mask. All she has to do is slide through until she comes to an opening on the other side of the wall. Then she can push out the grate, and, voila, she's inside. It's easy."

It took a half-hour. It took forever. Sunnye sat at a study carrel. I paced back and forth in the pinkish gloom. Then the doorknob turned, and we were in. Trouble led the way. We crept down the narrow staircase. The steps were stone, and felt slick and worn beneath our feet. Then Sunnye pushed open a door, and we entered directly into the prohibited space of the dimly illuminated closed stacks.

Row after row of tall shelves stretched back into the shadows, seemingly into infinity. I had a sudden eerie sense of disconnection from the present, as if we had somehow escaped the confines of time and matter and entered simultaneously into all the worlds pressed in ink and bound into these volumes, as if we had penetrated the collective consciousness of brains long since reduced to scattered molecules of insensate matter.

"Where's the librarian's office?" Sunnye asked.

Her voice slammed me back into the present, and I scrutinized the darkness. "I'm disoriented. Where are we? East? West?" It was only the second time I'd been in the closed stacks. The big fluorescent tubes that lit them during the day were turned off, but every twenty feet or so a naked sixty-watt bulb cast a faint illumination. Then my eyes caught the distant red glow of another Exit sign. "If we make our way toward that Exit light, I bet we'll find it. There's a door leading from the stacks directly into Rachel's office."

We crept through the tortuous aisles of books, then Sunnye opened the door to the curator's office, turned on a desk lamp, and started issuing orders. "Amanda," she directed, as she booted up Rachel's computer, "you take those file cabinets. Karen, the desk. A systematic search should give us some idea if anything fishy is going on with these librarians."

The desk was set up against the wall and strewn with scrawled-over printouts and pink telephone-message slips. A rank of plastic file holders lined its back edge, stuffed with directories, manuals, catalogs, manila folders and envelopes. How Rachel could function amid such disorder was incomprehensible to me. "What am I looking for?" I asked helplessly.

"A signed confession saying 'I killed Elwood Munro' would be good. If that doesn't jump out at you, just use your brain. Check for something that's not where it's supposed to be, something that doesn't belong where it is. Whatever." Sunnye was distracted by her futile attempts to access Rachel's computer files. "Now, what would a librarian's password be?"

"*Due date*," I suggested.

Keys clicked. "Nope."

"*Late fine?*"

More clicking. "Nope."

"*Book.*" I was reaching now.

She tapped the keys. "Bingo," she said. "I'm in."

"You're kidding?" I stared at her. Sunnye clicked "My Documents" on the virtual desktop and began scrolling.

I shrugged and turned to the actual desktop. A systematic search, huh? I could do that. Beginning at the left, I plucked out tightly wedged folders from the desk racks, sorted through their contents: *acquisitions; deaccessions; cataloging; pre-cataloging; systems management; personnel.* Boring.

Next came rare book and manuscript catalogs. I leafed through them. Whew! The prices! Book collecting had become a high-end business, indeed. An anonymous *Treatise on the Police of London*, By a Magistrate. First American Edition, 1798. $1,000. An perfect American first edition of Sir Arthur Conan Doyle's *A Study in Scarlet* in original wrappers. $17,500. And, oh my God, a mint copy of the first edition of *The Maltese Falcon*. $35,000! "Lookit this, guys," I exclaimed. They ooohed and ahhhed.

The computer manuals were next, not nearly so interesting. I opened the closest. Incomprehensible. I shook each one. Nothing hidden between the leaves.

Then I tackled a series of battered interdepartmental mailing envelopes. The nearest and fattest was wedged tightly in its own plastic niche. I eased it out and unwound the string closure: a ream of paper bound by wide rubber bands. The cover sheet identified the document as Systems Management Operational Draft. Great. More computer gobblety-gook. I set it aside and reached for the next envelope. Then my eyes, even in the dim light, noted an anomaly in the thick systems management draft. Whereas the cover sheet was the bright white of standard computer paper, the pages themselves were yellowed at the edges. Hmm. I edged the thick document over closer to the desk lamp and began to remove the rubber bands.

Sunnye glanced up from the computer monitor. "You got something?"

"Probably not." But even to me the attempt at non-chalance was unconvincing.

Amanda abandoned her file cabinet. "What is it, Mom?" She peered over my shoulder.

I pulled off the second rubber band. The cover sheet fell away. Underneath, a thick old-fashioned typescript tied in off-white cotton ribbon. The yellowed page was densely typed on an old-fashioned manual typewriter, with several cross outs and a few handwritten corrections. The title read "The Maltese Falcon."

"Jee-zus Christ," Sunnye whispered. "Will ya look at that!"

"So, it wasn't Munro, after all," I exclaimed. "*She's* the one who took it!"

"*Who* took *what?*" Amanda asked.

Neither Sunnye nor Amanda knew the *Maltese Falcon* manuscript had been stolen. Its loss was so potentially embarrassing to the college that it had been hushed up as if it were a state secret. While Elwood Munro's death had brought the book thefts to public attention, so far, the stolen manuscript had remained a dark administrative secret.

I sat on the rolling desk chair and brought my partners-in-crime-fighting up to date. "I hate to say this," I concluded, "but it looks as if Rachel may have stolen the Hammett manuscript, then hid it here in plain sight in this...mess. When the brouhaha dies down, she'll be able to sneak it out of the library."

"Rachel? I've met this woman, right?" Sunnye asked. "She dresses like a milk-maid—all that pale, loose-woven stuff?"

"Sounds like Rachel."

"But," Amanda broke in, "if she stole the manuscript, does that mean she's the killer?"

A shudder ran through me: Just last week I'd spent hours with Rachel, and we'd ended up together in a remote and lonely location. But then I tried to imagine Rachel harming me—or sneaking up behind Elwood Munro and bashing him over the head. "Rachel? Never. She's such a gentle person. Why, Sunnye, you should have seen her with your dog. Trouble loves her."

At the sound of his name, the animal lifted his head and scrutinized me with wise brown eyes. I was still focused on the pages in my hand. "I don't know why the manuscript would be on her desk unless she took it. But I can't imagine why she would do that."

"Desperate for money," Amanda said.

"In cahoots with Elwood Munro," Sunnye suggested.

"You have any idea how much she could get for this?"

She laughed. "As much as she wanted, I imagine." The novelist had taken the manuscript from me and was turning pages reverentially. "This is a unique item, especially if these revisions are in Hammett's own hand. A real rarity."

I pushed it. "How much is 'as much as she wanted'?"

"Oh, I don't know. Fifty, a hundred thousand. Maybe more." She flicked the price away as if it were inconsequential. "Even a million wouldn't be too much; a million is nothing to some people. It would all depend on how much some person of means—some obsessed collector—was willing to pay, and pay under the table, too, this being stolen property. He'd have to keep it solely for his private pleasure, but there'd be someone…" She ran a light finger over the page and trailed off dreamily.

I must have given her a sharp glance.

"Not me," she said. "No way I'd take that kind of risk."

"Oh, no?" I felt my eyebrows pucker.

"Trespass is one thing," she continued, soberly. "Receiving stolen goods is altogether something else."

"You better call Charlie," Amanda broke in. "If there's any possibility this Rachel woman is the killer, we've got to tell him."

"Ye-e-es. But, you know, when it comes right down to it, I'm not absolutely convinced she's the biblioklept."

"The *what*?" Amanda frowned at me.

"The book thief, at least the one who stole the manuscript. Rachel's not the only person on campus to have easy access to rare books and manuscripts. There's Nellie Applegate. She's in and out of this office every day. So are the work-study students. I hate to say it, but Peggy Briggs is a library runner. She could get her hands on anything she wanted. And if ever anyone needed money…"

"Peggy…" Sunnye said, "hmm…and she disappeared right around the time of the murder."

"Right after she discovered the body."

"Really? Then you found her backpack in Munro's house…."

"Yeah. And the night before that—the evening of the reception—she was behaving oddly. She was standing in a doorway in the library lobby, carrying an envelope exactly like this one." I tapped the empty interdepartmental-mail envelope. "Now I'm asking myself whether or not she had the *Maltese Falcon* manuscript in it? And, if she did, was she in cahoots with Rachel?"

"Was *who* in *what* with me?" The overhead light flared on, and Rachel Thompson stood in the doorway, a ring of keys in her hand and an astonished expression on her flushed face. "What the hell is going on here?" she exclaimed.

Chapter Twenty-Six

Hearing Rachel's voice, Trouble jumped up from his place at Sunnye's feet. His mistress motioned him down again. He obeyed, but gazed longingly at Rachel.

The librarian strode over and snatched the manuscript from Sunnye's hand. She looked closely at it, then gasped. "Where'd you get this?" she exclaimed.

"Right where you put it," Sunnye said, sharply.

The dog's wide brow furrowed at her tone. He looked from his owner to Rachel, then back again.

"What are you talking about?" Rachel turned pages, checking the manuscript for damage. "This was stolen from the library."

"Yeah? Stolen by you and hidden in plain sight. That's a corny old ploy stolen from Poe."

"I don't know what you're talking about."

"We found the *Maltese* manuscript on your desk, Rachel," I explained. I picked up the stretched-out manila envelope, pointed to the empty slot in the desk rack.

Rachel's brow matched Trouble's in puzzlement. She turned to Sunnye. "What is this, Ms. Hardcastle? Some kind of wacked-out publicity stunt? Did you plant this here so you could pretend to find it? Get press for being a gen-u-wine private eye?"

I jumped in before Sunnye could respond. "Listen, Rachel. Sunnye doesn't have any phony reason like that. This is why we're here—the police think she killed Elwood Munro, but she didn't. We're helping her investigate—"

"Investigate?"

"Yes. She's just looking for evidence to exonerate herself."

"*Just looking?* Ransacking my desk? In a restricted area? After midnight? And, Karen, you went along with this ludicrous scheme? Breaking into the college library? Are you out of your mind?"

I shrugged: *Maybe.*

"We didn't exactly *break in.*" Amanda spoke for the first time. "We were already in the library. We just…stayed." Suddenly looking exhausted, she sank into a desk chair in a corner by the bank of file cabinets. No mention of having slithered through a filthy heating duct.

With narrowed eyes Rachel scrutinized Amanda. "Who are you?"

"She's my daughter." I stepped between the librarian and Amanda. "Leave her out of this."

Rachel jerked her thumb at Sunnye. "How do you know she didn't kill that man, Karen?" she said. "Just because she says she didn't? The celebrated Sunnye Hardcastle can do no wrong?" The librarian flourished the manuscript. "Don't let her dupe you. She probably stole this in the first place."

"That doesn't make any sense. How could she have gotten in here?" But, then, of course, there were no locked rooms for Sunnye Hardcastle; she could go wherever she wanted.

Rachel reached for the phone. "I'm calling Security."

I shook my head. "You can call the campus cops if you want to, Rachel, but if you do, you'll get Sunnye and me in a lot of trouble, and we're telling the truth."

Sunnye was tired of letting me take the lead. "Anyhow, Ms. Thompson, what are *you* doing here this time of night? You love your job so much you come in at, what, one-twelve a.m.?" She stood with her feet apart, hands loose at her sides. A shooter's position. My heart sank. I should have known Sunny Hardcastle would have a gun somewhere on her person.

"Can't we just forget about all this?" I pleaded inanely. "Before things get any worse."

Rachel eyed Sunnye warily. "I *do* come in at all hours—I live right down the street from the college. Tonight I was on my way home from…a date and stopped by to pick up an order form I'd forgotten." She wore a grey linen pant suit and a scarlet band in her dark hair: fairly dressy for Rachel. I remembered seeing her enter Rudolph's earlier that evening hand-in-hand with Paul Henshaw. Paul, a rare-book dealer. Had the two of them…? "And, no, Karen," she said, glancing over at me. "We can't *just forget about all this*." She reached for the phone on her desk.

Rachel's calm reason was beginning to shake my confidence. Was it indeed possible that I'd been duped by Sunnye into helping her get her hands on this invaluable manuscript? Or, on the other hand, was Sunnye right, and Rachel had taken advantage of her position to conceal it in a place so visible no one would ever think to look there? Or, had Peggy…?

Rachel picked up the receiver.

"I'll take that." From the darkness of the closed stacks, a new voice joined in. All heads swiveled toward the door. A shadow detached itself from the larger penumbra of books and bookshelves, stepped forward, took on the shape of a man. My God! It was Dennis O'Hanlon! "Put the phone down and give me the manuscript," he said, hand extended.

We froze in position: Rachel by the desk with the manuscript; Sunnye by the door to the stacks; Amanda slouched in the wheeled desk chair, half-hidden by the file cabinet; me all the way over by the reading-room door through which Rachel had entered.

"How'd *you* get down here?" Rachel asked. She looked dumbfounded.

"*You* showed me how, Ms. Thompson. Now, hand it over," he said, flexing his outstretched hand. Framed in the doorway, Dennis looked large and powerful. "I said, *now*. Come on, Ms. Thompson. You know I've been authorized by the college to investigate the thefts from your library. You cooperate and things will go easier for you."

"But...but, I...I didn't steal it." She clutched *The Maltese Falcon* to her chest.

"Uh, huh. Right. Karen, Sweetheart..." He stepped further into the large office. "You take that manuscript from Ms. Thompson and bring it over here. And...be careful. She may be armed." One second there was no weapon in his hand, the next a lethal-looking little automatic had materialized.

"Dennis," I protested.

"Mr. O'Hanlon," Rachel cried, indignantly. "I had nothing to do with this."

Dennis had the proper credentials, a compelling air of authority, and the gun, but I didn't leap to obey him. Something was out of sync here. He had told me at least twice that Avery Mitchell had taken him off the case. And Avery had told me that Dennis had backed out on his own. Now, here, tonight, he was claiming to *represent* the college.

With the clarity my brain can occasionally achieve under stress, I recalled everything I knew about Dennis O'Hanlon. I remembered the hungry eyes of the young Denny that day so long ago when we'd caught the big fish. Then I superimposed on that memory the equally hungry eyes of the mature Dennis as he'd sat at Rudolph's bar earlier that evening, expounding his philosophy of life: *There isn't a lot I wouldn't do for money.*

The words resonated in my brain. Paul Henshaw, who should know, had said that on the rare-book black market the collector's item now clutched to Rachel's breast could command a small fortune.

Three possible suspects in the murder of Elwood Munro and the theft of *The Maltese Falcon* manuscript stood before me: Rachel, Sunnye, and Dennis. Each had motive, means, and opportunity. Rachel had a taste for luxury, as exhibited by the new BMW, and she had, of course, free access to all the library's collections. Sunnye was an avid collector of American first editions, and what could be more collectible than the inscribed manuscript of the premiere American classic detective novel. And, Dennis...well, Dennis...there wasn't a lot he wouldn't do for money.

I decided to play along with him. "Now, Dennis," I said, giving the P.I. an innocent's wide-eyed stare. "I don't think a gun is necessary. Surely Rachel understands the consequences of her actions. Let's just call Security as she suggested. Then we can get this all sorted out." I moved toward the phone.

"Security? Not a chance." He considered me with a level green gaze. Then he sighed: things had gotten more complicated than he expected. "I didn't want to do it this way, Karen, but like always you're too smart for your own good." The gun, as if it had a life of its own, moved slowly, even reluctantly, from Rachel to me. I sucked in a deep breath. The shiny automatic then jerked toward Sunnye at the door, ordering her further into the room. She obeyed without protest, and my heart froze. Where was the feisty Kit Danger when we needed her? We stood at an impasse until Dennis sighed again. "I'm leaving here with this manuscript, ladies, and if you three know what's good for you, you're not gonna give me any grief."

You three? Only *three?* Then he hadn't seen Amanda slouched in her chair by the file cabinets. And, indeed, when I slid my eyes over toward her, she had vanished into the shadows. I exhaled with relief. At least my daughter was safe.

But Trouble hadn't vanished. The big Rottweiler was at Sunnye's side, a menacing snarl beginning to emerge from between bared teeth.

"Keep that dog back," Dennis snapped at Sunnye, "or he gets it first."

Sunnye glared, but she grabbed Trouble's leash and pulled him up short. I kept expecting her to do something—anything—to save us: lunge at Dennis, kick him off his feet, sic the dog on him. But she just stood there. Maybe she was marking time.

Maybe she had simply given up.

A moment of intense silence ensued as four sets of eyes focused on the private investigator and his gun: mine, Rachel's, Sunnye's, and Trouble's. Three women and a ferocious dog ranged against one renegade male.

We could have taken him if it wasn't for the gun. The gun was the equalizer—the cold steel equalizer.

Dennis broke the silence. "That little twerp, Munro, I fingered him as the book thief right away. You gotta admire his nerve; he just about owned this library. Broke into vaults, locked offices, closed stacks—wherever the books were that he wanted. Went in through ventilation ducts, elevator shafts, over steel security gates. But I don't think he was alone in it. He must've had an accomplice to tell him where things were, to cover up for him. Was it you, Ms. Thompson?"

"Me? I hardly ever saw the man. It was Nellie who..." Her eyes widened, and she proceeded pensively. "It was Nellie who assisted him when he needed anything. I sometimes thought she—"

But Dennis wasn't interested in Nellie Applegate. "You know, that stupid little dweeb could have really cleaned up on all those books, but he never sold even one of them. He was some kind of nut—took them just to...*have* them. Like owning thousands of books would make him smart."

"Looked pretty smart to me," I mused. "Even brilliant. The focus and comprehensiveness of that collection—"

He laughed. "And you only saw the one house—" He broke off as if he realized he'd said too much.

"There's more than one?"

"Shit!"

"Dennis," I persisted, "did Munro have more than *one* stash of stolen books?"

"Karen, shut up, will you. You see, I have a different take on rare books than Munro did. I look at them and I see... portable cash. He lived on trust funds, I found out. *Trust funds!* Well, ladies, this..." He stepped forward and snatched the manuscript from Rachel's hand. "This will enhance *my* trust funds."

In the murky light he stood silent for a moment, staring at me with eyes the color of used dollar bills. Then he shook his head and sighed. "Jesus H. Christ, Karen, like I said, I didn't want it to come down to this. I thought I could just walk out of here without...but things seem to be getting out of control."

Sunnye spoke for the first time since Dennis's appearance. Her words were low and level. "Did you kill that poor man, Mr. O'Hanlon?"

He spun toward the novelist, the muzzle of his little automatic swinging in her direction. "Kill him? He fell, didn't he? Library steps, damn unstable." Straightforward? Sardonic? His tone was unreadable.

Rachel broke in. "But, when used properly, they're not—"

Suddenly, a crash resounded. On the far side of the room a computer monitor exploded into thin shards. Shattered glass flew everywhere. I leapt back. Rachel screamed. A heavy tape dispenser ricocheted off the broken screen and skidded to a halt at my feet. Amanda must have hurled it from her hiding place behind the file cabinets.

Dennis swiveled toward the disturbance, a bullet from his gun smashing into the already pulverized computer screen.

"Hold it right there, O'Hanlon," Sunnye barked, without a second's lag time. I hadn't seen her reach for it, but in her steady hand she now held an efficient-looking black handgun. "One move and you're a dead man."

I recognized the line from *Stormy Weather*, when Kit Danger faces down Yves Dupin, international saboteur. Or was it from *Bad Attitude*, when the evil industrialist Nindy Falkoff threatens the life of Pauline Albright, crusading public service advocate? Or was it from—

But Denny feinted to the right, then dodged left, pivoted out the door and vanished into the shadowy stacks, pages flying from the loosely tied manuscript in his grasp. A bullet exploded from Sunnye's gun, whizzed through the door and lodged with a thunk in a thick, corded, leather-bound volume on the first set of shelves, about five feet above the floor. Heart level.

From four or five tiers away, a responding bullet cracked the door's glass panel right beside my forehead. I screeched and threw myself down.

"My God," Rachel shrilled, "he's firing from behind the incunabula!" She'd been scrabbling across the office floor, trying to recover a few fly-away manuscript pages.

I dragged her down before she could dash out to save her precious early printed books, but Sunnye was already beyond my reach, sprinting into the shadows after Dennis. Another shot cracked, ricocheted off a metal book truck with a reverberating ping. Sunnye's gun responded: boom! My ears rang: In the enclosed space the detonation was deafening.

From behind the desk, I grabbed the phone and yanked it down beside me. Pressing 911 with a spastic finger, I caught a glimpse of Amanda as she emerged from behind the bank of file cabinets, slithering on her belly in the direction of Sunnye's big leather bag. It took a second or two for me to realize what she had in mind. "Amanda, no," I yelled, but she had Sunnye's backup gun out of the bag and cocked, and was already halfway through the door into the stacks.

The tinny telephone voice said, "Emergency Operator. Hello? Emergency Operator." I dropped the receiver and jumped up. "Get back in here, Amanda," I ordered.

Behind me, I heard Rachel's voice breathlessly informing the operator of gunplay in the college library.

"Get. In. Here." My voice was commanding, but to no avail. My daughter crouched behind the wounded book truck, then slunk out of sight around the shelves.

"A-man-da!" I shrieked. But she was gone. "Goddamnit."

Another shot. A book flew off a shelf and landed broken-backed at my feet.

I snatched up the phone again and called Charlie on his cell. "College library. Dennis O'Hanlon." Another bullet pinged off a metal shelf. "He's got a gun." I slammed down the receiver and dived under the desk.

A period of silence ensued: Thirty seconds? A half-hour? Amanda was out there. I had to do something. I crawled from the cover of the desk toward the office door and peered out into the enormous chamber that housed the stacks.

Manuscript pages littered the side aisle, marking Dennis's flight like a trail of incriminating footprints. Sunnye lurked at the far end of the center aisle. I could see her, in Kit Danger's lethal demi-crouch, silhouetted in the lurid red light of the Exit sign. Trouble skulked at her side. Shadows hung from the high shelves, and the close air choked with silence. Spotting her prey, Sunnye steadied her arm and took aim. Before she could fire, a detonation sounded from the far side of the room. I saw a flash, heard a bullet whiz by. Sunnye dodged behind a shelf and vanished from my sight. The bullet clunked into the concrete wall where only seconds earlier she had stood. Once again, silence.

Amanda! Where was Amanda? I slipped off my shoes and padded noiselessly down the side aisle in my thick socks, keeping close to the wall. I checked each rank of books as I passed. I had to find my daughter. Suddenly I was brought to a halt. A loaded book truck blocked my progress. In the dim light of a sixty-watt bulb, I could see it was marked *Reshelving*.

Then I spotted him. At the end of the nearest rank, Dennis waited, braced against the wall, for Sunnye or Amanda to make a move. He was all muscle and stealth. Then a slender silhouette materialized in the semi-light of the office door. Amanda! The gunman aimed, but Sunnye stepped around the edge of the tier and distracted him. "Over here, O'Hanlon!" He swiveled toward her. His reflexes were swift, but I saw it in slow motion, his balance altering as he shifted weight to his left foot and swung himself smoothly around, pistol at the ready. I felt my breath quicken and my shoulder muscles tense. I lurched toward the book truck and gave it a mighty shove. It sped toward Dennis O'Hanlon like a bullet from a .45 Magnum and slammed him off his feet, books flying in every direction. Then, a snarl. A massive shadow launched itself from Sunnye's side. Dennis screamed only once as Trouble brought him down.

"*Gotcha*!" cried Sunnye Hardcastle. Kit Danger triumphs again.

Chapter Twenty-Seven

"I almost lost him among all those books," Sunnye said. The police had commandeered the librarian's lounge for interviews, and Sunnye had enthroned herself in a comfortable armchair. The room was illuminated by ceiling-mounted fluorescent tubes. Someone had made coffee, then burned it, and the bitter scent hung, nauseating, in the air. Rachel, Amanda, and I sat lined up on a low yellow plastic couch like ducks in a carnival shooting gallery. I just wanted to take Amanda home and put her to bed. Her earlier burst of energy had dissipated. She was wan, with dark smudges shadowing her eyes. But there was no getting out of this little party. A hastily awakened Avery Mitchell had pulled up a chrome-framed chair across the room, and the presidential frown was aimed directly at me like a marksman's rifle; I was in big trouble now. Charlie Piotrowski and a uniformed trooper had also commandeered a couple of the bent-chrome chairs with their brown upholstered backs and seats. Schultz, so ripely pregnant she almost sent me into sympathy labor, was perched on a plain oak bench. She'd have difficulty rising from anything more comfortable.

An ambulance had taken Dennis O'Hanlon to Enfield Regional Medical Center to be treated for dog bite. Dennis would live; Sunnye had called the Rottweiler off before he could do serious damage. But for now the P.I. was mildly sedated, capable of answering only the most rudimentary questions. Rachel had scurried to gather up the *Maltese Falcon* pages, a number of which were creased and dirty from being trod on during the gunfight or sprayed with blood from the outlaw P.I.'s wounds. I didn't want to think about what these forensic traces would do to the manuscript. But who knew? Maybe the blood spatters—and the story that went along with them—would render it even more valuable.

Sunnye had held Dennis at gunpoint until the first troopers arrived, refusing to relinquish him even to the campus security officers. She was bold, brave and strong, and everyone was extremely impressed. As she narrated her story of derring-do in the closed stacks, I sighed and stared out the narrow, leaded casement window of the lounge. "Maybe Dennis O'Hanlon didn't do it," I said. Sunnye's voice halted. Schultz ceased taking notes. Every head in the room swiveled toward me.

"Well, of course," I elaborated, turning back to the group, "he did try to steal the *Maltese Falcon* manuscript last night. No question about that. But what if that was simple opportunism? He was prowling around, heard us talking about the manuscript, decided to commandeer it. What I mean to say is, what if Dennis didn't kill Elwood Munro?"

"Wha—?" Sunnye jerked forward in her comfortable chair. "But he said—"

"He didn't say anything about killing anyone. You're much too quick to jump to conclusions, Sunnye. This is not one of your novels."

She widened her grey eyes at me, affronted.

"Keep talking, Karen," Charlie Piotrowski said. He'd arrived on campus three hours earlier, greeted me with an enormous sigh, ran a hand once over my disheveled hair, then treated me with the same professional detachment as he accorded everyone else in the room.

"That, tonight? That gunplay? I don't think he planned that. He didn't expect any resistance from us—three helpless women—just wanted to get away with his loot. As it turned out, he might well have ended up killing us." I shuddered, then returned Charlie's straight gaze. "But murder afore-thought? I don't know." I paused to organize my thoughts. "No matter how much money Dennis could get for that Hammett manuscript, it couldn't possibly be enough on its own to make murder worth his while. Munro's, or ours. He'd have to vanish, work up a new identity—"

"Not if he'd succeeded in killing us," Sunnye interrupted. "Not if he got away with it. Who would have connected him—a private eye from Lowell—with the bodies of four women in the Enfield College library? He could have just gone on with his life and sold the manuscript at his convenience."

"He didn't start out with the idea of killing us," I replied, though I couldn't be absolutely certain about that. "The gun was just for intimidation until he could escape."

"Those were fake bullets zipping past my head?"

"No, they were all too real. But by then he had no choice. You fired first."

"You did, Ms. Hardcastle?" Charlie's voice lacked all inflection.

Sunnye bit her lower lip as she tried to recall the exact sequence of the night's events. "I thought *he* shot first."

"He shot the computer." Amanda spoke up for the first time. "After I pulverized it."

"I heard what you did with that tape dispenser, Amanda," Schultz said. "That was quick thinking."

My daughter shrugged off the praise. I fervently hoped she'd gotten the notion of a career in police work out of her system.

"When Dennis showed up in my office the morning the conference began," I said, "he told me it was his first time on campus. Ever. That was a lie. He'd been hanging around, checking things out, at least a couple of weeks before that. Monica Cassale saw him in the library."

An utterance something like *hrrumm* escaped Avery's lips. I glanced over at him. He frowned, then gave me a magisterial nod: *Continue.*

"What if he'd already identified Munro as the biblioklept, followed him to Chesterfield, and found that enormous stash of books? He was a...greedy man. Stealing—especially from a thief—wouldn't tax his conscience at all."

"That would account for those unidentified tire tracks in the driveway," Charlie mused.

"Last night he inadvertently let something drop." I paused to think it through. "When I said the collection Munro had assembled was extraordinary, Dennis blurted out that I'd only seen *one* of the houses. Then he shut up fast. So what I'm thinking is—what if there's yet another hoard of purloined volumes in yet another Book House?"

"A second Book House?" Charlie spoke first, then Avery, so it sounded like an echo in the room.

"I'm just saying, *what if?* Depending on what Munro had collected there, if Dennis found it and was the only one to know about it, he might have had multiple millions in found money, hundreds, maybe thousands, of rare books just waiting for him to cash in on them whenever he wanted to. *That* would make it worth his while to disappear, to become someone else. He could put together quite a nice life on the illicit proceeds. *Trust funds*, he said." I paused. "But even if that *is* the case, it doesn't necessarily mean he's the killer."

Sunnye broke in. "But, if you're right, and O'Hanlon didn't know about the manuscript on Ms. Thompson's desk until he heard us talking about it, who put it there?"

"Your guess is as good as mine."

It was after eight o'clock when my daughter and I were allowed to leave the library. The campus was just stumbling to life for the day. A bleary-eyed fair-haired kid on his way to breakfast would have collided with Amanda if she hadn't straight-armed him out of the way. I sidestepped two young women holding hands, deep in conversation. We were halfway to the parking lot when I abruptly recalled that I didn't have a car on campus. I stopped cold. "Shit. No car."

"Wha..." Amanda paused in mid-step. "God, was that just last night when Sunnye and I picked you up? It feels like a millennium. How the hell are we gonna get home?"

A familiar hand gripped my shoulder. "I understand you need a ride," Charlie said.

I turned around. We stared at each other. There was a whole lot remaining to be resolved between us. A moment half as long as death ticked by. "Yeah," I said. "You offering?"

He hesitated. "I can't do it," he said finally. "Got to talk to Ms. Thompson some more. I'll get a patrol car to drive you. But I just wanted to say—"

His cell phone rang. He grimaced, checked the read-out, shrugged at me in apology, and answered. "Yeah?" He listened intently, then frowned and glanced over at me out of the corner of his eye. "You're shitting me? No kidding? Well, I'll be...Okay. Right. Got it."

He tucked the phone back in his jacket pocket. Then he took a deep breath and shook his head as if life were sometimes too much to believe. "Karen..." he said, and gave Amanda a sidelong look. She developed a sudden all-consuming interest in a border of crocus shoots pushing their way through damp earth and wandered away. Charlie placed his hands gently on my arms. I wasn't cold, but I shivered anyhow. His eyes as they looked straight into mine had the warmth and color of fine brewed coffee. "What I said yesterday? About maybe not having room in my life for a woman like you? I want to apologize. I don't know what got into me—I should get a mouth transplant. You're the best thing that ever happened to me. It's just that…I don't know. Sometimes it scares me, what it all means.…"

"Me, too," I replied, and swallowed. My throat was very dry.

"Yeah?" He smiled at me, but he had that far-away look he gets when he's thinking hard. Absently, he fingered the cell phone in his pocket. "You know, I just got an idea… maybe some way to let you know how sorry I am. Big-time. But I need a couple of days. I gotta get things cleared up here. Karen, babe, can you give me, say, the weekend to work it out? And then…after that…then we'll really talk about us."

I barely made it home, showered, donned clean clothes, and ate a tuna sandwich Amanda threw together, before it was time to rush back to campus and teach. When I returned to my office after class, Peggy Briggs was waiting for me in the hallway, holding Triste by the hand. Peggy had had her hair cut extremely short by someone who knew how to do it right. She and the little girl wore matching pale-green sweaters. They looked well-fed and relaxed. They did not look like people who had at any time been in mortal danger.

I gawked at her. "Where the hell have you been, Peggy?"

She gave me a newly confident smile. "May I come in, Professor?" I opened the door, and she stepped into the room. Triste bounded over to the green vinyl chair, her blond curls flying. Her slight body was nearly swallowed up by the soft cushions, but she bounced twice, then settled down in the big chair with dignity. "Stephie said you were looking all over for me. I'm sorry if I worried you."

I motioned Peggy to the Enfield-crest-embossed captain's chair. "Are you okay?" Somehow Peggy's self-assurance made me feel presumptuous about ever having been concerned.

"I'm more than okay. I'm…wonderful."

"Really?"

"We've been in Manhattan, Triste and I, staying with Stephie's parents. Did you know her mother is a literary agent?"

I thought back to a conversation with Earlene. "I knew she did something in publishing."

"Yeah, well, she's great. I wrote this book?...about my sister?..."

"I know."

"You do?" She frowned.

I nodded. I wasn't about to let her know Earlene had told me.

"Well, Stephie sent her the manuscript, and she actually read it. Then she called Steph and told her to get me down there—to New York. She thought the book was a...a hot property. She was going to auction it off, and she wanted to meet me. And I just, well, I just stayed....I didn't tell anyone where I was, because I couldn't really believe it was all going to work out."

I stared at her. I could feel a grin begin to curve my lips. "She sold your book, didn't she?"

Peggy grinned back. Triste bounced on the chair. "It's going to be published next year."

"Wonderful!"

"I got a big advance. We're going to move out of my mother's place. I've already found a new apartment. Triste can have her own room. I can quit my job in the library and concentrate on my studies. But..." She glanced at me sideways. "I'm afraid I'm going to fail your course. I missed two classes."

"Three, I think." I furrowed my brow. "But maybe we could call your visit to Manhattan a field trip, or 'distance-learning.'"

"Seriously?" She was fumbling in a big, bright canvas bag.

I nodded. "Seriously."

"That would be wonderful, if it could all work out. You know, it's so funny—at the hospital when my sister.... Well, some preacher started quoting scripture at me. He was this little thin wizened-up guy with a sour puss on him like you wouldn't believe. So he comes into the ER waiting room right behind the doctor. The doctor tells me Megan's dead. I'm screaming and wailing, and the parson starts mealymouthing at me. "'Miss Briggs,' he says. 'You must remember that the Good Book tells us that all things work together for good to those who love the Lord.' I wanted to rip his head off!"

"Of course you did. I would have, too." I could feel the ripping impulse in my own fingers.

"But you know, Professor, I think in a way that preacher turned out to be right. If I hadn't gone into such a black funk...what the shrink called a *clinical depression*...after Megan died, I would never have ended up in counseling, would never have signed up at GCC, would never have gotten the scholarship to this fancy school. Would never have written this book. So for me and for Triste things are going to be much better because she died. In an...ironic way, I guess 'all things do work together for good to those who—'"

"To those who *make* them work together for good," I interrupted. "Give yourself some credit, Peggy. *You* made this all happen."

She looked at me, slant-eyed, as if she suspected that might be true but was afraid to quite believe it. Then she retrieved a bulky manuscript from her bag and held it out to me. "Would you like to read this?"

"Oh, yes." I took it from her.

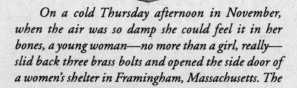

On a cold Thursday afternoon in November, when the air was so damp she could feel it in her bones, a young woman—no more than a girl, really— slid back three brass bolts and opened the side door of a women's shelter in Framingham, Massachusetts. The

shelter was in a large wood-frame house that had recently been painted a creamy white and fitted with new green shutters. The young woman peered out into the street, saw no evidence of danger, and took a tentative step. The bullet hit her cleanly in the chest, severing her aorta, sending a vivid red spray onto the grey cement of the sidewalk, spattering the frosted late-autumn grass with crimson blood.

She was my sister....

On Saturday night Sunnye, Amanda, and I indulged in one last retro meal, spaghetti and meatballs. In the morning I would drive Amanda back to school and probably not see her again until graduation. We hadn't talked at all about what she would do then. She was twenty-two, a grown-up, as she kept insisting; I had to learn to keep my mouth shut about her life. Sunnye was going with us as far as Bradley International Airport, where she would catch a flight home to Colorado.

When we finished eating, Sunnye stacked dishes and carried them into the kitchen; she could be surprisingly domestic when she wanted to be. On the far side of the pass-through window she stood at the sink, scrubbing her hands like a surgeon about to pick up a scalpel. Then she fetched her capacious bag to the table and reached into it.

"Karen," she said, her dark grey glance not quite meeting my eyes, "I've never been very good at asking for help, or very gracious about accepting it. But I want you to know I appreciate what you've done for me—braving those reporters, providing a refuge, interceding with the cops. So, here—" With a mock flourish she pulled out a hardcover book in a hot-pink dust jacket, a copy of her first novel, *Rough Cut*. "This is for you, Karen. It's a first edition," she said. "I'll sign it if you like."

I was stunned. "Sunnye, I can't take this." Hadn't she said these things went for three thousand dollars?

"Why not? You told me you lost yours."

"But this is much too valuable." My head was spinning.

"Nonsense. Look, I'm signing it. *From Trouble—with Love*." At the sound of his name, Trouble raised his head and adored Sunnye with his very best doggie gaze. "Now, don't go and give this copy to the Salvation Army."

"But, but, Sunnye, I can't—" I was itching to get my hands on the gaudy volume.

"Mom, shut up," Amanda interjected. "Take the book, and say *thank you very much* to the nice lady."

It was late Sunday afternoon before I heard from Charlie again. In a quick, hushed call he told me to dress rough and warm and meet him at the Blue Dolphin. And not to ask questions. When I bridled at his officiousness, he suggested in the gentlest of manners that I might be forever sorry if I didn't do as he asked. So I shut up, pulled on jeans, an Enfield sweatshirt, an old denim jacket, and the ubiquitous Spring-time-in-New-England mud boots.

"So, what's up?" I asked as I slid into the diner's narrow booth across from him.

"Hello, babe," he said. "I missed you."

"Did you? I'm glad. Me, too. You." But I attempted to read his eyes, looking for signs of trouble. Something lurked there. Not trouble, though. Could it be—mischief?

"Good. Let's get something to eat. Then we're gonna take a little ride."

"Where to?"

"You'll find out." He gave me a crooked smile, and said, cryptically, "You should be able to figure it out, anyhow. You seem to know everything."

Even when we'd finished hot roast beef sandwiches, and were on our way...somewhere...in his Jeep, Charlie wouldn't tell me where we were going. "Just call it a little mystery trip," he said, and chortled. We didn't travel far. He pulled to a halt in a weedy field adjacent to a secluded old house on the outskirts of Enfield. A patrol car and two plain grey vans were parked in the dry, overgrown field. The vans just about broadcast themselves as government issue. The house was stone and stucco with a portico and two turrets. At one time the residence had aspired to a welcoming elegance, but the overgrown hard-pan-dirt driveway with its narrow parallel ruts suggested that its days of hospitality had expired with the demise of the carriage trade.

I sat in the Jeep, transfixed by the sight of the building in front of me. "Christ Almighty, Charlie. Is that what I think it is?"

"Depends on what you think it is."

"The second Book House, of course."

"Yep." He was grinning at me. His little surprise. "Thanks to you and your hunch. Remember that call I got on the cell the other morning? That was Agent Mathes of the FBI team that's handling the Chesterfield site. I'd told Mathes what you said about another house. She confronted O'Hanlon with it, and he gave it up right away. Seemed to think cooperating with the Feds is gonna make things go easy for him." He laughed. "Must have helped that, somehow, he got the idea he was in the frame for Munro's death."

"My God, the place is enormous." This impressive dwelling was three or four times the size of the little white house in Chesterfield. "You think they're going to let me in there?"

"Damn well better." He spoke with feeling. "Without you we would never have found it. Would've sat here moldering until O'Hanlon served his time and came back to plunder it."

I paused with my hand on the Jeep's door handle. "What's going to happen to him?"

He gazed at me quizzically. "He should go away for a good long time. It seems he's been nothing but trouble his whole life, your old classmate. And, now, add grand theft, breaking and entering, menacing, assault with a firearm." He gave me an intent look. "Do you care?"

"Hell, no. I don't think he intended it to happen, but in the end he probably would have killed us all. And, for what? The greedy bastard!" I sat for a few seconds, still gripping the door handle. Maybe it wasn't quite true that I didn't care. "But, Charlie, the hell of it is, I really did want to believe in him. He played the macho private-eye so…beautifully. And, besides, we were kids together. He ate at my mother's table. We were in the same Goddamned home-room! I wanted to believe he'd made it out of the cesspool we were born into through hard work and smarts—and honesty. Like I did." I gave an abrupt laugh as the irony hit me. "God, I'm so stupid. He told me nothing's ever what it seems to be, but I wanted to think he was…the real thing."

"The real thing?"

"You know. Like a character in a book."

Charlie's brow furrowed, as if there was something contradictory about what I'd just said.

I went on. "A tough-guy P.I. A…shamus with a hard-boiled code of honor."

"A male Kit Danger?" Charlie laughed.

"Yeah. I guess."

He still had the quizzical expression. "That's all, huh? You sure? He's a damn good-looking son-of-a-bitch, that O'Hanlon. Women must—"

My eyes grew wide with indignation. "What do you think I am, Charlie Piotrowski?"

He just continued to look at me.

Okay. I was a woman. Nuff said. I glanced over at the conspicuously inconspicuous government vans. "You really think the FBI will let me—"

His hand sliced the air straight across. "Don't worry about the Fibbies. I fixed it. You're not really here. Okay? Get out of the car. We have two hours."

Twelve rooms full of books, but the crown jewel for me was the collection of British detective fiction that filled the mahogany-paneled library. I walked into the room wearing latex gloves, gawking and gaping like a bibliophilic tourist. It was a grand, if threadbare, space, strikingly different from the modest farmhouse parlor that held Munro's American collection: fourteen-foot paneled ceilings, wall-to-wall, floor-to-ceiling bookshelves with sliding ladders, recessed leaded windows with worn red-velvet cushions on the window seats, a crystal chandelier, begrimed and dripping with cobwebs, a Persian rug the size of the New York Public Library. And books, of course. Row upon row of books. From nineteenth-century triple-decker classics bound in lustrous morocco to lurid 1950's paperbacks.

Here was an original set in green wrappers of *Oliver Twist; or the Parish Boy's Progress* by Charles Dickens, 1838. I was in such awe, I didn't dare touch it. On the same rank of shelves stood rows of flimsy yellowbacks, cheap nineteenth-century editions published to be sold in railroad stations. Carefully I plucked out a thin saffron-colored volume: *Recollections of a Detective Police Officer*, by someone who called himself "Waters." Eighteen pence. It was in immaculate shape, still in its paper wrapper. A cheap read, all right, but somehow preserved for fifteen decades. A cherrywood bookstand boasted a first edition of *The Hound of the Baskervilles* by Arthur Conan Doyle. Its bright red cover with a silhouette in black of a massive dog hunched dramatically against a rising moon highlighted a full shelf of the adventures of Sherlock Holmes. Early twentieth-century editions in hues of orange, blue, green, and yellow were shelved against the end wall: *Gaudy Night* by Dorothy Sayers, *The Mysterious Affair at Styles* by Agatha Christie, *The Body in the Library*, also by Christie. The adventures of Lord Peter Wimsey, Monsieur Hercule Poirot, and Miss Jane Marple. Further down the shelves I pulled out an Ian Fleming first edition, *Goldfinger*, its paper dust-jacket featuring a skull with golden coins in its eyes and a red rose in its mouth. Bond. James Bond.

I turned a beautiful Graham Greene in my hands. I'd read somewhere that a first edition of *Brighton Rock* with a perfect dust jacket had sold for £50,000. It hadn't made any real impact at the time. But that was then. This was real.

"Well?" Charlie queried, after my initial perusal.

I placed the Greene back on its shelf. I had tears in my eyes, not so much because of the books, but because Charlie had actually brought me here despite all the misgivings he'd expressed about involving me in his work. "Thank you," I said. "This is wonderful. Thank you, thank you. I know it couldn't have been easy, getting me into this place. But you trusted me enough to bring me to see this...it's...it's..." I reached up and stroked his cheek, truly at a loss for words.

Chapter Twenty-Eight

We spent the night at Charlie's little yellow house in Northampton. What else could we do, we asked ourselves, but love and respect each other and try to work things out? I left very early, while he was still asleep, and drove back to campus to pick up an anthology I needed for my class prep. Love and crime and books were all very nice, but I still had to earn my living. It was almost six when I entered the quad from the parking lot. Everything was hushed and motionless, as if a neutron bomb had just depopulated the campus. The pale peach sun was rising behind the turreted roofline of the library. I stopped, transfixed by the exquisite sharp contrast of stone and light. Next to the beautiful old building, the foundational walls of the new library under construction stretched away into the shadows. This fifty-million-dollar edifice was about to rise into being as a state-of-the-art, twenty-first-century electronic information-technology center. Oh, yes, and as a repository for that soon-to-be-outmoded information technology, the book.

My hours with Charlie had put me in a mellow and meditative mood. I stood there alone in the dawn and mused. The Book, as book historians called it, as if there were a single entity that somehow transcended individual volumes. My thoughts went back to the mystical feelings I'd had the night

I'd illicitly entered the stacks. All those minds preserved in all those books, long-dead, but still vigorous and alive: Chaucer, Shakespeare, and Milton, of course, the usual suspects, their names stamped in gold on leather spines. But also humbler fare: Chandler and Hammett and Anna Katherine Green. Even the pseudonymous authors of the ephemeral press, such as Ned Buntline and Bertha M. Clay. All of them inscribed in ink on paper and held in trust for the present and the future. And who had done the keeping? Librarians with lost names, nowhere stamped on book spines. Generation after generation of custodians of the book. Decades, centuries of individuals dedicated to transmitting the accumulated cogitations and imaginings of the collective consciousness. Dim, dusty, ghostly, now, those librarians of the past, but, then as now, with absolute power over books. Live, vivid people like Rachel, as well as insubstantial wraiths like Nellie Applegate. Nellie, who was so…interested in… Elwood Munro, book thief extraordinaire. Wait a minute! Nellie! Had anyone seriously questioned Nellie?

I called Charlie from my office and woke him up.

"Where'd you go, babe?" he asked groggily.

"What about Nellie Applegate?" I demanded.

"Huh? Applegate? The librarian? That little grey woman who looks like—"

"Yeah. Her."

"What about her?"

"Couldn't she be the one who stole the manuscript? She'd have access to all the library keys and to Rachel's office. She would know how sloppy and shortsighted Rachel is—that she might not even recognize the manuscript in all that junk on her desk. And Nellie's been behaving so oddly lately…"

"Like how?" He seemed to be at least half-awake now, maybe even shifting himself up out of those tangled sheets.…

"Almost…distraught. She was infatuated with Elwood Munro—Bob Tooey, as we knew him. He was an inoffensive-looking little man, but she couldn't keep her eyes off him. She ogled him from the reading-room desk as if he were Apollo descended from Olympus. If he did have an accomplice in stealing those books—"

"Applegate would have been perfectly placed to get him what he wanted," Charlie said.

"Yeah. I think the library has pretty good security against intruders, but I'd be surprised if they worried about their own staff."

"I think it's time," Charlie said, sounding as if he had actually gotten out of bed, "that we had a little talk with Ms. Nellie Applegate."

Charlie surprised the hell out of me by asking me to ride along to Nellie's place on Hill Street. He wanted someone who knew the librarian in case she freaked out. He'd asked Rachel first, and she would only go if I went. I rode with Rachel in the BMW. Paul Henshaw's BMW actually, she confided to me, lent to her while the Nissan was in the shop. It was six, and the sky was beginning to lighten over the Pelham hills to the east. Nellie lived on a narrow commercial street in a seedy part of town. I'd never been there before, but the neighborhood made me feel right at home: the turned-over garbage cans, the shabby corner grocer's, the three-story frame houses with their rickety ranks of porches. We climbed a narrow set of stairs to Nellie's apartment above Pratt Liquors. A blotchy orange cat streaked past us as we reached her landing. Schultz rang the bell set into the doorframe. When there was no response, she pounded on the door. "Police business, Ms. Applegate. Open up."

From inside came a sudden high scream that increased in volume and shrillness, then, just as suddenly choked itself off. The cops glanced at each other. I could feel a sudden spurt of tension in the drab vestibule. Charlie waved Rachel and me peremptorily toward the stairs. Rachel quickstepped halfway down. I descended two or three steps, then halted well within the line of sight.

"Ms. Applegate, you all right?" Charlie called. No response. He rattled the doorknob. Locked. Gripping the knob, he put his shoulder to the door and shoved. It didn't budge. He turned to the hefty trooper who had accompanied us. "Kick it in."

The beefy blond grimaced, but squared off anyhow. Before he could launch himself, the door opened from inside, and Nellie Applegate stood there with a still-steaming teakettle in her hand. She wore a grey bathrobe in some pilled fabric and pink slipper socks. She looked like a walking nervous breakdown, her face blotched and strained, the greying hair unkempt.

"It was the freakin' teakettle," Schultz tittered in nervous relief. "And here I thought someone had a knife at her throat."

Nellie set the hot kettle down on the polished surface of a maple bookcase. "What do you want?" she whispered.

"We need to ask you a few questions, Ms. Applegate. Can we come in?"

Silently Nellie stepped aside, and the three cops entered, leaving the door open. I slid into the small living room behind them. Rachel remained on the stairs.

"Ms. Applegate..." Charlie gazed at her, slit-eyed, assessing. "We understand you knew Elwood Munro, the man who was found dead in the library stacks."

Nellie didn't respond. This policeman's massive bulk seemed to terrify her.

"We already know all about you and Munro, Nellie," Charlie continued in an off-hand manner. He leaned toward her, suddenly paternal, consoling. Good cop. "You might as well get it off your chest. You'll feel a lot better."

She slid, boneless, into an armchair and cowered there, trembling. Who could tell what this brute of a man might do?

"No one's going to hurt you," Charlie assured her. "Just answer our questions and you'll be fine."

She sank further into the cushions, as if her body were anticipating total meltdown.

I nudged him aside. He balked; I could feel the resistance in his arm muscles. I treated him to a wide-eyed stare: *Let me handle this*. After a second or two, he shrugged, strolled over to the window, and stared down at the cracked sidewalks.

"Nellie," I said, "I know you knew Mr. Munro, because I saw you talking to him." I hadn't, but she couldn't know that. "He was a handsome man. So strong and...powerful." I grinned: Just us girls together. "At least I thought he was attractive. Didn't you?" I hoped I wasn't piling it on too thick.

She nodded. "I loved him," she whispered.

I nodded back and perched on the padded arm of the chair, making my next remark exquisitely casual. "So, how long ago did you find out he was stealing books?"

Her eyes were fixed on mine. "It wasn't until he asked me to—" She broke it off, her expression suddenly horrified, and covered her mouth with her hand.

"You helped him, didn't you?" I kept my voice sympathetic.

Her mouse-brown eyes were riveted to mine. She nodded again. "He was the first man who ever really loved me."

That pissed me off. I may be naive, but I like to think that the library is the one pure institution we have left, the one that still exists solely to serve the public, the one we can trust absolutely to pass on knowledge from one generation to another. Now here was this weak, dishonest...seduced... librarian. This custodian of the book who'd failed her trust. I had to bite my tongue, but there was one more thing I needed to ask while I still had her talking. I barely managed to keep my voice even. "How could you love a man who stole books

Nellie? Or did you stop loving him when you found out he was a crook?"

Her eyes widened.

Speculatively, I said, "Maybe that's why you killed him."

She jumped out of the chair and squeaked. "I didn't kill him! He fell!"

Charlie pivoted on his heel and strode back toward us. Nellie cringed. "He fell, did he?" Charlie said. "Tell us about it."

Nellie Applegate had indeed caused Elwood Munro's death, but completely by accident. The night preceding the library reception, at his instruction, she'd stolen the *Maltese* manuscript from the showcase in the foyer and had "hidden" it on Rachel's desk. After the reception, she'd arranged to meet Munro in the closed stacks and hand the manuscript over to him. When she entered the stacks, he was balanced on the very top of the movable library steps, stretching to reach a volume on the highest shelf.

"I called his name," she choked. "I guess I startled him. He turned toward me—fast. I keep seeing it over and over again. He's on the top of the steps trying to get one of those Erle Stanley Gardners. When he heard my voice, he swiveled. He just *swiveled*. It goes over and over in my head like a bad movie. It happened so fast. He didn't even yell. Just grunted and went down. Then there was that awful crash—like a crate of books. I never heard anything so horrible in my life.

"I ran over to him, but he was...gone. Gone. Just gone. I keep seeing it—his neck at that weird angle. I can't stop seeing it." The tears started then.

Charlie handed her one of his ubiquitous packs of tissues. "Why didn't you report it?"

She flinched at his expression. "He was...gone." She mopped her eyes, but it didn't stanch the flow. "There was nothing anyone could do for him. And I was afraid..."

Charlie remained silent, but his lips were tight. Bad cop, now?

"Afraid of what?" I asked. Schultz and the trooper were mere onlookers. Rachel stood inside the open doorway, gaping at the scene.

"Afraid the police would find out that I'd stolen that manuscript from the showcase. Afraid I'd lose my job. Afraid...I'd be charged with murder. But it wasn't my fault. He just swiveled and—" She was back into the rewind.

"Tell us about the stolen books," Charlie said. "You help Munro with that, too?"

She nodded. "Until I met him, I thought love was something that just happened in stories." Then Nellie couldn't speak for sobbing.

"But you didn't even report his death? Jeezus Christ!" Charlie's face was a study in shades of incredulity. He was neither good cop nor bad cop now, just his own person. And appalled. He turned away from Nellie Applegate and motioned to Schultz with his thumb. "Take her in. She's got more talking to do."

The body in the library: A murder that wasn't a murder. A killer who wasn't a killer. A librarian who stole books. A private eye who was really a crook. And Sunnye Hardcastle, crime novelist, who had been bold, and brave, and strong—and had gotten the story all wrong.

Epilogue

The door to my office opened, and Charlie Piotrowski walked in. He held a Starbucks cup in each hand. "You busy?"

"Not if that's for me." I held my hand out for the coffee. "Come on. Give it over."

He handed me the cup with a grin and settled into the green chair. They fit each other nicely, big man, big chair. He unzipped his dark-blue jacket, shrugged out of it, and picked up his own coffee cup from the side table. "So...I spent the morning talking to that pathetic little woman. You want to hear her story?"

"Nellie Applegate? Sure." I sipped the steaming dark brew.

"Well, I don't think there's any doubt about it—Munro's death was an accident. It's nuts, really. What a freaky way to die. The guy could leap across shattered factory skylights, but he broke his neck falling off a three-foot high set of rolling library steps."

"What's going to happen to Nellie?"

"She'll be charged with grand theft, unlawful failure to report a death. Manslaughter? I doubt it. All depends on the grand jury findings. It's sad, really. The whole thing is damn sad. Munro, too. Applegate told me the weirdest stuff about him." He took two brown packets out of his jacket pocket, ripped them open, and stirred raw sugar into his coffee.

"Oh, yeah?" This I wanted to hear.

"Seems the guy was an orphan. His mother committed suicide when he was a baby. Applegate didn't say anything about a father, so maybe there wasn't one in the picture. Munro was raised by his grandmother, some kind of religious nut. They lived one of those narrow, shriveled-up lives some people seem to need. The only book Grandma allowed in the house—that little place in Chesterfield—was the Bible. I mean, I'm no shrink, but this has got to mean something, right? She monitored all his reading, even his school books. Publicly humiliated him in front of his schoolmates by screaming at his English teachers about the books they assigned. She thought—I'm quoting Applegate—'indiscriminate reading exerted an evil influence on innocent souls.'" He sipped coffee. "When Munro was in his teens, Grandma died, and, surprise, surprise, she had money stashed away—"

"That's where his trust funds came from."

"So he dropped out of school and started buying books. He ran out of space, so he bought another house. When the money was no longer enough to support his habit, he figured out a way to get books without paying for them."

"He became a biblioklept."

"If that's what you call a book thief. So Applegate's statement ties things up pretty good as far as BCI is concerned." More coffee. "But there's one loose end that worries me. None of this explains what happened to Peggy Briggs."

"Oh!" I slapped my forehead. "I didn't tell you. She's okay. She showed up here Friday." I recounted Peggy's story.

"Well, good, that clears that up. By the way, you'll be happy to know that, according to Applegate, Peggy's out of the scene as far as any involvement with Munro goes."

"I knew that all along," I said. I heard voices in the hallway and remembered that my office hours started in a few minutes. "But what was her backpack doing at his place? I didn't ask her."

"Ms. Nellie stole it for her sweetie. Munro wanted Peggy's car—get this—because of the bumper stickers. The bumper stickers! He was gonna steam them off, put them in a scrapbook he had."

"I'd rather be reading," I recalled slowly. "It makes a crazy kind of sense."

"The guy had gone big-time squirrelly. That's the way I see it. To get the car, he needed Peggy's keys. Which were in the pack. Which Ms. Applegate pinched for him." He shook his head. "That poor deluded woman even drove the stolen car out to his place for him." He put the Starbucks cup back on the table. "You know, in my work I see a lot of crap, but this is one for the books. Here's this sad little mouse of a librarian, and she falls big time for a book crook, breaks the law for him, puts her livelihood in jeopardy, then accidentally gets him dead. Now she's going to jail. The things people do for love." He shook his head, this strong, smart man, baffled by the mysterious transgressions of the human heart. "Who was it said, 'I won't play the sap for you'?"

I looked over at him with a half-grin. "Don't worry, Charlie. I won't ever ask you to."

FOUR FOR A BOY
A LORD CHAMBERLIN MYSTERY
by Mary Reed and Eric Mayer
ISBN: 0-7434-8690-0

Gang-plagued streets, politicians plotting each other's downfall, poverty and homelessness existing side-by-side with manifest wealth—no, this isn't modern-day Washington, D.C., but rather 6th-century Constantinople.

After a philanthropist is murdered in the city's Great Church—where he'd gone to visit a controversial stature of Christ—John the Eunuch, Lord Chamberlin to Byzantine Emperor Justinian the First, is assigned to ferret out the killer... and maybe also to act the role of a spy in a web of rivalries involving the current and future emperors.

To receive a catalog of other Poisoned Pen Press titles,
please contact us in one of the following ways:

Phone: 1-800-421-3976
Facsimile: 1-480-949-1707
Email: info@poisonedpenpress.com
Website: www.poisonedpenpress.com

Poisoned Pen Press
6962 E. First Ave. Ste. 103
Scottsdale, AZ 85251